D1518201

Masquerade
Book Two of the
Unchained Trilogy

Maria McKenzie

Cover Art by Renae Denbow

Edited by Lisa McKenzie

Copyright © 2013 Maria McKenzie

All rights reserved.

ISBN: 1484900162
ISBN-13: 978-1484900161

ALSO BY MARIA MCKENZIE

The Governor's Sons

"...McKenzie proves herself to be an effortless storyteller who sympathetically portrays the ironies and hypocrisies of those precarious times...Realistic, multifaceted characters make for an especially engaging novel."— *Kirkus Reviews*

Escape: Book One of the Unchained Trilogy

"...the book is a joy to read. What warms the heart is Daniel and Lori's simple love for each other and their strong trust in God. It literally shines through Maria's writing...A very simple, compelling and historically authentic read."— *Maria Mohan's Book Blog*

Visit or contact Maria at
www.mariamckenziewrites.com

Dedication

For Daddy, the dreamer

ACKNOWLEDGMENTS

Again, many thanks to Lisa McKenzie – Great friend and teacher, amazing writer and all around incredible human being!

To my talented writer friends who have provided invaluable feedback for *Masquerade*: Elaine Olund, Melissa Booth, Miguel Trejo, Andrea Rotterman, Marissa Perry and Barbara Timmons.

To Paula McKenzie Nahm – Your eagle-eyed sharpness never ceases to amaze me!

To Earl Hughes – Thank you again for all of your insightful input!

Special thanks to Renae Denbow for another beautiful artistic creation, to my mom for her input on the past, and to my husband for his inspiration and advice on the male perspective!

Introduction

The Story of The Unchained Trilogy

Fade to white...Just who do you think you are? Steven Jordan thought he knew, until his grandmother Selina Manning threw a grenade that put his identity in question. She reveals a secret: her grandmother was a black woman, born a slave. Yet Selina has lived her entire life as white.

Will Steven ever accept this root hidden beneath his family tree, or choose to leave it buried? Uncertain of what he'll find, he delves into the past to learn where the secret began.

The Unchained Trilogy is an explosive three book series of love, deceit, emotional destruction and in the end, forgiveness. It spans a time period of one hundred and forty two years, with *Escape* (Book One) opening the series in 1856, and *Revelation* (Book Three), closing it in 1998. Time does move fast in this family saga, and since there are several years to cover, some purposeful time gaps do exist to move along the narrative. For a brief overview of the entire trilogy, here's what to expect in every story:

Book I, *Escape*: The year is 1856. Lori is a black woman, born a slave, but Daniel Taylor, a young abolitionist from a wealthy merchant's family, falls in love with her, and risks his life to help her in a daring escape.

After overcoming torturous trials and challenges, Daniel and Lori have a family. However, their youngest daughter, the beautiful and treacherous Lavinia, chooses to pass as white. But will she ever find true happiness while hiding behind a mask?

Book II, *Masquerade*: Lavinia runs away from home at age seventeen to pursue a life of decadence as an actress. Married to a powerful showman in New York, Lavinia weaves one lie after another, doing whatever it takes to keep the truth about her "Negro" mother a secret.

Selina Standish, born during her mother Lavinia's second marriage, learns the truth about her ancestry as a young girl. But Selina is convinced by Lavinia never to acknowledge her "Negro blood." However, Selina finds this difficult after meeting her "Negro" relatives, whom she comes to love. Eventually, Selina makes a choice that binds her heart and troubles her future.

Book III, *Revelation*: In 1998, one-hundred year old Selina Standish Manning reveals a secret that she's carried for nine decades like a painful chain bound around her heart. Now, near death, Selina tells her family the truth about her black ancestry.

Her relatives are surprised by this

revelation, and her grandson, Steven, struggles to accept that black blood courses through his veins. One moment he's an average white guy of European descent, and now this! Despite Steven's initial misgivings regarding the secret, he and the rest of his family are eager to hear what Selina has to say, and their lives are forever changed as the past is revealed...

"And, after all, what is a lie? 'Tis but the truth in a masquerade."

Alexander Pope

Prologue
Spring, 1889

"Now, not only will you have to speak with an accent," Vernon said, closing the script he'd just read with his new wife, "you'll have to speak slowly." Beginning to feel groggy from the soothing sway of the locomotive, he yawned, then placed the script on the center table in front of him. "You gotta keep in mind that the sailor has taught your character English, and it's a new language for her."

"Oh, Vernon, I realize that." Lavinia clutched her husband's arm. They sat on a green velvet love seat in his private rail car. "Sometimes you talk to me like I'm a child."

Vernon chuckled. "Sometimes I forget you're old beyond your years."

"I'm seventeen, hardly a child."

"Well, to an old man like me—"

"Oh, Vernon...you're not *that* old."

Her words were sweet, Vernon thought, but at fifty-four, he was old...and probably losing his mind. Since he'd married Lavinia only days earlier, not a moment had passed when he hadn't questioned himself about what he'd done. She was young, beautiful and determined—and he was in love with her.

Vernon Hargraves, owner of New York City's premier theater company, The Hargraves Players, had never considered himself a marrying man. But that had all changed, once he'd set eyes on Lavinia Taylor. Who would've thought that Vernon's desire to buy land in California, would instead result in his gaining a wife?

"Vernon," Lavinia arrested his thoughts, "what should I wear in the production?"

He looked into his young wife's eager face, one of unearthly beauty with high cheekbones, sensual lips, and cat-like green eyes that sparked wildly with excitement. Vernon smiled, patting her hand. "My seamstress will fix you up in some clothes that are—island-like."

"Island-like?"

"Yeah. Sarongs and such."

Lavinia's emerald eyes widened. "Sa— sarongs?"

Vernon's rotund middle joggled as he

laughed. "They're long pieces of fabric that you wrap around the waist."

Lavinia's mouth opened in wonder, then she giggled. "That's scandalous! What about the rest of me?"

"You'll be well-covered." He squeezed her hand. "Your costumes will only be suggestive of the South Pacific. And your hair," he gazed at the thick black tresses piled high, "you'll wear it down. With your exotic look, and your...mystique, the starring role in *Hidden Splendor* is just right for your debut."

"My debut!" Lavinia exclaimed. "Oh, I can't wait! Vernon, you're just too good to me! Do you think people will love me?"

"Of course," Vernon's eyes began to grow heavy and he leaned his head back, "but none as much as I do..."

****

In moments, Vernon was asleep. His large belly rose and fell, and his rasping snores kept time with the rhythmic chugging of the locomotive.

Using a lace-edged handkerchief, Lavinia patted dust from her brow. The heat from the train ride and its bitter smelling ash didn't faze her. She was too busy dreaming about her future plans. Lavinia lusted for the role of the island girl and wanted more than anything to reveal her talent to the world.

4

"Mrs. Hargraves." One of Vernon's servants, an Irish girl in prim and proper black attire, approached Lavinia and bowed slightly. "Dinner will be served in thirty minutes."

Lavinia suppressed a giggle. This maid suspected nothing. The thrill of a white servant kowtowing to her, as if she were a rich and powerful white person, was only too exhilarating!

She raised her head in a masquerade of white superiority. "Very well, then. Thank you."

The maid returned to the car's dining room, leaving Lavinia alone with Vernon once more. Soon, she'd need to wake her husband for the evening meal. But that slipped her mind. Instead, Lavinia's thoughts gravitated back to *Hidden Splendor*; not the play itself, but the title, which so brilliantly reflected her circumstances. She'd successfully escaped from California, and was now journeying to New York in search of the hidden splendor that awaited her!

Gazing at Vernon, she took notice of his black suit. He wore the color of mourning, which to Lavinia was rather symbolic. It represented the death of her old life. Lavinia was attired in purple. She remembered her mother saying that purple was the color of royalty, and now, Lavinia felt resurrected as a queen!

The locomotive swayed as it went around a curve. Vernon's balding head lolled to the side. He snorted loudly, as drool oozed from the corner of his mouth. Removing her eyes from him, Lavinia gazed at the car's elegant furnishings, varnished mahogany wall paneling, and the heavy red drapes trimmed in gold brocade. Then she peered from the window at the mountainous terrain and barren landscape under a setting sun of orange, pink and gold.

Good riddance, California, Lavinia said to herself. So what if her father was a powerful white man because of his land and money? Her mother was nothing but a lowly ex-slave, and because of that, Lavinia's life had nearly been ruined. Even though she looked white, Lavinia would never be thought of as anything more than Negro, and she was too pretty and too smart to stand for that!

She wouldn't miss her home, and she certainly wouldn't miss her parents — they'd never understood her, nor her dream of becoming an actress! And Lavinia would never forget the hurtful things they'd said to her before she'd run off with Vernon!

"Being an actress is barely one step above being a prostitute," Mother had said. Lavinia's lip twitched at the thought of her mother's blackness — blackness Lavinia had despised and disowned. And Father had called Vernon filth. That was before he'd told Lavinia that the stage was right where she belonged, because she'd acted like a whore! "Running after that man like a common strumpet," he'd said, "then selling yourself to him in a loveless marriage...You disgust me!"

Lavinia raised her chin, holding back the burn of tears inflicted by those scathing remarks. How dare they! Married in North Carolina in some kind of Quaker ritual, her parents' marriage wasn't even legally binding. But, Lavinia thought smugly, hers was. Vernon had appeared in California as if by magic to rescue her. Now, not only would he make her an actress and star, he'd give her a brand new life in New York — as white.

Chapter 1
Two Years Later
New York City, 1891

"So, Melinda," Andrew said to his beautiful female companion, "what did you think of *The White Company*?" They'd just finished a sumptuous meal at Sherry's in New York City, at 37th Street and Fifth Avenue. Andrew had had filet de boeuf, Melinda, poulet en casserole, and both had enjoyed baked Alaska for dessert.

Over the hum of soft conversation, silverware clinking gently on china, and the melodious sound of a Schumann quintet for piano and strings, Melinda said, "I love any great adventure novel, and I thoroughly enjoyed *The White Company*! To me, it's one of 1891's best books. I couldn't stop reading it," she laughed. "I devoured all three volumes…"

On their table sat a low centerpiece of red roses next to a slim lamp with a scalloped shade of frosted glass. Crystal chandeliers glimmered from above, suspended from ornately carved ceiling beams, while triple-armed brass sconces glowed from large scrolled columns.

The soft gas-lights enhanced Melinda's innocent beauty. Diamonds glistened at her ears, and the beaded pink silk she wore complimented the rosy hue of her skin. Her chestnut hair, swept up with a fringe of bangs in front and tendrils at the sides, shimmered with gold highlights.

With every little movement, her beaded gown and earrings twinkled shyly like distant stars in the night sky. She reached for a cut crystal goblet and took a sip of wine. Andrew knew she enjoyed Chateau Lafite Rothschild, so he'd ordered a bottle. But since he rarely drank, he'd only nursed one glass through dinner.

Andrew Standish, dressed in white tie and tails, was one of New York City's most eligible bachelors, and Melinda Jennings was a lovely intelligent girl, a graduate of Miss Porter's School, and the daughter of a banker. Andrew had met Melinda not long after her debutante ball. He'd called on her once before, although he couldn't remember when. His brother,

Julian, liked Melinda, and said she was perfect for Andrew because she was a level headed girl—but, in Andrew's opinion, Melinda could hardly compare to Lavinia Hargraves.

Melinda smiled, glancing briefly at the red roses, then, with a well manicured hand, smoothed the white linen tablecloth. Aside from the delicate bone china coffee cups and matching water and wine goblets, their dishes had been cleared away.

"...I must say," she continued, "John of Hordle was by far my favorite character, because of that sarcastic wit of his! Also, I believe..."

As Melinda continued talking, Andrew pretended to listen interestedly. Although beautiful women were at his disposal, he seldom called on the same one more than once or twice, because as far as Andrew was concerned, his heart belonged to Lavinia Hargraves.

Andrew realized his eyes had wandered to one of the elaborately carved columns when Melinda said his name. An MIT educated architect and contractor, he'd been studying the scroll work while thinking of Lavinia.

"Andrew," Melinda said again, slightly annoyed this time.

"Yes, Melinda," he flashed a charming smile, "you were saying?"

"I was *asking* what you thought about the

book."

"It was a fine work and very…" Andrew trailed off when he saw Lavinia Hargaves and her husband enter the restaurant. Melinda glanced over her shoulder as Andrew's eyes veered past her.

The head-waiter escorted the couple to a table. Lavinia was a sheer vision to behold as she strode by the mirrored walls among the admiring gazes, stares and gasps of Sherry's theater-loving patrons.

"Lavinia Hargraves," Andrew said in awe, "not only is she the greatest actress in New York, she's by far the most beautiful."

Her hair was twirled high, intertwined with jewels, and she wore a sequined lavender gown with thick tufts of feathers surrounding her bare shoulders and hemline.

"Her dress seems rather vulgar to me," Melinda said.

Melinda's shoulders were covered by capped sleeves and she lacked what it took to create truly breath-taking cleavage. Ignoring her, he said, "My friend, Justin Glass, the theater critic, says she's the greatest actress since Sarah Bernhardt. He wrote a glowing review of her last performance here. It was back in November, *The Taming of the Shrew*. Did you happen to see her in that production?"

"I was with *you* when you saw it! You'd called on me that evening!"

"Oh, yes, Melinda, of course. Wasn't she magnificent?"

Melinda sighed, frowning. "I suppose she was."

"I haven't seen her perform since then, and with her spring tour approaching, I won't see her on stage in New York again until May. I've never seen a finer actress. If I were an actor," Andrew said, "I'd like to play Petruchio to her Kate. I've never seen a more stunning creature."

Melinda sat back, crossing her arms. Her diamond earrings refracted the light, scattering a small shower of light beams across the table.

"The very presence of Lavinia Hargraves never fails to electrify me—uh—I *mean*—all those around her," Andrew said awkwardly, noticing his dinner companion's disgruntled expression.

Melinda's cheeks burned red. She stood up. The sudden movement made her beaded gown glitter angrily. Andrew rose with her. Keeping her voice low to prevent a scene, she said, "Andrew, I'll see myself home."

"Melinda, darling—I—I..."

"You needn't see me to the door," she hissed sharply.

"I'm sorry," was all Andrew managed to say, as Melinda turned to go—yet he really wasn't sorry to see her leave. Sitting down again, he watched Lavinia as she slowly, and a

bit seductively, removed her long lavender
gloves. Then she acknowledged those she
knew with a slight bow of her head, as a queen
might acknowledge her subjects.

Andrew Standish had fallen in love with
Lavinia Hargraves two years earlier when he'd
first seen her perform in *Hidden Splendor.*
She'd become a star that night, and Andrew
had decided that one day she'd become his
wife. He just hadn't known she was married at
the time.

Her last name was Hargraves; he'd seen
that in the theater program. But Andrew had
assumed that the young woman was perhaps a
great niece, third cousin, or other family
relation of Vernon Hargraves. After the
production, however, he felt sickened upon
hearing the truth.

Vernon had married Lavinia in secret.
However, he'd not "unveiled" her until her
first appearance as the star of *Hidden Splendor.*
At the close of the first night performance
Andrew had attended, Vernon himself, had
introduced Lavinia to the audience, as not only
his stunning new discovery, but also his wife.
Andrew had then resigned himself to the sad
realization that he couldn't marry her — at least
not yet.

Stars attended after theater meals of fowl
and wine, called bird and bottle suppers,
during the theater season, and Lavinia and

Vernon usually went to Sherry's, Delmonico's or one of the other restaurants in the nearby Broadway hotels. To find out exactly where they'd go, Andrew would bribe one of the stage-hands. But when Lavinia dined out during the off season, he had no way of knowing where she'd turn up. Tonight he'd been lucky—luckier still, now that Melinda was gone.

Gazing toward Lavinia, Andrew finished the last of the Chateau Lafite in his glass. Then, savoring the wine's delicate flavor and appreciating its almond and violet aroma, he slowly drank two more glasses.

Unencumbered by a female, and emboldened by the wine, Andrew decided that he'd make the best of an opportunity. He'd have a chance to meet Lavinia, and stand only mere inches away from her. He summoned his waiter. Andrew knew Vernon through real estate business, and as a patron of the arts, Andrew had made contributions to the Hargraves Theater. Tonight he'd manage to wrangle an introduction to the old man's wife.

****

Once seated, Vernon gazed proudly at Lavinia while she nodded regally toward their acquaintances. Her sequins sparkled and flashed along with the diamonds that dangled from her ears and the crystals that were twirled through her raven hair. The frothy feathers surrounding her shoulders made her appear as Venus beginning her rise from the sea foam.

Lavinia was his prize, and he'd made her a star. Vernon had spoiled his young wife and invested time and money in her career, perhaps at the cost of neglecting his daughter, Carrie.

"Carrie should have come with us tonight," he said.

"You asked her." Lavinia smiled tightly, nodding toward an actress friend. "But she chose not to. It's not your fault that your daughter *detests* being around people. And besides, Carrie feels only a mere shadow in my presence."

"Well, regardless of how she feels being out on the town with us, or you in particular," Vernon said, "she needs to get out more. That would help lift her spirits."

Lavinia smirked. "She needs to get out more so she can find a husband, if that's even possible at her age."

"Now, Lavinia, don't—" Vernon began. But he was interrupted by the appearance of a waiter in a short white jacket and black bow tie. He carried a bottle of wine.

"Pardon me, Mr. and Mrs. Hargraves," the waiter said, "a gift, compliments of Mr. Standish." He glanced across the restaurant in Andrew's direction. Andrew tipped his wineglass toward the Hargraveses, and they nodded in return.

The waiter held one hand under the bottom of the bottle and rested the neck on his forearm. With the label facing Vernon, he read, "Lacryma Christi, vintage 1889." After uncorking the glimmering red wine, the waiter served it to Lavinia and Vernon, then discreetly disappeared.

Lavinia fingered the heart shaped locket around her neck, then leaned toward Vernon. "So just who is that Mr. Standish," she asked. Vernon grunted a response that she barely heard. "What did you say?"

"He's one of our theater's biggest contributors." Vernon was coherent this time, but he provided no further information.

Lifting his glass, Vernon peered in Standish's direction. As the younger man stood up and began walking toward him, Vernon downed the wine like grape juice. It was bad enough that Standish had given them wine, Vernon thought, but now he was headed to their table.

Vernon could deal with Standish on business terms, but with Lavinia by his side, he'd rather the young man keep his distance. Vernon was worth a few million, but Standish was worth several more. Also, Standish was trim, over six feet tall, and sturdily built. His skin was fair, his hair a thick auburn, and his eyes sea green. With an aquiline nose and strong jaw line, Standish had the good looks of an actor, along with a winning smile and natural charisma.

Even worse, Standish was a gentleman, born in England, the son of a duke. But Andrew didn't use the title. He'd been in the States since childhood and considered himself a New Yorker through and through.

Aside from being a theater lover, Standish didn't engage in the same kind of fun that Vernon enjoyed. Standish didn't gamble or smoke, and with the exception of a little wine, he didn't drink. He rode a bicycle for recreation, boxed, and even had a gymnasium in his West Side brownstone.

As Standish approached, Vernon tried to exhibit the calm disposition of a confident old man with a beautiful young wife. However, he couldn't help but feel self-conscious about his thinning hair, bulging stomach and the twenty plus years he had on Standish. Both men wore white tie and tails, but Vernon's protruding front made him look more like a penguin. Sucking in his gut, Vernon stood to greet him.

"Andrew Standish," Vernon said, forcing himself to sound gregarious.

Standish shook his hand. "Vernon, it's nice to see you this evening, and," his eyes met Lavinia's, "your lovely wife. I don't believe I've ever met her." Vernon grimaced slightly, then introduced them. After kissing Lavinia's fingers, Andrew said, "Mrs. Hargraves, I must say you're not only the most beautiful actress I've ever seen, but also the most brilliant."

"Why, thank you, Mr. Standish." Lavinia glowed in the wake of Standish's admiration. "My husband tells me you've made substantial contributions to our theater. And just what do you do?"

"I own real estate throughout the city, as well as Truelove and Standish Contractors."

"I see...and you build what?" Lavinia asked.

"Skyscrapers, exclusively. I'm going to rebuild this city with steel," Standish said confidently.

Vernon observed his wife as she gazed up at Standish, and he wasn't pleased. It wasn't just the man's looks and breeding that threatened him. Upon learning of Standish's wealth, Lavinia's emerald eyes didn't merely sparkle, they ignited. With each bat of her lids, the flame grew brighter. And Vernon didn't like the way Standish looked at Lavinia, either. His eyes watered, not with tears, but carnal hunger.

"Do forgive my manners, Mr. Standish," Lavinia said, "thank you for the wine. It's quite good."

"I'm glad you're enjoying it. Lacryma Christi is my favorite and I chose that vintage because that's the year you became a star."

"Oh?" Lavinia glanced at the bottle. "So it is. Well, do tell me, what does Lacryma Christi mean?"

A low laugh rumbled in Vernon. "You may not want to know," he grumbled under his breath.

"Tears of Christ," Andrew replied.

The glow left Lavinia's face. Her eyes widened slightly. The flame died down in them. Vernon watched as her once beaming countenance darkened. He knew what she was thinking: Her Bible toting parents were convinced she'd burn in hell for becoming an actress, and now she was even being reminded that Jesus was crying over her decision.

"If you'll excuse me," Lavinia said, stiffly. She stood up and left the table, her sequins creating a flurry of flashes and flares.

As she walked to the ladies room, Vernon smiled satisfied, feeling triumphant.

Andrew was left dumbfounded. With a look of confusion, he said, "Did I..." but he seemed unsure of exactly what to ask.

"Thanks again for the wine, Standish." Vernon dismissed the younger man with a slap on the back. "Now, you go on and have yourself a nice evening."

CHAPTER 2

After a warm bath in the claw foot tub, Lavinia sat at her vanity in a red satin bathrobe. She removed her makeup with Atkinson's Rose Cold Cream and a cotton cloth, while Vernon stood behind her in pajamas and a blue silk lounging robe.

He placed both hands on his wife's shoulders. "You're the most talented actress on the planet." Bending to kiss her neck, his balding pate glistened in the mirror's reflection, illuminated by the gas sconces mounted on each side.

"And every man thinks you're the most beautiful woman in the world."

Lavinia only smiled at her husband's compliments while wiping away the heavily scented cold cream smeared on her face.

"I didn't like the way that Standish fellow

looked at you tonight."

"I'm trying to forget about that Standish fellow," Lavinia scoffed, "and how he gave us that bottle of Jesus's blood to drink!"

Vernon stood tall, laughing. His large belly jiggled. "It was called Tears of Christ."

"Then why was it red? Blood, sweat, tears, whatever! That wine — it was like a sign or something."

"It didn't mean a thing. Just put it — *and* him — out of your head."

"I will, and the sooner the better."

Vernon started for the door. "I'll be back in a little while. I'm going up to check on Carrie."

"Why do you have to check on her now?" Lavinia smirked.

Vernon stopped, turning toward his wife. Her eyes still remained in the looking glass as she cleaned away the last of her makeup. "She seems a little down," he said.

"Oh," Lavinia huffed. "Since we've been married, Carrie's always seemed," she moved her gaze to Vernon, then mimicked, "a 'little down.'"

"Lavinia," Vernon said, impatiently, "she's still my little girl, and —"

"Little girl? She's twenty-four!"

Vernon sighed. "You know what I mean. She had me all to herself before I married you and —"

"And would you *change* being married to me?" Lavinia snapped.

"Never." Vernon smiled, almost melting as he looked at his prize. "But I need to see how my daughter's doing."

"Fine," Lavinia, said sharply, watching him leave the room.

Turning back to the mirror, she began applying Hinds Honey and Almond Cream to her face. "That mousy little thing is hopeless," Lavinia fussed to herself. "Carrie should be married with a family of her own, but all she does is sit in her room and write! And she's *always* sad! At least she's *seemed* that way for the past two years that I've lived here!"

As Lavinia finished massaging the cream into her skin, her mind began to wander. Two years, she reflected. Had it really been that long since she'd escaped from California and that hell-hole she'd once called home? Lavinia sighed contentedly, then picked up her hairbrush.

Destiny had been good, she thought, while running the brush through her thick black tresses. It seemed like only yesterday that she'd arrived in New York, but so much had happened since then.

Lavinia smiled, remembering how it hadn't taken her long to adjust to New York City's fast pace. Living among its aggressive, obnoxious and overcrowded inhabitants had seemed almost intoxicating, and Vernon's opulent lifestyle was another easy adjustment.

Vernon lived in a massive limestone mansion that resembled a castle. He had servants for everything, but they were all Irish, so none suspected her of being anything but white. After all, according to the press releases written by Vernon's press agent, Lavinia's mother was Spanish, which accounted for her very dark hair and the slight olive caste of her skin.

Negro servants would have studied her hair and complexion, then whispered behind her back, causing her to live in fear. Lavinia exhaled in relief. She wasn't worried in the least about what Vernon's maids thought of her, but she'd made no attempt to endear herself to any of them.

Vernon's lavish four-story dwelling was situated near West End Avenue. Although the décor was gaudy and extravagant, Lavinia didn't mind. Indeed, she'd made it even more gaudy with the new furniture she'd purchased.

The first floor drawing room had a large mahogany sofa and matching chairs with elaborately carved leaf and scroll ornamentation and ornate gold and purple upholstery. A large table made of rosewood and brass was in the center of the room along with two enormous tiger skin rugs.

The dining room was adjacent to the

drawing room. Leather covered walls and decorative red velvet hangings surrounded an intricately carved Chippendale sideboard and dining room set. Large potted palms were placed in each corner and a huge fireplace was along one wall.

On the second floor was the master bedroom with an adjoining parlor, dressing room and master bath. In the sleeping quarters, mirrors flanked the large brass bed. Carrie's bedroom was on the third floor, along with three other guest bedrooms. The multitude of servants required to operate the sprawling household had their rooms on the fourth floor.

Aside from the house, what had been most exciting since her arrival in New York was her reception by the public as an actress — and star! Vernon furnished her with roles that showcased her stunning beauty and extraordinary talent. From Shakespeare to modern dramas, any role she played never failed to draw a full house.

After she'd appeared in her first play, the papers declared, "Lavinia Hargraves is a hit," and "a dynamic sensation that set the stage on fire with her very presence." Lavinia put down her hairbrush. She stared at herself in the looking glass while mentally reciting those quotes. She couldn't remember the exact publications, but she'd never forget the words.

Hidden Splendor was the production, and she'd performed in it near the end of 1889. It was a chaste romantic drama in which Lavinia had played an island girl who falls in love with an American sailor. She'd become a star that night. There were too many good reviews, and Lavinia couldn't possibly remember them all, but one she could still quote verbatim was written in the *The New York Times Dramatic Mirror*. Vernon received it weekly and he'd read her the review upon its arrival.

"Lavinia!" he'd called, "Listen to what Gerald Matthews wrote about you in the *The Mirror*. 'Who was the exotic temptress with the extraordinary range and superb acting ability starring in Vernon Hargraves's latest production, *Hidden Splendor*? No other than his new bride, Lavinia Hargraves! She is spectacular, beautiful and talented. This critic waits in eager anticipation to see her next role! She is the jewel in the crown of the Hargraves Players and she is, indeed, the not so hidden splendor of this production!'"

Now embarrassed, Lavinia recalled how, at then seventeen, she'd jumped up and down while squealing with delight, "I'm great! I'm great!"

Remembering the criticism she'd received from William Winter, the dramatic critic for the *New York Tribune,* Lavinia smirked. Winter condemned her and the play. She'd never been able to erase his words from her memory, yet Lavinia's smirk widened to a smile. Even though he'd despised her, Lavinia had to admit that she'd rather liked his review.

"The wanton beauty alone of that Lavinia Hargraves defies the limits of common decency," he'd self-righteously declared. "Her searing portrayal of an island vixen, in the already salacious production of *Hidden Splendor* leads the audience, as well as her doltish co-star, Emmett Forester, within mere inches of hell's fiery furnace."

It was said by the publisher of *The Dramatic Mirror* that William Winter could

unearth impurity from the quotations of the stock market.

However, Lavinia was convinced the man just didn't like her! His reviews were always antagonistic. Lavinia sighed. Or perhaps he loved her, and was trying to woo her with negative praise. Whatever the case, it didn't matter. Regardless of what Winter said, audiences flocked to see her in droves, and from this, Lavinia had realized that there was no such thing as bad publicity.

With the exception of Winter's prose, her reviews were stellar and the papers loved writing about her. She'd been interviewed by the *New York Times* recently and the clipped article still lay on her dresser.

After walking to retrieve it, she gazed at

the words:

This esteemed player has no formal training but can easily portray any personality on stage. She can effortlessly display warmth and serenity, or wild, reckless passion, her emotional scenes leaving audiences overcome and yearning for more. She can make an audience weep as she emotes heartfelt sobs, her voice sounding as though flooded by a river of tears.

Setting down the paper, Lavinia raised a brow. No one knew that to shed such realistic tears, all she had to do was think about being Negro, and how her life would be ruined if anyone knew. As for her lack of formal training, she'd told the reporter, "My acting comes from my heart." The article had concluded by saying: Lavinia Hargraves is one of the greatest emotional actresses of our time.

Lavina walked to her dressing room, still floating high on those words. She removed her robe, then slipped on a pink silk nightgown edged in white lace. The bodice was embroidered with pink and blue butterflies. Gazing in the full length mirror, she admired her reflection.

Without makeup, and not even wearing an evening gown, Lavinia still possessed a beauty that startled even her sometimes. "I'm the most beautiful woman *I've* ever seen," Lavinia said to herself, "as well as the greatest emotional actress of our time."

CHAPTER 3

Vernon trudged up to the third floor. Although Carrie kept her feelings to herself, Vernon knew what was going on inside his daughter's head. When she was upset, she'd close herself away and write. To her, writing was almost like crying.

Vernon felt a little guilty thinking about the positive side to this. Carrie's melancholy mood caused her to become a more prolific writer. Her plays were well loved by the public and received praise from the critics. They'd earned good money. Yet Vernon would rather see Carrie happy.

Since he'd married Lavinia, Carrie had withdrawn more and more. Now it was to the point that she'd barely leave her room. The spring tour was about to start, and Vernon didn't want to leave town without having a heart to heart talk with his daughter.

"Carrie?" Vernon knocked on her door.

"Come in, Daddy."

Vernon opened the door. Carrie sat at her roll top desk. Down her back flowed long blond hair. That was Carrie's best feature. As she turned to look at him, Vernon thought it a pity that the horse face he'd given her didn't quite match the ingénue-like tresses she'd inherited from her mother.

Carrie's mother had been a beautiful actress, but Carrie was plain, with bovine eyes and a slim hooked nose. Her mouth was long and her lips full, yet she did posses a beautiful smile, even though her teeth were large and slightly spaced.

Regardless of her ordinary appearance and reed thin figure, Carrie was still Vernon's little girl, and he knew of no one more beautiful on the inside.

"I knew you'd still be awake—and writing." He smiled. Carrie was dressed for bed in a pink and white robe that she wore over a simple white nightgown. "When's that play gonna be finished?" Vernon asked. "Just the other day a critic asked when I'd be presenting another work by the talented Carrie Hargraves."

A slight smile lit her face. "It's almost finished."

"Good. I think I've got the casting all

figured out!"

Carrie's little smile disappeared. "With Lavinia starring, of course."

Vernon didn't respond. Instead he took a seat on the pink chaise longue not far from her desk. This made Carrie almost laugh. Vernon chuckled, knowing that the sight of his large frame on her fainting couch amused her.

"Carrie," Vernon eyed her seriously, "I know the past couple of years haven't been easy for you. But in the last few months you've rarely left your room."

Carrie glanced away. "I'm fine, Daddy. It's just that—it's takes some time to—get used to Lavinia. Her living here—has made my life—a little different. But since you're happy—"

"Carrie," Vernon interrupted, "you're not a very good liar. I *don't* think you're fine."

Carrie played with the pink cord of the robe tied around her waist. Then, looking at Vernon, tears pooled in her large eyes. "I've tried to accept your marriage to—Lavinia—but I can't. Life goes on, though, so I just try my best to live it..."

She paused for a long moment. "I'll never forget the first day she came here...You'd sent me a telegram from California telling me you'd married. Then you arrived in New York—and brought her home to meet me—before the two of you left on your honeymoon to Europe."

Carrie took a deep breath. "When I was introduced to your new wife, she conveyed to me that *she'd* be the queen of this household — and that I was no better than a scullery maid."

"Lavinia said no such thing!" Vernon exclaimed.

"She didn't use words, Daddy. Lavinia arrived here resplendent in queen's blue satin, like royalty. Upon first seeing me, her nose rose high — and she sneered. Then — she extended her fingers — but from the look in her eyes — it was as if she wanted me drop to my knees and *kiss* her hand, rather than shake it."

"Carrie, you imagine too many things; I was right there! I didn't see any of what you're talking about. And that was a long time ago. Let's talk about now. I think if we discuss everything you're trying to hide, you might feel a little better."

Carrie's pale face reddened. "Daddy, you're aware of what I'm hiding! But my main concern is you. You came back from that tour married to a young girl — a child almost — and you hardly even knew her! You love her, but does *she* love you?" Vernon was silent. "Does she *care* about you?

"You *know* Mama never stopped loving you!" Tears spilled down Carrie's cheeks. "Year after year you promised to marry her — when the time was right. She waited through every one of your affairs, and in the twelve years after I was born, up until she died, the time was never right!"

At this, Vernon felt more guilt. Carrie had implied more than once that her mother had died from a broken heart.

"When I talk about Mama," Carrie swiped away tears with her fingertips, "you always say that's water under the bridge. But if you'd loved her half as much as you love Lavinia, she might still be alive. You wouldn't marry *Mama*, but you married a complete stranger!

"Daddy—since you married Lavinia, you've been drinking more. For a while you weren't drinking as much. I don't care about Lavinia not liking me. It used to bother me a little, because no one's ever *dis*liked me. But what does bother me—is how she feels about you." Then Carrie mumbled softly, "You're just her ticket to stardom..."

Vernon chose not to acknowledge what Carrie had said about Lavinia's sentiment toward him. He knew his young wife didn't love him. Physically, things had slightly improved. She didn't brace herself before lovemaking anymore. As if enduring a ritual of torture, Lavinia used to grab onto the spindles in the brass head board and tightly shut her eyes for the duration of his amorous activity. But she'd finally adjusted, somewhat, though she'd never once expressed pleasure.

Lavinia was, however, genuinely fond of

her husband. She'd told Vernon many times how much she admired him, how proud she was to be his wife, and how impressed she was by the way he managed his theatrical company. Lavinia never tired of asking him questions about the theater, and she loved hearing him explain every detail. Although appreciative of her pride and admiration, what Vernon truly craved was Lavinia's love.

"Maybe you could try being a little nicer to her," Vernon said.

"Nicer?" Carrie said incredulously. "I *am* nice to her—I'm nice to everybody! I couldn't be cruel if I tried!"

Vernon hesitated. "You know she hates it when you call her—'Mother'." He watched as Carrie stiffened and pursed her lips. He hadn't overlooked his daughter's passive jabs toward his wife. "She's told you to call her Lavinia."

Carrie sighed. "All right. I won't call her 'Mother' again. But other than that, I've been as nice as I can be and she *still* hates me! She calls me 'that mousy little thing', she disparages my writing—so I just stay out of her way. I can tolerate Lavinia, as long as I'm not around her!"

Carrie dropped her eyes to her lap. "That's how I feel...that's the truth...I've probably said too much. And I'm sorry, Daddy, if I've hurt your feelings."

Vernon walked to Carrie and gently

squeezed her shoulder. "I wanted you to tell me what you were holding in," he smiled, "and you let go of quite a bit."

Carrie gazed up to her father, returning his smile.

Sadly, Vernon reflected, everything Carrie had said was true. "Lavinia's not the easiest person to know, but she's got my heart, and I can't do anything about loving her. But I do want you and Lavinia to—at least be friends."

Carrie frowned. "Friends? I hardly think she wants to be my friend. That does work both ways. But—I do have an idea—it's an idea for a play—for her."

"That's my girl!" Vernon said excitedly. "Lavinia will be thrilled to have a play written just for her!"

"I know," Carrie said, flatly. "Daddy, I'm not beautiful like the women you've known or your actresses—"

"But honey," Vernon stopped her, "you're more beautiful than all of them put together, because you're real, and you've got a heart. Actresses just wear a bunch of powder and paint—and that makes 'em look like what they ain't!"

Carrie nodded with a slight smile, then sighed. "Well, I don't want to be an old maid forever. I hope there *is* someone special out there for me."

Vernon bent to kiss her forehead. "There

is, and he'll be the luckiest man in the world when he finds you. But he better treat you right, or there's gonna be trouble!"

Carrie laughed.

"Now that's more like it! You stop being sad. Come by our room before we turn in and tell Lavinia all about that play you're writing for her."

Carrie looked down as though ashamed. "It's not a very flattering piece of work."

Vernon chuckled, not surprised by her confession. "You think you can change it up some?"

"For you, I will. I'll need a little time to rethink the story, but I'll come tell you about it as soon as it *is* flattering."

****

"Carrie's writing a play just for *me*?" Lavinia asked Vernon in their bedroom. She lay comfortably on a purple chaise longue edged with gold brocade. Wearing her red robe, she perused a script for *The Masked Ball,* her first spring touring production.

"That's what she told me," Vernon said, "and she'll be down later to tell us all about it." He reclined on their turned down bed, propped up on two large feather pillows. With his sprawling girth spread across the ruffles and frills of the bedding, Vernon resembled a walrus.

Not bothering to look away from her script, Lavinia said, "Well, well. I just can't wait to hear what that mousy little thing has to say, because she barely ever says a word!"

"Lavinia," Vernon said sharply, "Carrie has a name! Respect her enough to use it."

Glancing at her husband, Lavinia raised a brow. "Aren't you the touchy one? You've spoiled her. You dote on her entirely too much. Just like Father doted on my sister, Olivia. He gave *her* everything."

"I'm all Carrie has."

"But you won't be around forever. Then what'll she do? She's an old maid, a spinster! It's time she finds a husband and gets out of here." Lavinia closed the play and tossed it to the floor. She said nothing for a moment, then leaned back against the velvet upholstery. Gazing at the ceiling, she asked, "Did Carrie ever write a play for Andrina Styles?"

"No."

"Good!" Lavinia sat up. Catching Vernon's gaze, she said, "That tramp hates me, and I know why! Andrina told me more than I ever needed to know about your *affair* with her!"

"That was over a long time ago." Vernon shook a cigarette from a pack of Duke's Best, then struck a match to light it.

"Apparently, she's still carrying a torch for you."

After inhaling, Vernon blew out a thin stream of smoke. "She's just jealous because of all the attention you get from the audience and the critics." He took another puff, then smiled slyly, patting the spot beside him on the bed. "Maybe before Carrie comes down, we can…"

She knew what he wanted, but she'd rather talk about the theater and all his upcoming productions for her. The marital bed — the price she paid — was revolting. In between theater seasons they were home earlier in the evenings and to her dismay, Vernon was extremely amorous.

He wanted her almost every night. However, if he were a little tipsy, he'd be less likely to feel the urge to indulge. Lavinia rose, then strode to the black marble table not far from her chaise longue. On it sat a cut crystal decanter. She removed the stopper, then poured bourbon into two crystal tumblers.

Lavinia had discovered that as long as she kept Vernon steadily imbibing throughout the day, that by bedtime, a drink or two would put him to sleep in an instant. She'd noticed that over the past two years, his tolerance to alcohol had lessened.

"Have a drink with me, darling?" She asked seductively, although she had no intention of drinking the bourbon she'd poured for herself. But since Vernon hated to drink alone, she'd pretend to take small sips.

Lavinia's parents had never allowed liquor in the house, and when she'd married Vernon, she'd been eager to try it. She'd found she only preferred wine, and only then on occasion.

As Lavinia walked toward him, Vernon reached toward his nightstand to put out his cigarette. The tiny figure of a Negro child holding a cigar stood at one end of his rectangular metal ashtray. Dressed in baggy clothes, the boy wore a bowler hat on his bobbing head. Extinguishing his cigarette, Vernon eyed Lavinia and the whiskey, while the ashtray boy nodded enthusiastically.

Vernon took the tumbler from his wife, and without hesitation, swallowed the entire drink. Lavinia smiled sweetly, pretended to take a sip of hers, and then walked to the other side of the bed. After placing her glass on the nightstand, she'd never touch it again. While fluffing her pillows, Lavinia hoped it wouldn't be too long before Carrie arrived, or Vernon fell asleep.

When she'd made herself comfortable, Lavinia suddenly remembered the previous topic of their conversation. Becoming angry all over again, she said, "I've got more talent than that Andrina Styles. I'm younger, more beautiful, and married to *you*! She has good reason to hate me. But she's absolutely despicable to me, and even has the nerve to act like *she's* better than *I* am." Peering at Vernon suspiciously, Lavinia continued, "I know you two were *lovers*, so just what *did* you tell her about me?"

"The same as what I've told the press agent to write. You come from a wealthy family out West. Your father was from a well-to-do Southern planter's family, and your mother was from Spain, but they're both dead."

****

Carrie walked slowly down the dim hallway, the only light coming from sconces lining the wall. The floorboards creaked slightly, but Carrie slowed her pace as she approached her father's bedroom.

The door was open just a crack, yet when Carrie was about to knock, she stilled upon hearing Vernon's voice.

"I didn't mention anything about your Negro mother, if that's what you're thinkin'. I haven't told a soul. That's our secret, remember? I meant what I said, Lavinia. No one will ever know, I promise.

"Sometimes," he slurred slightly, "I wonder about your folks…what they'd think about you bein' an actress and all. There they sat with their rich pious selves out in California lookin' down on me. I'm used to bein' looked down on by pompous asses like your pa, but not by no nig…niggra, like you're uppity ma."

"As far as I'm concerned, my parents *are* dead," Lavinia said bitterly. "Don't ever speak of them again."

Carrie's heartbeat quickened with excitement, and she smiled in triumph. Relishing the fact that she now had the power to destroy Lavinia, Carrie waited a few moments before knocking.

"That you, Carrie?" Vernon asked, upon hearing a rap on the door.

"Yes, Daddy, it's me."

"Come in," Lavinia said coolly.

When Carrie walked in, she remembered how masculine her father's bedroom had once been. But Lavinia had feminized it by draping the bed with gold ribbons.

It still galled Carrie to know that her father shared his bed with such a horrid woman— and a Negro at that! And Carrie was further distraught to see an empty glass on her father's nightstand. An identical one was on Lavinia's side, its amber contents untouched.

"I won't keep you but a few moments," Carrie said softly.

"You gonna tell us about your play for Lavinia?" Vernon asked.

"Yes," Carrie said. But before she began, she gazed toward Lavinia's vanity. Something glimmered not far from it on the Oriental carpet.

"Mother—I mean—Lavinia," Carrie said, walking toward the shiny object, "I think a piece of your jewelry is on the floor." Bending to pick it up, Carrie saw that it was Lavinia's locket. She stood, holding the trinket high to admire its delicate beauty. The encrusted diamonds and rubies glistened.

"Oh," Lavinia said, "my locket. Just set it on my dressing table, will you?"

"Of course." Carrie placed it carefully on the vanity.

"It must have slid off the edge of the table. Your father's given me so much jewelry since we've married, I hardly ever wear that locket anymore. But it is a beautiful piece, and precious to me. It's an heirloom." Lavinia paused for a moment. "My father gave it to me—because I was his favorite daughter."

Carrie tipped her head. "I thought you were an only child."

"I did have a sister," Lavinia said quickly, "but she died."

"Oh." Carrie's brows rose in surprise. "I'm sorry. So—your parents *and* your sister are dead? How did they die?"

Lavinia eyed her suspiciously. "I'd rather not talk about that!" she barked.

"Forgive me for upsetting you. But didn't you tell me once that the locket's been passed down for several generations on your father's side?"

Again, Lavinia peered at her with apprehension. "Yes. And just why are you so interested in my locket all of a sudden?" She asked sharply.

Carrie felt the hair on the back of her neck bristle. "I — I was just curious — that's all. It's so lovely, you should wear it more often. But — enough about that." Vernon's eyes appeared heavy. "Daddy's just about to fall asleep. The title of my work — by the way — is related to jewelry. I'll tell you what it is after I've told you the story, so you'll better understand its significance. Perhaps both of you could — act out this brief scene."

Handing one page of her script to Lavinia, Carrie said, "You're Anna. Your husband is angry, but you don't care." Then Carrie walked to the opposite side of the bed. Vernon's eyes had completely closed, and just as she was about to nudge his shoulder, Lavinia stopped her.

"Carrie, *please* don't wake your father! He needs his rest. You and I can act out the scene."

Disregarding Lavinia's protest, Carrie shook her father's shoulder. "Lavinia, Daddy can go right back to sleep after he reads this. He loves acting out my plays before he casts them. This will give him a head start."

Vernon stirred, smiling sleepily at his daughter. "You want me to act, honey? Who do you want me to be?"

"Your name is Patrick," Carrie said, "and you're an enraged husband." Lavinia smirked leaning toward Vernon so she could share the script with him. "And Lavinia, of course, is Anna, your wife—just like in real life."

"Ready?" Vernon asked Lavinia. After she nodded, Vernon cleared his throat and began reading the role of Patrick to Lavinia's Anna.

Patrick: *Anna, you were nothing when I found you, and now you'll be nothing again!*

Anna: *But I care not, because I have something greater! Something that your money could never buy.*

Patrick: *You'll come crawling back to me! You'll see. When poverty walks in the door, love flies out the window!"*

Anna: *Despite what you think, Patrick, I'll be richer than I ever was with you.*

"Anna exits stage left," Lavinia read. Then with a pinched face she asked, "So—what happened prior to this, and what happens next?"

"Anna is very beautiful," Carrie replied. "That's why Patrick married her, yet he's unfaithful, because he doesn't love her. He's very rich, and gives Anna lots of material possessions, including a perfect strand of gleaming white pearls. But Anna's life is sad and empty with him, because the only thing he won't give her, is his love.

"So Anna leaves Patrick for a poor man, named Nathan. Nathan can only afford to give her a small token. But despite the lack of material things, Anna is truly happy and fulfilled with him, because she has his love.

"The title of your play comes from that small token Nathan gives to Anna to symbolize his love. It's a single Majorca pearl, one of those beautiful dark pearls that comes from Spain."

"And just what *is* the title of my play," Lavinia asked impatiently.

"*The Black Pearl.*"

Lavinia winced upon hearing '*black*', and that was the reaction Carrie wanted. "I'd originally entitled it *Love's True Beauty*," Carrie smiled innocently. "But *The Black Pearl* is a much more fitting, don't you think? Especially since your mother was...a Spaniard?"

CHAPTER 4
NEW YORK CITY, 1894

The actors were in a replica of Cleopatra's palace. Gauze drapes lined the back of the stage and two huge columns stood on each side with large potted palms in front.

...Here is my space,
Kingdoms are clay; our dungy earth alike
Feeds beast as man; the nobleness of life
Is to do thus...

Kenneth Tyler recited his lines to Lavinia as they performed their first dress rehearsal of Shakespeare's *Antony and Cleopatra*. He thought himself the perfect Mark Antony with his dark haired good looks and lanky frame. Several actresses had described his smoldering sapphire eyes as deadly, because they'd pierced the heart of many a woman.

A dagger was strapped to Kenneth's waist and sandals were on his feet. He wore a woolen tunic with decorative body armor and shoulder plates. The stage directions called for an embrace, and as usual, Lavinia stiffened when his arms encircled her. He continued holding her as he said the rest of his lines.

> *...when such a mutual pair*
> *And such a twain can do't, in which I bind,*
> *On pain of punishment, the world to weet*
> *We stand up peerless.' "*

"I want both of you to walk to center stage while Kenneth is talking," Vernon's voice boomed from the front row. "Stop at center stage when it's time for the embrace." Kenneth and Lavinia nodded in his direction.

Now Lavinia pulled from Kenneth and spoke as Cleopatra. She wore a black braided wig adorned with beads, and a long white muslin sheath, its broad collar decorated in elaborate jewels made of paste.

> *Excellent falsehood!*
> *Why did he marry Fulvia, and not love her?*
> *I'll seem the fool I am not. Antony*
> *Will be himself.*

"Walk away from him some, Lavinia,"

Vernon directed. Lavinia did as she was told. "Now, Kenneth, approach her from behind, grab her arm and turn her to face you."

As Antony, Kenneth followed Vernon's instruction, then muttered under his breath, "I'd much rather grab something else."

"Did you say something?" Lavinia whispered.

Kenneth shook his head with a leering smile. "I was merely thinking out loud." From here, Kenneth went straight to his lines and grabbed her arm.

> *But stirr'd by Cleopatra.*
> *Now for the love of Love, and her soft hours,*
> *Let's not confound the time with conference harsh;*
> *There's not a minute of our lives should stretch*
> *Without some pleasure now. What sport to-night?*

He gazed at Lavinia and raised a brow. "I could think of many," he said only loud enough for her to hear.

Caught off guard, Lavinia forgot her line. Kenneth mouthed the word "hear" to get her started. *"Hear the ambassadors,"* she said somewhat distracted, and then Kenneth concluded his scene with her onstage.

> *Fie, Wrangling queen!*

Whom everything becomes — to chide, to laugh,
To weep, whose every passion fully strives
To make itself in thee fair and admir'd!
No messenger but thine, and all alone,
To-night we'll wander through the streets and
note
The qualities of people. Come, my queen,
Last night you did desire it.

Directing his last line to the actor playing the messenger, a young man wearing a simple white tunic, Kenneth said, "*Speak not to us.*"

As he and Lavinia exited the stage, followed by the messenger, Kenneth placed Lavinia's hand on his dagger, then said for her ears only, "perhaps you can unsheathe my dagger."

"That line's not in the script, Kenneth!" Lavinia snapped, once they were backstage. "Nor was that other one. *You* should know that performing Shakespeare is certainly *not* the time to add dialogue at your leisure!"

Kenneth almost laughed as she walked away from him to observe the remainder of Act I, Scene I from the wings.

****

With the rehearsal complete, the entire cast and crew strode onto the stage. Kenneth watched as Vernon lumbered toward center stage to join everyone.

"Bravo, everyone," Vernon exclaimed enthusiastically, his hog's belly protruding from beneath his vest. "And Lavinia—flawless as always!"

"Mr. Hargraves, what about my Kenneth?" Jenny Green said, as she bustled behind him, her cockney accent just as thick as Kenneth's when he wasn't performing. She'd sat next to Vernon during the rehearsal. "Wasn't he superb?" Kenneth listened as his doting fiancé sang his praises.

Vernon turned to face her. "Of course, and he and Lavinia are still magic together, even in a tragedy!" Vernon chuckled, then yelled toward Kenneth, "Stealing him from Theodore Johnstone's Players in London was the best financial move I ever made." He grasped Jenny's hand in a paternal gesture and then kissed it. "But I saw you first as Ophelia."

Jenny smiled. "That was a long time ago. I'm so busy with my two girls, the theater's a distant memory."

"Never too late to make a comeback." Vernon winked at her, then clapped to get his company's attention.

Male actors milled about wearing togas and tunics, while the women cast members were costumed in long white muslin with simple beaded collars and black braided wigs. The crew, in modern dress, held conversation alongside the ancient Egyptians.

Kenneth had overheard Vernon's remark to Jenny while he'd spoken to Joel Hancock, the actor playing Caesar. When he and Hancock had finished their discussion regarding the beginning of Act II Scene II, Kenneth gazed toward Lavinia.

He supposed he should feel at least a little guilty about Jenny giving up her promising stage career for him, but he didn't. Now, too preoccupied with Lavinia, he hardly thought of Jenny at all.

Vernon dismissed the cast and crew. Tomorrow would be a day off, but he expected them the day after for another dress rehearsal. As everyone meandered from the stage, Kenneth watched Vernon approach Lavinia. The old man stood akimbo with his large gut thrust forward.

Hargraves towered over his beautiful, young wife, and Lavinia, as Cleopatra incarnate, gazed up at him, her green eyes rimmed in coal black liner. They stood at the opposite end of the stage, so Kenneth couldn't hear what Vernon said to her, but Lavinia looked at him as a pupil would a teacher, not a wife her husband.

If Kenneth had the chance, he'd like to explain to her that she shouldn't be so stiff whenever any physicality was required. Lavinia was a brilliant actress, but Kenneth was exasperated by her tenseness whenever he did more than hold her hand. Only a small amount of affection could be shown on stage, but even a chaste embrace was difficult for Lavinia.

They'd first been paired together two years ago in *The Black Pearl*, and that production had been a screaming success. Since then, audiences had craved more plays with he and Lavinia starring together as a romantic couple.

Kenneth's eyes roved over Lavinia's delectable body as she talked with Vernon. While he imagined just what he could do with that body, to bring out Lavinia's best, Jenny grabbed his arm.

"Kenneth, love," she smoothed her green silk dress over rather expansive hips, "I thought we could dine at the Astor this evening."

His fiancé's looks certainly couldn't compare with Lavinia's, not now anyway. But at one time Jenny had been a stunning actress. With thick hair of reddish gold and wide eyes of sea green, she was still quite pretty. Yet motherhood had transformed her into a somewhat frumpish woman whose fashionable clothes tried, but failed, to conceal a once wispy figure now bordering on fat.

Despite Kenneth's blatant indiscretions, Jenny was as faithful as a lap dog.

"We might as well enjoy our last few days of freedom while me mum's here to watch the girls," Jenny smiled.

Beatrice and Samantha, were hers and Kenneth's chubby daughters, three and four respectively. Jenny's mother, Endora, had been visiting from England so he and Jenny could enjoy some time without their fussy, whiny brats. However, Endora would be leaving in a few days. Because of Kenneth's affairs, Jenny no longer allowed any female servants to reside with them.

"Jenny," Kenneth said, distracted, gazing once more toward Lavinia, who was still listening intently to Vernon, "that sounds fine—just fine. Why don't you go home and change, then meet me there?"

"I can wait for you to change from your costume. We can leave together."

"Jenny—I might be a little while. As a matter of fact, before you go to the Astor, stop at Tiffany's and buy yourself a little bauble."

Jenny sighed, crestfallen.

"That's supposed to make you happy," Kenneth said, lightly pinching her cheek. "Perhaps a ruby to match your lips." Kenneth bent to kiss her full lips, something he still enjoyed about her.

"Very well, then," Jenny relented, after his brief tokens of affection. "But don't keep me waiting too long."

Kenneth gave her a quick peck on the cheek, then hurried her away. When Jenny was completely out of sight, he searched for Lavinia. Yet now the stage was completely empty. Lavinia was nowhere in sight.

Kenneth rushed to his dressing room. After shedding his tunic and war gear, he changed into his day clothes, a black suit with vest and cravat. Grabbing his bowler hat, he walked down the hall to Lavinia's dressing room.

Putting his ear to her dressing room door, he only heard female voices, Lavinia's, and her maid, Amy's.

Kenneth smiled at the memory of Amy. She'd been a sweet little piece. Quiet and not much to look at, yet she'd been a tigress in the bedroom. Kenneth walked to the wings in search of Vernon, but only encountered a few cast and crew members on their way out. Vernon was nowhere to be found. Good, Kenneth said to himself, walking back to Lavinia's door.

He knocked. "Lavinia," he said through the closed door, before our first night, I'd like to discuss a way to bring greater depth to our performances."

"Wait just a moment," Lavinia replied. Seconds later, she invited him in as Amy, finished buttoning the back of her turquoise dress.

Amy flashed Kenneth a flirtatious smile, which he ignored. No use leading the poor girl on. He had no desire to revive their short-lived affair. There were greener pastures to explore.

Amy rolled her eyes, then let out an irreverent snort as she adjusted the fabric over Lavinia's bustle.

While Lavinia checked her reflection, she asked Kenneth to have a seat on a satin chair near her dressing table. When she turned from the mirror, Amy brought over a very large hat, decorated with white stuffed birds and ostrich plumes. "So, Kenneth," Lavinia said, "just what do you suggest we do to improve our performances?"

"Lavinia," he glanced at Amy, who was about to assist her mistress with the hat. Amy shot him a nasty glare in return. "If I may," Kenneth said, "I'd like to speak to you alone."

Lavinia hesitated, then took the hat from her maid. "Of course. Amy, if you wouldn't mind." She motioned the girl to the door. Amy trudged out. Passing Kenneth, she turned up her nose, then loudly slammed the door behind her.

Bending to place the hat on a matching chair opposite Kenneth, Lavinia said, "It appears Amy doesn't like you."

"I'm not here to discuss your girl."

"All right, then." Lavinia stood tall, placing hands on hips and smiled. "So, tell me what you had in mind."

Kenneth took a deep breath, as though mustering nerve. In all his years of philandering, he'd never had the gall to approach a boss's wife. "Where's Vernon," he asked cautiously.

"He went home. He was quite exhausted after today's rehearsal."

Kenneth rose, tossing his bowler to the vacant seat, then swaggered toward Lavinia. "I've hesitated to address this—for obvious reasons. Audiences love us together, but our performances are lacking something. We could make them better if ..."

Lavinia raised a brow. "If what?"

Sidling close to her, he said slowly, "If you would unsheathe my dagger."

Looking confused, Lavinia said, "There's that line again. Just what do you mean?"

"I mean—I'd like to slip my key into your lock."

"But I've already let you in here—you don't *need* a key!"

"I take it you've never heard of a double entendre."

Lavinia blinked her eyes in question. "A double *what*?"

She so wanted to be worldly, Kenneth reflected laughing, but was still an innocent in so many ways.

"What's so funny?" Lavinia asked sharply.

"I won't beat about the bush any longer,

Lavinia. I believe that your performance, as well as mine, would vastly improve if — we made love."

Lavinia's eyes widened. Raising her chin she said, "Kenneth! I'm a married woman!"

"Yes. But you're married to an old man — an old man that you *don't* love."

She backed away from him slightly. "My marriage is none of your business!"

"Your marriage lacks passion, and, no, that's none of my business. But improving my performance — and yours, *is* my business. Lavinia, this is the perfect way." He moved closer to her, all the while gesturing dramatically with his hands. "We can only show but so much of our '*love*' on stage. But if you experience being with me in a way that can't be displayed to the audience, the *feeling* — and depth of emotion we have behind closed doors, can transcend to the stage. Trust me."

This was a ploy he'd used many times with his leading ladies, so many times in fact, that he'd actually come to believe it himself.

"Has Vernon ever made you scream — in ecstasy?" Kenneth asked.

Lavinia's face contorted in shock, but then an inquiring gaze flickered across it. "How dare you ask me such a question! My — my marriage is a sacred union."

"I've never known you to be so self-righteous. You're a much better actress than you're pretending to be now. You're not offended by what I've said, but you are curious. And you never did answer me. Has Vernon ever kissed you," Kenneth grabbed Lavinia's waist, pulling her close, "like this?"

Holding her tightly, he kissed her with searing passion, pressing his body firmly against hers. Half-heartedly, Lavinia tried to push him away. "Kenneth," she gasped, "please—"

"With pleasure." Kenneth knew she wanted more, and kissed her again before she could finish her feigned protest. Finally, her body melted into his, and Kenneth felt victorious as she returned his embrace, *and* his kiss.

When he slowly pulled his lips from hers, Lavinia was breathless.

She disentangled herself from his arms. "That's—that's not what I meant."

"But it is what you wanted," Kenneth said slyly. "I know Vernon's never kissed you like that. And he's never touched you in places that could make you—wildly euphoric, has he?"

Lavinia was silent for a moment, then, "You think you could?"

She'd decided not to feign insult any longer. Kenneth smiled. "Most definitely. Lavinia, I know how to play a woman like a fine instrument. And you, my darling, are no less than a Stradivarius. We're magic together now," he said, opening his arms in an exaggerated theatrical gesture. "Just think what we'd be if—"

"I'm no fool, Kenneth." Lavinia crossed her arms, eyeing him cynically. "You just want to sleep with me, that's all." She turned away from him to look in the mirror. After checking her hair, she picked up the enormous hat.

"I won't deny that. I'm *dying* to sleep with you. But that's not all." From behind, he approached Lavinia, took the hat from her hands, then threw it back to the chair. Placing an arm around her waist, he said, "I swear, Lavinia, our performances would be even more explosive," he kissed her neck, "volcanic even—if we made love." She leaned comfortably against him. He moved both hands to her breasts. "I have a suite at the Imperial Hotel—where we can rehearse. Meet me there tomorrow at two."

He pulled a brass key from his pocket. Placing it in her hand, he said, "Dress plainly, so no one will recognize you, and use the side entrance. We wouldn't want to stir up a scandal." Continuing to kiss her neck, he worked his way toward her ear.

Lavinia pulled from against Kenneth, then slowly turned to face him. "I'll take what you've said under advisement."

He looked at her aghast. "You sound like

we've been discussing a business proposal!"

"Haven't we? If I do agree to what you're proposing, *I* have everything to lose — and so do you — if Vernon ever finds out."

"But darling, I won't tell a soul. Discretion is my middle name," Kenneth said with a sneaky smile. "If Vernon, or anyone else, ever suspects something, just deny it. That's how the game is played." He winked. "And you're a great actress, you can be convincing."

Lavinia shook her head with a wicked smile. "Why on earth does poor little Jenny put up with you?"

"Forget about 'poor little Jenny.' Don't give her a second thought." He laughed. "I never do."

"Well — I may, or may not show up tomorrow. This is a rather weighty decision for me, so you'll just have to wait and see."

"But — but if you don't come, you'll never know what you've been missing! And you won't be with just any bloke," Kenneth said dramatically, "you'll be with me — *Kenneth Tyler!*"

Lavinia yawned. "If you've said all you have to say, Kenneth, you may leave now."

****

Lavinia gazed at Kenneth. He'd fallen asleep after their first tryst at the Imperial and now lay on his back. He was a beautiful man, and his profile lovely to look at. She'd been worried about sneaking out to meet him, but now she was glad she had.

Spent from their amorous activity, Lavinia felt oddly exhilarated as well. She couldn't sleep. Her head was spinning from what she'd just experienced, and she was eager for more.

Now she understood what her mother had explained long ago. Lavinia had been about eleven when her brother David had told her and Olivia about the facts of life. He'd learned about the process from one of the hands at the ranch. Then he'd been more than happy to share that information with his sisters.

Simple Olivia had been mortified, but not Lavinia. Living on a ranch, she'd figured out on her own that the human process of procreation couldn't be that different from what dogs and farm animals did. While observing them, Lavinia had concluded that the males appeared to be more interested and determined, while the females merely endured the ordeal.

Mother had been appalled to learn what David had described to his sisters. She'd tried her best to repair the damage by telling them that lovemaking in marriage was a gift from God, to be mutually enjoyed by both husband and wife.

Although Vernon was well satisfied after lovemaking, Lavinia had never enjoyed being with him that way. But with Kenneth, she'd thoroughly relished the experience — despite not being married to him! But could something that felt so wonderful really be wrong? Lavinia felt just a twinge of guilt, but then decided to cast all thoughts of sin, Vernon, and Mother right out the window!

Giggling, she pulled the sheet and satin comforter up to her chin. Kenneth had pleased *her* by stirring things within her that Lavinia didn't even know existed. Plus, his being young and handsome only added to the overall excitement of the equation, which had equaled a volcanic sensation, just as Kenneth had promised.

Although Lavinia felt no love for Kenneth, she saw no reason for her trysts with him to stop. These discreet private rehearsals would surely add greater depth to their performances. How could they not? What they did today, and would continue to do in the future, Lavinia decided, was strictly for the benefit of their art.

CHAPTER 5

"Oh, Daddy," Carrie wailed, "you have to get well. You have to eat!" Although she begged Vernon to take food, Carrie, being too distraught over her father's health, had barely eaten anything herself for the past few days.

Carrie's pale blue dress hung loosely on her slight frame, and her blond hair fell in a thick braid down her back. Recently, Vernon had taken a turn for the worse. Carrie hoped he wouldn't notice her pallor, the dark circles under her eyes, or how gaunt she'd become. He was too ill to be worrying about her.

Holding a forkful of scrambled eggs, she tried to feed Vernon from a tray. He lay propped up on pillows in bed, but refused to eat. The scullery maid had just removed a soiled bedpan from the room and replaced it with a clean one, yet a slight stench of urine still hung in the air.

Vernon had taken sick during the production of *Antony and Cleopatra*. That had been months ago, and now Lavinia was involved in rehearsals for another play, *The Country Wife*. Although Vernon had heard rumors about Lavinia and her co-star, Kenneth Tyler, Carrie knew he didn't want to believe them.

Her father, now bedridden and frail with a jaundiced complexion, had been diagnosed with cirrhosis of the liver, and warned by his doctor to abstain from alcohol. However, that didn't deter him from asking for it, and Carrie suspected that before he'd become debilitated, Vernon had been drinking heavily behind her back, perhaps in an effort to blot out the truth. Carrie had no reason not to dispel the rumors she'd heard regarding her stepmother.

Vernon turned away from the food she offered. "If I die, I'll feel a hell of a lot better." A few seconds later, his gaze met hers, and Carrie saw tears in his eyes. His whites glistened, glassy and yellow. "Honey, you were right. Lavinia never did love me. She cared for me a little…at least at one time…"

Carrie stifled a sob as she wiped away his tears with a handkerchief.

"Truth is…I don't think Lavinia can really care about anybody. She only wanted what I could do for her. Now the theater is all that matters to her...but it's probably the only thing that ever has mattered to her..." Vernon took the handkerchief from Carrie and covered his mouth. For several moments, a rasping cough rattled his emaciated form.

"I love you, Daddy. Please eat something. You need your strength. I'm here to take care of you — I'll *always* be here!"

Vernon looked at her, his eyes filled with sorrow. "Carrie, I don't want to live anymore, and I don't want you wasting your life taking care of me."

"Daddy, you've provided for me my whole life! Now it's no less than an honor for me to care for you!" Carrie couldn't hold back her tears any longer. As they ran down her cheeks, she wiped them away with the back of her hand.

"I never knew dealing over a sick old man was an honor." Vernon smiled, then squeezed his daughter's hand. "Now, Carrie, stop that bawlin'. You're gonna be fine. You're well provided for; it's all spelled out in my will. But you'll meet a good man — someone who'll take care of you. And love you. You won't have to worry about a thing."

"But Daddy, I don't want you to die! You can't — not yet," she sobbed. "It's not your time to go!"

"Oh...I disagree," Vernon said sadly. "So to make things more tolerable for me... how's about a little whiskey?"

"No! And you know better than to ask!"
Carrie scooped up more eggs and held them to
his face. "Eat this instead!"

"Well—I could uh—use a dose of medicine
right now—maybe after that—I could eat."

Carrie eyed him disapprovingly. The
medicine relieved his discomfort, but also
contained a large amount of alcohol. "Daddy,
the doctor said only one dose a day and you
had some less than two hours ago! I'm not
going to let you kill yourself! Don't you care
about your theater anymore? Who'll make
sure the Hargraves productions are the best if
you're not around?"

"Honey," Vernon gently pushed away the
fork Carrie held, "Lavinia can take care of
everything. She's a born businesswoman. She
can manage anything, and when I'm gone,
she'll take over the management. Nobody can
make my theater more profitable than she can
with her star power and brains." He closed his
eyes.

Feeling helpless, Carrie lowered the fork
with one hand, and softly squeezed his
shoulder with the other.

Vernon's eyes opened slightly at her touch.
"Carrie...don't you worry about a thing..."

"I'm not worried about myself," she said
quietly, "I just don't want to lose you."

Carrie heard the bedroom door open, but

didn't remove her eyes from Vernon. Her father, however, struggled to look past her. Then his face brightened. Carrie knew that could mean only one thing.

Taking a deep breath, she turned to see her step-mother. Lavinia wore a simple gray dress. She carried a handbag and a stack of papers she placed on the black marble-top table. Lavinia coolly approached father and daughter.

"Carrie," she said crisply, "I need to speak to your father — alone."

Carrie's grip tightened on the fork. She wanted to stab Lavinia with it. Her father's wife hadn't felt compelled in the least to alter her schedule so she could care for her ailing husband. A few weeks ago, Lavinia had even said, "Carrie, you're doing a fine job as nurse. Keep up the good work."

Since Vernon had become so ill, Lavinia had moved to a different bedroom. Now Carrie slept on the purple chaise longue in her father's room so she could be there for him at all times.

Pursing her lips, Carrie felt her neck muscles twitch. "Lavinia, I'd rather you *not* talk to my father now. I'm trying to give him some food to build up his strength." And besides, Carrie thought, Lavinia's presence would only upset him, causing more harm than good.

"Carrie," Vernon said, "I want to talk to my wife—I don't want to eat right now."

Carrie hesitated, then put down the fork, though it took a great deal of restraint. Taking the bed tray, she excused herself from the room.

****

Vernon slowly propped himself higher on his pillows. "You're back early from rehearsal...At least I think you are...I'm not too good at keeping track of time these days."

Lavinia smiled stiffly, not acknowledging whether or not she *was* back early.

"How are you feeling?"

"Better," he paused, "now that you're here."

Gazing at Lavinia, Vernon longed to believe she'd never been unfaithful. But he knew the truth. He was more than three times her age. Pairing her with a young, handsome leading man hadn't been a wise decision, but it had seemed like a good idea at the time. The people loved them, and marketing Lavinia as Kenneth's onstage love interest had generated boatloads of cash.

Now Vernon hovered near death because of that fateful business arrangement, and he'd found solace in drink when he'd heard the rumors. Lavinia had constantly denied her husband's accusations.

"Tell me again..." Vernon began to cough. "Tell me again...all those rumors aren't true."

"Vernon," Lavinia slowly sat down on the bed next to him, "I've told you time and time again, not to believe idle gossip. Especially from actresses—like that Andrina Styles—who are merely jealous of me." Vernon held his wife's hand and gave it a gentle squeeze. Lavinia pulled her fingers from his grasp and stood up. "Are you—comfortable?" She asked.

"Comfortable as can be expected."

"Is Carrie still taking good care of you?"

"I couldn't ask for a better nurse—except you."

"Well..." Lavinia began, "as you always say, 'the show must go on.' Now, is there anything you need? Anything at all?"

Feeling broken, he said, "Just you."

"Oh, Vernon—I'm here for you—when I can be."

"That isn't enough," he said bitterly. "So, how's about somethin' to drink instead?"

Lavinia gasped. "Vernon! You shouldn't."

"I know you got somethin'..."

"Oh..." Lavinia clicked her tongue, then started toward the black marble-top table. "Perhaps—just—a *little* won't hurt."

After opening her handbag, Lavinia pulled out a flask. Though not a drinker of spirits, she kept this supply available just for Vernon. In the intricately engraved metal hip flask, she carried only the highest quality vodka, so Carrie would never discern her father's indulgences. Vernon had taught Lavinia that the finer the vodka, the harder to detect on the breath.

Lavinia strode back to her husband. "Now, darling, you shouldn't have this, but I hate seeing you deprived of something you love." While cradling his balding head with one hand, she held the drink to his mouth with the other. He drank the vodka as if it were mother's milk.

Pulling his lips from the flask, he rested against Lavinia. She immediately eased him back to his pillow.

Vernon remained quiet for several moments, but then said, "You're a cold hateful woman." The disease had ravaged his body so severely that drunkenness set in quickly, loosening his tongue. "But I still love you. The first time I laid eyes on you, I stripped you naked...in my mind...I did all kinds of things to you..."

Lavinia arched a brow. "Do you want more to drink?" Not waiting for an answer, she raised his head, positioning the flask near his mouth again.

"You tryin' to kill me?" He eyed her with a vicious glare, but grabbed the flask and drained it anyway.

"Don't be absurd!" Lavinia balked. "Of

course I'm not trying to kill you! It's just that *Carrie* doesn't allow you any spirits at all."

Turning up the flask one last time, Vernon sucked it dry, then thrust it at Lavinia. "That's because she cares about me! You never have!"

"Darling—I—I've always been *more* than fond of you—I care for you and I've appreciated everything you've ever done for me."

"Then give up the theater...and stay with me," he pleaded. "I don't have much time."

Lavinia let out a deep sigh and frowned. "Vernon—I can't—we'd lose a fortune! People *want* me and they pay good money to *see* me. I can't let them down."

Vernon slumped against his pillows. "But you can let me down."

"Carrie's here for you."

"She isn't my wife! 'In sickness and in health,' that's what a marriage vow says!"

Lavinia took a deep breath. She walked to her handbag and tucked away the flask. "I need to go."

"Go? You just got here!"

With her back to him, Lavinia said, "Darling, how you do lose track of time." She turned to face him. "I've been here quite a while. Arguing will only further deplete your energy, and besides, I—I need to do some shopping for the upcoming production. The— uh—seamstress showed me her patterns for the Restoration costumes — and we're going to choose some fabrics."

"Cold blooded viper," he muttered, "I know you're going to see that Kenneth Tyler."

Lavinia crossed her arms. "Vernon, do you think I'd leave you, sick as you are, to carry on with another man behind your back?" Her voice dripped of innocence. "I'd never do such a thing, and I certainly don't know what kind of a woman *would*!"

"That isn't true. I know you and I know you'd do it!"

"Vernon, you have my word." Lavinia picked up the stack of papers she'd brought into the room, then strode back to her husband. Sitting on the bed, she slipped an arm under him and pulled him close. "Darling, you've been the very best husband to me. No one could have been more wonderful."

Vernon leaned his head against his wife. Her words soothed him like warm oil. Now feeling drowsy and dazed, the alcohol and arguing had sapped what little strength he had. His eyes closed and he began to nod off.

"Vernon," Lavinia said softly, "you've made my dreams come true. Everything I have, I owe to you. And I — I've grown to love you."

"What?" Vernon asked. An edge of hopefulness tinted his voice, and he struggled to open his eyes.

"I've grown to love you."

"You — you have?" Vernon asked, unsure if what he'd just heard was real or a dream. Yet when Lavinia nodded, his eyes welled with tears.

"I was only a young girl when we met, incapable of loving you as a woman — but now I am a woman, and I've grown a woman's heart."

"Lavinia — I love you so much..." His eyes closed as he relished the feel of her body next to his.

"I know, darling." Lavinia kissed his forehead. "Now, I — I know you're tired," she removed her arm from him, "but I have a few papers that I — need you to sign."

Groggy, he tried to open his eyes again, but couldn't. "What are they?"

"Just some contract renewals. Elizabeth Ward and Jason Henry prefer that you sign their contracts. Even though you've given me complete permission to do so, they're afraid that if I sign them they won't be legally sound."

Vernon chuckled a little. "Well, I'm not dead yet...or maybe they just don't trust you." His eyes were still closed, but feeling euphoric from Lavinia's declaration of love, he said, "No matter...I'll do whatever you want."

She placed the pen in his hand. "Just sign here, darling."

His eyes opened slightly as he signed where Lavinia asked, but he failed to read the papers. Afterwards, his head lolled to the side in Lavinia's direction. Through slitted eyes, he watched his wife walk back to the marble-top table and grab her handbag.

When she started quickly for the door, he called to her, his voice weak. "Lavinia, lie with me."

She stopped abruptly, then slowly angled toward him. "Vernon — the doctor said — it's not safe for you to — stir up those feelings."

"But, I — I just want to feel you — next to me…"

Lavinia glanced at the clock on the faux marble mantle, then walked back to the table to set down her things. "For just a little while," she said coolly.

Lavinia approached the bed, removed her pumps, then pulled back the covers. She hesitated, studying the bed, as though inspecting the cleanliness of the linens. And afterwards, she cautiously slid in beside her husband. Moments later, Vernon dozed off, but when he woke to his own snoring, it was just in time to see Lavinia slip from the room.

CHAPTER 6

"Is the old man dead yet?" Kenneth called to Lavinia from the bedroom of their hotel suite; the same one they used for every "rehearsal." He'd heard her come in and lock the door.

Lavinia strode from the elegant sitting room to the bedroom. Kenneth's side of the bed was turned down and, as usual, he was already undressed and waiting for her.

"No." Lavinia walked to the opposite side of the bed. She still wore her black cloak and a large picture hat as she sat down on the gold satin comforter. "Kenneth, this has been going on between us for months. You don't expect anything permanent from me, do you?"

Kenneth almost laughed. "Permanent? You mean as far as what we have? Gosh, no! Why? You weren't expecting anything from *me*, were you?"

"Not at all."

"Good. Why do you ask?"

She sighed. "Vernon wants me to take leave of the theater — and care for him."

"Well, you are his wife."

"I know." She shrugged her shoulders. "But I *can't* give him that. He has Carrie. *She* can deal with him. And besides, I'm just not ready to give up everything I have for him."

"Even though he's given you the world?" Kenneth said, goading her as devil's advocate.

"You're one to speak!" she spat coldly, spittle flying from her lips. "Sleeping with his *world* famous wife after he propelled your career to new heights and fattened your bank account!"

"Touché, my dear. All I'll say then, is that when I do get around to marrying Jenny, it'll be when I'm ready to give her some of myself."

"Some? Not all?"

"Isn't that the pot calling the kettle black?"

Lavinia appeared stung by his words and shot him a nasty look so disarming it took him by surprise.

"Why are you looking at me like that? What did I say?"

She pursed her lips. "Nothing."

Kenneth laughed. "If looks could kill, I suppose I'd be dead now."

"Marriage to Vernon was my idea. He

knew I didn't love him."

"Do you think you could ever love anyone? You'll be a widow soon. It's only a matter of time. So could you ever love anyone enough to marry again?"

"Never."

"I suppose marriage isn't for everyone," Kenneth said. "Neither are children, for that matter. But at least I won't have to contend with our brats for a while. Jenny's been with the girls in London on holiday to visit her mum."

"I remember when she left. I was shocked she'd leave you alone for such a long time."

Kenneth laughed. "I promised I'd be good. Or maybe Jenny's just finally decided that there's no way to fight my wicked ways — whether she's around or not. Regardless, she arrived back home last week, well rested from a very pampered voyage. But the girls are still overseas, and will be for a few more weeks. Jenny thought we needed some time alone."

"And here you are with me," Lavinia said snidely.

Kenneth ignored her comment. "Jenny wants to set a date for the wedding, but I'm just not ready to do that yet."

"Isn't she tired of waiting? Hasn't it been five years?"

"She loves me, but once we're married she'll expect me to be faithful. So now I'm —

sowing my wild oats."

"Do you think you *can* be faithful?"

"I don't know. I doubt it. She's lived with my infidelities this long. If she finds me being untrue after we are married, it'll come as no great surprise. She knows what she's getting."

Lavinia shook her head. "The poor dear."

"No, my darling, Lavinia, she'll have the reward of being the wife of the *great* Kenneth Tyler."

"Now, that's not much of a prize, is it?"

The truth of Lavinia's tongue was like the hot sting of a bee. He *was* no prize and he'd tried to keep that a closely guarded secret behind his charm, good looks and money. He was an actor; he had no education. He played make believe for a living, and he'd squandered more money drinking and dabbling in narcotics than he cared to remember. He'd indulged in more women than he could count, and he'd fooled them all into believing he was something special, something to be prized. But he hadn't fooled Lavinia, or Jenny. Jenny knew him almost better than he knew himself, but she loved him, regardless.

Kenneth smiled wryly. "I don't know why I subject myself to that poison tongue of yours. It must be your devastating beauty that keeps me coming back. Speaking of which, there's a beautiful sky blue silk number with lots of feathers in the bathroom waiting for you. Go slip it on and slip into—character." He smiled.

She looked at Kenneth seductively. "I'll be back."

Not long after Lavinia disappeared into the bathroom, Kenneth heard the door to the suite open. Before he could grab his bathrobe to see who was there, Jenny walked into the bedroom.

"So," she said, standing at the foot of the bed, "it's Lavinia this time, isn't it?"

Jenny had always been so gentle and sweet, but for the first time, Kenneth was seeing her angry. He loved her wide green eyes; they so perfectly accompanied her reddish gold hair. Her eyes were so wide, in fact, that she appeared in a constant state of surprise. But now the wide eyes were narrowed. They bore into his like the dangerous eyes of a woman scorned one too many times.

"Jenny!" He fumbled with the sheets, trying to keep his privates and skinny white legs covered. She'd seen it all, but now he felt vulnerable and awkward being caught in this predicament. "You're the only woman for me," he said quickly. "You know that, don't you? And how did you get in here? How did you find me?" Each question stumbled upon the last.

"I followed you and I bribed the maid! But it took me a while to find one who'd take a bribe, and that was only after I'd told her that my husband was cheating on me! So just where is your slutty whore?"

"No one's here but me," he said loudly enough for Lavinia to hear. Hopefully, she'd locked the bathroom door. "And I'm not your husband yet, so I'm not *really* cheating on you," he protested. "Jenny, do you honestly think I'd have the audacity to sleep with Vernon's wife?"

"I've learned not to put anything past you!"

"What does it matter? We'll be married soon."

"Soon? You said that last year. Do you even love me, Kenneth? I tell you countless times each day I love you, but you've never once said that to me!"

"Darling, you know I do."

"Then say it!"

"I love you — there, are you happy now?"

"No, because you don't mean it. It's been Lavinia for months now, hasn't it? Your affairs never last this long. Do you love her?"

"No!"

"But you keep coming back to her. Even if you don't love her, you'll start seeing someone else. I can't take it any longer, Kenneth. I can't even cry about it anymore; I've no tears left. And now I've realized that the only way I can ever have you — is in death. Then you'll never be in another woman's arms."

"Jenny! What are you talking about?"

"This." From her handbag, she pulled a pearl-handled revolver, a .32 caliber Iver Johnson.

Kenneth broke into a cold sweat as Jenny pointed the gun at his head.

"You've humiliated me year after year. But no more! If I can't have you in life, I'll settle for you in death."

Feeling his heart beat like the fast paced rhythm of a snare drum, Kenneth said, "Jenny, you're crazy! I—I know you won't pull the trigger because—you love me, don't you?"

"That's exactly why I'll pull it. So I can have you all to myself!"

****

Overhearing Jenny from the bathroom, Lavinia's heart raced. Pull the trigger?! With her ear pressed firmly against the door, she couldn't believe the scenario playing on the other side. However, Lavinia was sure of one thing—*she* couldn't die at the pinnacle of *her* success! And if she did, for what? Kenneth? How could she have been so stupid?

Perhaps he could wrestle the gun from his jealous—and seemingly deranged—fiancée. Lavinia wondered how she could escape from this mess, and then worried if Jenny would come after her in the bathroom.

Realizing that the top of her dress hung loosely around her waist, Lavinia quickly pulled it up, over her chemise. Slipping her arms through the sleeves, she was thankful she hadn't worn a corset.

Fumbling to button the back of the dress, Lavinia looked for a blunt object to fend off Jenny in case she did try the door. She eyed the sink. The thick bottom of a crystal tumbler would have to do; if necessary, Lavinia would break it. Broken glass would be a more deadly weapon against a woman who was stark raving mad. With tumbler in hand, Lavinia pressed her ear against the door once more.

****

"But—but," Kenneth stammered, "what about—Samantha and Beatrice?"

"Our children?" Jenny asked, facetiously. "Well, it's nice of you to think about them for once. It's a bloody shame it takes a gun pointed at your face to conjure them to your mind. You're a worthless wretch of a father." She moved closer to him and lowered the gun toward his chest. "I'll shoot—but I can't bring myself to shoot your beautiful face."

Kenneth felt himself shaking as she moved toward him. Pressing himself against the elaborately carved headboard, he said, "Now—Jenny—you're a fine actress—no one can hold a candle to your Ophelia—but now you're scaring me. A gentle creature like you couldn't possibly know how—"

"I'm not acting! I *am* sane! I'm perfectly capable of using this weapon—and I intend to! Kenneth, I'm no better than you, because I've been a twit for loving you. I planned it this way—with the girls overseas—they'll be better off without both of us."

Still pointing the gun at Kenneth, Jenny glanced toward the bathroom. Taking a few steps backwards, she saw that the door was closed. "I—I know that—*Lavinia*, your smutty harlot, is hiding in there. I'm not stupid as you think. You say you're alone but that door is closed. I should kill her before I kill you, shouldn't I?"

"Jenny, don't be stupid—" Kenneth started.

"I *have* been stupid—for far too long! But I won't kill your tramp, because this is between us." She walked back to the foot of the bed, aiming the gun at his heart. "It'll be you and me—alone. I won't bring her along to interfere with us—after it's done. You'll be mine—mine alone." Jenny spoke as though in a trance. Trembling, she squeezed the trigger.

Jenny screamed at the loud pop. Kenneth screamed when the bullet grazed his shoulder, then plowed into the mahogany headboard, splintering the wood. Not believing what she'd done, Kenneth looked at her, too dumbfounded to speak.

"Oh, bloody!" Jenny cried, and fired again.

****

This time the bullet nailed Kenneth in the chest. He slumped to the side. His eyes remained opened in stunned disbelief, and the white sheets turned crimson as blood flowed from his wound. Too shocked to believe she'd just killed her lover, Jenny fell to her knees. She slowly placed the barrel of the gun in her mouth — then pulled the trigger.

****

After the third shot, there was silence. Lavinia waited a few moments to make sure Jenny wasn't lying in wait. After a short while, Lavinia was convinced Jenny was no longer a threat, but a corpse. She steeled herself to come out of hiding. Upon opening the door, Lavinia was immediately accosted by the stench of blood.

She stumbled over the carnage, holding her dress high so as not to stain the hem. Her body shook as she took in the sight of blood and brains scattered about the room. Seeing Kenneth's bright blue eyes still open wide, Lavinia's stomach convulsed in dry heaves. She thanked fate for an empty stomach, otherwise she would have left evidence of her presence.

Lavinia heard shouting outside the hotel

room, and people running down the hall.

"It sounded like gunshots!" she heard a man yell.

Panicked, Lavinia ran to the bedroom window. The fire escape was located a short distance away. Lavinia would have to climb from the window and maneuver herself onto it.

"It must've come from this room!" Another voice boomed from outside in the hallway.

Lavinia reached for the window latch, but the lock was stiff and difficult to turn. As she struggled to open it, someone began pounding on the door. "Is everyone all right in there?"

Frantic, Lavinia's hands shook, as she continued to fight with the latch.

"I have a key," a female voice said.

As Lavinia heard the jingle of keys, the lock on the window finally popped. She raised the pane high, while at the same time hearing, "We're unlocking the door! Is anyone in here, is everyone all right?"

Not looking down, Lavinia clambered from the window and lowered herself to the fire escape.

"Open the door, Zelda," were the last words she heard before starting her frenzied descent down the metal ladder.

CHAPTER 7

Vernon made no effort to acknowledge his daughter as she walked in the room with his usual breakfast tray of soft boiled eggs and *The New York Times.*

Propped on pillows, he stared straight ahead at nothing. His complexion seemed a bit more yellow today, Carrie observed, and his eyes more sunken.

"Daddy—I hate to see you so sick. You'll feel better if you eat something. I have a soft boiled eggs and—"

"I'm not hungry. I don't want any food. I just want Lavinia," he said quietly.

"I don't know where Lavinia is." Carrie took a deep breath, trying to hide her frustration. "Maybe she's still asleep. She was gone most of yesterday afternoon and I don't know when she came home." Setting the food on the black marble table, Carrie said, "Daddy — I — I have some bad news."

Vernon finally looked at her, his sad eyes questioning.

"It's about Kenneth and Jenny. It seems that — that Jenny completely lost her mind — because of Kenneth's — philandering." Carrie remained silent for several seconds, then added, "She killed Kenneth, and then committed suicide."

"Damn," Vernon said softly, lowering his head.

"She killed him at The Imperial. Apparently, he was there with — another woman..."

Raising his eyes to Carrie's, Vernon swallowed hard. "Who was — the other woman?"

"She wasn't there when the police arrived — but the window was open near the fire escape." Carrie picked up the newspaper, then walked to Vernon's bedside. "Daddy, there's an article all about it in this morning's *Times*."

Vernon sat up slightly taking the paper. After reading it intently for a few moments, he stopped to re-read one part out loud. "It says here, 'a resident in the hotel saw a mysterious woman descending the fire escape, and a passerby saw someone near the hotel who resembled actress Lavinia Hargraves, prior to the discovery of the bodies...'"

Vernon lost his grasp on the paper. It slid from the satin comforter to the floor. As he eased back into the pillows, a tear slid down his cheek.

"Daddy," Carrie squeezed his shoulder.

"Leave me be, Carrie..."

"But, Daddy, I—"

"Honey, I want to be alone..."

"Daddy, I'm here for you! I love you. You'll get better—I know you will—if you'll let me care for you!" Carrie sobbed, but Vernon closed his eyes, ignoring her.

****

Devastated, Carrie later regretted that she'd ever shown her father the paper. As she'd predicted, the news had confirmed his suspicions. It had also broken his heart. That evening, Vernon Hargraves breathed his last.

CHAPTER 8

Lavinia rushed to the doorway of the drawing room as Carrie screamed over and over again, "This can't be true!"

To keep the servants from overhearing their heated exchange, Lavinia quickly closed the pocket doors.

"This can't be true!" Holding her father's last will and testament, Carrie sat in one of the gold and purple chairs. "First, my father dies, and now you tell me *I* have nothing, because he's leaving everything to *you*? You're lying!"

"Carrie, darling," Lavinia walked calmly from the doorway, "you see the will."

"Yes—but—but Daddy told me I'd be well provided for!"

Lavinia sat down in the matching chair opposite her step-daughter. "Apparently, your father changed his mind."

"But he told me that shortly before he died!" Carrie threw the document down on the rosewood table between them. "You never loved my father! You never cared for him! And after all he did for you — you never treated him any better than dirt!" Suddenly, Carrie shot up, glaring down at Lavinia. "*You* killed him! You don't deserve a dime of his money! And I know about you — I know what you are!"

Lavinia stiffened.

"You're a Negro!"

Lavinia raised her chin, performing as best she could to appear unaffected by the truth of this detrimental accusation. "Carrie, darling, sit down," she admonished sweetly, as though addressing a child. "Due to your father's — untimely demise — it seems that you've become — unhinged."

Red faced with bovine eyes wide, Carrie stood defiantly, refusing to sit. "I am no such thing! I overheard my father talking about your parents — they're wealthy — they live in California!"

Lavinia's heart beat wildly, yet she maintained her composure. But what if Carrie actually took it upon herself to go West and track them down? Lavinia pushed that thought aside, and instead focused on the task at hand.

She smiled pleasantly. "So — you're saying

I'm a Negro—from a rich family? Since when do Negroes have any money? Poor, dear, Carrie...I hate to see you so delusional."

"That's not true—"

"Perhaps making up all those stories— your plays—is interfering with your... perception of reality."

"I despise you! You're depraved! Vile— malevolent—pure evil!"

"Do you feel better now," Lavinia asked, unfazed, "having gotten that nasty little tantrum out of your system? I'm your stepmother, Carrie. I'm here to help you, and I realize that you don't know *what* you're saying."

Carrie's chest rose and fell rapidly. "I know exactly what I'm saying!"

"Well..." Lavinia eyed her sharply, "I know exactly what you *did*. And *that*, combined with your father's death, has crippled your mind."

Carrie shook her head, appearing confused. "What—what are you talking about?"

Lavinia crossed her hands in her lap. "What else *could* I be talking about, dear?"

"I—I don't know!"

"Come now...I know *all* about it...your procedure," Lavinia waited, watching Carrie's big eyes widen further. "Yes...your abortion—I know..."

Carrie crumpled to her chair in tears.

"You poor dear. One of my actresses told me about that detestable boy. After he...deflowered you...he married someone else. That actress only told me to get a starring role. She'd used the same butcher for her procedure—but nearly bled to death. Yet you, Carrie, you were lucky—however—there *is* the possibility that you may *never* conceive again."

Carrie cried into a handkerchief, but tried to stifle her sobs.

"I never told your father," Lavinia said. "I didn't want to sully his image of you as chaste and pure as the driven snow. That would have broken his heart."

"You broke his heart!" Carrie wept.

"Carrie, you can speak ill of me all you please, but I do want to assist you in this trying time of need. Although your father changed his will, I'm giving you this." Lavinia pulled a check from her pocket and placed it on the table. As if Carrie were blind, Lavinia pointed out the amount. "Five thousand dollars."

"What have I ever done to you?" Carrie sobbed. "Why do you hate me?"

"I don't hate you, dear. How could I? I never told your father about your past, and I'm giving you a generous sum of money."

"But I know you changed his will!"

"I did no such thing," Lavinia blinked in wide-eyed innocence, yet her mind ran wild. She still feared the police would somehow connect her to Kenneth's murder. Already questioned once, she'd managed to convince them she'd been nowhere near the scene of the murder. Now there was the possibility of Carrie siccing lawyers upon her. "You have my word," Lavinia said, "and besides, changing a will...is nothing you could prove."

"That day — that day you had a stack of papers and —"

"Contract renewals."

"I don't believe you!"

Lavinia hesitated. "Then believe the will."

"This just can't be…" Carrie cried.

"Your father's dead now and you can't change that. Nor can you change what he's stated in his will. You have resources, Carrie, dear. Your father paid you handsomely for your plays, and I'm aware that the apartment building he gave to your mother is now in your name. He said once that there's a vacant furnished apartment waiting for you. You just hadn't chosen to live there — yet. So, you have a place to stay. And you must have *some* money in the bank. You never leave your room to spend anything.

"In addition, the apartment rents will generate some income for you. And then there's the five thousand dollars I'm giving you. That should be enough for you to make a brand new start. Consider it like a dowry. A girl doesn't have to be beautiful to catch a husband, but a little money never hurts."

Carrie looked at the check. "A little is right. Compared to what my father had, this is nothing."

"Be thankful for what I am giving you. Five thousand dollars is a lot of money."

"But—"

"No buts, or everyone just might find out about that sordid little liaison you had with that boy. Now gather your things. You can easily be out of here by tomorrow evening."

Carrie stood slowly to look down on her father's widow. "I didn't think I could ever hate anybody...but I hate you! Daddy's dead. Kenneth and Jenny are dead. All three are dead because of you!" Her voice trembled and her body started to shake. "You leave nothing behind but a path of death and destruction. That'll be your legacy!"

Lavinia shot up from her chair. Her back straightened beyond the restraint of her corset. "How dare you speak to me that way!"

"How dare *I*?" Carrie's voice had risen to the level of hysterics. "Everyone knows you were sleeping with Kenneth!"

"That's preposterous! Why, our—our relationship was strictly professional!"

"Professional?!" Carrie almost laughed. "And you say *I'm* unhinged? Your nothing but a whore and a liar!"

Lavinia's face burned and her eyes

94

narrowed to slits. Carrie turned white as a sheet.

"I'll be gone for two hours," Lavinia hissed. "You be out of here when I get back, and if I ever see you in this house again, I'll destroy you."

In tears, Carrie fled to the pocket doors. Before opening them, she looked back at her step-mother. "I'll remember you when I write my next play! I'll call it *The Nigger!*"

CHAPTER 9
WINNABOW, NORTH CAROLINA
WINTER 1895

While Lavinia rode in a hired carriage, her mind wandered back to a childhood memory. She must have been about ten years old the night she'd listened outside her aunt's library door. Lavinia couldn't be seen, but she remembered the conversation vividly between her father and his sister, Sarah.

Lavinia's family had traveled to visit Aunt Sarah and her husband, Uncle James, in Oberlin, Ohio. Both were abolitionists. Mother and Father had stayed with them after Father had helped Mother escape from Dancing Oaks Plantation, and then married her in a Quaker safe house.

Everyone else had already gone to bed on this particular night, except Aunt Sarah and

Father, who'd stayed up late talking. But Lavinia had been unable to sleep. After hearing voices in the library, she'd crept down the stairs. Eavesdropping on grownups had always proved to be informative.

"I received a letter from Annabelle," Aunt Sarah had said, and then paused for a long moment. "Hers...and Aunt Lucinda's financial situation is rather desperate. So I've sent them some money." Upon hearing this, Lavinia's father nearly combusted.

"After what they did to Lori?! They can starve in the streets for all I care! Aunt Lucinda flogged her near to death because she could read, and Lori will carry those scars on her back to the grave!"

"Daniel I know — and I'm sorry for that. But, perhaps they've paid the price. They're war widows, and Annabelle lost both of her children to smallpox, and —"

"Those tragedies happened years ago," Daniel said. "But maybe they're still paying for what they did. At least Dancing Oaks wasn't burned to the ground like Annabelle's place and they have a roof over their heads."

"It wasn't burned because the Union Army used it as a hospital. Aunt Lucinda suffered through that, as well as everything else."

"Sarah, you reap what you sow..."

Coming back to the present, Lavinia thought about her white relatives. They'd

always fascinated her. Not Aunt Sarah and
Uncle James, but her southern family,
Annabelle and Aunt Lucinda, the ones she'd
never met. Which was why Lavinia was now
in Winnabow, North Carolina, on her way to
visit Dancing Oaks Plantation, or at least what
was left of it. Her relatives, however, had no
idea she was coming—they didn't even know
who she was, yet she wanted to surprise them.

Lavinia had fantasized about these people
her entire life. They'd lived in a grand house,
dressed in the finest clothes, surrounded
themselves with luxuries, and had been waited
on hand and foot by slaves. Lavinia sighed,
thinking of the grandeur of it all, and how she
would have loved being a southern belle.

Lavinia had taken a private rail car from
New York to Wilmington with two maids and
several trunks; she'd spent a week there. Then
she'd taken the steamer to Winnabow where
she was staying at a charming inn. She'd
arrived just a few days earlier, but in that time
she'd learned her way around the community
and asked questions of the townspeople that
verified what little information she had
regarding her father's family and their land.

Lavinia wasn't exactly running away from
New York, but after Vernon's death she'd
realized what it was like to have no family.
Vernon had loved her, but now he was gone,
and Lavinia had no one. She'd rather die than

go back to California. Being alone and white was preferable to being a well-to-do Negro with loved ones alive and well.

Although her theater people had been like family, once the scandal broke, and Vernon died, they didn't seem to trust her. Then they'd all deserted her by moving on to different companies.

And worse yet, following the murder-suicide, audiences were wary about attending anything with the Hargraves name attached to it. Lavinia chose not to let the unfortunate occurrences she'd endured set her back in any way. She'd decided to lay low for a while, and then make a comeback in a year or so. In time — people would forget, and besides, she reflected, audiences had loved her once, so surely, they'd love her again.

Now, as Vernon's widow, she had plenty of money. And with no theater to speak of, she had plenty of time. But feeling alone, she'd decided to venture South, in search of relatives.

Her parents hadn't talked about her father's family plantation much. They claimed Dancing Oaks stirred up too many bad memories. But Lavinia did know that Father's mother, Rebecca, had been born and raised there. Lavinia had never met Rebecca or Rebecca's husband. Both of her father's parents had died while he was still in his teens.

However, what Lavinia had learned about Rebecca was that she'd married an abolitionist and become one herself before Daniel was born, henceforth, Daniel, Lavinia's father, had been raised as an abolitionist.

Lavinia's mother, Lori, was raised as a slave at Dancing Oaks until she was around six. But then for some reason, she was given temporarily to Rebecca by her brother Elijah, who lived at Dancing Oaks and maintained the plantation. Lori's temporary stay turned into ten years, long enough for Rebecca to have her tutored, and long enough for her and Father to fall in love. The two were just about the same age.

After Rebecca's death, Mother was sent back to Dancing Oaks. Father, at eighteen, went there too, and tried to protect her. Father had never revealed much about his Uncle Elijah's wife, Lucinda. He'd referred to her more than once as "that cruel woman" on the rare occasions her name popped up in conversation.

But, Lavinia rationalized, Lucinda had had to be cruel to keep her slaves in line. If I'd been a plantation mistress, Lavinia said to herself, I would have been cruel, too—out of necessity.

Annabelle, Lucinda's daughter, was even more of a mystery. All Lavinia knew was that she was just as cruel as her mother, only beautiful. Father had referred to her as cold, in looks and disposition, because of her very fair skin and white blonde hair.

Thinking back to the conversation she'd overheard as a little girl, Lavinia remembered Aunt Sarah's response to Father, regarding their Aunt Lucinda's dire straights.

"Daniel," she'd said, "how can you call yourself a Christian? I know the way Aunt Lucinda treated Lori, and all of her slaves, was deplorable, but like it or not, she is family. I know it's difficult to forgive her past ways — but I'm fortunate to have so much. I wouldn't feel right not sending them anything. I believe I'm doing what Jesus would have done. Remember, He said, 'Forgive them; for they know not what they do.'"

"Lucinda knew exactly what she was doing when she tried to kill Lori!" Father had said angrily.

The arguing continued, but Lavinia must have fallen asleep. The last thing she recalled was Father carrying her to bed, tucking her in next to Olivia, and kissing her goodnight.

The next morning she saw Father give Aunt Sarah what must have been a check. He'd said, "Don't dare mention this is from me. Deposit it into your account, then send them a check with your name on it."

Aunt Sarah had smiled. "So, you've had a change of heart?"

"It was Lori's idea. I suppose she's more

righteous than I'll ever be. And we prayed about it together," Father had said.

That was thirteen years ago, Lavinia thought. The fact that Lucinda had ordered her mother flogged near to death barely fazed her. Instead Lavinia mulled over the current financial situation at Dancing Oaks. Without slave labor, it would never be what it was; and she'd learned from the locals that vast amounts of acreage had been sold off. What remained was worked by share croppers. Lucinda was even considering selling the place because it was getting too hard for her to maintain. Lucinda and Annabelle would be more than willing to accept any money she had to give, Lavinia thought smugly, and she'd already written them a check.

Gazing at the large leafless oak trees and the dirt road from her carriage window, she wondered what it would be like to finally meet these southern kin. Father had asked Aunt Sarah not to write any news of him to these relatives after his and mother's escape. So they couldn't possibly know if Daniel was alive or dead. And Lavinia was certain that they'd never think that, as a grown man, her father would choose to spend his life with a Negro slave.

Lavinia had cooked up the perfect scenario to serve to these people so they'd accept her without hesitation. And she longed for that.

This was the rich planter family she'd never known. But they were mentioned in her biographies that appeared in the press. Now she wanted to know them, and they'd welcome her with open arms.

True, she was an actress, and these were genteel southern people, but things weren't like they used to be around these parts before the war. They'd easily embrace a rich relation with money to share. And establishing ties with this upstanding white family, of one time high social standing, would validate her as white.

They'd never suspect the true identity of her mother, because she looked just as white as they did. She could easily explain her jet black hair as being inherited from her fictional Spanish mother, who was also written about in those press biographies.

She looked forward to enjoying winters in the South with her "new family." And she hoped that one day they would accept her invitation to visit, or even live with her in New York.

Perhaps today they'd welcome her at once, and then insist she go back to the inn, collect her things, and stay with them for the duration of her visit in North Carolina. How nice it would be to spend Christmas with newfound family.

Chapter 10

"Ma'am," the driver shouted back to her, "this is where the Calhoun property starts."

Lavinia thanked him, and peered through the window again. She could only imagine the past splendor of the plantation. As the carriage passed through the unkempt drive of live oaks, she wondered if there had ever been any formal gardens about the grounds as she'd envisioned. There were none now, only some fallen trees and overgrown areas of disarray.

Once at the entrance of the mansion, the driver helped her alight from the carriage. She instructed him to wait, then blew out a deep breath, surveying the dilapidated property. Lavinia slowly walked up the crumbling steps to the front door.

What surely had been a majestic house at one time now looked aged and humbled, like a toothless old man in rags who'd once been a rich young dandy.

The exterior was dirty and in need of paint. Cracks were visible, some shutters missing, and the columns rotting and peeling. Lavinia could give them all the money necessary to fix up the place and have it appear as it did before the war, which must have been glorious. They could then sell it, and make quite a bit of money.

Lavinia could help her relatives tremendously, she thought, and they'd be so glad she'd come to provide them aid. Lavinia took a deep breath as she approached the door. She grabbed the large brass knocker, pounded it gently, and waited.

Moments later, the heavy door slowly creaked open. "May I help you?" An elderly woman with thin gray hair and an abundance of wrinkles stood facing her. She looked haggard and tired as she leaned on a cane, her humped back visible to Lavinia.

Could this be Lucinda? Lavinia wondered. She was nothing but an ugly old hag, almost chinless, with no visible lips to speak of, wearing a drab gray dress. Draped around her shoulders was a black moth-eaten shawl. If this were Lucinda, Lavinia mused, she'd never been a great beauty. And although times were hard, Lavinia had never imagined Lucinda looking this bad—nor answering her own door.

"Hello," Lavinia said, "I'm looking for Lucinda Calhoun."

"What can I do for you?" Lucinda suspiciously eyed Lavinia's green velvet dress and matching hat, complete with ostrich plumes.

"I'm Lavinia Hargraves, from New York."

Lucinda tried to straighten her crooked back. "No Yankees are welcome here," she said sternly, starting to shut the door.

"But, Mrs. Calhoun," Lavinia put a hand on the door to keep it from closing, "or rather, Aunt Lucinda—I'm your nephew Daniel's daughter."

Looking Lavinia coldly in the eye, Lucinda said nothing.

"May I call you Aunt Lucinda?"

"No. And just what are you tryin' to pull, girl?"

Placing jewel encrusted fingers over her heart, Lavinia said, "Why, I'm not trying to pull anything. Daniel Taylor is my father. But he died recently." Lavinia paused, noting the look of surprise, then satisfaction, that stirred in the old woman's eyes. "I've practically felt like an orphan since his passing," Lavinia continued, "and I've felt compelled to look for you. I—I've so desperately wanted to find his side of the family—down here in the South—and establish some—family ties."

"Well," Lucinda said shortly, "just who's

your mother?"

"Oh, my mother? Her name was Cristina Maria Conchita Fernandes—from Segovia...Spain."

Lavinia had dreamed up a splendid fictional mother in preparing for her role as the orphaned half-Spanish actress. "But my mother died when I was very young. My father met her while traveling abroad. He fell in love with her, and brought her back to his home so they could marry. But you see—all of her relatives are in Spain. North Carolina is— so much closer than—going overseas to Europe, of course—and my father had some very fond memories of the South." Lavinia paused to see if Lucinda believed any of what she was saying.

"Go on," Lucinda said.

Her cold gray eyes unnerved Lavinia. "Well, it's just that I've always wanted to *know* my southern family—here—in the United States. With my parents—gone—and no brothers or sisters—I'm hoping to be a part of *your* family." Lavinia smiled, as she thought of a new storyline to perform that incorporated the check. Giving it as an act of charity might insult the old woman.

"But the main reason for my visit is this," she said. "My father wanted you to have something." She pulled the check from her beaded handbag. "On his deathbed, he asked that I give this to you—as a peace offering. He was sorry for his—past indiscretions here, and hoped he could make it up to you. This check is in the amount of three thousand dollars."

A sharp glint lit Lucinda's beady gray eyes as she eagerly took the check. She smiled, revealing near toothless gums. "Three thousand dollars, eh?" She folded the check and stuffed it in the bosom of her dress. Trying to straighten herself again, Lucinda said, "That boy did cause us grief. I'm glad he finally realized the error of his ways." A haughty air had seeped into her voice. "His repentance certainly puts a whole new light on things. Come in, Mrs. Hargraves, and sit down for a while." Lucinda hobbled toward the parlor and Lavinia followed. "Annabelle," Lucinda called. "Put on a pot of tea. We have a guest."

Lavinia took in her depressed surroundings. The hardwood floors were buckled, missing varnish and bare of carpets. The roof must have needed replacing because circular rainwater stains were arrayed across the ceiling, and the dingy walls appeared puckered. The place probably hadn't been painted since before the war.

The parlor was sparsely furnished with only a sofa, chair and table. "Have a seat." Lucinda motioned her toward a red velvet chair. Tufts of stuffing peeked from the torn fabric of the seat cushion.

"Why, thank you," Lavinia said politely, spreading her skirt to sit.

"So your father wanted us to have three thousand dollars? And you traveled all this way to make sure we got it, and you don't even know us." Lucinda painfully lowered herself to the sofa. The wooden claw foot at the opposite end was chipped and a tad uneven. It left the floor slightly with Lucinda seated on the other side.

"Oh, but I feel in my — very heart of hearts that I *do* know you. And more than anything, I want you to know me."

"I'm willing to do that," Lucinda said, "and I'm sure my daughter, Annabelle, is, too. So let's start by hearing all about you."

"Oh!" Lavinia practically squealed with delight at the interest taken in her by Lucinda. "Perhaps you're not familiar with my name down in these parts. But I'm a rather well known actress up North."

Lucinda squinted her face, doubling its wrinkles. "An actress?"

"Yes, ma'am. Nowadays — acting is becoming a much more respectable profession."

Before Lucinda could respond, a middle aged woman walked in the room carrying a pot of tea and cups on a tray. She wore a faded blue frock with a frayed hemline, but she had the fairest hair and skin Lavinia had ever seen. Deep lines were etched in her brow, probably from worry and hard work, and her face was wrinkled like the creases in a sheath of white linen left to dry in a heap.

"Hello," the woman said coolly. She eyed Lavinia with caution while placing the tea on the table.

"Annabelle, dear," Lucinda said, "this is some kin from up North. She's come to visit and brought us money."

"I'm Lavinia Hargraves." She extended her hand to Annabelle, all the while drinking in her cousin's appearance in search of some family resemblance. Although whiter than most white people, Annabelle was not the southern belle Lavinia had fantasized her to be. Her hand was rough, and she was no longer beautiful. Annabelle's earlobes, however, seemed the one part of her body still delicate and unravaged. Studying them, Lavinia thought with glee, they resemble mine!

"Mrs. Hargraves," Lucinda began, but Lavinia interrupted her.

"Please, I'm family, call me Lavinia." She smiled, sitting back comfortably, as Annabelle served her tea from a cracked porcelain pot.

"Lavinia's giving us three thousand dollars." Lucinda pulled the check from her bosom. At the mention of the dollar amount, Lavinia observed Annabelle's furrowed brow lift in surprise. After Annabelle had finished pouring tea for everyone, she sat next to her mother. The couch's uneven claw foot stomped against the floor under Annabelle's weight.

Taking the check from Lucinda, Annabelle examined it, then asked Lavinia, "So, just how are you related to us?"

"The young lady says she's Daniel's daughter," Lucinda answered for their guest, "and she's an actress from New York."

Annabelle's lip twitched and her eyes narrowed. "Daniel's daughter...and an actress,,," she said slowly. The room fell silent as Annabelle scrutinized Lavinia with a disdainful gaze. Lifting her chin, she said, "Daniel *embarrassed* us *tremendously* by what he did."

Lavinia stiffened, but kept a pleasant smile affixed to her face. Then Annabelle's cold blue eyes bore into hers. "Why my cousin was so entranced by that *black* slave girl is beyond me, but it was *shameful* the way she *whored* around with him."

Lavinia pursed her lips and took a deep breath. "My word. He—he never went into detail about—his—his actions."

"Annabelle, watch what you say," Lucinda said. "Lavinia doesn't need to hear such things about her father. And besides, he married a white woman. Lavinia's mother was from

Spain."

Lavinia relaxed a bit, but when she reached for her teacup, Annabelle stood up quickly and the sofa's claw foot left the floor again. "Don't you touch that cup!"

"What?" Lavinia asked, surprised by her cousin's command.

"And get out of that chair! You can leave through the back door! How dare you come in here and expect me to—to *serve* you while you take advantage of my mother! You can't fool me!"

Astonished, Lavinia couldn't speak.

"Now, Annabelle," Lucinda admonished, "what in the devil's wrong with you? There's no reason for you to be rude like that, talking nonsense! She's kin, and she's come a long way to give us money."

"I don't know what she's up to, but we don't *need* her money!" Annabelle crumpled the check, then threw it in Lavinia's lap. "Don't you see, Mother? She's nothing but a white nigger—just like the ones who lived in your mother's house!" A look of horror crossed Lucinda's face, then Annabelle said, "She's Daniel's daughter—by that *wench*!"

"I—I'm—no—Negro," Lavinia sputtered. "My mother was from Spain!"

"That's a lie," Annabelle seethed.

Lucinda squinted her eyes, looking more closely at Lavinia. "Well, I'll be," she said, the corners of her mouth downturned. Grabbing her cane, Lucinda struggled for a moment to stand. "Get up," she said to Lavinia, who rose slowly, clutching the check thrown at her moments earlier. "I've seen enough white niggers to know one up close," Lucinda said. "But I suppose I was blinded by all that money. Now get out and leave us alone! We don't want you here, and we're not desperate enough to take money from a nigger."

"But, you're wrong about me!" Lavinia protested. "I'm white! I'm as white as you!"

Annabelle laughed without smiling. "Not by a snowball's chance in hell," she said frostily.

"One drop stains you," Lucinda added, "and as dark as that girl was that your father ran off with, you're plenty stained."

"Lori is not my mother!" Her mother's name escaped before she could stop it, but now it was too late.

The two women eyed Lavinia like she was nothing more than a worthless field hand on an auction block. "Lori," Annabelle said bitterly. "I'd forgotten her name."

"Yes," Lucinda nodded with lips downturned even further now, "that's what it was. So if that darkie's not your mother, just how did you know her name?"

"She—she was a servant to my father for years. She and her husband were in his employ."

"You're quite the actress, aren't you?" Lucinda said.

"She's nothing but a filthy black liar, masquerading as something she's not," Annabelle sneered.

Lavinia tried to hold back her tears. "I wanted to help you."

"We don't need your help," Annabelle said. "So you can just take your nigger-actress whore money and go back to New York."

"I have a legitimate stage career," Lavinia declared, "and my company is esteemed and held in high regard!" The scandal wasn't something they would've have known about.

Waving her arms dramatically, Lavinia raged on, "Your men are dead and your place is in ruins! I'm a very wealthy woman and I could give you all the money you need to fix up this dump!" Furious, she uncrumpled the check, tore it to shreds, then threw the pieces at their feet. "You'll be sorry you were so cruel to me!"

"Out!" Annabelle pointed her toward the backdoor. "The only thing we're sorry about is you coming here. Don't *dare* darken our doorstep again."

****

Bitter tears burned Lavinia's eyes, as she left Dancing Oaks in her hired carriage. "I hate my mother!" she said to herself. "She follows me everywhere! Why can't I escape from her—why does her blood have to curse me?"

Looking at the war torn remains of the plantation, Lavinia suddenly realized how ridiculous it was of her to come here at all. In the first place, there was the matter of her being a "white Negro." If Annabelle had noticed that easily, others around these parts might see through her, as well.

And what did a little one horse town like this hold for her, anyway? "There's nothing here for me," she said quietly. Not a soul recognized me, the great Lavinia Hargraves, she reflected, not even in Wilmington. I'm a New Yorker. That's where I belong, and I'm going back there to live an even greater life than I had before!

CHAPTER 11
NEW YORK
1896

At home in New York, Lavinia pondered her circumstances over breakfast in bed. Although wealthy from Vernon's fortune and real estate, she'd had no theater income for quite a while, since there were no productions to generate money. Much was needed to reinvigorate her career, hire new players and renovate her theater in order to cleanse it from the scandal.

She took a sip of coffee just as a knock sounded at her bedroom door. "Come in," she called, placing her cup on the bed tray. When the door opened, Lavinia saw her lady's maid waiting there. Gazing at the clock over the fireplace, she said, "You're late!" The portly woman wore a bonnet, and had a coat on over her street clothes. "And why aren't you in uniform?"

"I've come to say that I'm quitting, Mrs. Hargraves."

"Quitting?"

"Yes, ma'am. I considered not coming in at all, but decided that wouldn't be proper."

"But Hazel Mary—"

"It's Mary Hazel, ma'am."

"Can't you at least stay until I hire someone to take your place?"

"No, ma'am. As of today, you've seen the likes of the last of me. I can't take working any longer for someone who has such an abrasive nature."

"Abrasive nature? I'm a woman alone! I have to be abrasive to survive!"

"As I recall, ma'am, you were just as abrasive when Mr. Hargraves was alive, but when he was around, things here were a bit more tolerable. Now, if you'll excuse me, ma'am, goodbye." The woman left, shutting Lavinia's door behind her.

Scowling, Lavinia sat back on her pillows and took another sip of bitter black coffee. No theater people, no family, Lavinia thought. She had no one! Not even a trusted servant to confide in.

She heard the doorbell and tried to suppress the welling dread she felt deep down inside. Despite her other worries, one nagging thought disturbed Lavinia more than anything else — Carrie.

What if Carrie *did* expose her and come after her with lawyers and take away all of Vernon's property?   Every time there was a visitor, Lavinia feared the worst. She jumped with a start, almost spilling her coffee, when she heard a second knock at the door.

"Yes?" she asked nervously. It was the new parlor maid. The young girl was slender with dark brown hair. Her gray dress was ruffled at the bottom and she wore a long white apron and puffy white cap. Lavinia couldn't remember her name.

"Mrs. Hargraves, there's a Mr. Andrew Standish to see you." The maid walked to the bed and presented his calling card. The tenseness left Lavinia as she pushed aside thoughts of Carrie and focused on the card.

It was a photograph card with the name Andrew Standish penned in calligraphy. The name hadn't registered at first, but the small grainy photograph on the left appeared familiar. Then Lavinia remembered the tall, handsome auburn haired man she'd met while out with Vernon one evening. Andrew Standish — of Truelove and Standish Contractors. Now it was all coming back to her.

Vernon had told her only a little about Standish, but what Lavinia remembered most was that Standish was worth millions because of his property and construction business!

"Thank you—Mae."

"It's Maeve, ma'am."

"All right, then, Maeve. Show Mr. Standish to the drawing room and offer him some coffee. Tell him I'll be down shortly and then come back," Lavinia snapped. "Hazel Mary—Mary Hazel, whatever, quit, so I'll need you to help me dress."

"Yes, ma'am," Maeve said.

"And take this!" Lavinia motioned to her bed tray.

Before Maeve was out of sight, Lavinia was out of bed, yanking open her closet doors. She pulled out a brilliant gown of cranberry red, but then thought better of it. Casting aside the colorful creation, she grabbed a simple black crepe with puffy sleeves and black lace ruffles down the front. Vernon had been dead six months, but she'd only worn black for about two, if that.

After Maeve returned, she assisted Lavinia with her corset and dress, then styled her mistresses hair, piling it high using hair pins, and placing a large tortoise shell comb in back to help hold Lavinia's thick tresses in place.

"Thank you, Maeve."

"Yes, ma'am. Will there be anything else, Mrs. Hargraves?"

"No, you may go."

After Maeve left, Lavinia took a look at herself in the mirror. She'd prefer to be wearing something low cut and colorful, but today she'd play the role of Vernon's widow, still prostrate with grief — yet still gorgeous!

****

When Lavinia entered the drawing room, Andrew was seated in one of the purple mahogany chairs. A fire crackled in the fireplace, warming the room. He stood as she approached him, her hand extended.

"Mr. Standish," Lavinia said, as he kissed her hand.

"Mrs. Hargraves." He smiled.

"Please, Mr. Standish, sit down." Lavinia sat in the matching chair opposite his. "I do remember meeting you once, I believe at Delmonico's, with my husband."

"Yes, Mrs. Hargraves, that's right. I did meet you, but it was at Sherry's."

"Oh, yes," Lavinia said pleasantly, "you're right. So, how may I help you today?"

"I want to extend my sincere condolences to you upon Vernon's unfortunate passing." At the mention of Vernon's name, Lavinia's eyes watered. She pulled a lace handkerchief from her pocket and proceeded to dab at the corners of her eyes. "Mrs. Hargraves, I didn't mean to upset you."

"That's quite all right, Mr. Standish. It's

just that—I do miss him, surprisingly so." She caught her guffaw. "I—I mean, I'm surprised it's *possible* to miss someone, as much as I miss my Vernon."

"Mrs. Hargraves," Andrew said, "I'm so sorry for you for your loss. I wish there was something I could say or do to ease your pain."

"Pay me no mind." Lavinia smiled the brave smile of a grieving widow. "But I do appreciate your condolences."

An awkward silence hung between them for several moments, then Andrew cleared his throat. I did come here for a reason, Mrs. Hargraves." Wearing a black suit, he sat tall and confident. "I have a business proposition for you. I want to buy your theater."

"Buy my theater?" Lavinia's eyes widened, as she considered his proposal.

"The building and the company."

"My word," Lavinia fluttered her eyes.

"I understand how dedicated you are to your work—"

"I live and breathe for it."

"I'd offer you ample compensation, as well as allow you to maintain full creative control."

"I do wish to—revitalize my career. Everything will be so difficult for me—without Vernon. He handled the finances and travel arrangements—"

"I'd have people for that, Mrs. Hargraves." Lavinia toyed with the idea of selling the theater. The money would be good. She liked the idea of having complete control *and* being the star. And though she possessed a sharp business mind and was perfectly capable of handling finances and travel, she realized a man liked to see a woman helpless, a damsel in distress, so he could rescue her.

"Mrs. Hargraves, I realize what I'm proposing requires some serious thought — so perhaps we could discuss this further — over dinner this evening."

Lavinia smiled, trying to suppress the sudden urge to jump up and down like a school girl. "Why, that would be lovely, Mr. Standish."

"Marvelous. I'll pick you up at seven and we'll dine at Delmonico's."

Trying not to sound too giddy, Lavinia replied, "I can hardly wait."

CHAPTER 12

Lavinia's black gloved hand slipped through Andrew's arm as his carriage drove them to Delmonico's. Over the fast clip clop of the horse's hooves, Lavinia gazed into Standish's eyes while he explained the current skyscraper his company was building. They'd passed the construction site only moments earlier.

Playing the part of a doe-eyed girl, impressed with Andrew's manly exhortations regarding his work, she feigned deep interest. But her mind wandered. Standish was quite a fellow. So charming, and so very rich! Healthy, young, and pleasing to the eye.

She could easily tolerate his company—but *love* his money. And what a nice accoutrement he'd be for her arm. Lavinia Standish—that had a nice ring to it, she thought, and no

"Hargraves taint." The Standish Theater presents Lavinia Standish starring in…

Lavinia forced herself to stop daydreaming, yet the prospect of a new life with Standish was exhilarating! Her heart was about to burst at the excitement of an evening out. She'd felt awkward being seen in public because of the scandal; in addition, she was supposed to be in mourning. However, she had no intention of mourning the acceptable two-year standard.

Their carriage arrived at Twenty-Sixth Street and Fifth Avenue around seven-thirty. It had been a long time since Lavinia had been to Delmonico's, and she'd missed being seen by an adoring crowd. As the door was opened for them, Lavinia swept through the entrance.

Tonight, Lavinia felt at ease on Andrew's arm. He was an upstanding man of integrity and well respected. She imagined that by now, enough time had passed for the scandal to be a distant memory.

An attendant waited to take their wraps. Andrew took off the silk top hat and Inverness cloak he'd worn over his black tuxedo and white tie. Lavinia was draped in a long black mink. Once it was removed, she couldn't help but notice Andrew admire what lay beneath.

She wore more black, although it could hardly be considered mourning attire. Her gown was an off the shoulder velvet, decorated with large sequins and an abundance of black feathers about the shoulders and back. Smaller sequins ornamented the bodice, complementing her generous powdered cleavage, and she'd draped a long diaphanous shawl of black tulle below her feathered shoulders.

As the headwaiter escorted Lavinia and Andrew to their table, there were a few stifled gasps and veiled stares as some of the customers recognized her. Lavinia relished the sensation. She wasn't nearly as hungry for food as she was for attention.

On the way to their table, they passed a decorative fountain in the center of the room bordered by colorful flowers. The water flowed soothingly, sparkling in the dim light. While they walked amidst stares and gasps, Lavinia caught a glimpse of herself in the mirrors that lined the walls. She appeared no less than royalty.

Once seated at the mahogany table, she removed her long black gloves. But not as she would have following a grand entrance at a bird and bottle supper. This time, she took them off them subtly and gracefully, as if performing a private show, just for Andrew.

Andrew crossed his arms on the white linen tablecloth. He leaned closely toward Lavinia, admiring her. Diamonds dripped elegantly from her ears and her hair was pulled away from her face. A long cluster of spiraling curls fell alluringly over one shoulder.

"Mrs. Hargraves, you're absolutely gorgeous," he said. She'd noticed that he'd tried to keep his eyes from dropping to her chest. The tops of her creamy breasts were pushed high, nearly overflowing from the sequined velvet, begging to be admired. She didn't mind if he looked.

"Why, Mr. Standish, how you do embarrass me," she said.

"I'm sorry. I'm actually a bit embarrassed myself for acting like such a schoolboy. But I'm in awe of your beauty. I do hope you're enjoying yourself, and please, call me Andrew. May I call you Lavinia?"

"Of course. And yes, I am enjoying myself, Andrew. I haven't been to Delmonico's in months. The last time I was here — I — I was with Vernon."

Lavinia pulled a black lace handkerchief from her sequined evening bag. So as not to ruin her make-up, she didn't allow her eyes to water. However, she did dab at them gingerly. In the subdued lighting, Andrew wouldn't notice her lack of tears. Yellow shades imported from Paris surrounded the lights.

"If the memories are too painful here," he said concerned, "we don't have to stay."

"Oh no, Andrew!" Lavinia protested

126

quickly, but then added calmly, "I mean—dining here is fine, I assure you. Being here—with you—will keep my mind off of other things, and the atmosphere," she smiled, gazing up for a moment at the silver chandeliers hanging from the frescoed ceiling, "is as divine as the food."

A waiter appeared by their table. "A bottle of Lacryma Christi, for you this evening, Mr. Standish?"

Lavinia stiffened. She'd forgotten about that wine called Jesus Crying or something, and when Andrew glanced toward her, he must've seen the look of horror on her face. Lavinia quickly replaced it with a strained smile. Lacryma Christi was only a name, she forced herself to think, and didn't really mean anything.

"Tonight," Andrew said to the waiter, "we'll have Dom Perignon."

"As you wish." The waiter bowed and disappeared.

"I'd forgotten your aversion to the name of my favorite wine." Andrew smiled. "Perhaps you'll explain that to me one day, but tonight champagne is in order because we have something to celebrate."

"We do?" Lavinia asked. "And just what might that be?"

"A new beginning?"

"A new beginning—of what?"

"Your theater, of course, under my management."

Lavinia hesitated. "Mr. Standish— Andrew—I thought we were to discuss that further this evening. I still have yet to make up my mind."

The waiter reappeared, poured the champagne, and vanished.

"A toast," Andrew said, as he picked up his crystal flute, "to your new theater."

"But," Lavinia gently placed her hand on his to lower his glass, "what if I decide I *don't* want to sell my theater to you?"

He looked her firmly in the eye. "Then I suppose I'll have to marry you."

At this, they both laughed.

Lavinia was glad to see that the evening was progressing just as she'd wanted. This man, she decided, was more than just interested in her theater, and he'd just tested the waters, as only a rich and powerful man could, by throwing out a marriage proposal.

"Andrew, surely you jest! Why, we don't even know each other."

"Then now is a good time for us to get acquainted. I've always wanted to know how you became involved with Vernon. I mean no disrespect when I say he was—so very different from you."

Lavinia raised her chin slightly and sighed. "I suppose we were different. He—came to see my father regarding some business once," she said evasively.

"What does your father do?"

Lavinia pursed her lips. "He had a business out West — but, Andrew, I'd rather not talk about my parents, they're dead." She dabbed at her eyes again. "My mother died when I was a little girl and I lost my father when I was seventeen. I'd met Vernon not long before that.

"He was such a kind man. And after my father died — well — we married — and he took great care of me. Oh, Andrew," she looked down, distraught, "I just can't talk about it anymore."

"Forgive me, Lavinia. I'd forgotten that your parents are deceased. I'd read that in the papers. Have you any brothers or sisters?"

"No." She gazed at him forlornly, placing the handkerchief against her heart.

"So you have no one?" Andrew held one of her hands. With the other she wiped away imaginary tears.

"Not a soul, and losing Vernon on the heels of the — other great tragedy I endured — the murder suicide of my co-star and his lovely fiancée — has just been too much for me."

Lavinia lowered her voice. "Something that's hurt quite deeply — is that some think I was — involved — with Kenneth — romantically. Andrew," Lavinia implored him with sorrowful eyes, "I hope *you* don't think that. I can assure you, in all honesty, that my relationship with Kenneth Tyler was nothing more than professional."

Her gaze dropped for a moment. "Perhaps I should be flattered that some think otherwise. Could our love scenes have appeared *that* convincing?

"No one ever suspected Jenny of having problems with her—sanity. I can't imagine what drove her—to do such a horrible thing. Jenny was quite gifted; she'd stopped performing because of her children—perhaps that caused her emotional strife. Oh, Andrew, I keep asking myself why so many bad things have happened to me—and why so many all at once? I—I just don't understand."

Andrew still held her hand. Squeezing it gently he said, "Lavinia, I know how difficult it is to lose those close to you. As a boy, I lost both of my parents. My aunt and uncle raised my brother Julian and me, but I felt helpless after my parents' deaths, especially my mother's. When she died, I wondered who would ever love me like she had. That was a frightening thought for a young boy.

"Despite that, my aunt and uncle loved us as if we were theirs. They had no children of their own, so they spoiled us. I don't know what we would have done without them. Perhaps Julian and I would have managed somehow." He held up two crossed fingers. "Because the two of us—we're thick as thieves. No one can make it through the tough times alone." Gazing deeply into her eyes, he said, "Lavinia, I'm here for you, and for what it's worth, I never believed you to be involved with your co-star."

She smiled, feeling relieved. "I'm so glad you understand."

He lifted his champagne glass. "Shall we?" After Lavinia lifted hers, Andrew said, "To us." They clinked glasses, entwined arms, and drank. "Now," he set down his glass, "after we're married, I say we have lots of children."

He was perfect, Lavinia thought, except for that. "Andrew, if we *were* to marry, there's something you need to know. I—I can't have children."

Andrew was taken aback only momentarily. "Well—there are lots of orphans out there that need loving homes."

Lavinia took a deep breath. "Andrew, you don't understand. I'm physically capable, but my—work—the acting and the touring—once the theater is rejuvenated under your management—should we get married—all of that will keep me very busy."

This didn't deter Andrew. "Lavinia, one day you'll change your mind. Maybe not right away—but every woman wants children—they're a precious gift. Don't be so quick to think you don't want any at all."

Lavinia hesitated. "Perhaps you're right," she lied. "Maybe — one day."

"I'd like at least five." Andrew smiled with a wink. "Darling, if you don't mind, I told my brother Julian we'd stop by after dinner. I'm eager for him to meet you. He and his wife Serene have seen several of your plays. If we're not too late, their children might still be awake."

"Their — children?" Lavinia asked tightly.

"They have two boys," Andrew smiled, "three and five — oh, and one on the way."

Lavinia forced a smile. "I'm sure — meeting them — will be *lovely*..."

Chapter 13

"Uncle Andrew!"

Lavinia heard a shrill little voice call from upstairs.

"Is that you?"

Lavinia watched as Andrew smiled. He sat next to her on a red velvet sofa edged with gold brocade.

"Excuse me," he nodded to her, and then to his brother Julian and Julian's wife, Serene, seated across from them on a matching loveseat.

As Andrew walked from their living room, Julian said in a gruff voice to Lavinia, "Brigid, their nurse, just put them to bed."

"It's me," Andrew called up from the hall, "your favorite uncle!"

"Their only uncle," Julian grumbled under his breath.

"Xander," the little voice shouted, "I told you! Come on!"

"Hold on, you two!" A husky female voice called from above.

"Let us go!" A younger sounding voice protested.

"It's all right, Brigid," Andrew called to the husky voice. "I want to see my nephews, and I have someone I'd like them to meet. I'll send them back up in a moment."

"Glory be to God, Mr. Standish," husky voiced Brigid replied, "you indulge the children entirely too much! I don't think your brother will be pleased with me for letting them—"

Julian sighed. "It's all right, Brigid," he yelled. "Loose them from your clutches." Serene smiled sweetly, patting her husband's hand.

"Very well, then," Brigid said. "Behave yourselves!"

Lavinia stiffened upon hearing the pitter patter of clumsy little feet running down the stairs.

"Uncle Andrew!" the little voices squealed in unison.

Seconds later Andrew walked back into the room carrying a small, giggling boy in each arm. Lavinia's heart raced as she eyed the two chubby, pink cheeked redheads. Using her acting skills she forced her sweetest smile, while fighting against instinct to flee as Andrew approached her.

"Mrs. Hargraves," Andrew said, "allow me to introduce my nephews, Alexander and Philip."

Sitting stiffly with a broad faux smile in place, Lavinia took a deep breath. "Why, aren't they the most *precious* little cherubs I've ever seen!" Her tone was steeped in sugar.

"She's very pretty, Uncle Andrew," the older boy said. "So pretty she doesn't look real."

Andrew laughed.

"Uncle Andrew, may we touch her?" the younger boy asked.

Lavinia sat petrified, trying to keep the artificial smile affixed to her face, as the boy squirmed to get down from his uncle's arms and attack her. His nose was runny. The snot would ruin her black velvet dress! She detested the feel of little hands all over her. She'd hated her days teaching at the Westmore School, surrounded by children touching her and playing with her hair.

Thankfully, Andrew held fast to the wriggling child. "Alexander," he said, "both of you will just have to take my word that Mrs. Hargraves is made of flesh and blood, just as you and I..."

While Andrew continued talking to the boy, Lavinia caught a glimpse of Julian studying her. He wasn't admiring her beauty, nor looking at her in a salacious, lustful way. She would have preferred that. Instead, he sat with thick arms folded across his large chest cynically scrutinizing her, as if she were nothing more than a common criminal.

Feeling self-conscious, Lavinia wondered if her looks were fading due to the stress of the scandal, or worse yet, if Julian was suspicious of her ancestry?

Serene was unaware of Julian's disdainful gaze upon Lavinia. She only smiled pleasantly as Andrew spoke to her children. Her sweetness reminded Lavinia of Olivia—and that thought alone made her want to retch. But Lavinia did pity the poor woman, pregnant again, her stomach bulged like a watermelon beneath her gown.

"Now, darlings," Andrew said, "off to bed!" He carried the boys away and sent them back up the stairs.

Lavinia was ready to escape. When Andrew appeared again, she said in a honeyed voice, "Andrew, darling, it's getting late..."

****

After he'd said goodnight and procured another dinner date with Lavinia, Andrew bounded down the stairs of her West Side mansion to his carriage, breathing in the cold night air. "Back to my brother's house," he ordered the driver.

Julian's brownstone was on the West Side as well, and not far from Andrew's. To both brothers, the West Side seemed more exciting than the aristocratic East Side, with its boring afternoon teas, formal dress dinners and stiff evenings at the Metropolitan Opera.

Andrew preferred the excitement of a Broadway show and the company of a sensuous actress over an evening with a debutante. As his carriage passed the Dakota, Andrew remembered a party taking place there tonight. His friends, the Sokolowskis, were entertaining Mark Twain. Perhaps Andrew would put in a late appearance after leaving Julian's. Having been with Lavinia for a good part of the evening, Andrew was too excited for sleep.

When the driver arrived at Julian's home, Andrew quickly alit from the carriage and approached the door. It was unlocked. All the servants were asleep, but Andrew knew his brother had expected his return. He never could wait until morning to hear Julian's opinion of his lady friends.

After placing his top hat and cloak on a coat rack in the large reception hall, he walked upstairs to the first floor. "Julian?" Andrew called quietly.

"In the living room. Come in here and sit down," Julian said, as Andrew walked in and took a seat in a large red velvet chair. "I know you're eager to see what I thought of that actress you brought here."

Julian sat on the sofa, a satin bathrobe pulled closed over his pajamas. A snifter of brandy was on a mahogany end table beside him. Julian was handsome in a gruff sort of way, but hardly dashing like his younger brother. At 6'3" he was one inch taller with a larger frame and slightly pudgy stomach. Dark haired and dark eyed, Julian sported a thick moustache.

Serene sat next to her husband, looking radiant, as always. In a green satin bathrobe with a collar of cream-colored ruffles, she simply glowed. Deep auburn hair tumbled in tight waves to her waist and her hazel eyes sparkled. Serene appeared in a perpetual state of bliss, which only intensified in Julian's presence.

Settling back in his chair, Andrew smiled at her. "And I have the honor of hearing your opinion, as well?"

"I think she's lovely," Serene said.

"But that's not all you said," Julian countered gruffly.

The two were a perfect match, Andrew thought. Years ago, however, Andrew had fallen in love with Serene first. Since losing her to his brother, Andrew had been in search of the perfect woman—and he'd found her, when he'd fallen in love with Lavinia. Finally, after six years of longing, marrying her was possible.

For a moment, Andrew gazed at Serene's swelling stomach and felt a slight pang of jealousy. He wanted to possess the same things as his older brother, a beautiful wife he loved and lots of children.

"So? What did you think?" Andrew asked, his gaze passing between them. "Isn't she beautiful, wonderful and magnificent?"

Julian looked seriously at his brother. "I didn't like her," he said flatly.

Andrew leaned forward suddenly. "You didn't?" He asked dumbfounded. "But why?"

"I tried to like her — for you," Julian said, "but I couldn't. You've carried on about her for six years. I've read about her in *The Mirror* and *The Times*. I've seen her plays — and she's good. She's an actress, she likes to talk about herself, as she did this evening, telling us about every production she's ever appeared in. I suppose that's only natural for someone like that. But anyone that self-centered can only be in love with one person — herself!"

"Nonsense, Julian!" Andrew said. "Lavinia's just self- confident and strong. She lost both parents at a young age, then she married Hargraves."

"And there's only one reason she would've

married that shady Hargraves character to begin with!" Julian exclaimed.

"Serene, darling," Andrew said, ignoring his brother, "what did you think of her?"

"She's a beautiful woman and a talented actress, and—"

"And you said you could tell she didn't like the children!" Julian said. Serene looked down sheepishly.

"Truly, Serene?" Andrew asked, crestfallen.

Serene's eyes met Andrew's. "What I said, was that I could tell she's not used to being *around* children. And some women may not be warm toward other people's children, but when they have their own that all changes. Besides—a woman's heart grows with every child she has."

"So—did you like her?" Andrew asked hopefully.

"As I said, I think she's lovely."

"Well, I'm suspicious of her!" Julian protested. "She doesn't sit well with me at all."

"But Andrew's smitten with her," Serene said.

Julian threw up his hands. "He was smitten with that other actress too! What was her name, Fiona Henderson? Beautiful girl, but the intellect of a tree stump. That Melinda Jennings, there was a level headed girl who would've been just right for Andrew! But no, he's obsessed with actresses! And he's been known to lose his head too easily where women are concerned.

"Now, this Lavinia, she's not just any woman! You have to watch her. She's smart — shrewd and conniving — and I don't trust her!" Julian eyed Andrew sharply. "What about the scandal with that actor fellow?"

"She assures me she had no part in it," Andrew said.

"And you believe her?" Julian asked, taking a sip of brandy.

"I have no reason not to."

Julian hesitated, placing the snifter back on the end table. "It's your life, Andrew. But just remember, she's already buried one husband."

MARIA MCKENZIE

Chapter 14
New York City
Spring, 1897

WHACK! Andrew's hands, sheathed in a
new pair of Draper and Maynard boxing
gloves, struck the black leather heavy bag with
a series of forceful punches. The five-foot sack
weighed about a hundred pounds and swung
slightly left to right and back. It hung,
suspended from the ceiling, by a chain, which
loudly jingled and clanked in response to each
of Andrew's bashes. BAM!

He'd gotten out of bed at six. Now in his
gymnasium, Andrew was in the midst of his
morning calisthenics routine. It had been an
unseasonably warm night. The heat had risen,
making the gym akin to an oven, even with the
windows open. Sweating profusely, Andrew

was clad in an undershirt, tucked into belted pants.

The Greek term teleos, Andrew reminded himself, meant becoming all that one was created to be, and he aspired to the classical ideal of perfection, a standard of excellence expressed through body, mind, form and spirit in ancient Greece. Yet now he felt only the primal rage of an animal. WHAM!

Andrew and Lavinia had been married almost a year, and her new life with him—and his money—was providing her a splendid existence. They'd sold Vernon's mansion, choosing instead to live in Andrew's four-story brownstone, wired with electricity, at Central Park West and Eighty-Sixth Street.

Andrew's equipped gymnasium, on the fourth-floor near the servants quarters, contained several pairs of wooden dumbbells that varied in weight, a medicine ball, a set of Indian clubs, and a rope-and-pulley weightlifting system.

However, the equipment of choice to express his internal fury was the black leather heavy bag. After all he'd done for Lavinia, she showed him no appreciation, whatsoever! WHAM!. When they'd married, Andrew had actually thought Lavinia would stop working—at least eventually. BAM! And want to have his children! WHACK!

He knew she loved the theater, and was

perhaps the most talented actress of all time — and he loved that about her. Yet now it was time for her to be a wife and mother, and to love her husband *above* the theater! But Andrew couldn't tame her. FWAM!

Whenever he'd bring up the subject of children, Lavinia would only say sweetly, "Soon, darling, but not just yet."

Hoping to expedite her decision and his desire for little ones, Andrew refused to wear French letters. Lavinia, however, wasn't at a loss for alternative ways to kill off what he'd provide to make babies. She'd learned quite a few methods from the worldly women of the theater, and tried everything from sponges to suppositories. Yet her preferred contraption was the douching syringe, which she referred to by the unladylike name of "the pisser." And she used that vulgarity just to irritate Andrew. BAM!

Why couldn't she be more like Julian's wife, Serene? That's what Andrew wanted, a mate who adored him, and would glory in the fact that she was the mother of his children.

The new Standish Theater, formerly The Hargraves, now seemed both child and lover to Lavinia, and it thrived on Andrew's money. WHACK, WHAM, BAM! She'd spared no expense in renovations to create a stunning showplace. Truelove and Standish Contractors, *his* company, had made a few structural design changes to the facade to create a much grander entranceway, including the addition of large Baroque columns.

On the inside, Lavinia used a vibrantly glowing color scheme of dark green, bronze, and gold. The velvet covered seats, which had been a subdued maroon, were now reupholstered in bright red.

After Lavinia's theater had been transformed into a more modern looking playhouse, she'd inaugurated it by presenting free programs, using some of the most popular players of the day.

"William Faversham," Andrew muttered, WHAM, "James K. Hackett," BAM, "Francis Wilson," WHACK!

Although the heavy bag wasn't a living being, Andrew wished it could feel pain. Thinking of all those men, Andrew's punching increased to a maddening pace. Had his wife slept with them? It was rumored that she'd slept with that Kenneth Tyler before his murder. When Andrew had begun courting her, he'd refused to believe that—then! WHAM, FWAM, BAM! What did Lavinia take him for, another Hargraves?

Julian had insinuated that Lavinia only married the old man for his money and what he could do for her. At thirty-five, Andrew hardly considered himself old, but he was rich, and his money had done quite a bit to resurrect

Lavinia's scandal-ridden career.

Any wariness Faversham, Hackett, or Wilson might have had regarding the scandal seemed to vanish at the sums of money she'd been willing to pay them. Of course the money came from Andrew's pocket, and if she'd been sleeping with them, why would they *not* agree to appear in her productions? WHAM, BAM!

Andrew pushed those thoughts from his mind. Lavinia wouldn't be unfaithful — that's what Andrew wanted to believe — yet *he* couldn't satisfy her. His punches grew quicker and more hostile. *He* couldn't compete with the stage! WHACK!

Just last night after they'd made love, Lavinia said, "Why darling, that almost made me feel as alive as I do when performing. To me, the stage is really the only place where I truly feel alive." WHAM, BAM, WHACK!

How dare she! Exhausted, and pushed to the stressful limit, out came a primal scream. "Arghhh!" He didn't care who heard him. His anger simmered — boiled! He had every right to feel this way.

Andrew left the heavy bag and moved his attention to the brown leather medicine ball. He kicked it. The sand-filled sphere rolled a good distance until it thudded against the wall. That's when Andrew realized the pain in his big toe from the hasty punt. Limping toward the dumbbells, he relished the discomfort.

Throwing his boxing gloves to the floor, Andrew picked up a thirty pound pair of dumbbells. He curled one arm up, lowered it, then repeated the motion with his opposite arm. Lavinia did admire his muscles, when she wasn't spending his money.

Huffing in a deep breath with each motion, Andrew thought about the past several months. By late last year, his wife's questioned involvement in the murder suicide of Tyler and his lover was far enough in the past to be forgotten, according to Lavinia.

Yet if anyone still harbored ill thoughts about her because of it, she didn't care. Lavinia's main concern was putting on good plays with good casts. There, she'd succeeded. Once again, the public flocked to see her performances, and she received the much needed praise and adoration she craved.

Lavinia's industriousness in the theater and the interminable tours had taken a toll on Andrew. At first it had been exciting being married to *the* Lavinia Hargraves. He'd even toured Europe with her. But once had been enough and he'd only lasted two weeks of the three-month tour.

He'd come to the conclusion that he didn't really understand theater people, and had nothing in common with them. A strange lot, they seemed happy only when pretending to be someone else, and when themselves, sought happiness through the excesses of dope and alcohol. Lavinia didn't involve herself with narcotics or drinking, aside from an occasional glass of wine, but she thoroughly immersed herself in the characters she played.

Andrew had completed twelve repetitions with the dumbbells. He put them down, then sat on a bench, pausing for a while before doing more. Sounds drifted in from the open windows. The slow clip clop of the horse pulling the milk wagon, the rumble of streetcars, and the hearty mantra of "Read all about it..." from a newsboy.

The heat was exhausting, or was his relationship with Lavinia draining the life from him? Her heart was in the theater, not in her marriage, and Andrew questioned if she still loved him, or if she'd ever loved him at all.

Was his money the only thing that had attracted her to him? He didn't want to believe this. In spite of everything, he *did* love her. And, perhaps, if they had a child, their marriage would flourish as much as the theater. A child might even put her heart in their marriage and save it. At least, that's what Andrew hoped.

Gazing at the heavy bag, Andrew decided on another round. He strode to it, took a stance, and raised his fists. Then, he commenced punching, only this time with bare hands. WHAM, WHACK, BAM! The pain felt good.

Chapter 15

Lavinia lay in bed feeling queasy. Having just vomited in a porcelain bowl, she'd rung for the maid.

"Darling," Andrew said, "you've been ill now for over a week."

Usually, Lavinia was still asleep when Andrew left for work. But she'd been waking early the past several mornings with an unexplained illness that seemed to pass by mid-afternoon. Andrew, dressed for the day in a black suit and gray cravat, had just finished breakfast.

"I'm fine," Lavinia said, propping herself up on feather pillows.

There was a knock at the door. Andrew called, "Come in." It was the scullery maid, a young girl in a simple gray dress and white apron. She rushed in quietly and removed the soiled bowl on Lavinia's nightstand, replacing it with with a clean one, then discreetly left the room.

"You're not fine," Andrew said. "I spoke to Dr. Davenport yesterday, and he's coming to see you this morning." Andrew brought over a satin bathrobe and helped her slip it on over her pink nightgown. "He should be here soon." Andrew sat down next to her.

"Then I need more than a robe!" Lavinia sat up quickly, but then the nausea overtook her. "Oh..." she collapsed against the pillows, sighing.

As if she were a porcelain doll, Andrew tied the satin ribbons of the wrap snuggly at her neck. Lavinia felt almost suffocated by this gesture. "There," he said, "now you're well covered."

"Andrew, I don't *need* Dr. Davenport! Whatever I have will run its course."

The last thing Lavinia wanted was to be seen by a doctor. She didn't want her greatest fear confirmed. The fear that she could be — with child. Lavinia dreaded the very thought of a baby. But perhaps she could will herself not to be pregnant.

"It's like the cold I had in February," Lavinia said. "It would come, I'd recover, then it would come back. You remember."

"I only remember worrying about you."

"Regardless, I finally managed to rid

myself of that bug for good. Now, this is probably the same sort of thing—so I'll be fine. Then I can get back to the theater. I can't afford to miss any more rehearsals for the new play. I've already missed three!"

"Lavinia, you've been working too hard. You need a rest from the theater. Then you'd recover quickly from whatever's ailing you. The world won't end if you miss a few more rehearsals."

"You just don't understand!" she snapped. "And I haven't been working too hard. This illness, or whatever it is, will go away. It always does."

"But even after the nausea subsides," Andrew said, "you're still not yourself. When was the last time you ate a substantial amount of food?"

"I just haven't wanted to eat much of anything." This was true, but not eating certainly couldn't be beneficial for a baby, Lavinia had rationalized. If she were pregnant, the child might starve—and then, cease to exist.

"Well, darling, I want you healthy, permanently, and not sick every morning." Andrew moved limp strands of hair from her face then lightly touched her cheek.

"I'll be fine!" She pushed away his hand. "Stop worrying about me! As long as I'm healthy for the approaching premiere in two weeks, I'll be happy."

"Lavinia, I'd like you to be happy—just
being with me. Your theater doesn't leave you
much time for your husband. I want to see
more of you. After all, you're married to me,
not the theater."

There was another knock at the door. "Mr.
Standish," Lelia, the parlor maid said from
outside their room, "Dr. Davenport is here."

Andrew approached the door and opened
it. Lelia wore a full length white apron over a
gray dress with leg of mutton sleeves. "Thank
you, Lelia. Would you please escort him up?"

Once Lelia was out of earshot, Lavinia
glared at her husband. "You tell that man to
leave! I'm fine!"

"No, my dear, you're not." Andrew
walked toward her, then lovingly stroked her
hair. "If I didn't care for you, I wouldn't have
sent for him."

Moments later, Dr. Davenport, with gray
hair and ruddy cheeks, peeked in the room.
"May I come in?"

"Dr. Davenport!" Andrew said.

"Good morning, Andrew, Mrs. Standish."
He shook hands with Andrew and nodded
toward Lavinia. "Though you're not feeling
well, may I say you're looking as beautiful as
ever."

"Why, thank you, Dr. Davenport," Lavinia
said sweetly, though she felt trapped and

powerless in the presence of Andrew and his co-conspirator. "I can assure you, though, I'm quite well."

"Your husband's mighty concerned about you." The short man approached the bed. After placing his little black bag on the nightstand near Lavinia's clean vomit receptacle, he asked, "What's been ailing you?"

"Well, for about the past week or so, I've been nauseated in the mornings, and feel depleted of energy, but by mid-day, I feel somewhat better."

"She's also lost her appetite," Andrew added.

Dr. Davenport placed a hand on Lavinia's forehead, then held her wrist for a few moments, looking at his watch. "No fever and a normal pulse," he said, satisfied. Peering at Lavinia over his little round spectacles, the doctor gently pressed her abdomen in three different spots. "No pain?" He asked. Lavinia said no.

Dr. Davenport took his stethoscope from his medical bag. Once more, keeping his eyes fixed on Lavinia's, he gingerly slipped the diaphragm beneath her satin robe and listened to her heart for several seconds. Standing straight, the doctor smiled. "Mrs. Standish, you're as healthy as can be, but I suggest you start eating. Your symptoms only indicate that you're pregnant!"

Lavinia's worst fear was confirmed. She had to convince the doctor, as well as her own body, that a pregnancy couldn't be possible. Yet before she could say anything, Andrew was putting his arms around her and kissing her cheek.

"Darling, I'm so happy! We're going to have a baby!"

Lavinia pulled from her husband's embrace. "Why, this—this can't be, Dr. Davenport. I—I've taken precautions."

"Precautions aren't always reliable, Mrs. Standish. When was your last cycle?"

As though in mourning, Lavinia said, "It's—a month late."

"And you haven't suspected anything?" the doctor asked.

"I can't say my cycle is always—regular."

"Well, I think we can all rest assured that you're pregnant! But, to be on the safe side, I can take a specimen from you and test it on a rat. If your maid could bring up a pot—"

"That won't be necessary, Doctor," Lavinia said, repulsed. "I trust your word."

The doctor looked at her with a twinkle in his eye. "I think you might have had a slight suspicion about this. Women's intuition, they say. Now, Mrs. Standish, you'll need plenty of rest, and you'll want to maintain a healthy diet with lots of milk, eggs, meat and cheese. You're eating for two now!"

At the mention of all that food, Lavinia felt a slight wave of nausea.

Andrew smiled broadly. "I'll see to it that she's pampered and waited on hand and foot, even more than she is now!"

"Mr. and Mrs. Standish," the doctor bowed slightly, "I think my work here is done."

"Thank you so much for seeing us this morning, Dr. Davenport! I can't think of any better news to start my day!" Andrew exclaimed triumphantly. "I hope it's a girl — though I'd be more than happy to have a boy!"

Lavinia's lower lip protruded in a pout while her husband vigorously shook the doctor's hand. He made no effort to contain his excitement.

"You know," Andrew remarked, "I've had my own suspicions, Dr. Davenport, that's why I was so eager to get you over here!"

The two men laughed. Lavinia, with arms crossed tightly over her chest, felt the laughing was at her expense.

"Well," Andrew patted the doctor on the back, "let me see you to the door."

Andrew escorted the doctor downstairs, leaving Lavinia alone to contemplate her predicament. She detested the idea of having a child. It would interfere with her life, the theater, everything!

Lavinia *had* told Andrew that her having children would be fine, at some point in the future, but she'd lied. She'd only said that so he wouldn't hesitate to marry her. Having children was important to him, but having his money was important to her. She didn't want children, but now here she was expecting! How could fate be so cruel?

There was a way to stop it, but how could she now? When she'd first had an inkling about three weeks ago, she'd thought about going somewhere far, far away, where her face wasn't known. Then she could've had the "procedure" done, and no one would have ever known.

Yet time with the theater hadn't permitted that, and besides, she'd convinced herself that she was imagining things. Then the nausea had begun. Now, with Andrew well aware of her condition, Lavinia was mired by this deplorable circumstance—and there was no way out!

Her husband returned to the bedroom, oblivious to her state of despair. As he rushed to embrace her, he said, "Darling, you can't believe how ecstatic I am." She didn't return his embrace. "I hope we have a girl who's just as beautiful as you are. I'll spoil her mercilessly.

"I even have some names picked out, that is, if you like them, too." Lavinia pulled away, turning her back to him and leaning into the pillows. "Don't you want to hear what they are?" he asked, crestfallen at her unresponsiveness.

"What?" she asked like a sullen child.

"Both name's are befitting a princess. The first is Loraline."

From over her shoulder, Lavinia shot him a nasty glare. "Loraline? Why *that* name? It sounds too much like—" she stopped herself before she blurted *Mother's name*, then took a deep breath. "Under no circumstances will a child of mine be called that!"

"Darling, you needn't be so vehement. How about Selina, instead?"

"Fine," Lavinia said tightly, turning away once more.

"Of course, if it's a boy, I'll be just as thrilled, though I can't seem to decide on the perfect name. But, perhaps—when I see him, I'll know exactly what to call him. Or, I should say, *we'll* know what to call him."

"*You* want the baby, *you* name it."

"Lavinia," Andrew gently squeezed her shoulder, "aren't you the least bit happy?"

"No. I'm not happy at all!" Sitting up to face him, she declared, "This is all your fault!"

"Well, it had better be my fault—I enjoyed every moment of it! Lavinia," Andrew paused for a moment, "I'm rather astonished by your reaction."

"I don't care! If it weren't for your— unbridled passion, I wouldn't be in this situation! I know when this happened!" She said, as though accusing him of a crime. "If you'd just released me when you'd finished, instead of kissing me — and holding me — I could've taken care of things — in time!"

"Lavinia!" Andrew laughed. "The way you run off after lovemaking annoys the devil out of me, and I've been tempted to throw out that pisser of yours! I want to hold onto you and kiss you each and every time. So, darling," he said, playfully kissing her hand and then working his lips up her arm, "perhaps this is your fault. Can I help it if you stir within me such 'unbridled passion'?"

She pulled her arm from him. "I don't want this baby!"

"Lavinia!" Andrew grasped her shoulders, eyeing her seriously. "Children are a gift, a precious gift from God. We should be celebrating. I know you don't want children now, but once the baby's born, you'll change your mind.

"You'll love him, or her, with all your heart. And your heart will grow. It'll grow a little more with each baby to make sure you can give each child all the love it needs."

"I don't want this one and I certainly don't want any more! And what you just said sounds like something silly, stupid Olivia would say!"

"Who's Olivia?"

"Nobody! And the only thing that'll grow is my stomach. There's nothing to celebrate." Lavinia started to cry. Few things reduced her to tears. But this—a pregnancy, nearly unraveled the fiber of her being. She had no control over the child that would take over her body for the next several months—and her existence for years to come. "My life is over...I'll be fat and ugly," Lavinia wept.

"Darling," Andrew said, wiping away her tears with a handkerchief, "a new life is beginning in you, and a new phase of life—is starting for us. If I'm calculating correctly, February of 1898 will be a happy time for us both, as our first child is born. And, darling," he smiled, "you'll look absolutely beautiful while you're pregnant."

"I'll look like Lillian Russell!" she cried.

"The Great American Beauty! She *is* stunning, isn't she?"

"She looks like a sow!" Lavinia continued to weep. "Now get out and leave me alone," she pushed Andrew from the bed, then grabbed the clean bowl, "so I can vomit in peace!"

Chapter 16
February, 1898

Rivulets of perspiration trickled from Lavinia's hairline down the sides of her face, as labor pains, sharp as a thousand knives, tore through her. She wore a white cotton nightgown, its bloodstained fabric scrunched to her knees. Screaming, she pushed.

It was just past nine p.m. The heavy blue gray drapes in the bedroom were closed, and the brass chandelier, lighted by electric bulbs, illuminated the room.

"The baby's head is crowning!" Dr. Davenport said. He was sweating, too. He'd removed his jacket a while ago. Now his necktie was loosened and his sleeves rolled to his elbows. "You'll have to push a little harder, Mrs. Standish."

Breathing hard, Lavinia said, "I feel like

I've been pushing for hours—and the pain," she gasped, "I can't take it..."

Eva, Dr. Davenport's daughter, gently dabbed away the perspiration from Lavinia's forehead and cheeks with a cloth, then said, "Hold my hand, Mrs. Standish. Squeeze as hard as you can."

Lavinia squeezed the young woman's hand, then let out another scream.

"Push, Mrs. Standish!" Dr. Davenport yelled above Lavinia's cries. "The head is out, now the shoulders are coming!"

Finally, Lavinia released Eva's hand. She fell silent as the rest of the baby's body slid from hers.

"Oh, Mrs. Standish," the doctor said as the baby wailed, "she's a beautiful girl, with quite a head of hair, I must say! But as large as you were, I thought she'd be a little bigger. She's a tiny precious thing, but looks and sounds mighty healthy."

While the doctor cut the umbilical cord, Lavinia thought she could rest, but all of a sudden, more pains overtook her, the same kind she'd experienced during the baby's birth. Terror seized her. Even with a doctor present, childbirth was dangerous! I never wanted a baby, Lavinia thought, and now I'm going to die!

Lavinia drew in a deep breath. "Doctor, I feel more pain! Something's wrong!"

Dr. Davenport quickly handed the baby to Eva, then turned his attention back to Lavinia. "Heavens to Betsy, Mrs. Standish! Another head is crowning; you're having twins! Push!"

At this news, Lavinia screamed in pain and fury, as a second baby tore its way from her loins. Twins? She might just as well be dead!

Dr. Davenport laughed. "Mr. Standish will be thrilled to have not one, but two little girls to spoil!" However, when the doctor finished delivering the second baby, a look of surprise, or perhaps shock, crossed his face. Momentarily stunned, the doctor was silent.

"Doctor," Lavinia said out of breath, "is something wrong?'

"No, no — but it's — it's a boy! I was — just surprised not to see another girl."

The babies cried loudly in squeaky little voices, as the doctor and his daughter cleansed them. Collapsed against her pillows, Lavinia also cried, in deep heartfelt sobs.

"Every mother cries tears of joy." Dr. Davenport smiled. "Mrs. Standish, they're both beautiful, and just as healthy as can be," the doctor said, while he and his daughter swaddled the infants in blankets. "Eva and I will bring them to you in just a moment."

After the babies quieted down, Dr. Davenport and Eva whispered among themselves for a short while, prior to approaching Lavinia's bedside.

Before Eva handed Lavinia her daughter, Lavinia said, "What was all that whispering about?"

As Eva bent down to give Lavinia the girl she said, "We were only discussing how beautiful your babies are." Unsmiling, Lavinia took the child, unsure of exactly how to hold it. "If you'll excuse me, Mrs. Standish, I'll get your husband." Eva quietly left the room. Unable to bear his wife's screams, Andrew had been pacing downstairs in the living room for hours.

Lavinia held her daughter, wearily gazing at the rosy pink bundle, whose head was covered with silky black hair. A little girl, Lavinia thought. That's what Andrew wanted—at least *he'd* be happy. So, she sighed, this was Selina.

After a few seconds more, Dr. Davenport said, "Here's your son." Lavinia opened an arm to receive her second child. As the doctor gently placed her baby there, he said, "Your husband will be pleased to know he has a son, along with that little girl he wanted so badly."

Lavinia's breath caught as she looked at the boy. To her horror, he was dark.

Chapter 17

Lavinia stared at her son as though he'd fallen from the moon — the dark side. He was hideous! His head was covered in soft black curls and his skin was golden brown.

Upon seeing him, Lavinia's first reaction was how much she hated her mother! She stained me, Lavinia thought angrily, and now she's stained my child!

Lavinia had never suspected she'd pop out a pickaninny. She could see her sister, Olivia, having a mongrel that looked like this, but never herself. As fair as Andrew was, and as light as Lavinia was, she'd believed that to be an impossibility. Yet she'd been wrong.

Now stuck with incriminating ancestral evidence that could destroy her, Lavinia's mind churned as she tried to think of a method to do away with the child. However, looking at the little prune-like face, she had second thoughts. Perhaps that was a rather drastic measure — she was its mother. Lavinia just wasn't thinking clearly. After all, having just had a baby — two babies — she felt as if she were going insane.

The doctor hadn't said anything about the boy's color, Lavinia reflected, but surely he must've noticed it. Why had he looked so shocked upon first seeing him, and what else could he and Eva have been whispering about? She heard Andrew's laughter in the hallway, along with his solid footsteps, as he approached their bedroom. Her mind raced as she tried to think of an explanation for the baby's color — that subject was bound to come up, if not by the doctor, surely by Andrew.

"I hear your husband," Dr. Davenport said. "I'll leave you two alone for a little while with your children."

After the doctor left the room, Lavinia heard him congratulate Andrew, who then thanked the doctor for delivering his babies. Lavinia rolled her eyes as she listened to the last of the male backslapping ritual, before again concentrating on the creation of a fabrication.

When Andrew finally did burst into the room, she was so distraught by what he'd think of the boy's appearance, and by what she'd concoct about it, that she barely noticed him.

"Twins!" Andrew exclaimed, seeming doubly overcome with joy. "I still can't believe it!"

Lavinia raised her eyes to meet Andrew's. He was too far away to notice the boy's dark skin, but that wouldn't last for long. She braced herself for the worst.

"My wife," Andrew smiled broadly, "just as beautiful as ever—and my children, more beautiful than I ever could have imagined!"

Andrew still wore his day clothes. Although he'd removed his gray suit jacket, he'd kept on his vest and cravat. Despite his slightly mussed auburn hair and the stubble on his once clean-shaven face, he remained dashing.

Lavinia, on the other hand, felt atrocious. She lay dripping with sweat, surrounded by red stained cloths and bloody water filled basins, and she was sure dark circles rimmed her eyes from the ordeal she'd just endured. However, as Andrew quickly made his way toward her and his newborn babes, he seemed oblivious to his wife's appearance.

His whiskers grazed her forehead when he kissed her, yet he still smelled nice. Before he took Selina from her, Lavinia caught a hint of the clove and sandalwood in his cologne.

"Is this my daughter?" Andrew asked, holding the baby snugly. Lavinia nodded, fearing what he'd say when he got a closer look at the boy. "My beautiful Selina," he murmured. "You'll never want for anything." After a few moments more, he placed the girl back in the crook of Lavinia's arm. "Now, let me see my son!"

An air of triumph was in his voice. Not only had he gotten the girl he'd wanted, Lavinia thought, but in addition a son, as a bonus. Yet worry gripped Lavinia. She held her breath and almost trembled as Andrew eagerly reached for the boy.

For a long moment, Andrew cradled the infant in his arms and stared, saying nothing.

Lavinia's heart beat wildly. She felt as if she'd lose control, wet the bed and then —

"An angel," Andrew said quietly. "I shall call him Gabriel! He's a fine and handsome young man, with the face of a leader. Surely, he'll accomplish great things!"

Lavinia exhaled, relieved. Her husband appeared unfazed by the child's color — and was also too busy planning its future.

"Julian couldn't produce twins!" Andrew smiled, ever competitive with his older brother. "But even if he could, his wouldn't be nearly as beautiful as mine!"

Temporarily forgetting her quandary, Lavinia seethed. He boasted of *her* achievement, as if it had been his! A few moments of pleasure had been his only contribution, yet she'd done all the work!

Chapter 18
One Month Later

"Anna, I'm so glad you've come to call." Lavinia sat with a friend in the brownstone's elegant living room. "I don't think anything can prepare one for motherhood! It's probably the most difficult thing I've ever experienced — especially the nursing!"

"Chere, I've been wondering how you were." Actress Anna Held smiled. "And I must say, you do have glow about you, a motherly glow, despite all zat extra weight! But — you're nursing zem yourself?"

Anna's accent was French, and although she'd lived in France, Lavinia had heard the scandalous rumor that she'd been born a Polish Jew. As Lavinia hid her past, Anna tried to hide hers as well. That was one reason Lavinia liked her so much.

"Unfortunately, I *am* nursing them myself," Lavinia said. "I told Andrew I would for one month. But now I don't know what possessed me to say such thing!"

The parlor maid, Lelia, brought in a tray of cake and coffee, then quietly departed.

"Zat's dreadful!" Anna said. "Why didn't you hire a girl — a wet nurse?"

Lavinia poured coffee for them from a sterling silver pot. "I did, but she quit the day before the twins were born."

Anna's large brown eyes danced as she laughed. "Well, you need one." She helped herself to a slice of cake. "You don't want to further ruin your figure by nursing. No doubt your girl quit because of your temper."

"Perhaps," Lavinia sighed. "Regardless, I'm paying the price by suckling my own children. Andrew wanted me to, instead of hiring another wet nurse right away. He thought I'd — 'bond with the children' that way. Those are his words, but I've found it repulsive and I'm about to go mad!"

It was just past eleven o'clock. Anna, wearing a sporty burgundy suit and a matching hat decorated with a large bow and dyed feathers, appeared beautiful, fresh and vibrant. She smelled of gardenia. The sun, shining through the windows that faced Eighty-Sixth Street, highlighted the gold in her thick chestnut locks.

Lavinia, with hair loose and tumbling down her back, pulled her green velvet wrap more snugly about her to conceal the milk stains on her nightgown. She caught a whiff of baby and mother's milk wafting from her clothes. With the constant feedings, she rarely looked or felt fresh.

"Andrew begged and pleaded with me to nurse them," Lavinia went on, "so I said I would—mainly to shut him up. But, as of tomorrow, my month is over! And believe you me, I'm telling that man today that I demand a wet nurse—two—despite what he said about his sister-in-law, *Serene*. She nursed *her* children, and the sun seems to rise and set on whatever *Serene* says or does— though *I* think she's somewhat touched in the head!"

Anna smiled slyly. She ran her fingers over the arm of the heavily gilded Louis XIV sofa she sat on. "You don't know about Serene and Andrew, do you?

Lavinia raised an inquisitive brow. "No."

"I was told zat Andrew was once very much in love wiz her. But zat was a long time ago, chere—and he got what he deserved— always stealing his brother's girlfriends! When Serene met Julian, she fell in love wiz him!"

"Well—I suppose Andrew would *like* me to be like her—at least where the children are concerned, but that's not going to happen—it never will!"

"And why should it? You are you—a beautiful and brilliant actress! You are denying the public of your talent."

Lavinia longed for the stage, and what Anna had just said confirmed that her desire was *not* an ill-conceived notion. "You're right, Anna." Lavinia's gaze wandered toward the large gilt edged mirror hanging over the room's meticulously carved mantel. Then, meeting her friend's eyes once more, Lavinia said, "I've wanted to start performing again soon...and if I go back next month...I can participate in part of the spring tour, then completely jump in, come fall."

"Zat's the spirit!" Anna said enthusiastically. "While I'm starring in *The Little Duchess* this fall, you don't want to be stuck in the same tragic role of Mother! You tell Andrew zat nursing the children will cause them to have an unnatural attachment to you, or demand they be hand fed—your nurse could do zat. Then your breasts will no longer be your ball and chain!"

Lavinia's eyes welled with joy at the thought of her impending freedom. "I like that idea," she said. However, Lavinia smirked at the thought of Brigid. "I do have a decent nurse."

Andrew had hired her. Brigid O'Shaughnessy had been employed by Serene and Julian for five years to care for their boys.

Then she'd had to leave them due to her ailing husband. Now widowed, she was happy to again be working with children.

"You don't sound too fond of her," Anna said.

"Brigid is rather overbearing — but Andrew adores her — and she'll make my return to acting possible. She's more than capable of feeding the children." Lavinia inhaled deeply. "Oh, Anna, I so envy you."

Anna was "married" to American producer Florenz Ziegfeld Jr. They considered themselves husband and wife, but hadn't bothered with a formal ceremony. Anna still wasn't divorced from her first husband. Regardless, Ziegfeld was the boss and she was his star.

Vivacious and uninhibited, Anna was even willing to show her legs on stage — but Lavinia most envied her now, because she had no children to contend with.

"You have everything — and nothing tying you down or holding you back."

"Chere, you can have zat, too, if you want. My Liane is three — and being raised in a convent — zere, she has lots of mothers!"

Anna was by no means religious, another common bond between them. However, it was said she'd been anxious to escape the stigma faced by Jews in Europe. She'd converted to Catholicism after marrying her first husband, a wealthy Catholic, who also happened to be a much older Uruguayan playboy and gambler.

"A tempting idea..." Lavinia paused, envisioning a convent doing the mothering of her children. "But," she sighed, "Andrew would never allow that."

****

By five o'clock, Lavinia was exhausted. She'd hidden herself away in the bedroom to catch a brief nap, but before her head hit the pillow, she heard the babies crying. The other bedroom on the second floor was now the nursery. Lavinia pulled the covers over her head, as she heard Brigid's commanding footsteps and the infants' demanding cries coming down the hall.

Over the infants' screaming, Brigid called through the unlatched bedroom door. "Mrs. Standish!"

Lavinia sighed wearily. "Come in, Brigid."

The door was slightly ajar and Brigid pushed it completely open with her shoulder. She wore a white apron over a light blue dress, and had a puffy white cap on her salt and pepper curls. Brigid's energy knew no bounds, and she never tired of the babies. Smiling cheerfully she said, "I'm sorry to disturb you again, ma'am, but the children are hungry."

Brigid spoke with a heavy Irish brogue. At forty-seven, she was a tall, thick woman with broad shoulders. Her face was round and kind, and her eyes, a soft gray blue.

As an oldest child, she'd helped raise her nine brothers and sisters. After she'd come to America from Ireland with her husband at age eighteen, she'd worked as a nurse in rich households. Brigid had never had children of her own, but she considered her ability and enjoyment of working with them her gift.

Lavinia propped herself up on pillows. Then, as though preparing for battle, placed another on her lap, and one under each arm. After Lavinia opened her top, Brigid helped her situate an infant on each of the pillows strategically positioned beneath her arms.

Selina latched on immediately, and suckled contentedly, but Gabe, the *dark* one — the troublesome baby with colic — continued to cry. Lavinia began to cry, as well, something she'd done frequently since before and after the birth of the twins.

"There, there, Mrs. Standish," Brigid said, while helping the boy find his mother's nipple. Gabriel finally quieted, then sucked vigorously, pulling and tugging at his mother's flesh. "He's fine now."

Lavinia stopped her crying and looked down at the infants, listening to the boy's loud nursing, all the while feeling the yank and strain from each child. Until she could free herself from this, she thought, pouting, her life was over.

Brigid, on her way from the room, distracted Lavinia from her tragic musings. "Glory be to *God*, Mrs. Standish, that you and your babies are as healthy as can be!"

Lavinia's skin bristled every time Brigid invoked her impassioned, *Glory be to God!*

When Brigid reached the doorway, she stopped, then slowly turned toward Lavinia. "You should be thankful, ma'am, for such fine, robust children."

Lavinia said nothing. She only continued to glare down at the little beings that fed from her like parasites.

"But sometimes..." Brigid said, "I suspect you don't want them."

Lavinia shot the nurse a nasty look. "How dare you say that; I shall tell Mr. Standish," she snapped. What Brigid had said was true, but Lavinia didn't like the woman's tone.

Putting hands on hips, Brigid said, "If you want that I should resign, you take that up with him, ma'am. He warned me of your difficult disposition, and begged me not to quit before I even started working for you.

"I've seen and heard with me own two eyes and ears what a surly, sourpuss of a woman you are, and I would have left long ago if he hadn't pleaded with me to stay.

"Just today," she pointed her finger, continuing to scold Lavinia, "I overheard you mention to that actress friend that came calling, that you plan to go prancing back off to the theater in a month! Said it just as nonchalant like as you please, with nary a thought about your babies. 'Tis a shame indeed — and glory be to *God*, Mrs. Standish, that I'll be here to care for them!"

"Why — the — the nerve of you!" Lavinia sputtered. "I can easily replace you with a much more *respectful* nurse! Do you really think that you can get away with speaking to *me* that way?"

Brigid crossed her arms. "Yes, ma'am, as a matter of fact I do. 'Twas your husband that told me to let you have it, if need be, with both barrels loaded. Glory be to God that I don't believe in holding anythin' back, especially when it needs to be said. If Mr. Standish wants me to leave, I'll have me bags packed and ready within the hour." Brigid stood tall, pulling her white starched apron over her large bosom.

"Now, I'll be back shortly to relieve you." Brigid turned to go, leaving Lavinia speechless. "And by the way," Brigid angled to face to her employer once more, "as I was coming to you with the children, Mr. Standish arrived home from work. I'm sure he'll be up momentarily. You tell him everything I said. Now, if you'll excuse me, ma'am."

Brigid left the room, closing the door

behind her. Lavinia fumed. How dare Andrew go behind her back regarding Brigid's employment! Her anger continued to smolder, until Lavinia began to think more in depth about her situation — Gabriel's crying — and the new living hell of motherhood.

Lavinia sighed. She needed Brigid. The woman was a good nurse — superior in fact — though Lavinia hated to admit that. It would be most beneficial for the woman to remain employed here. Lavinia knew of one famous actress who'd had an inexperienced nurse and her child had died on account of that. But with a highly trained individual like Brigid, Lavinia rationalized that she could go back to the theater with no qualms about her children's care. And once she returned to acting and touring, she'd not even see Brigid that often.

Lavinia decided she'd learn to tolerate the woman's presence. She'd risen from one detrimental occurrence and couldn't afford another. Negative publicity regarding a murder scandal was one thing, but add to that the death of a child — or two — and her career would never recover.

Andrew opened the bedroom door, then closed it gently as Lavinia glanced in his direction. He strode in and removed his jacket and cravat. As he loosened his collar and unbuttoned the top of his shirt, he approached the bed. The sight of Lavinia nursing the babies always brought a smile to his face.

"Darling, you're a vision to behold." Andrew sat next to her.

"*You* try doing this all day."

"Lavinia," he smiled, "I would if I could."

She looked at him incredulously and began to cry. "I think you mean that! You're a deranged man!"

"Darling, you're not yourself."

"No, I'm not! And it's time we hire a wet nurse—two of them!"

"But you agreed to try nursing—at least for a while."

"I agreed to a month—and it's been a month—an eternity—I can't take it anymore! I looked like a sow while I carried them—now I'm nothing but a cow! I can't bear being sucked and pulled on all day! I'm tired of leaking and ruining my clothes. I refuse to be a human trough any longer! Besides, if I keep nursing—the babies will develop an unnatural attachment to me!"

"But I was hoping you'd become *maternally* attached to them," Andrew countered.

"It's either wet nursing or hand feeding!"

"Darling, you know Dr. Davenport doesn't approve of that! You can't improve on God's plan of mother's milk. Besides, we can't feed the children cow's milk or one of those other concoctions—diarrhea could kill them, that's why Serene nursed her children. But no wet nurse for her, she wanted to do it herself."

"I am *not* Serene!" Lavinia wept angrily. "And I demand those wet nurses—because—because my breasts just weren't made for this!"

Andrew wiped away her tears. "I'm sorry, darling...you've won," he smiled. "You will have your wet nurses." Always the consummate competitor, he added, "But it's a shame I *can't* nurse them. I'd do a much better job than any woman could."

"You sound like a lunatic!" Lavinia scoffed.

"I am crazy—for you and our children." He placed an arm around her shoulder and kissed her cheek. Gazing at the babies, he said, "Look darling, they've fallen asleep."

"Well," Lavinia huffed, "I'm not sure how long the boy will stay that way."

"Lately, he hasn't been crying as much," Andrew said. "Brigid thinks his digestive system is improving. Darling, let me hold them." Lavinia gladly maneuvered them into their father's arms, then closed her top.

"They're such beautiful babies." Andrew rocked them gently. "Selina looks so much like you. And Gabriel—he's handsome as a prince—straight out of *The Arabian Nights*! I'm amazed by his complexion."

Lavinia stiffened.

"It's marvelous!" Andrew continued. "I still can't believe that as fair as I am, I could produce a child with such color. But he couldn't possibly take after me. It must be the Spanish blood from your mother."

Lavinia hesitated, pursing her lips. "Ye—yes. She was—from the uh—very, very south of Spain."

"Close to Morocco?"

"Yes."

"So just think, darling, you probably have Moorish blood running through your veins."

"Moorish?" Lavinia looked at Andrew distastefully.

"Yes. The Moors, in Africa—like Othello."

"That's not true at all!" she said hotly.

"I'm only jesting, my dear, but I wouldn't care, regardless. People are people, as far as I'm concerned. A man's character and what's inside him are the important things."

"Well, you needn't worry about our children being Negroes."

"Darling," Andrew placed Gabriel safely by his mother, "I was only teasing you." When he rose from the bed with Selina and walked toward the bassinets, Lavinia looked down at the boy. Disgusted by his "*Moorish*" appearance, she turned away, then was shamed by the fleeting thought that, with all his digestive problems, cow's milk probably would finish him off.

Hearing the baby gurgle, Lavinia looked back just in time to see a large glob of spit-up roll from his mouth. It narrowly missed her robe. She quickly moved her velvet wrap away from the mess, then grimaced, as she sopped up the slimy ooze with a rag.

"Now that you're a mother," Andrew said, "I'm seeing more of you. I like that." Lavinia bit her tongue.

Andrew tucked Selina into her bassinet, then returned to the bed for Gabriel and placed him in his.   Afterwards, Andrew removed his shoes. He reclined next to Lavinia, then began kissing her neck and caressing her. "So, my darling," he whispered in her ear, "is this what your breasts were made for?"

She pulled away. "Andrew, it's too soon for that. And next month—I—I plan to go back to the theater. After all—it's the touring and performing—that makes me truly happy. I'm as pleased, as I—can be, with your choice of— *Brigid*, as a nurse. You like her, Julian and Serene speak highly of her, so I'm sure she'll do a fine job with our children, and while I'm away, she'll surely meet their every need."

Andrew looked at her aghast. "What about me?" His face flushed bright red. "I don't think Brigid will be meeting any of *my* needs!"

"Andrew—I'll see to it that we have—*some* time together."

"You've said that before, but when you're involved with that blasted theater, you only

allow me a fraction of your attention. I
suppose that's because I don't make you truly
happy!'"

"I'll give you more time—if I can," she said
weakly, straining to smile.

Andrew stood from the bed, angry.
Stalking from the room he said, "There should
be no 'ifs' about a wife giving her husband
time and affection!"

Chapter 19
New York City, 901
Three Years Later

"Brigid, are the children in the living room, dressed and ready for their photographs?" Lavinia called on her way down the brownstone's formal stairs. The staircase, constructed of ornately hand-carved black walnut, was an artistic masterpiece Lavinia deemed worthy of her majestic grand entrances.

"Yes, ma'am," Brigid heartily replied from the living room. "And glory be to God, they're the most precious little darlings I've ever seen!"

Lavinia, wearing a bountiful white feather boa around her shoulders, strode into the room attired in a white dress with three-quarter sleeves, trimmed in lace at the plunging bodice. The multi-tiered skirt was also trimmed in more thick layers of lace. Lavinia's hair, piled high in curls, was topped by a very tall hat decorated with more lace and white ostrich plumes.

She wore large pearl earrings, a long pearl necklace hanging almost to her waist, and a pearl and opal choker, patterned in a crisscross design, tight at her throat.

"Mother, you're beautiful," three-year-old Selina exclaimed. She sat on the gilded satin sofa with her brother. Brigid, in her blue dress and white apron, was sandwiched between them, holding open a copy of *Little Red Riding Hood*.

Lavinia ignored her daughter's remark for a moment, while she stood horrified, staring at Gabriel. The boy, who'd been squirming and bouncing his rump up and down on the sofa, stilled under his mother's scrutiny.

Abruptly taking her eyes from Gabriel, Lavinia turned her full attention on Selina. "Darling, you're beautiful, too, a living doll— my little me!" Her pet name for Selina. Lavinia approached her daughter, then bent down to rearrange the girl's long dark curls and adjust the oversized white bow in her hair.

Standing tall, Lavinia glared down at Gabriel. His dark brown curls looked neat. However, his skin appeared darker than it had first thing this morning. When the child lifted his arms, as though asking to be held, Lavinia ignored him. She scowled. "Brigid, what did I tell you about letting Gabriel play in the sun?"

Brigid put the large children's book down on the coffee table in front of her. "Ma'am, fresh air and sunshine are healthy for the children," she replied, a tad defiantly.

"He can play outside, just keep him in the shade!" Lavinia studied the boy's golden complexion in disgust. She sighed. "Perhaps it won't be too obvious in the photograph. But aside from that," she eyed Brigid sharply, "I thought you said *both* of them were ready!"

"I don't understand ma'am." Brigid glanced on either side of her at each of the children. Gabriel wore a white sailor suit with knee britches and Selina, a frilly white dress with lots of ruffles and lace. "They're dressed just as you asked for the photographs."

"But — *the boy* — he can't drag along that thing! It's falling apart and smells like a dead animal!"

Gabe's large dark eyes widened, filling with tears. He held his tattered blue baby blanket tightly to his chest and lovingly caressed it.

"It was bad enough that *both* of them sucked their thumbs! Their mouths could have been ruined if it hadn't been for the *quinine*!"

Hearing that word, the children started crying at the memory of the bitter medicine being applied to their thumbs.

Brigid put a loving arm around each child. "Now, now, Mrs. Standish, you mustn't upset the children! You want them happy for their pictures."

"Happy indeed! I can't be happy having a child of mine seen in public displaying that piece of garbage! Selina doesn't carry around that ragged doll any more."

"Only because you threatened to burn it," Brigid said tightly.

"Well, then," Lavinia crossed her arms, scowling down at Gabriel, "what can I threaten to do with that blanket? Rip it to shreds? Soak it in *quinine*?"

At this the boy began to cry harder. When Brigid put both arms around him, pulling him into her comforting girth, Selina quickly stood up. "Mother, I'll help him not carry it, I promise!"

When the girl reached to hug her mother, Lavinia snapped, "Don't touch Mother, you'll ruin her dress! Now," she addressed Brigid, "I'm leaving. The photographer will take some pictures of me first, then me with Selina, then Selina and Gabriel together.

"So Brigid, have the children there by two. My photos should be done by then. Make sure they're happy, free of tears—and free of anything that resembles *refuse*," she sneered toward Gabriel's blanket, now partially hidden behind the child's back.

Brigid took a deep breath and rose from the sofa. A disgruntled expression creased her face. "I'll do my best, Mrs. Standish, but *you've* apparently set the tone for the day!" When Lavinia smirked and turned to leave, Brigid followed her.

Once near the front door and out of earshot of the children, Brigid gently grasped Lavinia's arm. "Now, Mrs. Standish," she said quietly, "you do intend to have some pictures taken with Gabriel, too, don't you?" Her tone was steely, making her employer uncomfortable.

Lavinia hesitated. "Perhaps another time. I'm only interested in having Selina pose with me today — for some — mother/daughter photos." She pulled from Brigid's grasp, then left for her waiting carriage.

Chapter 20
New York City, Spring, 1902
Several Months Later

Andrew sat distracted, feeling tired and only halfheartedly looking at the watercolor rendering, painted by one of architect Henry Hardenbergh's artists. It portrayed an elegant hotel, and sat on an easel in one of the Truelove and Standish company meeting rooms. Andrew was lost in thought. His gaze moved to the wavy grain of the highly polished mahogany table. He could barely concentrate on what was being said about the painting.

"I believe I've captured your vision, gentlemen, for the finest luxury hotel in New York City..." Hardenbergh, standing by the painting, addressed financier Benjamin Burke and hotelier Frank Stansfield, along with Julian and Andrew at the brothers' Truelove and Standish Contracting Enterprise. Their office was at Broadway and Chambers Street in the Broadway Chambers Building.

Running a wooden pointer from the top of the painted image to the lower part, Hardenbergh continued, "The building will be eighteen stories high, composed of brick and marble, and designed in the French Renaissance style. It'll be organized along classical lines of base, shaft and capital. Here you can see..."

A divorce, Andrew thought ignoring the architect's words; that was the only option for him now.

Hardenbergh, a solidly built man with a handlebar moustache, tapped his pointer at the bottom of the painting. "The base will be a two story marble rusticated basement with one row of balustraded balconies. These will be under a sharp projecting coursing..."

Andrew hadn't wanted to resort to such a scandalous action, but he couldn't stand to remain in his marriage any longer. He'd only stayed with Lavinia for as long as he had for the sake of the children.

"Eight stories in yellow brick capped by two transitional floors of balustraded balconies will rise from the base," Hardenbergh continued. "A large cornice and a mansard slate roof of five floors with gables, dormers, and copper cresting would be above these floors. You'll notice that..."

Andrew had been willing to put up with little to no conjugal relations. Lavinia was either on tour, too tired after late nights of performing, had a headache, or was in the midst of her monthly bleeding.

However, one evening he'd caught her in the kitchen handling a piece of uncooked meat. Lavinia claimed she'd heard that their butcher was selling spoiled meat, so she was checking the brisket's freshness. When he'd asked about the strategically placed blood stains on her nightgown, Lavinia had merely said, "It slipped from my hands; that's where I caught it." She'd made no secret of not wanting more children, and now it appeared from that incident, that she'd resorted to faking her monthly cycle at times by smearing her night garments with bloody raw meat.

The lack of marital relations was one thing, but when she'd devastated Gabe, that was the last straw! Lavinia had taken Selina to the park one day, a rare occurrence, but she'd refused to take Gabe. "Brigid will take you later," she'd told him. Because of the boy's color, Lavinia favored Selina over her son, but she'd never made it so obvious until the park incident. That evening, Gabe had cried in his father's arms and asked, "Does Mother love me?"

That's when Andrew had contacted a lawyer. Lavinia was an unfit mother above all else, and after five years of marriage, he would divorce her and take the children.

Adultery was the only legal grounds for divorce in New York, and it had to be proven in open court. Andrew couldn't prove Lavinia had committed adultery, yet as much time as she spent away from him with her theater people, he couldn't prove she'd been faithful either. It would be Andrew's word against hers.

Although a divorce in his home-state didn't appear a possibility, Andrew had the means to go to Nevada. His lawyer had suggested that. The residency requirement there was only six months, and in that state, there were several grounds for divorce.

Hardenbergh finished describing the exterior and moved on to the interior with a different set of paintings. Andrew only heard bits and pieces of what the man was saying.

"800 rooms...500 baths...Ten elevators...Two floors of public rooms."

"No expense is to be spared for the Whispering Winds," the hotelier Stansfield, a thin eloquent man in his late forties, chimed in.

"And I want to know that only the finest materials are to be used," financier Burke added, chomping on a Cuban cigar that infused the room with its bittersweet aroma. An older man in his mid-fifties, Burke sat back in his large leather chair, with meaty hands clasped over his rotund middle.

"Gentlemen," Julian said, "you can rest assured that we're importing only the best for this project. Isn't that right, Andrew?"

Andrew snapped from his thoughts, meeting his brother's gaze. It was one of a school teacher admonishing a student for not paying attention. What had Julian just asked? Something about importing the best? "Absolutely," was all Andrew replied, hoping that was an appropriate response.

"Tell us about the marble, Andrew," Julian prodded.

"Uh—it's coming from Carrara—Italy. We're importing the white and blue gray that's quarried there."

"And the crystal?" Julian eyed him sharply.

"Waterford—from Ireland." Andrew realized he wasn't performing up to par in this meeting. No doubt Burke and Stansfield had noticed that, too. They directed all their questions to Julian, despite Julian's efforts to bring his younger brother, whose mind wandered like a lost sheep, back into the fold.

Andrew smoothed his face, feeling the stubble he'd had no time to shave this morning. He'd hardly slept last night while

mulling over his situation. Then he'd
overslept, missing his calisthenics routine in
addition to his shave.

"We're looking at a three year time frame
to complete this project," Julian gazed at
Burke, "and, as we discussed earlier, the
estimated cost will be around twelve million
dollars. We never cut corners at Truelove and
Standish."

Moments later, when Hardenbergh began
discussing the placement of crystal chandeliers
and marble fireplaces, Andrew's mind drifted
back to his dilemma.

As of now, Lavinia was unaware of his
intentions, as was Julian. Andrew had wanted
to make sure the contracts were signed with
Burke and Stansfield before scandalizing
Truelove and Standish with a divorce.

Now that the deal was sealed, he could no
longer postpone the inevitable. He'd tell Julian
today, and this evening, discuss the matter
with Lavinia. It was Wednesday and she'd
performed a matinee, so she'd be home, and
most likely not in an amorous mood.

Andrew sighed quietly. Lavinia would
never change. Aside from her maltreatment of
Gabe, what hurt Andrew most, was that at one
time he'd loved Lavinia more than life. He
could still remember the intensity of that love,
yet her feelings for him had been only
superficial, at best. Painful as it was to admit,

Andrew suspected that Lavinia had never loved him at all.

She'd only given him crumbs of her time, and she gave the children hardly any attention at all. He'd finally come to see her true character, although, for years he'd tried to deny the selfishness, self-absorption and deceptiveness that she'd demonstrated since the day he'd met her.

Finally, he'd realized that there was nothing left of their marriage to salvage. Moving his eyes to Julian, who sat confidently, while expounding authoritatively upon the upcoming project, Andrew envied his older brother's happy home and loving wife. All those years ago, Julian had been right. Lavinia was already in love, with herself—and married to her theater.

"If I say so myself, Henry," Julian said to the architect, "you've captured exactly what we want!"

Stansfield and Burke agreed.

"Andrew?" Julian asked.

"Yes, I—uh agree as well."

"Demolition starts on The Royale a week from today," Julian said. The Royale was the twenty year old hotel on the Fifth Avenue property the Standish brothers, Burke and Stansfield had purchased to build The Whispering Winds. "Once the site is cleared, we'll commence work on The Winds."

Just as the Royale was to be demolished, so
Andrew thought, was his marriage, leaving
behind an emptiness in his heart. However,
the Royale, a rather nondescript and unexciting
hotel, would be replaced with something
extraordinary and grand.

Andrew had his children, who were his
purpose for living, but would he ever have the
splendid marriage he'd always hoped for?
With Lavinia, he reflected, that was an
impossibility, but perhaps one day he'd find a
special woman to fill the void in his heart.

****

When the meeting ended, Hardenbergh,
Stansfield and Burke departed, leaving Julian
and Andrew alone in the meeting room. After
seeing the men out, the brothers stood by the
open door. Julian closed it, directing Andrew
to sit down with him at the table.

Catching his brother's inquiring gaze,
Andrew said, "I'm sorry—I was distracted."

"Distracted," Julian replied, "you were
hardly with us at all. Something's bothering
you, and it doesn't concern The Winds." He
raised a brow. "Trouble in paradise?"

Andrew hesitated, although now seemed
as good a time as any to bare his soul. "How
perceptive of you," he said.

"Just *how* serious?"

"Very...I'm divorcing Lavinia."

"You're what?" Julian said angrily. "That's more than serious—especially for business. Divorce won't set well with Burke or Stansfield!"

"That's why I've waited to mention it to you. Now that the deal is underway, they won't be going anywhere on account of me. I assure you, the divorce will transpire quietly, with the utmost discretion—out of state." An awkward silence hung between them for a few moments. "I didn't want to resort to this—but now I have no choice. Besides, is business more important than my life?"

Julian's face softened. "I suppose not. I've suspected things were—awry in your marriage for a while. It's none of my business what's happened between the two of you, but I disliked that woman from the start.

"Look what she's done to you! Only thirty-nine and you're graying at the temples! You've got circles under your eyes—and it doesn't even look like you shaved today! In my opinion, ridding yourself of her calls for a celebration."

Andrew winced.

Noting this, Julian's face reddened. "That was careless of me—I'm sorry—I didn't think of the children."

Andrew blew out a deep breath. "Her mothering skills rate far below those of a dog's, but a bad mother is better than no mother at all. I'm taking the children, but she can see them whenever she wants."

"So—what was Lavinia's reaction to all of this?"

"She doesn't know yet..." Julian's eyes widened as Andrew continued, "I'm discussing the matter with her this evening."

Julian reached to squeeze his brother's shoulder. "God help you. You have a place to stay—should she threaten your life."

Andrew smiled slightly. "I'm not counting on that drastic of a reaction."

"Well, if things do get heated," Julian stood up, gathering some papers from the meeting, "you know where I am. And, by the way, I'd planned to invite you your family to dine with us this evening. We *are* celebrating, but I hate to share my news on top of yours."

Andrew rose to his feet and stretched. "Tell me; I could use some good news."

"Serene's pregnant."

Andrew felt that familiar pang of jealousy at his brother's words, his brother's wife, his brother's steadily increasing number of children...

"We're hoping for a girl this time."

Andrew smiled stiffly. Though genuinely happy for his brother, the only word he could muster was, "Congratulations."

"Thank you—we'll celebrate with you another time. Now—I'm calling it a day. Are you leaving as well—for the uh—confrontation?"

"No," Andrew said, "I'll be staying a little longer. I need to prepare for a meeting I'm having regarding the West Street Project tomorrow. I'm aiming to be in better form than I was today." He'd also scheduled another meeting for this afternoon that he chose not to tell Julian about.

After the brothers said their goodbyes, Andrew walked to his office. He peered from an open window down onto the hustle and bustle of Broadway. New York City's streets were always crowded, jammed with people, street cars and horse drawn vehicles. Soot filled the air, along with the foul smell of ripening manure, and noise filtered through the atmosphere on all levels as elevated trains roared throughout the day.

New York was his home. It offered a life of challenge and excitement. But sometimes Andrew wondered, for the sake of his his children, what it would be like to live in a place that wasn't quite so dirty and crowded.

He pulled out the West Street documents from his desk, then made himself comfortable in an ornately carved revolving chair, upholstered in brown velvet.

Andrew liked keeping busy, not thinking about Lavinia. His work and children kept him sane. Putting down the project papers,

Andrew gazed at a photograph of Selina and Gabe near the front of his desk. Picking up the picture, he admired the two angelic faces that smiled at him from the sterling frame. Gabe wore a sailor suit, and Selina, with curls tumbling to her waist, wore a lacy dress.

How they were growing—they'd been three in this photograph but had turned four in February. Gabe, a dashing boy, appeared to become more handsome each day. Although a friendly, loving child, he wasn't nearly as talkative as his sister.

Quite bright, Gabe seemed to easily grasp the idea, as Andrew had explained, that steel buildings were like boxes made of vertical and horizontal steel sticks. The boy displayed a keen interest in building, and had already erected some rather impressive block structures. Andrew smiled as he thought about his son, and his precious Selina, whom he never tired of spoiling.

She was a precocious, and rather outspoken little thing, who had no trouble speaking her mind or Gabe's. Selina was a beauty, just like her mother, but thankfully, that's where the resemblance stopped. Selina was a compassionate and caring little girl.

"Mr. Standish?" Andrew's secretary, Elaine, knocked at his door, distracting him.

"Come in." Andrew placed the photo back on his desk. Elaine opened the door wearing a long sleeved white shirtwaist and navy blue skirt. "Yes, Elaine."

"There's a lady to see you, sir. She says she has an appointment with you. Her name is Carrie Hargraves."

Chapter 21

Andrew stood upon seeing the thin young woman enter his office. She wore a peach colored dress with a matching jacket. Ivory colored lace trimmed the large collar and willowy drooping sleeves.

The ensemble gracefully adorned her slim figure. Her thick blond hair was curled and piled on her head. Over it, she wore a simple picture hat ornamented by silk flowers in shades of peaches and cream.

Carrie Hargraves had the largest eyes Andrew had ever seen. She was by no means beautiful, but her shy smile was charming.

"Miss Hargraves." Andrew approached her; she smelled of rose water. Shaking her hand, he said, "It's so nice to meet you. Thank you for agreeing to see me." He escorted her across a red and gold Persian carpet to a set of brown leather chairs in front of his desk. "Please have a seat."

As he sat opposite her, she said softly, "I was — rather taken aback — that you wanted to see me — concerning a legal matter. I assume it involves Lavinia." Her voice trembled. "I must admit — I have been curious about her — since we — parted ways. How is she?"

"She's fine." Andrew paused for several seconds, observing the young woman's nervousness. Carrie clasped her white gloved hands tightly in her lap to keep them from shaking. Attempting to put her at ease he said, "I'm an admirer of your work, Miss Hargraves, but I don't believe you've written anything lately. I look forward to your next production."

Looking down, she blushed deep red. "Thank you, Mr. Standish. You're very kind. I've been so busy — I just haven't found the time to write. But I hope to — soon." Then meeting his eyes she said, "However — you didn't ask me here to discuss my plays."

Andrew smiled. "That's true, and I'll be honest with you." He hesitated, taking in a deep breath. "My intention — is to divorce Lavinia."

Carrie pursed her lips, and again dropped her gaze. "I'm sorry, Mr. Standish. I'm sorry for you — and Lavinia. She's been on my mind — and I've been — praying for her."

Surprised by this, Andrew said, "So, you were close to your step-mother?"

Carrie remained silent, then after several seconds remarked, "Quite the contrary, Mr. Standish—but the Bible says to pray for your enemies."

"Then—Lavinia mistreated you?"

Raising her chin, Carrie said, "Have you asked me here to sully Lavinia's character? I won't be a party to destroying someone. I couldn't live with myself. "

"Miss Hargraves, whatever you tell me won't go beyond Lavinia's ears."

"So you can threaten her with anything I say?"

Andrew paused for several moments. That was his plan, but hearing it verbalized sounded rather backhanded and devious. "Threaten is a strong word, Miss Hargraves.

"So it is..."

Slightly peeved, Andrew replied, "I'm only asking that you honestly answer any question I ask."

Carrie sighed, appearing conflicted. "The Bible also says that you reap what you sow— but it's not my place to pass judgment on anyone."

"Your judgment's not required, only the truth. So, how did my wife—act toward you?"

Carrie sat quietly for a few seconds. "I don't believe it's in her nature to be kind."

Andrew laughed slightly, without smiling. "I agree wholeheartedly with you. Is she worth your prayers?"

"My flesh says no—but God says yes."

They said nothing for a short while, until Carrie broke the silence. "I've been intending to—contact Lavinia about something—something I did that was wrong."

Carrie opened her reticule and pulled out a velvet pouch. "Mr. Standish—please give this to her. It's an heirloom—from her family—it was special to her."

Andrew took the trinket from its pouch. It was a simple heart shaped locket encrusted with jewels. Though lovely, it couldn't compare to the diamonds, rubies and emeralds that Andrew had lavished upon Lavinia. "I'll be sure to give it to her." He placed the locket safely in his pocket. "But how did it come into your possession?"

Carrie inhaled deeply, saying nothing.

"Did she give it to you—perhaps as payment for something?" Andrew asked.

Carrie shook her head. "If she'd given it to me—I wouldn't feel so awkward now."

Andrew prodded, "Is something—painful—involved, concerning it?"

After another long pause, Carrie said, "Mr. Standish, when my father died—Lavinia and I—had our differences. I was angry with her—and—I'm ashamed to admit this—but I stole her locket." She looked away from him, embarrassed.

"I took it out of spite, because, somehow, my father's will was changed. I was left with practically nothing from his estate. I've known all along that it was wrong to take the locket. But over the past few months, I've felt compelled to return it because," Carrie hesitated, "I've found new life in Christ. I've forgiven Lavinia for how — she treated me. But I've ignored God's prodding to tell her that."

Andrew sat back in his chair, listening. Though tempted to go back to the issue of her father's will, Andrew decided to let Carrie keep talking about God. That seemed to soothe her.

"I'm trying to live as God wants me to — but, I've failed this time. Mr. Standish — please tell Lavinia that I'm sorry. I'm sorry for taking her locket — and I'm sorry for all the things I said to her when we last spoke."

Andrew sat forward and gently grasped Carrie's hand. "You have my word."

Her large eyes filled with tears. Squeezing his hand, Carrie leaned close to him saying softly, "Thank you. I — I will talk to Lavinia myself someday — but there's more I have to forgive — not concerning her treatment of me — but — but other things. I need to keep praying — for guidance — and strength." Her eyes lingered on Andrew's a bit longer than necessary, then she drew away, removing her hand from his.

"Miss Hargraves, I understand your bitterness, and I admire your ability to forgive Lavinia. For all she's put me through, I'm not sure I'll ever be able to do that." After hesitating briefly, he backed up their conversation. "You mentioned that your father's will was changed. Do you know how?"

She sat quietly for several seconds. "No."

"I suspect you believe Lavinia changed it, don't you?"

Carrie studied her hands, remaining silent.

"Please answer me honestly, Miss Hargraves."

"Alright," her eyes locked onto his, "I did believe that. But it doesn't matter now. Lavinia gave me some money from the estate. And one of my father's apartments was in my name; I still own it. Also—I married a wonderful man." She smiled. "He introduced me to Christ, and that's what's given me the ability to forgive. When I think about the things I said to Lavinia—I feel almost sick. I hope she's willing to forgive me, as well."

"You hope she can forgive you?" Andrew asked in disbelief. "Besides the apartment you spoke of, do you own any other pieces of your father's property?"

"No. But the apartment's been all I need.

With my husband's income, we're doing quite well."

"But it sounds as if Lavinia swindled you out of your inheritance."

"Mr. Standish, I don't really know what happened with my father's will, and I'm not accusing Lavinia of anything. If it hadn't been for Lavinia, I wouldn't have met my husband. God brings good things out of bad.

"After my father died, Lavinia wanted me—" she stopped abruptly, then went on saying, "well—I left my father's house. I used to hide there, in my room writing. But leaving that life of solitude brought a husband to me." Glancing toward Andrew's desk, she saw the back of Gabe and Selina's photo. "May I?" Andrew nodded as she picked up the picture and turned it around. "Your children?"

"Yes," he smiled, "the only good thing to come out of my marriage."

Studying the photo for a long moment, Carrie said nothing, then, "They don't look at all alike—but they're beautiful."

Andrew thanked her, then stood up and walked behind his desk. "Do you have children?"

"Two girls."

"Are they what's been keeping you so busy?" Andrew asked as he pulled out his check ledger.

"Yes, and I love every moment of being

with them."

In his head, Andrew estimated the worth of Vernon's property that Lavinia had inherited upon his death. Then he began to write a check. "What's your married name?" He asked.

"It's McDougall."

Laughing, Andrew said, "That's a good strong Scottish name, so I know this won't be squandered." He handed her a check for double the amount of the property.

Carrie sat speechless. While slowly placing the children's photo back on his desk, she eyed the sum of money, aghast. "Mr. Standish—I—I can't possibly accept this."

"Miss Hargraves, or rather, Mrs. McDougall, I won't be able to sleep at night if you don't. When I married Lavinia, I was pleased to see the property she'd been left by Vernon. I didn't realize, however, that it wasn't rightfully hers. I believe this is a fair price."

"Mr. Standish, it's beyond fair!"

"But I'm taking into account the pain and suffering you endured through my wife's actions. Now, Mrs. McDougall, I insist you take this, for my sake, please."

"Mr. Standish, no I—"

"Mrs. McDougall, haven't you ever heard the expression, 'The Lord works in mysterious ways?'"

A radiant smile overtook her face. "I have."

"Well, this money is rightfully yours, for your property."

"Oh, Mr. Standish—all I can say—is thank you."

After a moment, Andrew said, "You can further thank me—by telling me how Lavinia treated your father."

Tears welled in Carrie's eyes again, this time spilling down her cheeks. "That's rather painful to talk about."

"I understand," Andrew said softly. "Would you care for some water—or perhaps—a brandy?"

Carrie, declined his offer of refreshments, then pulled a handkerchief from her reticule. "Although I've forgiven Lavinia for what she did to me," she said, "I'm still trying to forgive her—for breaking my father's heart." Andrew listened patiently. "He loved her so much— but she only loved what he could provide for her..."

As Carrie expounded upon her father giving his beautiful young wife the sun, the moon and the stars, a hard cruel reality struck Andrew like a sack of bricks. Hargraves had been a corpulent old man that Lavinia had used to achieve her dream—and he, himself, had been no different to her, as she'd used him to regain it.

"...But despite my feelings," Carrie swiped away her tears, "assure her that she can trust me. I'll be discreet."

This grabbed Andrew's attention. "Discreet—regarding what?"

Carrie's large eyes widened and she visibly gulped. Pressing fingers to her lips, she shook her head rapidly. "Nothing—it's nothing! Mr. Standish—I've told you about my relationship with Lavinia—and I've probably told you more than I should have about her marriage to my father." She rose quickly from her chair. "I have to go."

"Not yet you don't," Andrew walked from behind his desk to face her. Grasping her arms gently he said, "Whatever you've brought up is *not* nothing. I want the truth from you—not something you'll cover up with a lie. I can't claim to be in church every Sunday, but one of the ten commandments says 'Thou shalt not bear false witness.' I appreciate what you've shared with me, Mrs. McDougall, and I've compensated you for your loss—because I wanted to—it was the right thing to do. Now, I insist you tell me Lavinia's secret. I'd say you owe it to me."

When Carrie dropped her eyes to the floor, Andrew released her arms. She dug into her reticule, then handed him his check. "I don't want to *owe* you anything."

Andrew hadn't expected this, and now needed another tactic. Pushing her outstretched hand away, Andrew exclaimed,

"Mrs. McDougall, that money is yours!" His angry tone made the poor girl start.

"I'm sorry—but I'm the father of Lavinia's children! I have a right to know everything about their mother! Whatever information you have regarding Lavinia involves all of us—me, as well as the children!"

Fidgeting with her fingers, Carrie remained silent for several seconds, then said, "I'm sorry, Mr. Standish—my father knew the truth—I just assumed—you did, too. Perhaps—we should sit down."

At this, Andrew felt his knees weaken and sat with Carrie. What didn't he know about Lavinia? Was *she* the one who really killed Tyler? Perhaps she had a lover Hargraves tolerated and she'd continued to carry on with him behind Andrew's back. Or maybe she had another child hidden away somewhere—an imbecile in an asylum. Could she be a criminal, or infected with a disease, was she dying?

Carrie held one of Andrew's hands this time, and looked deeply into his eyes. "I know you're a man of character and integrity. That's what my father always said. He respected— and envied you. What I'm going to say shouldn't make any difference to you— regarding your children."

"My children?" Andrew's heart raced.

"God made us all," she continued, "and

beneath our skin, we're all the same."

"What are you trying to tell me, Mrs. McDougall?"

"Lavinia's mother..." she trailed off, as if uncertain of how to go on.

"What Mrs. McDougall? Was her mother a leper?"

"No—it's not as bad as that—or perhaps it's worse—depending on how you— perceive of things..."

"Please, Mrs. McDougall, you must tell me!"

"Lavinia's mother," Carrie almost whispered, "is a Negro."

Andrew listened in stunned disbelief. "Her mother is a Negro?"

Carrie nodded, letting go of his hand.

Andrew said nothing for a long time. He only gazed toward the picture of his children. Carrie hadn't turned it away when she'd placed it back on his desk. Looking at Gabe, Andrew now realized that that explained everything. The boy's color, Lavinia's ill treatment of him. Andrew would love his child no matter what, but this was a rather shocking revelation.

As his wife, why hadn't Lavinia ever told him? If Vernon had known the truth, wasn't Andrew entitled to that information as well? Andrew still couldn't believe what he'd just heard.

"You said *is* — meaning — she's alive?"

Carrie nodded again. "When Lavinia married my father, both of her parents were still living."

Andrew seethed, trying to suppress a growing rage. "Mrs. McDougall, tell me everything you know..."

Chapter 22

Andrew slowly approached his and Lavinia's bedroom. Walking inside, he saw her seated at her small mahogany writing desk in the corner of the room. The scent of lavender and honey filled the air, as Lavinia had taken a milk bath a short while ago to beautify her skin.

This particular evening, except for the loquacious prattle of Selina and Gabriel at the dinner table, little discussion had transpired between the adults.

Lavinia scribbled furiously on what looked like a script. Andrew said nothing as he watched her. Clearing his throat he asked, "What are you doing?"

"Rewriting a scene." She didn't look toward him, as she continued to write. "There's not enough of *me* in it."

Andrew didn't move far from the door after he'd closed it. Instead he propped himself against the wall next to it.

After several moments of silence passed, Lavinia, still not bothering to glance in his direction, said, "You say we never spend time together..." she paused to continue writing, "...and here I am, alone." Finally pushing the script aside, she walked to her vanity and sat down before the large circular mirror. When she began removing pins from her hair, thick tresses fell to her waist.

Despite himself, Andrew watched mesmerized, entranced by her beauty, as she commenced brushing her hair. "I was out back," he said. "I played with the children for a while, until Brigid brought them in for a bath. Then I stayed outside to think."

Lavinia said nothing in response. She kept brushing, not the least bit interested in his thoughts.

"Lavinia...we need to talk."

While Andrew gazed at his wife's reflection, he thought her still devastatingly beautiful. He dropped his eyes to the floor. It was safer not to look at Lavinia. From the start, her blinding beauty had prevented him from seeing beneath the surface, and throughout the course of their marriage he'd been severely burned.

Andrew wondered how many other lives

she'd ruined. Carrie had risen above Lavinia's treachery, but after talking to Carrie, Andrew realized that Vernon had died from a broken heart because of it. Then there was the case of that murdered actor. Was he actually involved with Lavinia, and did his fiancé kill him in a jealous rage on account of her?

Andrew asked himself how many lies his wife had told him? As cold and unfeeling as she was, learning the truth about Carrie's situation and Vernon's will hadn't been hard for him to believe.

Lavinia's cruelty knew no bounds. Only someone so heartless could reject her own family and pretend them dead. But to Lavinia, family wasn't important; Andrew could see this first hand. Between theater rehearsals, performances, parties and tours, Andrew and the children rarely saw her.

Raising his eyes, he studied his wife's image in the looking glass once more. Lavinia's back faced him. Her silk bathrobe, the color of lilacs, had a thick fringe of wispy feathers at the lapels. "You've never loved me, have you?" Andrew asked.

"Don't be silly." Lavinia dismissed his comment with a slight laugh.

Approaching her from behind, he said, "You've never loved the children either."

Lavinia continued brushing. "Andrew, you're speaking like a *dunce*! She sounded as if she were scolding a child.

Andrew's anger smoldered. "You're made of stone," he muttered.

Unfazed, Lavinia remarked, "Well, you have said my skin resembles alabaster—so I'll take that as a compliment." Still stroking her hair, she went on, "Andrew, you're in a foul mood. Go play with the children some more. I'm sure they're bathed and dressed for bed by now. They love it when you read them bedtime stories and tuck them in."

Andrew clenched his fists as years of repressed rage boiled inside him. "Look at me!"

Lavinia ignored him, slowly pulling the brush through her glossy tresses.

Suddenly, Andrew grabbed her by the shoulders. He pulled her from the vanity with such force, the bench beneath her tumbled backwards. With fingers digging deeply into her flesh, Andrew pressed his entire body firmly into hers. The vanity's mirror rattled and shook as he forced her against the dressing table's edge.

Throttling her shoulders he said, "You've never loved me and I've had *enough*! I'm *divorcing* you!"

Lavinia's eyes widened in shock.

"Divorcing me?" She struggled against his grasp. "Andrew, you're hurting me! But is that what you want?" Though his hands still held fast to her shoulders, Lavinia stopped wriggling, then gazed at him seductively. Slipping her hands onto his thighs, she rubbed them slowly. In a breathy whisper Lavinia said, "I've never seen this side of you — it excites me.

"Do you think I don't love you because I won't let you hurt me? Is that why you want a divorce? Hurt me, if that'll make you happy — and banish the ugly thought of divorce from your mind."

When Lavinia reached to kiss him, Andrew loosened his grasp on her shoulders. At the touch of her lips on his, he lost control. Kissing her savagely, Andrew held tight to her curves. His hands roamed roughly over Lavinia'a back and buttocks, then found their way to the front of her robe. He brusquely squeezed her full breasts, then began pulling open her robe to free them.

Finally remembering himself, Andrew released her, as though she were made of hot coals. Breathing hard, he stepped a few paces away, then set the vanity bench upright. Angry with Lavinia, as well as himself, he said, "I don't want to hurt you! But I do want a divorce."

Her sexual counterattack foiled, Lavinia glared at him through narrowed eyes. She didn't bother to close the robe. It was open slightly, where Andrew had tugged at it

seconds earlier, and now revealed the tops of
her breasts. With each breath they welled like
rising cream. Andrew had to struggle not to
look at them, as well as fight the compulsion to
touch them.

"On what grounds?" Lavinia said.

"You've alienated my affection."

"I haven't been unfaithful to you!"

"And you've denied me my conjugal
rights."

Lavinia laughed in what sounded like
disbelief. "*You* shunned *me* only moments ago.
Besides, I haven't denied you my body! It's
just that—there are some times I can't. If you
were a decent man—kind and sympathetic—
you'd see things differently! If Serene weren't
feeling quite herself—Julian would
understand. Just because she couldn't give in
to his needs—he wouldn't accuse her of
denying him his rights!"

"Leave them out of this. You're not
Serene, I'm not Julian"

"Fine then," she said crisply, "I *won't* give
you a divorce. Besides, I've learned from more
than one actress that it's impossible to get a
divorce in New York without one party
committing adultery—which *I* haven't!"

Andrew's heart raced angrily, but he
retained his composure. "There are other
places I can divorce you on numerous grounds.
Now, I know this is about my money. What

you brought into this marriage, you'll take away. You'll have Vernon's property, your theater, and I'll even give you enough money to keep the theater afloat for one year."

"And what will you provide the children?"

"I'm taking the children."

"You're taking them? Not Selina, you won't! Besides, you're being foolish! All of this talk about divorce is rubbish. It certainly wouldn't be good for your reputation or your business! An upstanding man of integrity and honor divorcing his wife? How would that look? No divorce, and that's final. If being married to me is so horrible — we'll live separately — I'll keep Selina here with me, and you can have Gabriel — *and* a mistress, lots of them, if you like."

"I don't want to live that way!"

"Every man wants to live that way, but you'd have your wife's permission."

Stunned by her comment Andrew remarked, "Have you no scruples?"

"I've scruples enough to survive!"

Andrew reached into his pocket, then held out the velvet pouch to her. "I have something for you."

"Is that what I think it is?" When she reached excitedly to grab it, he pulled it away. "It's my locket, isn't it?"

As Andrew slowly handed it to her, he said, "A Mrs. McDougall brought it to me."

Lavinia snatched the pouch, then eagerly
dug inside it and pulled out the trinket.
Letting it dangle in front of her she said, "I
gave up looking for this years ago! It's an
heirloom. I must have lost it at Vernon's
mansion. You said a Mrs. Mc something
brought it to you? One of Vernon's former
servants?"

"No," Andrew said while watching
Lavinia sit down at the vanity. She held the
locket around her neck, then gazed adoringly
at her reflection.

"You might know Mrs. McDougall by
another name..."

"Oh?" Lavinia said, showing no real
interest as she continued to admire herself.

"Yes..." Andrew paused for a long
moment,"...Carrie Hargraves."

Lavinia gasped, dropping the locket. It fell
on the vanity's mirrored glass tabletop with a
soft clack. Looking down quickly, Lavinia
fumbled to collect the trinket. After shoving it
in its pouch, she closed it away in a gold
Florentine box, then sat perfectly still, as
though preparing for her greatest role. After a
deep breath, she sat tall. Watching his wife's
reflection, Andrew noticed her straining to
smile. Slowly turning to face him, she casually
remarked, "Carrie—you said?"

"Yes," Andrew replied. He waited, giving
Lavinia time to reveal what she'd hidden about

herself, but apparently, that information was not forthcoming. After a few seconds more, Andrew said. "Miss Hargraves told me that she's forgiven you. She wanted to give that back. She stole it out of spite — after her father died."

Lavinia turned away from Andrew. Keeping her back to him, she didn't move as he spoke. "She asked your forgiveness for insulting you," Andrew said, then again waited for a confession that he knew would never come. "She's been praying for you."

Lavinia balked. "Like I need her prayers!"

"She also mentioned that you needn't ever worry about her divulging — the truth..."

Hearing this, Lavinia swirled quickly to face Andrew. Though her eyes appeared wild with fear, she blinked several times, then again forced a smile.

"The — the truth?" she said, in a thin voice. "That Carrie — why, everything she says is a lie. The girl's mad. You can see that! She stole my locket, for heaven's sake. And besides, she hates me! But from what I recall — we parted amicably — and I — I — have no idea what — *truth* she's talking about!"

"Take what I'm offering you. Vernon's property, though ill-gotten gains, is worth a good bit. And the theater will survive, especially if I bankroll it for a year. But if you don't agree to a divorce and give me both children—I'll expose you—as *Negro,*" he paused, watching Lavinia flinch as though she'd been prodded by an ice pick, "then I could divorce you on grounds of deception and not give you a thing."

"You wouldn't! That's impossible!"

"You're a Negro masquerading as white. When it becomes known what you did, swindling Carrie out of her inheritance, you just might end up in jail."

"How dare you threaten me! How dare you believe her lies! Why, that Carrie! You divorcing me was her idea, wasn't it?!"

"Your step-daughter quoted something from the Bible, 'You reap what you sow.' Now, here's something my uncle often said, 'You live by the sword, you die by the sword.' This is war, Lavinia. Surrender while you can. Once I'm through with you, if you don't end up in prison, you'll be lucky to find work in a minstrel show."

Lavinia balled her fists. Her face turned bright red. "Why, you—you want to ruin me! You *and* that *slut!*" Throwing her arms in the air dramatically, she declared, "I might as well save you the trouble." She stalked to the window, opening it from a few inches to its full height of three feet, allowing the smell of soot to infiltrate the spacious room.

"I shall throw myself from this window, leaving a bloody mess on your hands! Then you can explain to *our* children how you drove their mother to suicide!"

As Lavinia began to climb through the window, Andrew rushed to her, pulling her back inside the room. Slamming the window so hard the pane cracked, Andrew said, "Woman, have you lost your mind?"

There was a banging at the door, "Father, Father," Selina cried. "What's the matter?"

Andrew seethed, looking at Lavinia, who now wore a smug smile, and finally closed her robe.

"Come in, darling," Andrew said

Selina ran into the room, with Gabriel trailing behind her. He dragged along his blue baby blanket, but upon passing Lavinia, balled it into a tiny bundle he tried to hide under one of his arms. When both children stopped at Andrew's legs, Selina said, "Father, why are you and Mother fighting?"

Bending down, Andrew scooped the children into his arms and stood up. "We're not fighting, Selina, we're having a discussion."

"A very *loud* discussion," his daughter said.

"Father, will you come read a story?" Gabriel asked.

"Of course, but Mother and I need to finish our talk." Putting them down, he said, "Now run along to bed. I'll be there in a moment."

"Mr. and Mrs. Standish," Brigid appeared in the doorway wearing a robe over her night dress and a night cap on her head. "I'm so sorry! I put the children to bed a little while ago. I didn't—"

"It's all right, Brigid," Andrew said. "But if you wouldn't mind getting them settled again. Then I'll be in shortly to read a bedtime story."

"Of course, Mr. Standish." Brigid smiled, gathering the children and ushering them from the room.

Andrew closed the door behind them. Then, after a few moments of silence, Lavinia said, "You've turned them against me, haven't you?"

"What?" Andrew asked, not comprehending her.

"The children—they didn't even look at me! Just how long have you been plotting this divorce business with your new friend, Carrie?"

"Lavinia, we're through here. Now it's time to bury the hatchet."

"I'd like to bury it right in your heart!" She said viciously, as a few wispy feathers from her robe floated delicately around her.

"And what would I find if I tried to bury it in yours, *besides* an empty cavity?" Exasperated, Andrew exhaled. "Lavinia, if you don't give me a divorce and *both* children, I'll expose you as colored."

"You're only leaving me because of the blood that courses through my veins! Blood that I can't help being there!" She cried.

"That's not true!"

"You, who said a man's character is what's most important, not the color of his skin!"

"I wanted to divorce you long before I knew anything about you being a Negro. And though I'm taking the children — I want them to know the truth."

"What?! You can't be serious! I'm the way I am because of it! I've had to do whatever I could to hide it! Perhaps Gabe *might* understand, because of how he looks — but what about Selina, your *precious* little *princess*? Is she strong enough to handle the truth? Do you *want* her to be like me? Do you want to turn her into me?!"

Confused, Andrew dropped his gaze to the floor.

"Andrew," Lavinia's tone was cool and controlled, "the best thing for all of us, is to stay together. The children need their mother, but they don't need to know the truth about me — or themselves. We could continue to live under the same roof, and you could keep a mistress. With a discreet arrangement like that, the children would never know things weren't right between us."

Andrew remained silent for several

moments. Things hadn't been right between him and Lavinia for a long time, and what she was suggesting was a sordid arrangement. Aside from the mistress, it wouldn't be healthy to raise the children in a house filled with secrets.

If Carrie knew, perhaps others did too, and what if the children *did* find out later from someone else? That would be even more damaging. Selina and Gabriel needed to know the truth — from their parents, and they needed to learn it now, while young and innocent, not hardened by societal opinion.

Having learned the truth, Andrew had struggled with it himself since finding out. Science said that Negroes and whites were different. But how could he make sure his children were unaffected by the burden of Negro blood? He was at a loss of what to do.

Meeting her eyes, he said, "I'm going to tuck the children in, then I'm going upstairs to bed. That's where I'll be sleeping from now on. We're divorcing — I'm taking the children."

Turning his back on her, he slowly walked toward the door. Before leaving the room, he gazed at her once again, feeling a mixture of sympathy and hate. Lavinia appeared more hardened than usual, yet defeated, as she stood stiffly with her head held high and tears brimming in her eyes.

"If you try to stop me," he said, "you'll

suffer the consequences. "

"Andrew, no!"

Before Lavinia could protest further, he closed the door.

Chapter 23

"How would the two of you like to visit your grandparents?" Andrew asked a few days later.

The children squealed with delight at their father's question, while Lavinia blanched, horrified. They were dining at home on a Sunday evening under the light of an opulent crystal chandelier.

Giggling, Selina said, "How can we get to heaven? That's where you told us our grandparents are."

"My mother and father are in heaven, but," Andrew glanced at Lavinia, "not your mother's parents. I was mistaken about them. They're alive, aren't they darling?"

Lavinia's eyes narrowed as she she pursed her lips. Breathing in short quick breaths, her chest rose and fell rapidly.

"They live in California," Andrew addressed the children, "and that's where I'm taking you!"

Gabriel squirmed excitedly in the mahogany chair. "California! Cowboys live in California!"

Watching Gabriel wriggle, Lavinia exclaimed, "Sit still!" The boy immediately ceased moving. "Both of you," she said to Selina and Gabriel, "leave the table!"

After they skittered across the Oriental carpet and out of the room, Lavinia scowled at Andrew. "Just what are you talking about? Are you seriously going to drag my children off to California to—" she stopped abruptly when the scullery maid came in to clear away the dishes.

Andrew had eaten every bite of his roast beef, asparagus with hollandaise and herbed rice with butter, as had the children, yet Lavinia had merely picked at hers. Approaching Lavinia, the maid asked, "Are you finished, ma'am?"

"It's cold, take it away!" Lavinia snapped.

"May I bring you something else?"

"No!"

The girl took Lavinia's plate, then stacked the others underneath it. She moved slowly, careful not to chip her employer's china, though to Andrew, she seemed to be proceeding at a more deliberate pace than usual.

After the maid had finally finished and returned to the kitchen, Lavinia picked up the conversation where she'd left off. "Going to California with the children indeed! I won't allow it!"

"Listen to me, Lavinia. For several months now, I've been intending to travel there and explore the development opportunities. But I've felt an even stronger compulsion to go since Carrie told me that you'd left your parents behind there. She'd puzzled some of the pieces of your life together from what she'd overheard, and came to the conclusion that your father is a wealthy landowner."

Lavinia sat silently seething.

"I see you don't dispute that. Well, I feel it necessary to make their acquaintance, find out who they are."

"And you want to expose my children to them? The children don't need to know *those* people!"

Andrew wasn't sure what kind of people they were, especially Lavinia's mother, a Negro woman of all things. Was she the evil one Lavinia had taken after? He'd need to see for himself. He'd debated about taking the children with him, but eventually decided it was the right thing to do.

"I'll be the judge of that. My parents are

dead! Julian's my only family. The children need to know they have more than just us. And they need to know who they are. I don't ever want them to be ashamed of their ancestry. Alexander Pushkin was descended from an African and he was never ashamed."

"Alexander Pushkin didn't live in New York," Lavinia said through clenched teeth.

"Have you ever told your parents about Selina and Gabriel?" Andrew asked. His wife said nothing. "Perhaps they'd like to know that they have grandchildren. It seems cruel to deprive them of that. What harm can it do?"

"Harm? Selina and Gabe will be damaged for life! Associating with them—why— they'll—"

"Mother!" Selina ran into the room, "I can't find Gabriel. We're playing hide and seek."

Lavinia appeared frantic as her eyes darted around the room. Then, quickly raising the blue damask cloth, she peered under the table. Sighing in exasperation and relief, she said, "He's not in here, Selina! Now leave us alone! Father and I are busy."

Andrew smiled at his daughter and winked. "Look in my wardrobe." He then watched as Selina happily ran off.

Lavinia lowered her voice. "The children will be labeled as...

"Labeled as what, Lavinia?"

She said nothing for a long moment. "My

parents are what drove me away. No possible good will come from you and the children going there. You'll be sorry, you'll regret it!"

Lavinia appeared to summon tears as if on cue. "My mother...she was horrible... she'll scare the children...scar them for life!" Dabbing at her eyes with a blue cloth napkin, Lavinia wept on, "You'd never believe the dreams she caused me to have, brought on by her caustic words."

Unmoved by her dramatics, Andrew said, "My children will be fine. But I won't know anything — about the other side of their family — unless I venture there myself. I don't think I can trust anything you tell me. Now, I plan on being gone for at least two months. That'll provide enough opportunity for business, as well as time to meet your people."

"You're a fool to do this!" Lavinia said harshly, the pitiful voice and tears now abandoned. "You'll see! You'll wish you'd listened to me!"

Doubt gnawed at Andrew, and it intensified with Lavinia's words, sometimes outweighing his positive thoughts about the endeavor. What if he didn't like what he found in California? He didn't know if Lavinia's mother had been a slave or a free woman, and he still had a hard time imagining what a wealthy white man would have wanted with her. Had she been his maid? Was she even literate? Yet despite his unease, Andrew had to know what his children derived from.

He'd never been one to harbor prejudice, as long as Negroes kept to themselves and away from him, he now realized. In his wildest dreams he'd never imagined himself married to a black woman, however, Lavinia had probably bewitched him with voodoo magic or something she'd learned from her mother.

Andrew said, "When I return, we can start divorce proceedings. I'll need to set up residence in Nevada for six months, prior to the process being finalized, but that beats waiting a year. In the meantime, I'll need your help. I want to get some correspondence in order with your parents to make arrangements."

"This fiasco is *your* affair! I left California behind years ago. I never corresponded with my parents after that. For all I know, they are dead by now! But if they're not, and you insist on dragging my children off to California to turn them into Negroes, I won't lift a finger to help you! You can find my relatives all by yourself!"

Andrew hesitated, glaring at her. "So — do you want me to hire a private detective to find your family so even more people will be exposed to your past?"

Lavinia sat back, stiffly clasping her hands.

The muscles in her neck twitched as she raised her head. "Fine," she said tightly, then looked away. "I'll provide you with their address."

"I knew you'd see it my way," he said sarcastically.

Turning to meet his gaze, Lavinia's eyes seared into his. "Do you plan on exploiting my parents?" She asked.

Andrew felt his cheeks burn. Angrily throwing his napkin on the table, he said, "What are you implying?"

"Only that a cunning robber barren, such as yourself, would swindle them out of property for development." She wore a nasty smile. "A filthy rich man like you is always concerned about the bottom dollar—and whatever it takes to get it. Will you use the children somehow to make a deal? Isn't that what this trip is really all about?"

Andrew stood slowly, choosing not to acknowledge his wife's last blow. "If you'll excuse me." Irate, he trudged from the dining room, leaving his wife alone.

Chapter 24
Wilmington, California
Summer, 1902

Johnny Cahill gazed into the California sky for a moment before pulling on the reins to stop the buckboard. One of the two gray shire horses whinnied upon stopping near the train station in Wilmington. It had been slightly overcast earlier, but now the sun shone brightly, despite large puffy clouds floating lazily through the vibrant blue sky.

Climbing from the two-seater buckboard, Johnny wondered what the sky looked like in New York. That's where the Taylor's guests were coming from. Breathing in soot from the arriving train, Johnny assumed that's what most of New York smelled like.

He'd volunteered to pick up the visitors today, because he was — indispensable — yeah, he thought, indispensable. He liked that big fancy word. The school teacher, Mrs. Cummins, had taught it to him, and he was especially indispensable to her. She'd told him that more than once, especially after some unfortunate happenings at Charlton Place, her ranch, where he was gainfully employed as the general manager.

Johnny was also a big help to Mr. and Mrs. Taylor. He made sure of that. Mr. Taylor hadn't really liked him at first, but now he seemed to, at least a little, anyway. Johnny's stepmother's brother was Uncle Tommy Douglas, the former general manager of Charlton Place. Douglas was doing his sister a favor by letting Johnny work with him. Uncle Tommy had warned Johnny not to screw things up. And he hadn't.

Sure, Johnny'd gotten in trouble a few times. But that was before he'd turned over a new leaf, then come to California and started working with Uncle Tommy at Charlton Place. His stepmother was a good-hearted woman who wanted to see him continue down the right path. Her brother's position at a prosperous ranch sounded like a place where Johnny could thrive, and now Johnny was doing just fine. And he planned to be doing even better in the future.

Nobody knew what this Andrew Standish city-slicker looked like, but Johnny could spot an eastern dude, or a similar breed, in no time. He'd be darn near easy to find 'cause he'd have a little boy and a little girl with him.

After the train stopped, Johnny walked through the crowd of people, horses and wagons toward the first class cars. He'd been told Standish had rented a private rail car. The *gentleman* had traveled with servants, but they wouldn't be staying in California with him at the Taylor's. The Taylors had enough hired help to handle the whippersnappers. And besides, Johnny figured, no use of them seeing how Mrs. Taylor wasn't white.

It hardly took any effort to pick Standish out as he stepped off the train with the two kids. He *looked* rich, wearing spats, an expensive dark gray summer suit, and matching bowler hat. The young'uns were right cute little critters. The girl was a pretty thing, all gussied up with bows in her hair and a deep blue dress with frills. Looked just like the pictures of her mother he'd seen at Rolando. And there was no doubt the boy reached back to Mrs. Taylor to get his color.

Johnny approached them with his hand extended. "Mr. Standish?"

****

"Yes," Andrew said, shaking the young

man's hand.

"I'm Johnny Cahill, here for Daniel Taylor."

"Pleased to meet you," Andrew replied.

Cahill looked to be about thirty. He stood a hair over six feet, and his frame was sturdy and solid.

Selina tugged at Andrew's jacket. "Father," she said, looking at Cahill's attire, "he's another cowboy, isn't he?" Cahill had on a wide brimmed hat. His shirt was gray, and he'd worn a suede vest over it. The stacked heels and pointed toes of his cowboy boots were clearly visible beneath the hem of his navy blue trousers.

Andrew said, "the children have become fascinated by all the cowboys they've seen."

Cahill smiled a crooked smile. Probably one he thought ladies of all ages appreciated, along with his long lashed brown eyes. Cahill removed his hat, revealing golden blond hair that he shook from his eyes with a toss of his head. Bowing slightly toward Selina, he said. "I've certainly worked as a cowboy, Miss."

"Can I touch your gun?" Gabriel asked eagerly, looking at the weapon in Cahill's holster and the shiny tips of the bullets in his gun belt.

"Gabriel, what have I told you about that?" Andrew said sternly. "You don't need to be touching firearms."

Cahill squatted down to Gabriel's level. "You come visitin' here again, when you're a little older, maybe I'll teach you how to shoot. 'S'longs it's okay with your pa." Johnny winked at the boy.

Something about Cahill's manner sat wrong with Andrew. To him, the crooked smile appeared ominous, rather than charming. And his comment to Gabriel, though innocuous in matter, sounded sinister in tone. Or perhaps Andrew had read too many disturbing accounts about the Wild West and the wilder cowboys that populated it. If the Taylors were anything like Cahill, Andrew wouldn't plan on staying with them for long. But their letters had given him no indication to be wary, and neither had anything he'd learned about Taylor while in Los Angeles.

Mrs. Taylor had responded joyfully after receiving his first letter. She'd insisted that he and the children stay for at least a month. This was her reaction, despite the fact that Andrew had informed her of his impending divorce from Lavinia. Andrew had written of the importance he felt for the children to meet their grandparents, and Mrs. Taylor had expressed her eternal gratefulness for this.

She'd even apologized on behalf of her daughter. *Although I am not privy to the circumstances of your marital difficulties*, she'd written in a beautiful flowing script, *I realize that my daughter is troubled with an emotional affliction of some sort. I am truly sorry for the pain she must have caused you in your life. I am no stranger to that myself.*

Andrew actually found himself looking forward to meeting this woman, who now, through her words at least, didn't seem an illiterate black woman of devilry. His business acquaintance in LA had filled him in on Lavinia's father. "Honest as the day is long," Andrew's friend had said. "But just because he's honest, doesn't mean he's ignorant." Andrew had interpreted that as one who couldn't be taken advantage of.

Cahill stood up and replaced his hat. "Mr. Taylor sends his apologies," he said. "He was gonna come meet you himself, but had a business problem that needed tendin' to. I suspect he should be at his place by the time we get there, though."

Chapter 25

Lori gazed around the parlor, seeing that everything was neat and nothing out of place. Now was a happy time for her because she'd be meeting her grandchildren. But over a dozen years earlier, this room had held nothing but pain. That was when Lavinia had told Lori that she hated her.

"You've ruined my life! You've ruined my life — by being a Negro! And I hate you for that!"

Lori still remembered those words her daughter had hurled at her, just before running away with that despicable Hargraves to a life of depravity as an actress.

Lori took a deep breath. Focusing on the joy, she held back tears while pushing away the hurt that still cut like a jagged blade. She'd rushed around all morning and into the afternoon, trying to ensure perfection throughout the whole house for the family that was coming to visit.

Mr. Standish had corresponded that he and his children—Lavinia's children—had planned to stay in Los Angeles for a few weeks. *I've researched the area and arranged some business meetings with an acquaintance of mine, as we will be discussing real estate development there,"* he'd written. Then he'd gone on to say, *After concluding my business, I accept your generous invitation.*

Lori hoped Mr. Standish would consider extending his visit. She and Olivia couldn't wait to spend time with the children, and Lori's true desire was for them to stay for the entire summer, rather than only a month. Remembering Lavinia's anger, Lori felt a prick of pain in her heart. Gabriel and Selina were young, they couldn't be at all like Lavinia, at least not yet. Again, Lori forced herself not to think of such things.

The train bringing Mr. Standish and the children had already arrived in Wilmington and Cahill had gone to meet them. They'd be at the ranch soon. Hearing footsteps in the hall, Lori's heart began to race. She quickly glanced out the window, but saw no sign of the buckboard. Turning, she saw Daniel walk into the parlor. Letting out a deep breath, Lori felt disappointment, as well as a slight bit of relief.

She still hadn't finished checking on everything! "For a moment, I thought you were—"

Daniel began to laugh. "The company? How can a man alone sound like he's got two four-year-olds scampering behind him?"

"I suppose that was silly of me," Lori said exasperatedly. "Well, now that you've contended with your business matter, you'll only be in my way." Grabbing his arm, she steered him from the parlor. "Go sit out by the courtyard. You can keep watch there."

"Alright, alright," Daniel said, taking a newspaper with him as he headed for the veranda.

Lori gazed at the pink roses on the center table. She and Olivia had busied themselves making sure fresh flowers were in every room. Lori had also fussed over the servants, seeing that they'd prepared the cookies and candy she'd requested for the children, and that dinner was progressing as planned.

Lori wanted things to taste southern tonight, not Mexican. She'd asked Rosa to refrain from putting chilies in the cornbread, and she'd decided to prepare the grated sweet potato pudding and the pound cake herself.

She'd checked not long ago to see that the chicken was prepared to fry, the ham was baking, and the macaroni and cheese was ready to go in the oven. The black-eyed peas and the greens were simmering and fresh tomatoes were on hand to be sliced. Juanita had mastered the art of making lemon meringue pie, with much instruction from Lori, and a beautiful one she'd prepared waited in the icebox.

"Meez Taylor," Juanita had complained earlier in her sing-songy Spanish accent, "I theenk they like a Mexican feast better."

"Well," Lori had assured her, "tomorrow, you can fix your best Mexican feast, but not too spicy," she warned, "we don't want to make the children, or Mr. Standish, sick."

Sighing with satisfaction, Lori decided the parlor had passed inspection. It was spotless. From there, she walked down the hall to the side door that faced the courtyard. Stepping outside, she asked Daniel if he'd seen any sign of them.

"Not yet," he replied, keeping his eyes affixed to his newspaper. "Besides, I've only been out here a minute, if that."

"But, you haven't even been looking! You're too busy reading!" she scolded.

"I'm not deaf. If I'm not looking, I'll surely hear them. Lori, you've been working hard all day. Relax." Daniel patted the place on the bench beside him. "Why don't you come out here and sit with me?"

"Perhaps in a short while I will, but I still need to check on a few things."

"You've been busy checking on things all day. This Standish Yankee's just a man — *not* the Second Coming." Daniel had done some research on Truelove and Standish and found them to be one of the largest contracting firms in the East. "He might be rich as all get out, but you don't need to be working yourself into a tizzy over him. And I don't think the children will care one way or the other how the house looks."

"Daniel," Lori playfully pointed her finger at him, "you can downplay your enthusiasm all you want, but I know you're just as excited as I am about meeting our grandchildren!"

Daniel reached out his hand to her and she held it. "Lori — don't be — upset — if Standish decides not to stay the whole month. He's already been in LA for a while. He might get antsy...want to get back to New York. These parts aren't like what he's used to...not much excitement." Daniel paused, looking into his wife's eyes. "Or could be he's..."

"Uncomfortable." Lori sighed. "I know — I've thought about that."

"But it's downright admirable of him to do what he's doing," Daniel added quickly. "I've got to give him that."

"It is. He's a man of character. It's not every white man who'd want his family to know about its — darker side," she said wistfully. "We're not even *his* family."

"Well," Daniel said, "him being as rich as he is—he's got nothing to lose."

"Do you speak from experience?" She smiled.

"Even if I'd had close to nothing," Daniel pulled her to his lap, "for you, I would have risked it all."

Gazing into his eyes, she said, "You did." When he kissed her, Lori wriggled from his grasp, laughing. "Daniel, what if someone sees us?"

Running his hand over the persimmon fabric that covered her thigh, he said, "Guess they'll know that old folks like us still know how to kiss and spark." When Lori completely extricated herself from his arms and stood up, Daniel winked. "We'll have to pick up where we left off later."

"And right now," Lori called over her shoulder as she walked toward the door, "you just stay put and keep watch."

Back inside, Lori took one final look around the place. Striding down the hall, she hoped that all *would* go well with this visit. Words couldn't express the thrill she felt about meeting her grandchildren. Despite the heartache of Lavinia's absence, Lori couldn't wait to wrap her arms around Selina and Gabriel.

Grandchildren were something that she and Daniel had missed desperately. They'd enjoyed spoiling their son David's two children, but after last year's tragedy, David had decided to move his family to Paris. The children were in school and fluent in French, and David was writing and teaching English at the University of Paris. He and his wife, Janine, as well as their children, were living a different life now. A man was a man there, judged by his merits alone, David had said. No system of racism was in place to hinder a man's dreams and hopes. They'd made friends among the Parisians and the colored ex-patriots.

Living in France was just to be temporary. At least that's what David had said when they'd first moved there. But he and Janine were so enamored of their new lives that Lori feared they'd never live in California again. They'd only visited once since relocating there.

Then there was Olivia's situation.

Hearing her oldest daughter's footsteps on the stairs, Lori gazed up toward her.

"Flowers in every room." Olivia smiled, trying to sound and look cheerful. "Marigolds, begonias. Everything's perfect."

Lori hesitated for a moment. "Honey, I know all's not perfect with you. You can't hide from me that you're hurting."

Olivia's eyes welled as she reached the bottom of the stairs. When Lori embraced her, she said, "Mother, some days I'm fine, but then there are times like now, that I can't help but dwell on it." She pulled from Lori's arms, wiping her tears with the back of her hand.

"Are you up to being around Lavinia's little ones today?"

"Of course I am. I can't wait to meet them. Though I am a little envious; Lavinia doesn't even like children, yet she had two at one time!" They both chuckled.

Lori squeezed her daughter's shoulder, "Olivia, one day things will be different for you."

She sighed. "I hope so, Mother...I hope so."

"Lori!" Daniel called from the veranda. "They're coming!"

Lori and Olivia rushed to the parlor. They ran to the window facing the courtyard. They could see the buckboard, still a good distance away, as it approached.

Lori put one hand over her heart, while the other clutched Olivia's arm. Almost in a whisper, she said, "I can't believe this day is finally here."

Chapter 26

Andrew was amazed at all the property Daniel Taylor owned, or had owned at one time. While the buckboard trounced over dusty roads, Cahill had pointed out business and residential property that Mr. Taylor owned in the white and black communities of Little Ways. He'd then pointed in the direction of the Westmore College, a large white stucco building with a red tile roof, also in Little Ways. Cahill explained that Mr. Taylor had provided money and land for the colored institution, and that he'd founded it with a group of former slaves and abolitionists.

Prior to arriving in Little Ways, they'd ridden through two new towns, populated by shop-lined streets and one and two story frame homes, built on land that Taylor had sold to

developers. Then they'd gone through a wide
stretch of undeveloped land scattered with
pines and low growing willows that, Andrew
soon learned, was Taylor property as well.

After they'd passed through Charlton
Place, Cahill assured Andrew that it wouldn't
be too much longer until they arrived at
Rolando.

"We're just about there," Cahill yelled
over his shoulder to Andrew.

Andrew sat in the rear seat, holding Selina
in his lap, while Gabriel crawled over him, one
too many times, to enjoy the different views
from each side.

"Gabriel," Andrew said, grabbing the boy
firmly around the waist the next time he
skittered by. "Sit still for a moment."
Lowering his voice for only the children to
hear, he said, "Remember what I told you. I
expect you to be perfect little angels, seen and
not heard. Only speak when you're spoken to.
And you mustn't comment on how your
grandmother looks."

"Father," Selina said, "you told us her skin
was different, not light like mine. So what
does it look like?"

"Brigid says I'm golden," Gabriel said
proudly. "So is our grandmother golden too?"

That was a good question, Andrew
thought, because he honestly didn't know.
Other than an address, her father's name and

the number of siblings she had, Lavinia had provided no further information. Regarding her mother, she'd only said in a disdainful way, "we look nothing alike," which led Andrew to believe that she must be some shade of brown. But if she were the color of cinnamon or honey, Andrew had no clue.

Before he could respond to his children's questions, Gabriel shouted pointing, "I see the house!"

Selina, still on her father's lap, looked in the direction her brother indicated. "It's long," she said.

Andrew took in the sight of the adobe, a rather large and handsome dwelling. The spacious looking house, complete with upper and lower verandas, had two stories. The outside was whitewashed, while the window frames and veranda railings were painted red. Andrew wondered why Lavinia was ashamed of all this, then he remembered her mother writing of her daughter's emotional affliction.

As they rode through a high redwood gate and came closer to the house, Andrew saw a tall dark-haired gentleman. From the distance, Andrew could see that he wore a gold vest over a dark blue shirt. When the man walked down the steps to the courtyard, Andrew assumed that he must be Lavinia's father.

"I believe that's your grandfather," Andrew said, as the twins looked toward the man.

"Is he nice?" Selina asked.

"Darling, I'm sure he is," Andrew replied.

"Will he show us more cowboys?" Gabe asked, enthusiastically.

"Perhaps."

Selina raised her chin, while surveying the surrounding trees and flower gardens. "So where's our grandmother?"

"She must be in the house."

"Is *she* nice?" Selina asked, warily.

"I've never met her, darling, but I'm sure she is."

"Then how come she's not outside with our grandfather?" Selina probed.

"I don't know, Selina," Andrew said, "but we'll meet her when we get there."

Selina sulked. "Maybe she's mean and doesn't want to see us."

"I doubt that, darling."

"Will they have candy and cookies?"

"I don't know, Selina."

"My friend Eleanor's grandparents always give her candy and cookies. Isn't that something grandparents are supposed to do?" Selina asked.

"Some grandparents do," Andrew said.

"Well, I hope *they* do!" Gabriel exclaimed.

****

Lori gazed from the window with her

daughter as Cahill steered the buckboard into the courtyard. They watched as Daniel walked toward it to greet their guests. Andrew stepped down first.

Olivia gasped upon seeing his face.

Glimpsing her daughter's awestruck expression, Lori said, "I agree. He *is* handsome. Would be to any woman that's alive, I suppose."

Lori watched as Andrew lifted Selina from the wagon and placed her gently on the ground.

"Mother, she's beautiful, even more beautiful than her picture!"

Lori could hardly speak for a moment as she blinked away tears. "She looks just like Lavinia did — at that age."

When Andrew set Gabriel down, Lori exclaimed, "Oh, and look at that precious little Gabriel!"

Olivia smiled. "Sweet as an angel."

Raising a brow, Lori said, "I couldn't tell from the picture, but now I can see that he takes after me, doesn't he?" She and Olivia laughed. "How do you think she explained that?"

"Oh, Mother...your guess is as good as mine."

Both women continued to gaze quietly through the window, until Olivia said, "Mother, I'm going upstairs for a while. You and Father need some time alone with your grandchildren."

"Olivia, are you — all right?"

"I'm fine. I'll come down later to meet them. Right now, you and Father enjoy yourselves." Olivia smiled sadly, then left the parlor.

Lori picked up the skirt of her persimmon dress, a dress she'd had made just for this occasion. Its three-quarter sleeves were puffed at the shoulder and edged in lace, as were the neckline and ruffled hem. She couldn't wait to get outside and greet the children, but when she left the parlor and started down the hall, she stopped to check her reflection in a small mirror.

Lori's feelings of elation suddenly turned to fear. Lori hadn't told Daniel this, but after receiving a picture of the grandchildren, she'd debated as to whether or not to send a photograph of herself with Daniel to Mr. Standish. She'd decided against that, however, for selfish reasons.

Lori couldn't deny that her color might discourage him from coming. Although Mr. Standish was aware that she was Negro, it was safer to let him think she was light-skinned, which was probably what he'd assumed because of Lavinia's fairness.

Now riddled by anxiety, Lori wondered how her grandchildren would react to her.

Had they seen many Negroes? Had they ever seen any at all? What if they were afraid of her? She'd be devastated if they rejected her. Lori longed to run outside and embrace them, but fear held her back.

Lavinia had hated Lori because of her color, and Lori couldn't bear for daughter's children to hate her for the same reason. Praying softly, she recited from the Bible, "'There is no fear in love; but perfect love casteth out fear.' Lord, perfect me in Your love so that fear finds no place in me."

Chapter 27

Daniel approached Andrew with a firm handshake. "Mr. Standish, or may I call you Andrew?"

"Of course, sir," Andrew replied.

"Call me Daniel, and the pleasure is mine." He looked at the little faces peering up at him, then bent to pinch their cheeks. "Are these handsome children *my* grandchildren?"

Appearing coy, Selina tried to hide behind her father's leg. But Gabriel, with with a wide smile and twinkling eyes, said, "Hi!"

"Well, hello to you!" Daniel said. "I'm your grandfather. Let me hear you say that." He winked.

"Grandfather!" Gabriel yelled, then raised his arms for Daniel to lift him from the ground.

Obliging, Daniel hoisted him atop his shoulders. "You're a big boy," he laughed, "and heavy too."

"I like to eat! That's why I'm so big. Do you have candy and cookies?"

"Gabriel!" Andrew said, embarrassed.

"Of course we have candy and cookies. Don't all grandparents?"

"Yes!" Gabriel shouted.

"I'm so happy to finally meet you!" Daniel said to the boy on his shoulders. Then he smiled at Selina, partially concealing herself behind Andrew's leg. "And I'm happy to meet you, too, young lady."

Andrew gazed down, catching a glimpse of his daughter's face. Daniel had managed to coax a small smile from her.

Cahill and some of the stable-hands had carried the luggage inside. Now, as Cahill headed for the buckboard, he said, "Excuse me, Mr. Taylor. You be needin' anything else?"

"No, Johnny. But thank you for collecting our guests."

After Cahill said his goodbyes and headed back to Charlton Place, Daniel addressed the children. "You know what? We need go inside and find your grandmother, so follow me! She's been looking forward to your visit since we got your father's first letter."

As Daniel started for the house, with Gabriel on his shoulders and Andrew and Selina following behind, Mrs. Taylor appeared in the doorway.

****

Andrew was a bit surprised upon seeing Taylor's wife. Her skin was beyond cinnamon, beyond cocoa even. In its dark richness, her complexion was more like black coffee. Slim for her age, she appeared an elegant and striking woman with almond eyes and sensual lips. Although Lavinia had claimed no resemblance to her mother, Andrew could clearly see it.

Still slightly taken aback, he caught himself staring at the woman a bit too long. Fearing her color might unnerve the children, as it had initially unnerved him, he quickly glanced at Gabriel. The boy looked surprised, yet happy. Selina, however, continued to adhere to her father's pant's leg. As Andrew lowered his eyes to hers, she tugged on his jacket. Bending down, he heard her whisper, "Why is she so dark?"

"Shush," he said, softly, then thumped the back of her head with his thumb and forefinger to ensure her silence.

"Welcome—to all of you!" Mrs. Taylor's eyes brimmed with tears. Seeing this, Mr. Taylor set Gabriel on the ground, then approached his wife and put a loving arm around her. "I—I can't tell you how glad I am—that you're all finally here," she said, nearly choking on her words.

"You're our grandmother?" Gabriel asked, amazed.

Mrs. Taylor took a deep breath, trying to regain her composure. "Yes—yes I am. Now, let me meet all of you."

Gabriel ran to her and threw his arms around her waist. "Hello, Grandmother!" After pulling away, he held up his arms.

Mrs. Taylor laughed, then reached to pick him up. "May I kiss you?"

"Yes, please!"

At this, Mrs. Taylor covered his cheeks with kisses, making him laugh.

Placing Gabriel down, she then approached Andrew with a hug. "Mr. Standish, it's a pleasure to meet you." Looking at Selina, still slightly hidden, Mrs. Taylor smiled. "And I'll look forward to seeing all of you very soon." She then turned to lead them into the house.

Following Mrs. Taylor, Andrew saw Selina peer up to him with eyes wide and questioning. At this, Andrew pursed his lips, hoping her inquisitiveness wouldn't lead to embarrassment.

Once in the parlor, Andrew looked at the handsome couple who'd so warmly welcomed his family. Both were gracious and kind, and from the brief exposure he'd had with the Taylors, he was relieved to learn that they weren't anything at all like Cahill.

Andrew could see that Lavinia's mother was overcome with emotion, and he now felt foolish for ever thinking less than flattering thoughts of her, merely because she was a Negro. Andrew was, however, still shocked to see a woman such as Mrs. Taylor, in the station of a wealthy white landowner's wife.

Her dark brown skin glistened, and though she didn't look over forty-five, he knew she must be near her husband's age, because her hair, styled in a heavy roll on each side of her face, was almost completely white. Daniel, distinguished looking and handsome, had streaks of gray in his dark hair. Seeing him closely, Andrew guessed him to be in his sixties.

"I'm so pleased that you've come to visit with us, Mr. Sta—"

"Please, call me Andrew."

Mrs. Taylor looked kindly into his eyes. "Andrew, I'm so pleased that you and the children have come here—and, do tell me—how is Lavinia? Is she well—is she happy?" In his correspondence, Andrew had mentioned his marriage and pending divorce from Lavinia, but only briefly touched upon her stage career, though he'd sent some photos of her in costume, as well as a few of her theater programs.

"Mrs. Taylor—" Andrew began.

"Lori."

Andrew smiled. "Lori—she's doing well, and she's happy—because she's doing what she loves."

"Mother told Lina and me that she'd cry herself to sleep every night while we're gone," Gabriel said, "but I think she was only pretending. That's what she does all the time on stage!"

Lori's eyes watered again. She nodded, at the same time appearing happy and sad. "Later—I'll want to hear more about her. But now, I want to spend time with my grandchildren." She looked at Selina. The little girl, holding fast to her father's trouser leg, immediately dropped her eyes to the floor. "You're a beautiful young lady," Lori said, "but I know it's difficult being in a strange place. I'll talk to your brother for a while, and perhaps later, we can chat."

When she turned away from them to face Gabriel, Andrew saw scarring at the base of her neck and wondered what kind of accident could have caused that. Then he raised his eyes to the ceiling, constructed of timber beams and vigas. It creaked softly under the weight of soft footsteps upstairs.

"I'm Gabriel!" The boy smiled at his grandmother.

"I know your name," Lori said playfully. "And how old are you?"

"Four, and I hear you have candy! What

kind?"

"Gabriel, don't be rude," Andrew admonished.

"Oh, I have lots! Chocolates and peppermints, and some caramels too."

At the mention of each selection of candy, Selina moved further away from her father's leg. "Do you have chocolate covered nuts?" she asked. "Those are my favorite."

"I certainly do." Lori pivoted toward her. "Sweets for the sweet, they say. Of course, you'll need to eat something healthy before you start on the sweets." Stooping down to her granddaughter's level, Lori smiled. After several seconds, she said, "May I — hug you?"

Andrew held his breath. He noticed Daniel's posture stiffen. When Selina remained silent, Gabriel said, "You can hug me again!" Looking at the back of her neck he added, "And then I can kiss the sore spots on your neck to make them feel better."

"No." Selina smiled shyly. "It's my turn. You can hug me," she said walking into her grandmother's open arms. While Lori hugged her tightly, Selina asked, "Do I get kisses too?"

Releasing Selina from a snug embrace, Lori looked surprised. "As long as you don't mind."

Selina grinned. "I don't."

Lori hugged Selina again, then kissed her. Afterwards, she said almost in a whisper, "You so remind me of your mother...when she was your age."

When Selina pulled from Lori's arms, she looked at her grandmother for a long moment. "Your eyes are shaped like Mother's. So you really are my mother's mother?"

"I am."

"I'm glad you came to life again. We thought you were dead." Lori's eyes widened in surprise, but before she could say anything, Selina prattled on. "If you are our grandmother, then why is our mother white?"

"Selina!" Andrew scolded.

"You told me not to say anything about *her* skin, not why Mother's isn't the same."

Andrew's face was on fire. He knew he'd turned bright red. "Lori, please forgive—" he began.

"That's all right, Andrew." Lori smiled. "It's only natural that the children would have questions. Your mother," Lori said to Selina, "takes after her father."

Selina touched Lori's face and said, "So will you tell me then, why your skin is so pretty and dark." She then moved her hand to Lori's hair. "And why your hair is so puffy, white and soft."

Lori appeared to smile through welling eyes. "My hair is white because I'm old," she laughed. "But everything else is the way it is— because God made me like this."

Selina tipped her head. "Why?"

"Well—people are like flowers, aren't they? And flowers come in lots of different colors."

Selina nodded. "Like red, yellow, pink and purple."

"That's right," Lori agreed, "and people come in different colors, too, like white, black, brown, and yellow. Now, don't you think the world would be an awfully boring place if we all looked the same?"

After a moment, Selina said, "I guess so. Now may I please have some candy?"

Chapter 28

Andrew watched as a Mexican girl brought in candy on a white pedestal tray decorated with tiny flowers. Lori introduced her to Andrew as Maria, the servant she'd charged with the children's care. Maria was young, about seventeen, and wore her dark hair in a braid down her back. Her blouse was pink, with puffy short sleeves, and her skirt, bright red. After handing the treats to Lori, the girl quietly left the parlor.

The children, sitting on the sofa with Daniel between them, squealed with delight as Lori held the tray in front of them.

"Pecans, covered with chocolate," Selina exclaimed with a mouthful.

"Selina, you know better than to talk with your mouth full," Andrew scolded her. He stood by one the bookcases along the wall, observing titles that included Joseph Conrad's *Lord Jim*, Rudyard Kipling's *Kim*, Paul Laurence Dunbar's *The Sport of Gods* and Arthur Conan Doyle's *The Hound of the Baskervilles*.

"I just ate a caramel!" Gabriel shouted.

"Grandfather," Selina said to Daniel, "can you give me a piggy back ride?"

"Of course, young lady." Daniel laughed, then turned his back to her. "Climb on! It's a pity your Uncle David and his children aren't here to play as well."

After Selina scrambled atop her grandfather's back, he stood up. "Are they your grandchildren, too?" Selina asked.

"They are," Daniel said, looking over his shoulder at her.

"But then we'd have to share you!"

Daniel chuckled. "Selina, there's enough of me to go around!"

"Giddy up, Grandfather!" Selina playfully kicked her feet, as though kicking the shanks of a horse. Whee!" She laughed, when Daniel began walking around the center of the room.

Andrew watched amused, as Gabriel ran after them, and then, giggling attached himself to one of Daniel's legs. Meanwhile, Lori fed Selina more candy.

"Lori, I thought you weren't going to give them any candy until they ate some healthy food," Daniel chided.

"Oh, a little won't hurt right now," she said, as sticky fingers reached for more, "and the nuts are wholesome."

Andrew smiled, watching all of this. But then he gazed out of the room into the hallway. His heart skipped a beat when he saw her. Their eyes met as she walked down the hall toward the parlor. It was Lavinia.

For a split second, anyway, that's who he thought it was. Yet Andrew had been mistaken. As she came closer, the similarities vanished. Hers was almost the same beautiful face as Lavinia's, yet her beauty was softer, tamer, and more approachable.

Taller than Lavinia, and darker, her skin was smooth and golden. Her hair, a reddish brown, looked soft and full. Its thick tresses, pulled away from her face, tumbled gently down her shoulders in coils. The gown she wore, a shade of turquoise green, seemed to emanate warmth. That, along with her luminous brown eyes and comforting smile, put him completely at ease.

When she walked into the room, Andrew felt an incredible magnetic pull toward her. He began his approach, but stopped when the children gasped, grabbing her attention from him.

"She looks like Mother!" Selina exclaimed.

"Only darker," Gabriel added.

Seeing the young woman, Lori immediately put down the candy and rushed to her side. "Olivia, dear," she smiled, placing an arm around her shoulder, "Come meet your niece and nephew."

"She does look a bit like your mother," Daniel said, lowering himself to the floor to let Selina climb down, "but that's your Aunt Olivia. She'd appreciate a warm greeting from you."

The children detached themselves from Daniel and ran toward her.

"I'm Gabriel!"

"I'm Selina!"

The children shouted over each other, making her laugh. Andrew watched as she gracefully knelt down, as if on angels' wings, to give each of them a hug. "I'm so happy to finally meet you," she said, "and I'm *thrilled* to have a niece and a nephew! I heard so many happy sounds, I had to come down and see what all the joyous commotion was about!"

Her face was simply aglow. It beamed in a way that Andrew had never seen reflected from Lavinia's countenance, not even when she'd performed onstage. Glancing at Daniel and Lori, Andrew observed them both near tears watching their daughter with his children.

"We already have an aunt," Selina said. "Her name is Aunt Serene — but we like having another one!"

"I'm happy to hear that!" Olivia said.

"Why do you look so much like Mother?" Gabriel asked.

Olivia stroked her nephew's curls while his little hand played with the ringlets hanging down her shoulder. "Because I'm her sister."

"Well your skin is just like mine!" Gabriel's dark eyes sparkled as he placed his hand next to hers. "See!"

"You're right!" Olivia kissed her nephew's hair, then playfully touched Selina's nose. The children had warmed to her immediately, and Andrew watched amazed as Olivia displayed a natural ease with them. His chest felt warm, and he could swear his heart was melting.

"Darling," Lori said, touching Olivia's shoulder. "Come meet their father." When Olivia stood up, Lori guided her gently by the elbow in Andrew's direction. His chest, still warm, thumped like a stampeding herd as she approached him. "Andrew, meet my daughter, Olivia."

Olivia extended long beautiful fingers, which he grasped in a firm handshake. Andrew now remembered that Lavinia had mentioned that name once long ago. However, when he'd asked who she was, Lavinia had only said "nobody." But Olivia most certainly *was* somebody.

Trying not to let his eyes wander over

every inch of her ravishing figure, with its small waist and generous bosom, he said, "I'm pleased to meet you."

"The pleasure is mine," Olivia replied. "And your children are beautiful."

****

"Lavinia lives and breathes for her work," Andrew said after dinner, while sitting in the parlor having coffee with Daniel, Lori and Olivia. Olivia sat in a matching armchair next to him. Her parents sat facing them on a loveseat. The trip, combined with the excitement of meeting grandparents and a new aunt, had exhausted the children. Now upstairs in Lavinia's old room, Gabriel and Selina were tucked in bed, sleeping soundly.

"I believe she told me that the first time I dined with her," Andrew continued. "I should have taken her at her word. Little did I know that she had no room for anything else in her heart."

Andrew had been telling them all about Lavinia's stage career, and the life he'd shared with her in New York. They'd been eager to hear everything about her. Andrew, however, felt the discussion had dragged on long enough.

"There's not much more I can say about Lavinia, except that..." Gazing over at Olivia, Andrew forgot his train of thought. She smiled. Her beauty had entranced him, and he'd had to fight the urge to stare since meeting her. Now he felt compelled not to discuss the woman who'd caused him more pain than he'd imagined possible, and instead merely drink in Olivia's presence.

She had a soft sweetness about her that was beautiful and warm, and she loved children. Since Selina and Gabe had arrived, Olivia had shown them a form of affection they'd never known from their own mother.

Filling the silence, Lori said quietly, "Lavinia never performed in Los Angeles. The Hargraves Players used to come there, but Lavinia never did."

Forcing his eyes from Olivia, he glanced toward Lavinia's parents. Seeing the heartache she'd caused them was by no means pleasant.

"And her Standish Company never comes to Southern California," Olivia said bitterly.

"Lori and I were in San Francisco a few years back when they were on tour there, but..." Daniel trailed off.

"But we couldn't bring ourselves to attend a performance," Lori took a deep breath. "It would have been too difficult to see Lavinia and..."

Deciding to conclude the discussion of his soon to be ex-wife's legacy of affliction, Andrew said, "As far as I'm concerned, Lavinia is one of the greatest actresses of our time. No one can dispute that. But the theater is what's most important to her — not her family — not any of you — by no means her children, and least of all me — which is why I'm seeking a divorce."

Lori smiled as tears welled in her eyes. "That's understandable, Andrew, and though I don't know you well, you seem a fine man. I'm sorry Lavinia caused you such unhappiness.

"Since I learned of the — divorce — I've been praying that the two of you could somehow reconcile. I fail to understand why Lavinia wouldn't want to give up the theater when she has two beautiful children, and an ideal husband like you, Andrew. Is it at all possible — that living apart — for just a little while — might change things, and improve your marriage?"

"Lori," Daniel said, putting his arm around her, "I think you know the answer to that. There's not a man alive that can handle that girl. She's always been selfish and difficult."

"Well," Lori sighed, "she's certainly not doing what we'd envisioned for her, pursuing the siren song of the theater, but at least she's in good health — doing what she wants to do. I — I suppose acting isn't quite as — disgraceful — as it once was."

Andrew found himself amused by Lori's old fashioned sentiment.

"Lavinia's a grown woman," Daniel scoffed. "She's made her choices. She can do with her life as she pleases. All we can do is pray for her."

"How have the children taken to the news of the divorce?" Lori asked.

"I've told them that their mother and I will no longer be married," Andrew said, "but Lavinia isn't a constant presence in their lives. The theater keeps her very busy. So, when they'll visit her, it'll be no different than it was when we were married, except that we'll be living under separate roofs. That's how I've explained it. She's practically a visitor to them now. They say they understand—but, I suppose only time will tell.

"I moved in with my brother shortly before the trip. After the divorce is finalized, I'll find a permanent residence where I can live with the children. Their main concern was that Brigid, their nurse, would still be living with them, which she will. I couldn't raise the children without her."

"I see..." Lori pursed her lips, then began, "Gabriel seems to be aware of..." but then she stopped, and after a moment resumed, switching the subject. "Andrew, in your last letter you explained that you found out about us from the Hargraves girl, Carrie. But before that—how did Lavinia explain Gabriel's color?"

"First of all," Andrew picked up his coffee cup from the center table in front of him, "Gabriel's color has never been a concern of mine." After taking a sip from the white china cup edged in gold, he said, "But what Lavinia did tell me, was that her mother was from the very, very south of Spain."

They all laughed at this. Andrew's eyes lingered on Olivia. Her laughter was almost musical. Olivia seemed normal. Yet Andrew wondered if there was something beneath the surface he couldn't see. How could Lavinia be so — *Lavinian* – while Olivia wasn't.

"Back to the Hargraves girl," Lori said. "Something puzzled me. You mentioned that she sought you to give back something she'd stolen from Lavinia. I never trusted Vernon, he seemed a nefarious sort, but nevertheless, wealthy. So why was his daughter a thief?" Eliciting no response from him, Lori said, "Andrew?"

Finally tearing his eyes from Olivia, and putting his steam engine back on track, Andrew addressed Lori, whose brow now appeared furrowed. "By no means was Carrie a common thief. She'd taken Lavinia's locket, her family heirloom, out of spite."

Lori raised a recriminating brow. "Lavinia stole that locket from her sister. I gave it to Olivia when she became engaged."

Feeling as though thrown from a speeding

locomotive, Andrew turned to Olivia. "Your—engagement?"

Olivia breathed in deeply. "It's certainly no surprise," she said acerbically, "that Lavinia didn't tell you about Joshua."

"Joshua?"

"My husband."

For several seconds, Andrew said nothing. Although he hadn't seen a ring on her finger, Andrew should have known that a beautiful woman like Olivia wouldn't be unmarried. He glanced down, intently studying his black coffee, then raised his gaze to Olivia's. "So— when will I meet—Joshua?"

The room fell silent. Olivia's eyes glistened with tears. "I'm afraid you won't." Her voice broke softly. She stood. "I'm sorry. If you'll excuse me." As Olivia walked away, the ruffle of her dress swished quietly across the floor.

Mystified, Andrew watched her leave the room.

Chapter 29

"Olivia," Lori called, following her daughter into the hallway, but Olivia kept walking.

"Mother—please don't worry about me." Olivia didn't turn toward her. "I'm fine, really, I am." Grabbing the newel post at the foot of the stairs, Olivia looked at Lori over her shoulder. "I just need to go upstairs and compose myself. I'll be back shortly. Spare me the pain of living through it all again—while I'm gone—you and Father—explain things."

Lori nodded, but said nothing as she grasped her daughter's hand. Then Olivia slowly walked up the steps.

"You can never control when tragedy strikes," Lori heard Daniel say as she returned to the parlor. "Joshua was a doctor," he continued. "His office was next to my son's press, and one evening when Joshua was in his office later than usual, an explosion occurred."

Lori sat next to Daniel, then held his hand while he spoke.

"David's paper had reported some things that didn't sit too well with some in the white community. We think the intention of the explosion was to destroy the press, not to hurt anyone. But the blast destroyed both buildings," lowering his eyes, Daniel paused for several seconds, "and Joshua — was killed."

Dumbfounded, Andrew said, "Killed?"

Daniel nodded. "It happened about a year ago."

"And if her husband's death wasn't bad enough," Lori said quietly, "Olivia was eight months pregnant with their first child. On the day of Joshua's funeral, she lost the baby." Lori closed her eyes for a moment and shook her head. "Andrew — both of them had wanted children so badly — but Olivia had had some difficulties — three miscarriages before the last pregnancy. And we thought that child would be our miracle." Lori sighed, "Losing Joshua, and then the baby, took an incredible toll on her."

Andrew sat forward, clasping his hands. "I can only imagine her pain. I'm so sorry. Did you find out who was responsible?"

"No," Daniel said. "There haven't been any clues. We're assuming it was motivated by racial disfavor, but we don't know by whom."

"The press had been there for over ten years, before the explosion," Lori explained, "and we still own a large amount of property in this part of the county. I don't think anyone would want to anger us by harming our family."

Andrew nodded, then asked, "How is Olivia progressing—regarding her emotional distress?"

"She's fine, most of the time," Lori said, "but still healing."

Andrew stood upon seeing Olivia enter the room.

"I apologize for leaving so suddenly." She again took the chair next to Andrew's.

As he sat down, Andrew said, "I'm so sorry for your loss."

"Thank you." Olivia smiled pleasantly, yet she took a deep breath, appearing eager to change the subject. "Now, where did we leave off with the locket?"

"Your mother said Lavinia stole it from you," Andrew replied.

Olivia sighed. "After my engagement..."

Lori leaned forward, concerned that her daughter might cry, but upon seeing her laugh, Lori sat back, relieved.

"I would've given it to her if I'd known she'd wanted it so badly," Olivia said. "She'd run off and secretly married Vernon. Then, before she left California with him, she took the locket from my jewelry box. She left a note."

Lori crossed her arms. "And it said, 'I married first, so the locket is mine.'" She and Olivia recited this together in sing-songy voices, then laughed, while Daniel merely smiled, shaking his head at what now seemed almost comical family lore.

"So what did marriage have to do with the locket?" Andrew asked.

"It belonged to my mother," Daniel said, "but it had been in her family for years. It was given to her when she married, then passed on to me. I gave it to Lori as a wedding present."

"And when Olivia became engaged," Lori said, "I gave it to her."

"If only I'd known," Andrew said, resting his eyes on Olivia, "I would have brought it back to you."

"That's all right," Olivia assured him. "It's still in the family. Selina can enjoy it some day."

"Andrew," Lori said, "you were explaining that the Hargraves girl stole it from Lavinia to be spiteful."

"Yes. Your daughter — wasn't — particularly — nice to Carrie — during her marriage to Vernon, and after his death — Carrie was left with practically nothing — due to—changes in his will."

"Because of—Lavinia?" Lori asked.

"Carrie wasn't sure," Andrew said, "but that's what I think."

Lori's eyes dropped to her lap. "I can't believe I raised a child to act like that. I want to blame the way she is on the fever I had while I was pregnant with her. But—I don't really know if that's the reason Lavinia behaves as she does."

"Well," Daniel smirked, "I've become convinced over time, that there's some form of derangement in her mental organization."

"Daniel," Lori admonished softly. "Andrew, please go on."

Andrew smiled. "Carrie found me in order to return the locket. She knew Lavinia would have nothing to do with her."

"The girl should have kept it!" Daniel said.

Andrew leaned toward him, "Daniel, Carrie said something I'll never forget—she'd forgiven Lavinia, because she'd found new life—in Christ."

All remained quiet until Lori spoke. "When you live in Christ," she said, "you become a new person."

"I don't understand what that means," Andrew said, "but I hope to—one day."

Lori smiled. "It takes time spent with Christ to better understand what Carrie was talking about. Jesus can change your life. He can strengthen you with His strength."

"And He can enable you to forgive," Olivia added softly, "no matter how difficult your circumstances. He can heal relationships—and hearts. Some wounds are so painful—and cut so deeply—that only He can heal them."

Olivia sat silently for a moment. "Like losing my husband—and my baby. But His mercies are new each day. Every morning...He gives me the peace I need to go on living."

Staring at Olivia in disbelief, Andrew said, "I can't understand your peace after the tragedy you endured. You're saying that when those responsible for the death of your husband are caught, you'll forgive them?"

"I already have."

At this, Andrew had no response.

"In the face of adversity," Daniel said, "your faith strengthens. Lori was enslaved—"

"Daniel, please." Embarrassed, Lori stopped him. However, after a moment she reconsidered, realizing the power of their testimony. Taking a deep breath she said, "Go on—I don't mind."

Daniel gently squeezed her hand. "You're sure?" After she nodded, he continued. "I helped her to escape, but the first part of our journey happened while she was near death, bruised and bloodied from a flogging. We made it up North, and eventually out here, but we couldn't have done anything without the Lord."

"Lori," Andrew's eyes widened, astonished, "you were — tortured that way?"

Lori lowered her gaze, before meeting Andrew's eyes. Touching the back of her neck, she said, "Yes — Gabriel mentioned the sore spots here, but scars cover my whole back." Grimacing and red faced, Andrew appeared enraged. "Daniel and I — don't usually talk about that time, but sharing it shows what God can do in the most difficult situations. For us, He's what's most important in our lives."

"The vanity and riches of this world aren't enough to satisfy the soul," Daniel said. "What's here on earth is fleeting, but God is eternal. I find comfort through my faith. Lavinia hurt her mother countless times. She devastated us both by running away. But through God's grace — I've forgiven her."

"And so have I," Lori said. "Even though the pain of losing her still overwhelms me at times. But now I'm blessed to know her children," she smiled, "my grandchildren!"

Andrew sat thoughtfully, as though absorbing everything he'd heard. Then, he moved his gaze to Olivia.

"They say the Lord works in mysterious ways," she remarked.

"That He does," Andrew agreed, not moving his eyes from hers.

Chapter 30

The next morning, Andrew chose a seat next to Olivia in the dining room.

Daniel, sitting at the head of the table, addressed Olivia. "After breakfast," he said, "Andrew and I will survey more of the Rolando acreage."

Gazing at Olivia, Andrew thought she looked even more radiant than yesterday. Her dress, white with red roses, was edged in lace at the tiered hem and short sleeves. Andrew had had no trouble falling asleep last night, but thinking about Olivia was the last thing he remembered.

"Then I can provide even more fascinating insight as to how an agricultural ranch operates," Daniel continued, as two Mexican servants, Ramon and Diego, appeared, wearing gray shirts and black pants with red

sashes about their waists. Diego placed a small
bowl of red chunky sauce on the table, then
served everyone from a large platter filled with
bacon, fat sausages and scrambled eggs mixed
with green peppers and onions. Ramon put a
basket of round fluffy looking rolls on the
table, then served what looked like light
yellow gruel from a large bowl.

Selina and Gabriel, seated across from their
father and Aunt Olivia, giggled among
themselves as they looked at food unlike
anything they'd ever seen.

"That food might look strange to you,"
Lori said to them from the foot of the table,
"but it's mighty good."

"We eat bacon," Selina said, "and
sausages, but I've never seen any that look like
these."

"That's called chorizo," Olivia smiled.

"And what's this yellow stuff?" Gabriel
asked, pointing to the once runny substance
that had now congealed on his plate. Then
looking at the bread basket he asked, "And
what kind of rolls are those?"

"The uh—yellow stuff is—buttered grits,"
Lori said, "and those rolls are called biscuits.
They're delicious with butter and jam."

Andrew watched Olivia put the red
chunky sauce on her eggs, so he did the same.
She grinned at the children, then said to
Daniel, "Father, is it really necessary to bore

Andrew with more details about the ranch? You can't make dairy cows, alfalfa, barley or beans that exciting. Perhaps he'd rather do something else."

Andrew coughed, then took a long drink of water. "I'm sorry," he said, embarrassed, then wiped his mouth with a white cloth napkin. "This red sauce," his voice sounded slightly hoarse, "it's quite robust. I've never tasted anything like it."

"Oh, Andrew," Lori said, "I apologize. I should have warned you. Mexican food is rather spicy, but we've grown accustomed to it, and developed a taste for it."

"That's called salsa," Olivia said. "I couldn't live without it, but you might want to steer clear of it while you're here. It may not agree with you."

"I appreciate the advice," Andrew smiled. "Now, as far as learning how the ranch operates, I don't mind that at all. Business is business. And I've been talking to your father about buying some of his property. Not to pursue ranching, of course, but to develop the land. As I wrote, my business here is twofold. Most importantly, it's for the children, but secondly, I'm always on the lookout for business opportunities."

"Then tomorrow," Olivia said, "why don't you plan on visiting my ranch?"

"I'd be delighted!"

"I'll give you the guided tour myself," Olivia said. "We'll pack up the children in a wagon and take a picnic with us. We'll enjoy the scenery of the land, rather than the mechanics. You'll have your share of that today with Father."

"That sounds splendid," Andrew gazed at Olivia for a long moment. "I think I'm beginning to — fall in love — with California."

"We love California, too!" Gabriel said, "Don't we, Lina?"

Selina nodded enthusiastically. "May we please be excused?" She asked her grandmother. "We want to play outside."

Lori looked at their plates. Both of them had messed over the biscuits and grits, but they'd eaten all their eggs and chorizo. "I see you prefer the Mexican food to what we eat in the South." She seemed a little disappointed. "Well, as long as it's all right with your father, you may leave the table."

After Andrew excused them, Lori called for Maria to take them outside. When she appeared, Selina and Gabriel quickly ran off with her.

Catching Andrew's eyes, Lori took a deep breath. "Falling in love with California is easy." She sounded wary.

An awkward silence followed, then Andrew said, "Perhaps I — might even move here."

"That's rather hasty," Lori replied quickly. "You'd certainly need more time to make a major decision like that. And how would the children take to being so far away from their mother?"

Andrew dropped his gaze for a moment. Trying not to sound perturbed, he said, "As I mentioned last night, the children don't see that much of Lavinia. The theater takes most of her time, and she likes it that way."

"Andrew," Olivia said. His eyes met hers. "Stay here as long as you like. Mother told me she hoped that you and the children would consider staying the whole summer — so don't hesitate to extend your visit."

"I'll seriously consider that," Andrew said.

Chapter 31

After breakfast the next morning, Olivia dressed quickly in her bedroom for the wagon ride with Andrew and the children. She slipped on a white blouse, rust colored vest and black split skirt. The skirt was shorter than her mother would have liked, a few inches below the knee, instead of a few inches above the ankle, but Olivia didn't care.

"Some slaves barely had clothes enough to cover themselves," Mother had said once, "and you prance around in split skirts almost half naked and proud of it!" She was so old fashioned, Olivia thought, and didn't appreciate the mobility afforded by modern, less modest clothes.

She was beginning to detest living at Rolando with her parents. She had no trouble with Father, yet Mother seemed to become more over-protective each day. *You'll never get married again if...I don't want to see you hurt again, so never...*

Her fretting was endless, yet Mother's worries were preferable to living alone in the main house at her own ranch. The sinister events that had ocurred there not long ago put that out of the question.

Olivia sat on the bed and pulled on black boots. Then she grabbed her black bolero hat from the dresser. Olivia thought she was ready, until she glanced in the mirror. She put the hat down, then pinched her cheeks to redden them. Mother didn't approve of makeup. "One painted whore in the family is enough," she'd said, since actresses — and whores — were the only women who wore it.

The redness in Olivia's pinched cheeks faded quickly. She did have a few homemade concoctions that Mother seemed not to mind, at least not too much. So Olivia opened her top dresser drawer and frantically searched for her powder puff, a container of rice powder, and a little jar of beet juice mixed with cornstarch.

She found all the items near the back, since she rarely used them. Olivia dipped her finger into the beet juice mixture and rubbed a smidgen into each cheek. Then she worked a little of the color into her lips before hastily applying rice powder to her face with the puff.

Olivia wondered why she was bothering, and worse yet, why she was painting her face as if she were Lavinia. She grabbed a cloth and dunked it in her wash bowl, but before scrubbing her face, Olivia studied her reflection. She did look more youthful—and felt more beautiful.

After cleaning the finger tip she'd used to apply her makeup, she put the cloth down. She'd decided to keep her painted face. After all, she wasn't eighteen anymore. Adjusting the neck string on her bolero hat, she tried to convince herself not to be concerned about what Andrew thought of her looks. Although she knew he found her attractive, notions of becoming involved with him in any way were farfetched at best.

Olivia had almost come to believe that she'd never marry again. No finer man existed than Joshua; he'd been her dream come true. Olivia did want children, though having them with a young man would be preferable to having them with an older widower who already had grown children.

Sometimes she had to convince herself that she wasn't barren. If Joshua hadn't died, she wouldn't have suffered through the stress that caused her to lose that child. But what if children weren't in God's plan for her? This brought tears to Olivia's eyes, but she managed to hold them back.

Any man her age wanted to wed a young girl. Olivia blew out a breath. Maybe she'd live the rest of her years unmarried, and clinging to Joshua's memory. A depressing thought, she reflected, but as Tennyson wrote, "better to have loved and lost, than never to have loved at all."

Olivia was flattered by Andrew's attention. That was enough — or was it? Olivia couldn't deny her overwhelming attraction to him, which almost frightened her, leaving her to wonder, could she trust herself?

After putting on black riding gloves, Olivia quickly left her bedroom and hurried down the stairs. Andrew and the children waited in the foyer. Upon seeing her, Andrew said, "You look lovely."

Olivia's rapidly pounding heart disturbed her.

****

"This seems the perfect day to survey your ranch," Andrew said, as Olivia drove him and the children to Charlton Place. Selina and Gabriel rode in the wagon bed.

The wind carried the salty fragrance of the ocean. With mountains visible in the distance, Olivia rode on a dirt road dotted with locust trees.

Although Andrew attempted to take in the

lay of the land, his eyes strayed back to Olivia. Her astonishing beauty proved to be a distraction.

"Living here, I rarely complain about the weather!" Olivia laughed.

It was a sunny day, with seagulls gliding through the air, and despite a hazy scattering of long white clouds, the sky remained a dazzling blue.

When Olivia drove past rolling violet fields, Selina, begged her to stop. "Aunt Olivia! Look at all those beautiful purple flowers. I want to pick some for you!"

Olivia smiled. "Selina, that's very sweet of you, but those flowers are a crop I'm growing called alfalfa."

"That's a funny name!" Selina exclaimed.

"It may sound funny," Olivia said, "but it is pretty to look at. I'm growing it to feed my livestock."

Moments later, Andrew heard swift hoof beats approach them from behind. He glanced over his shoulder to see Johnny Cahill galloping to greet them on a paint horse, speckled with splotches of brown and white.

Olivia pulled on the reins to prevent her gray shire from going any further. "Good morning, Johnny!" she smiled.

Cahill halted his horse abruptly, only inches from the wagon. The animal reared up, circling its head wildly, as though objecteing to

the sudden stop. It's pink lips gnawed at the
bits in irritation.

"Selina, it's the cowboy again!" Gabe said,
scrambling to the other side of the wagon
where Cahill was.

Selina followed her brother. Each of them
wore short sleeved blue rompers with closed
toe leather sandals.

"Mornin', Miz. Cummins," Cahill said. He
tipped his hat, then flashed that crooked smile.
"You're lookin' a mite sprightly. I ain't seen
you lookin' this cheerful in a long time."

Eagerly eying Cahill's gun belt, Gabe,
smiled brightly. "Hi!" He shouted.

"How you kids doin' today?" Cahill asked.

"Fine," Selina replied, softly.

From his horse, Cahill leaned toward
Selina. "You sure look mighty pretty, Miss."
Selina looked down, then took a few steps
back. Standing behind her father, she placed
her arms around his neck.

"Don't be rude," Andrew said, patting
Selina's hands, "say thank you."

"Thank you," Selina mumbled.

"You didn't forget what you told me,"
Gabriel said, "that when I'm bigger you'll
teach me to shoot!"

Cahill laughed. "You gotta talk your pa
into that first!" When Johnny's eyes moved to
Andrew, his smile diminished. "Mornin', Mr.
Standish. You enjoyin' your stay 'round these

parts?"

Andrew gazed at Olivia for a moment, then saw a full blown scowl scorch Cahill's face. "Very much."

Looking Andrew up and down, he remarked. "You ain't all suited up like last time I saw you."

"Not for today's outing." Andrew wore a broad brimmmed hat and boots. His attempt at more casual western attire consisted of brown trousers and a matching vest worn over a white shirt, with no collar or tie.

"Is everything all right, Johnny?" Olivia asked.

"Everything's runnin' smooth as a whistle, ma'am, you don't need to worry yourself none."

"I never do, not with you around."

Cahill eyed Andrew sharply for a moment. "Thank you, Miz. Cummins, I appreciate that."

"Well," Olivia said, "we'd best be moving on, I'm just giving Mr. Standish and the children a tour of the place."

Cahill tipped his hat again, then winked at Gabriel. "Adios, amigo." While Gabriel giggled, Cahill gave Andrew a cutting smirk. "I won't keep you folks. Enjoy looking around." Turning his horse from them, he yelled over his shoulder, "There ain't nothing like this in New York." As he rode away, his horse kicked up large clouds of dust while galloping briskly down the dry dirt road.

Olivia flicked the reins to start her horse again. After a brief silence, Gabriel hugged Olivia, grasping her from behind like Selina held Andrew.

"Lina, don't you think Aunt Olivia looks more like me than Mother?"

Andrew glanced back, watching as Selina studied her brother and aunt.

"I guess," Selina said, "but I look more like Mother."

"*Both* of you look like your mother's children," Andrew remarked.

Gabriel took his arms from around Olivia. "Lina, I think Father should hug Aunt Olivia."

"I think you're right!" Selina laughed, placing one of Andrew's arms around her aunt's shoulder. "Hug her, Father."

Feeling awkward and a little embarrassed, Andrew removed his arm from Olivia, but only after he'd let it linger a second longer than necessary. "I'll hug her, if she doesn't mind."

Olivia smiled, but kept her eyes focused straight ahead as she drove. "I don't."

Andrew took a deep breath, but before he could raise his arms, Selina and Gabriel pushed him into Olivia. "Hug her now!" they said together. Trying not to make Olivia feel uncomfortable, Andrew gave her a brief embrace. To his surprise, however, she leaned close to him for a moment.

Gabriel clapped. "Hug her again!"

"I think that's enough hugging for now," Andrew laughed.

Distracted, the children paid him no attention. They ran to the rear of the wagon, as Selina shouted, "Deers!" She pointed off in the distance toward tall grass and yellow wildflowers where two fawns raised their heads from eating.

"Deer, Selina." Andrew looked too, not used to seeing wildlife. "Singular and plural are the same."

"Those are mule deer, Olivia said, glancing toward the animals, "because they have large ears like mules."

"There's the mother!" Gabriel yelled, seeing a doe run off with the fawns. "Maybe we'll see another deer family if we keep looking."

With the children occupied, Andrew said, "I don't think Mr.Cahill likes me."

Olivia dismissed this with a slight laugh. "I wouldn't be too concerned with what Johnny thinks of you."

"I'm not, but what do you think of him?"

"Johnny? Oh...he's not very polished, but he's sharp. The type who's good with figures and details. Johnny's been managing the place going on three years now, and he does a substantial amount of work for me."

"Such as?"

"Well, he's in charge of bookkeeping, supervising the foremen and making decisions regarding the crops. I've become quite dependent on his opinions about weather and pest problems. I'll ask Cahill what he thinks about something, and then ask Father. Nine times out of ten, their answers are the same.

"When I, or we, Joshua and I, took over the operation of the ranch, Cahill's uncle, Tommy Douglas, was the general manager. Father had known him for years. He'd worked at Rolando before coming here, and my father trusted him implicitly! Johnny is Douglas's nephew, actually his sister's stepson. So Tommy asked if we'd be willing to hire him as an assistant. My father didn't really like Johnny at first— but—"

"Does your father like him now?" Andrew asked.

"Oh, he doesn't mind Johnny. Father sees that he's quite capable and knows what he's doing."

"And Cahill's never disappointed you?"

"Never. I've told him many times he's indispensable. His uncle was killed on a day off in Los Angeles. After that, Johnny insisted he could take over as general manager. He practically begged for the position, so Joshua and I decided to give him a chance. Johnny grabbed the reins; stepped right in and took his uncle's place. He's been doing a fine job ever since.

"After Joshua died—Johnny was there for me. He was concernd about my well being, always asked if I needed anything...Hard as it may be for you to believe, he was very kind to me during that difficult time." Olivia smiled. "I'm sorry he doesn't seem to like you. Perhaps—he's not fond of New Yorkers," she teased.

"I don't doubt that," Andrew said.

Chapter 32

"Grandmother packed fried chicken. Now my stomach's growling for it!" Gabriel said.

Andrew had been too preoccupied admiring Olivia's beauty, as well as the scenery, to think about food. But now, a little before noon, his children felt differently.

"And I shall die if we don't eat," Selina announced.

"Dramatic, just like your mother," Olivia laughed.

Selina frowned. "Is that bad?"

Olivia raised her brows in surprise. "No, sweetheart—you're just very expressive—and make your feelings known. That's not bad. And since I don't want you to starve, I think I can find a shady spot for lunch."

Several minutes later, Olivia drove the

wagon down into a grassy valley scattered with blue lilac shrubs. She pulled alongside a towering pepper tree with fern shaped leaves that droopped like curtains from its winding branches.

As a gentle breeze swirled around them, Andrew inhaled, smelling lilac, orange blossom, and honeysuckle. He helped Olivia from the wagon, but the children jumped off, running away to explore.

Over the grass, Andrew and Olivia spread a Mexican blanket woven with broad stripes of red, blue, black and green. Afterwards, Andrew carried the large picnic basket from the wagon, and then Olivia unpacked the contents of cold fried chicken, bread, cheese, pickles, fresh fruit, and cookies.

Without being called, the children appeared almost magicallly, then ate ravenously, relishing the joy of eating the chicken with their fingers. Once they'd devoured several fresh figs and sugar cookies for dessert, Gabe set about industriously collecting sticks.

Selina, meanwhile, plopped down comfortably in her father's lap. As Olivia used a cotton napkin to wipe her niece's greasy fingers, Selina said, "Father, is something wrong with Aunt Olivia?"

Olivia stopped cleaning Selina's hands for a moment and looked at her. "You think something's wrong with me?"

"There must be," Selina replied.

Andrew, taken aback by his daughter's remarks, said, "No, darling, there's nothing wrong with Aunt Olivia. Why do you ask?"

"You keep staring at her!" At this, Olivia turned red. "Oh no!" Selina exclaimed, looking at her aunt's red cheeks. "Now she's blushing since she knows you stared at her!"

Andrew felt his own face flush.

"Father, why are *you* blushing? You're not being stared at — she is! Why?"

Chagrinned, Andrew hesitated. "It's just that — Aunt Olivia — is very beautiful."

Selina pursed her lips. "It's *rude* to stare."

"Then, Selina, my dear," Andrew laughed. "I'll do my best to — mind my manners."

"Good. You've learned a lesson, then." Selina wriggled from Andrew's lap. She yelled to her brother, who held a large bundle of sticks. "Gabe," she pointed to the pepper tree shading Andrew and Olivia, "let's climb this tree."

More than willing, Gabriel immediately dropped his sticks and ran to his sister.

After they attempted a few tries at climbing, Andrew lifted the children, one at a time, about six feet off the ground and set them in a large crook of the tree. He let them stay there for a few moments, then lowered them to the ground and watched them run off to play.

Now alone with Olivia, Andrew tried his best to act as though the earlier exchange with Selina had never occurred. While Olivia watched her neice and nephew playing, Andrew helped himself to one more eyeful of her. She'd removed her hat, revealing reddish brown hair that glistened gold under the sunlight beaming through the leaves of the pepper tree. To break the silence, Andrew took a breath to start a conversation, but Olivia spoke first.

"I hope you're enjoying your stay here," she said. Andrew gazed around him. "In California, I mean."

"I am—very much." Another silence followed. "The land here is beautiful."

Olivia smiled. "It is—and now there are lots of developers from the East coming out this way to buy it up."

Andrew returned her smile. "Present company included."

"I certainly didn't mean to imply anything negative by that," Olivia said quickly. "Father's sold lots of land to them—and prospered significantly. So I, personally, have nothing against land-grabbers."

Slightly taken aback, Andrew said, "I hope that's not how you think of me."

Olivia blushed slightly. "Of course not. I didn't mean that to slip out. You don't seem at all like a typical robber baron." Putting fingers to her lips, Olivia grinned. "Again, I'm letting my words get the better of me—please don't take offense."

"I won't—but you must know that while I was in L.A., I did have some business dealings with H.E. Huntington."

"H.E. Huntington!" Olivia exclaimed. "He is a land-grabber!" She laughed.

"He's—actually a business acquaintance, from New York," Andrew said. "When H.E. learned I'd be coming this way, he suggested I time my visit to coincide with his. He wanted me to see the prospective land, and of course, his trolley system. H.E. mentioned that there are plans to move a line out this way soon.

"Even though I'd always wanted to travel out this way, I had no idea I ever really would. But a couple of years ago, H.E. told me something I've never forgotten. He said that any bright young business fellow couldn't make a mistake in coming to southern California."

Olivia angled her gaze from Andrew toward the children. They played a good distance away, happily rolling down a grassy hill. "I suppose that's true," Olivia said. "And it's inevitable that anyone involved with land development in southern California would have to deal with Mr. Huntington. He has so many interests here. Father's sold him land. "

Both were quiet for a few moments. Although Olivia had seemed lighthearted about his "land-grabbing" business dealings, Andrew wondered if, because of that, she thought any less of him.

"I must make it clear," he began, "that my company has always been generous and fair with its employees. Ironworkers on up. As for land grabbing, if I see an opportunity to buy a piece of property that appears valuable to me, I buy it at a fair price. My brother and I own a good deal of rental property in New York. We make sure that the buildings are well maintained, and the rents reasonable. So rest assured, Olivia, I'm not a robber baron, a land grabber, or a slum lord, for that matter."

"That's good to know. But would you have told me if you were?" She winked playfully.

"You'll have to trust me."

"I do," Olivia said seriously, "otherwise, I wouldn't bring up what I'm about to discuss with you — it's something I've been thinking about for a while."

"What is it?"

She gazed down, tracing the colorful stripes of the blanket with her finger. "I've decided — that I'm going to sell my ranch. Since Joshua died, I don't want it anymore. Josh let Cahill and me handle the ranch while he did his medical work. During the school year, Cahill practically handles everything, since I'm busy teaching."

Clasping her hands, she was quiet for a moment. "Joshua was never a rancher at heart. He loved helping people more than anything."

Feeling competitive for Olivia's attention as she spoke of Joshua, Andrew stretched, flexing his muscles.

"And since he died," Olivia continued, "I've lost my enthusiasm for ranching. I just want to teach now. I told Father that unless he wanted this property, I'd like to sell it, and he's fine with that."

"Then perhaps," Andrew said, "in addition to buying some of your father's land, I'll buy your ranch, as well. You let me know your price, and I'll get my funds in order when I go back to New York. Just don't accuse me of being a land grabber."

"I won't!" She laughed. "I'll be glad to sell you this place, and—I suppose—you'll do some conversion of sorts—subdivide, then sell at a much higher price. You have no interest at all in agricultural production, only the profits from land sales."

Andrew felt his face flush slightly. Feeling a little defensive he said, "I am a business man; and you said you wouldn't accuse me of being a land grabber."

"I didn't," Olivia insisted. "I'm sorry if it sounded like I did. But what I said was true—

wasn't it?"

After an uncomfortable moment, Andrew replied, "I suppose."

"I've learned quite a bit about developers through the land Father's sold, and I've learned how they operate," Olivia said. "At one time Father owned fifty-thousand acres, but he's downsized considerably. Now each ranch only has a few thousand. Whoever buys this place will develop it anyway, so it might as well be you. I've been ready to give it up for a long time."

Andrew's mind wandered for a moment. Not only would he like to grab Olivia's land, he'd love to grab her body. He'd take whatever she was willing to give up.

"I don't—even stay out here anymore," she said, pulling him from his sordid thoughts. Olivia reached for a navel orange, then began peeling it. "Andrew, I feel—almost silly telling you this—but—after Joshua died, strange things started happening at the house—at night time. I heard odd sounds—like footsteps on the roof—and rattling chains. My housekeeper and her husband, and a few of the ranch men, live in rooms located in the wings on either side of the house. I trust them all—at least I thought I did, until the noises started.

"There's no inside entry to the house from the wings, but if someone wanted to get in and harm me, I'm sure it would be easy enough to find a way. When I asked about the sounds, no one else said they'd heard them. The men volunteered to take turns keeping watch for me every night, including Johnny.

"He doesn't live in the wings, though. He's got a cottage about a mile from my house, but some of the men told him what was going on. He was upset that I hadn't informed him myself — and he assured me he wouldn't let anything happen to me. Johnny's the one that arranged a night watch schedule — and once the men started patrolling, the noises stopped.

"So, after that, I told Johnny to call off the night watches. Mainly because I couldn't keep imposing on him, and all the men that way. For all I know, those sounds could have been my imagination. But I became so nervous about sleeping in the house alone — that I started living with my parents again." Olivia finished peeling the orange and tore it in two. Handing half to Andrew, she said, "I'm no braver than a frightened little girl."

"I don't blame you for moving," he said, concerned. "You need to be safe. And there's no safer place than being with those you love." He gazed at her, feeling the need to protect her, as well as the need of wanting her.

Chapter 33

"Olivia," Lori said, sitting at the foot of the dining room table. She glared at her daughter, seated next to her. They were alone after dinner, as Andrew and Daniel had left the table to take the children outside to play. "Mr. Standish has only been here a short while, and you're all but throwing yourself at him!"

"Mother!" Olivia blinked with unbelieving eyes.

"You told him to extend his visit—"

"But that's what you wanted—for the children to stay for the entire—"

"And then you invited him to visit your ranch without a chaperone."

"Chaperone? It was an outing with the children!"

"It wasn't appropriate!"

"Appropriate! I'm a grown woman!"

Lori clicked her tongue. "You'd have to be

blind not to see the way that man looks at you!"

Olivia took a deep breath and stood up angrily. "Maybe I *like* the way he looks at me! I'm an old widow—thirty-two going on thirty-three, and it's been a long time since any man's looked at me like he has."

"Olivia, that's not true! There are several suitable gentlemen who've expressed an interest in you—and none of them are divorced! Let no man put asunder, that's what the Bible says."

Olivia's mouth tightened. "I meant to say that any *desireable* man has looked at me! Besides, the gentlemen you speak of are widowers, and not one is under fifty. Before long I'd be a nurse, not a wife! If Andrew finds me attractive, so be it. Perhaps I find him attractive too!"

Lori's hand flew to her heart. "Olivia, how can you say such a thing? He's a married man!"

"Soon to be divorced!"

"Yes! And if that isn't horrible enough, he's soon to be *divorced* from your sister!"

"She doesn't want him!" In tears, Olivia fled the room, but her mother followed closely behind.

Lori grabbed her daughter's arm. "Olivia—think—think about what you're doing! At the dinnner table, Andrew went on and on about the wonderful time he and the children had today—and you sat there beaming like a young girl in love. You're a delightful eyeful to him, nothing more. He married one Negro woman not knowing what she was. He won't make that mistake again, especially when there's no mistaking what you are!"

"Mother, why are you—"

"I know you're overly emotional right now, with all the tragedy you've experienced," Lori interrupted. "You can't replace Joshua— but you shouldn't even entertain the idea of becoming involved with Andrew. It woudn't be proper. I want what's best for you, and Lavinia's soon-to-be divorced husband isn't. You don't know what could happen between them in the future—they do have two children together. You'd be setting yourself up to get hurt all over again."

"Mother—*you're* the one who's overly emotional! Who said anything about becoming involved with him? It was only a wagon ride!" Olivia tore from her Mother's grasp and ran upstairs.

Chapter 34
One Month Later

In the early morning hours, Andrew stood on the veranda of the Rolando Ranch house thinking about the decision he'd made and why. He and the children had been in southern California for about seven weeks. They'd spent an entire month with the Taylors but Andrew had chosen to extend their visit for a couple more weeks. Not only had Andrew fallen in love with California, he'd fallen in love with Olivia.

Watching the ruby red sun glimmer above the horizon, Andrew reflected that falling in love with her wasn't something he'd planned to do; it just seemed to have happened. Andrew wasn't sure if her feelings matched his, but if they did, he wished to pursue a courtship with her, and eventually marry her.

However, he could already hear his brother telling him what a fool he was. Julian and Serene wouldn't harbor any prejudice toward Olivia for being Negro. Sworn to secrecy about Lavinia's ancestry, they didn't like her any less for it, not that they *could* have liked her any less. One of Julian's closest friends at MIT had been a colored fellow from Boston. Unable to pursue a career in America, he'd moved to Europe. Now, quite successful in Austria, he owned a contracting company there, and at least once a year, he and his Austrian wife visited Julian in New York.

Yet Andrew believed Julian would think he'd jumped from the frying pan into the fire, by marrying a woman he'd known only briefly — who also happened to be Lavinia's sister!

"Maybe she's just like her sister — only worse," he'd say. "You just don't know it yet, because you lose your senses when you fall in love!"

Although Julian didn't have a problem with his one colored friend and didn't dislike colored people in general, he'd made it clear that, in his opinion, Negroes, with a few exceptions, like his friend, were inferior to whites. And Julian would surely point out that that's how most white people felt. "Just think of the hard time you'll have if you marry her," he'd say. "She can't exactly *hide* the fact that she's colored — like your first wife did so successfully."

After much introspection, Andrew had to admit something to himself. Although he preferred to think that he actually did believe a man's character lay beneath the skin, deep down, before meeting Olivia and Lori, his true feelings had been somewhat similar to Julian's. And now he thought about the rest of society.

Adhering to the acceptable standards of society hadn't been something Andrew tended to concern himself with. With his money and connections, he considered himself invulnerable. He'd already married an actress, and now was divorcing her, but would marrying a colored woman be pushing beyond the restraints of invulnerability?

Julian's was the voice of doubt that plagued Andrew. "She'll be bad for business...Some will think you've lost your mind...How will you be accepted socially...What about the children...And if you have children with her, what will they look like..."

Andrew sighed. Perhaps thoughts of loving Olivia and marrying her *were* foolish. He'd pondered this more than a few times, but couldn't refrain from thinking about her, or from constantly wanting to be near her.

Daniel had succeeded against the odds, Andrew reflected, and during a much harder time, so why couldn't he? Daniel and Lori were an upstanding couple, respected in the community with a number of friends, black and white. Andrew thought about this for a long time before deciding that he was invulnerable enough to marry Olivia. As a powerful white man of wealth and influence, he believed he'd suffer no major repercussions.

While the sun rose high, Andrew realized that not being with her wasn't an option. At that moment, he lowered his head and began to pray with fervency, something he'd never done, that God would make a way.

After several minutes of prayer, Andrew outlined his plan. It was his intention to move to California with Selina and Gabriel. They enjoyed living here, and they loved their Aunt Olivia. Before he could visualize a location for his southern California office, he was interrupted by a slight tug on his trousers.

It was Selina. Freshly awake and bright eyed, she wore a little red bathrobe over her nightshirt. Looking up at him, she said, "Father, since you and Mother won't be married anymore, will you marry aunt Olivia?"

Andrew reached to pick her up. Kissing her cheek, he said, "We'll see, sweetheart."

Chapter 35

Making sure Olivia watched, Andrew swam in broad strong strokes, a good distance from the shore. Now he stood, in water up to his shoulders, looking toward her. Smiling, she appeared impressed, as did the children, who stood next to her on the sand, jumping up and down clapping.

Wading back to shore, Andrew paused. The ocean, waist deep now, sloshed around him. When would be the perfect time? He asked himself. When would the opportunity present itself to him to tell Olivia that he loved her? Andrew watched as she walked on the beach with the children. Gabriel's bathing costume, a black unitard, resembled his father's.

Olivia began waving to him. She and Selina wore black as well, but their attire, short dresses with short puffed sleeves worn over bloomers, was more cumbersome in the waves. "Come out of the water!" Olivia yelled over the crashing waves and the squawk of seagulls. "Selina and Gabriel want you to help them build sandcastles!"

Andrew strode from the water, enjoying the pull of the current and the thrashing of the blue green waves around him. The Pacific was a bit rougher than the Atlantic. Breathing in the salty ocean spray, he neared the shore. The sand, firm and white under a cloudless sky, stretched for miles like a floor on either side. The children ran to him, splashing through frothy water surrounding their ankles.

"Come on, Father!" They shouted together.

Each child grabbed one of his hands, then began running, pulling him toward Aunt Olivia, who sat smiling on the shore with tin pails and shovels ready to start construction. The warm wind blew her hair, which sparkled as though adorned with diamonds. The sun shone on droplets of the Pacific adhering to her tresses, making her appear an angel in the ocean mist.

"My help wasn't good enough!" Olivia laughed. "They said you build things for a living so you'd build a much better castle than I ever could."

Selina knelt beside her. "We didn't mean

to hurt your feelings, Aunt Olivia," she said sincerely.

Gabriel sat on Olivia's other side, then put his arms around her. "Honest we didn't."

Hugging Gabriel back, then encircling Selina with one arm and pulling her close, Olivia smiled. "Children, my feelings aren't hurt! Your father is a builder, and I'm not that good at building at all, not even with sand."

"We'd never want to make you feel bad," Gabriel said. "We love you, Aunt Olivia."

"Yes, Aunt Olivia," Selina said. "We love you very, very much!"

Tears glistened in Olivia's eyes. "I love you, too."

Seeing her tears Gabriel asked, "Why are you sad?"

"I'm not," Olivia smiled. "Sometimes when you're very happy, you cry. And right now I'm very happy to know that you love me." The three of them hugged.

Andrew marveled at his children. How easy it was for them to express their love for her.

"Father," Gabriel said, "all four of us should hug, and you tell Aunt Olivia that you love her, too!"

Andrew knelt down and embraced all three of them. "Olivia — I love you..."

****

Andrew watched amused as Selina yawned, declaring, "But Father, I'm not sleepy."

"Me either," Gabriel said, blinking heavy eyes.

Andrew and the children sat with Olivia at her round dining room table in the Charlton Place ranch house.

"Your father's right, children," Olivia smiled. "That trip to the beach wore both of you out and you need a nap. Your grandmother has a nice outing planned later this afternoon at the carnival, so you need to rest."

"Can we go back to the beach tomorrow?" Selina asked. "I want to collect more shells and play in the waves."

"And can we have lunch at your house again?" Gabe said. "I really liked the empandas!"

After Olivia had taken all of them surf bathing at the beach, they'd come back to Charlton Place. This was the first time they'd been inside her house, and they'd come here for sandwiches Olivia's housekeeper had prepared. The woman had also made empanadas, cookies that resembled spicy fruit turnovers. The children loved them, but both had eaten one too many and complained of stomach aches. Despite this, Andrew thought, they were ready to come back and gorge themselves again tomorrow.

"I think we'll do something different," Andrew said.

"But perhaps, sometime next week," Olivia said, "we'll go to the beach and — "

A knock sounded at the front door. "Who could that — " Olivia gasped, standing quickly. "Oh, no!"

"What's wrong?" Andrew asked.

"That's Johnny. I was supposed to meet with him today." She looked at her wristwatch. The setting was engraved white gold. A length of black ribbon, cut and stitched at the ends, served as a wristband. "Now, as a matter of fact. I completely forgot. Andrew, please excuse me." She left the table, then called over her shoulder, "Take the children upstairs. There's clean linen on the bed in the first room on the right. They can nap there."

Andrew picked up Selina, who no longer complained of not being tired. After putting her arms around her father's neck, she buried her head in his shoulder.

"Come on, young man," Andrew said to Gabriel. "Upstairs for a nap."

"I'm a big boy, I don't need a nap." He yawned, following his father from the dining room. "But, maybe I'll just rest my eyes for a little while."

Andrew saw Cahill and Olivia talking in

the entrance foyer. When Andrew started up the stairs, Selina was sound asleep in his arms, but Gabriel waved enthusiastically at Cahill. Andrew nodded in greeting. Although Cahill granted the boy his crooked smile, all Andrew received was a cold glare in return.

Andrew walked to the designated bedroom, then tucked the children into the large double bed. By the time he left them, both were breathing heavily, bringing a smile to his face.

When Andrew reached the bottom of the stairs, Olivia was still talking to Cahill. Andrew strode past her to the parlor, then gazed at a collection of family photos hanging on a wall by the bookcase.

Olivia had shown them to him earlier. The children had enjoyed looking at two family photos that included their mother as a young girl, but had shown little interest in the others. Like Selina and Gabe, Andrew had been most fascinated by Lavinia's images. Daniel and Lori were in a recent picture, but he couldn't remember the names of the other relatives seen in the photographs — aside from Olivia's dead husband, whose name was seared into his mind by envy.

There was a white couple about Daniel and Lori's age. They lived in Ohio. Another picture showed Olivia's brother and his family posed in front of the Eiffel Tower. And then there was Joshua. He wore a black suit and tie. From this photographic portrait, he appeared a handsome, very dark, broad shouldered man.

"I'm sorry about that," Olivia said.

Andrew turned from the wall upon hearing her voice as she entered the room. "At the end of each month, I meet here with Johnny to discuss the end of month numbers. I rescheduled our meeting for a week from today. It won't take that long. I could have met with him now, I suppose...but I didn't want to be a horrible hostess."

Andrew smiled, then moved his gaze back to the wall of photos. "I was — a little surprised to see Lavinia's pictures here."

In one, she looked about fourteen and stood with her siblings behind their seated parents. Lavinia appeared a virtuous girl, innocent and demure, in a dark dress, its high collar trimmed in lace. In another, she was a small child in white sitting in a rocking chair. Her brother stood on one side of her in a suit with knee britches, while Olivia, also dressed in white, stood on her sister's opposite side. Lavinia sat tall, wearing a serious expression for a girl of about four. Even then, she appeared to be playing a role, perhaps a queen surrounded by her subjects.

"She *is* family," Olivia sighed. "But don't believe I haven't thought about cutting her image from these," she laughed. "That would be petty of me, though. We can't choose our relatives, can we?"

"No," his eyes moved to Joshua's photo, "only our mates." He paused for a moment. "You still...miss him...very much..."

"Yes..." Olivia gazed lovingly at her husband's picture.

Andrew felt pangs of envy riddle his insides. That sensation was foolish, he told himself. The man was dead, yet she looked at his photograph with a yearning Andrew wished she felt for him. Now she seemed to have forgotten Andrew's presence. He cleared his throat, attempting to break the hold the picture had over her.

Taking her eyes from Joshua's image, Olivia said, "I don't cry when I think about him anymore—well, not lately. I reflect on the happy times." A glowing smile brightened her face. A smile Andrew hoped would one day light her face for him. "That eases the pain some..."

Could Andrew compete with the memory of a dead man? He'd competed with many men among the living, in matters of love and business, and won. But would he have a chance against a memory held so tightly in Olivia's heart? Would she measure him by Joshua's standards? Would he even favorably compare?

If competing against a dead man wasn't

bad enough, Andrew was also competing against a Negro, something he'd never imagined. And not just any Negro, an exceptional Negro, a physician, upstanding and admired by his many patients, so Andrew had been told by several in the community of Little Ways, both black and white. From Joshua's photo, Andrew was jealous enough of his looks — but had he been stronger, more virile?

To be polite, Andrew said, "Tell me about him." Olivia looked surprised that he'd expressed interest. Yet he knew she'd be delighted to ramble on and on about him, as any woman would about a man she loved.

"You — really want me to?"

No, Andrew thought, but he needed to size up his competition. Regrettably, he bit out, "Well...sure."

For several seconds, she hesitated. Olivia didn't need words to express her love for Joshua. Her shimmering eyes and smile spoke volumes.

"He was...amazing...I could tell you all about — but I won't bore you." Andrew was relieved. "But the years we were married," Olivia said softly, "were the happiest of my life."

With those words, Andrew felt as if she'd plunged a dagger through his heart. "Olivia, you're young and beautiful," he said. "You do plan to marry again..."

Olivia was silent for a short while. "I—I—haven't given it that much thought. But...I do...wish I had my own children. I suppose that's still possible."

Hearing this, Andrew felt a small triumph. He turned his back to her, hiding a partial smile, then mumbled almost inaudibly, "What was Joshua like?"

"Pardon me? You asked what he was like?"

Turning to face her, Andrew nodded.

"Well...he...wasn't talented...in matters of business." She paused briefly. "But... he was kind...and compassionate."

Another dagger slowly worked its way in. Did she see any kindness and compassion in him, or was he only a calculating, underhanded land-grabber to her?

"Olivia, what about me?" Andrew said. "Do you consider my abilities to make money and employ men bad things?"

"No, Andrew, those are good things, and you're a good man. I could tell by the first letter we received from you. Lavinia drove you away. I'll never understand why she couldn't appreciate you."

Andrew stood quietly for a few seconds. Looking down at his fingers, not realizing he'd been fidgeting with them, he said, "The fact that I'm white—does that bother you?"

"No. My father's white...and...in a way, you remind me of my father."

Feeling hopeful, Andrew's brows rose in surprise. "Really?"

"You're both bold, you know what you want, and you go after it. You don't let obstacles stand in your way. You knock them down and keep going. Joshua was like that— to an extent." She exhaled deeply. "It's just so much harder when you're colored. Negro men have to fight further obstacles put in place by powerful white men, just like..."

"Like me?" Dagger number three found a snug place next to dagger two.

Olivia pursed her lips, embarrassed. "I *was* going to say that—but you're not all white men. I'm sorry. Forgive me?"

He smiled. "Of course."

"Andrew—I'll hate to see you go—you *and* the children," she added quickly. "Could you extend your trip perhaps even another week or so? I have no right to ask that—I know the children miss their mother—but I'll miss—I mean—I wish you weren't leaving."

Losing himself in the deep brown depths of her eyes, he said, "I'd rather not go at all..."

Olivia lowered her gaze for a moment as a rosy blush blossomed beneath her honey brown skin. "What—what about you, Andrew? I'm sure you'll...re-marry..."

"I hope to."

Olivia touched Andrew's arm. He covered her hand with his.

"I'll pray that God blesses you with a caring woman," Olivia said, "one who'll love you and your children. But especially that she'll love you, as I know you'll love her."

"Pray also — that she'll be like you."

Blushing again, Olivia moved her hand, but Andrew held onto her fingers, then kissed them before letting go.

"I — I should wake the children," Olivia stammered.

"But they've only been asleep for a few minutes."

"Oh." She glimpsed at her wristwatch. "So they have. Then I need to — um — check with my housekeeper about something."

When she turned to leave the room, Andrew grabbed her arm, forcing her to face him. "You're running away from me. Remember, when I see something I want, I go after it."

Olivia pulled from his grasp, smiling. "You're such a bandit," she teased.

Placing his hands on her shoulders, he said, "But you've captured my heart." Then he lowered his face to Olivia's and kissed her.

Chapter 36

The warmth of Andrew's lips filled Olivia with wanting, and as his kiss deepened, she felt the warm rush of need. Stepping close against him, Olivia wrapped her arms around his neck, breathing in the spicy scent of his cologne. As the fervor between them increased, Andrew moved his hands from her shoulders, then encircled them about Olivia's waist. He held her tightly. Kissing her with overwhelming intensity, Andrew pressed his muscular chest into the softness of Olivia's breasts, which welled above the stiff corset beneath her blouse.

Could she trust herself not to do anything foolish? She was nothing to him, but she wanted him. Lust of the flesh — that wasn't right. Besides, she didn't want to be a "white man's delightful eyeful," as Mother had so eloquently pointed out. Olivia wanted marriage, what she had with Joshua. And that was impossible with Andrew.

He'd been married to Lavinia, who was younger, more beautiful, fair — and fertile. Olivia shouldn't even be kissing Andrew, but it felt so right...and so...good...

Feeling the swell of his desire jolted Olivia to her senses. She pulled from his lips, then gently pushed him away. Breathing hard and feeling dizzy, as well as euphoric, she forced herself to say, "Andrew, please stop."

Andrew was breathing hard too, but at this, he took his arms from her and stepped back. "I'm sorry."

However, Olivia felt oddly disappointed that he hadn't protested her rejection. She actually wanted him to keep kissing her. "I hope you're not *really* sorry," she blurted.

He looked at her questioningly. "For overstepping my bounds as a gentleman."

"Oh...well...Andrew, it's not that I didn't want to kiss you — I did — it's just that — that I — that I can't..."

"That you can't forget about..."

Her eyes welled but she managed to hold back her tears. "About Joshua? He's dead...I know..."

"Olivia, I'm sorry. I shouldn't have mentioned — "

"Andrew, you don't need to apologize. Joshua has nothing to do with my feelings for you...I can't *stop* thinking about you...I *want* to be with you every moment. But I realize that things couldn't — I mean — you're still married — my sister is the mother of your children — and you're divorcing her."

"Olivia," Andrew said, looking at her for several moments, "I know you have reservations about me, but my feelings for you are honorable. We haven't known each other long...but I love you."

Olivia was silent, then asked in disbelief, "What?"

"When I first saw you, I was smitten. When I watched you with the children, I started falling in love with you."

Still unbelieving, Olivia felt her heart pound. "You love me? But — Andrew — you can't — "

"I'm sorry it bothers you that I'll be divorced. Your mother's disapproval is apparent. I can only hope — "

"I'm not my mother," Olivia said, putting a hand to her head. "Of course she'd have a conniption fit if...but what about *me*? I'm not white! Doesn't *that* bother you?"

"No."

"But you live in New York."

"I've decided to live here."

"What?"

"Olivia, I can leave New York behind, permanently. I want my life here with you."

"But—what about the children?"

"They love California."

"What about Lavinia? She—she—she's the children's mother!"

"Lavinia's desire is for the stage, nothing more. Olivia—do you want us to live here?"

"Yes! I mean no. I mean things couldn't possibly work between us!"

Andrew hesitated. "Olivia, I've known my share of beautiful women. But now I'm ready to be committed to someone for life. I wanted that when I married your sister.

"I'm thirty-nine. I don't want to squander any more time and I regret the years I wasted with Lavinia. The children are the only good thing to come from my marriage to her. Olivia, I'm telling you all of this, because you *are* what I want. I was beginning to think I'd never find that. And now that I have, I'm not giving up— unless you tell me—that you don't want me."

"I can't do that."

"Then marry me."

For several seconds Olivia said nothing. "M—marry you?" She walked slowly to a turquoise sofa near the bookcase and sank down. Andrew sat next to her. "Andrew— you're—you're not even a free man yet. I—I need time to think about this. And so do you. Do you realize how different your life would be — if you married me?"

"Olivia, I have thought about that.
But — with my resources — I've decided that's
not an issue to be concerned with."

He paused for a long time, looking deeply
into her eyes. "I won't beg you to marry me,
Olivia, but please think long and hard about it.
I'll leave you alone for a while. I saw a nice
rocking chair in the room with the children."
He glanced toward the bookshelf. Walking to
it, he pulled off a copy of *To Have and to Hold*.
"I'll go read for a while."

When Andrew left the parlor, Olivia felt
confused, light-headed, elated — and scared.
Was it really possible to marry him? The
children loved her as aunt, but would they love
her as step-mother? What would her own
mother say? What would her sister do?
Would his family even accept her?

Her eyes moved to the bookcase, only to
see the bold red letters on the spine of *The
Scarlet Letter* staring back at her. Olivia buried
her head in her hands. Is that what she was, an
adulteress? Andrew was after all, still
married — and she'd kissed him.

It had been scandalous and humiliating
enough for her parents when Lavinia had
eloped with a shady theater person and run off
to become an actress. How much worse would
it be for Olivia to marry Lavinia's *second*
husband after he'd *divorced* her?

What would people think? If it were ever known that she and Andrew had fallen in love before the dissolution of his marriage to Lavinia, would they look at Olivia and imagine a scarlet A emblazoned on her chest?

Letting out a long deep breath, Olivia leaned into the soft back of the velvet sofa. Gazing up at the timber covered ceiling, she wondered what to do. Then time stood still while she continued to contemplate every conceivable problem...as well as the feel of his touch...

****

Upon hearing the children run down the steps, Olivia glanced at her wristwatch. Over half an hour had passed since Andrew had left her alone. The children scampered into the parlor giggling. Each climbed on to the sofa, one on each side of their aunt, then hugged her around the waist.

"Please, oh please, oh please, Aunt Olivia, marry Father!" Gabriel said.

At the same time, Selina cried, "Yes, Aunt Olivia! You must! Please, please, please! Marry him!"

As the children squeezed her, Olivia heard Andrew's heavy footsteps. Moving her eyes from Selina and Gabe, she looked toward the doorway. When Andrew walked in, he smiled sheepishly. *He* wouldn't beg her to marry him,

Andrew had said, but apparently, he wasn't above asking his children to.

Chapter 37

"So you're pleased with the surveyor's report?" Daniel asked Andrew the next day as they rode a buggy into town to make a bank deposit. The bay horse galloped at a fast clip, while the wind blew strongly, stirring up dust, as well as the scent of ocean air, wild flowers and manure.

Before heading into town, Daniel had driven Andrew around his and Olivia's property where the surveyor had staked off the acreage Andrew would purchase.

"Completely, and you're agreeable to my price?" Andrew said as the buggy trounced over the bumby dirt road.

"I am, and Olivia says she's happy with what you're willing to pay for all of her acreage."

"She is. And I'm assuming that all of the men working for her won't have trouble finding employment once I start development there, though it won't be for a while."

"They shouldn't. There are other ranches, smaller ones, orchards, and with all the commercial development springing up in these parts, they should find good jobs. I can vouch for all of them."

Andrew remained silent for a few seconds. "Even Cahill?"

Daniel leaned against the black leather covering the buggy bench and smirked. Swatting the horse's rump, he said, "Maybe. Why do mention him?"

"Just curious. I believe Olivia said you didn't like him—initially."

"Well," Daniel hesitated, "he's proved himself to be a capable general manager—but at first, I had some reservations about him..."

The only sounds between them for several moments were swift hoofbeats and the jingle of reins. Then Andrew asked, "Such as?"

Daniel sighed. "I told Olivia and Joshua I didn't like Cahill because he was guarded about his past. And to me, he seemed too ingratiating, not genuine. But they wanted to give him a chance anyway.

"Olivia's been pleased with him, and Joshua was, too." Daniel stared straight ahead down the dusty road, then met Andrew's eyes.

"Perhaps I was wrong in my — initial assessment of him. But...something about his uncle's death...has always bothered me. Tommy Douglas was a fine man — and the prior general manager of Charlton Place."

"So — what happened — regarding Douglas's death?"

Daniel hesitated, moving his eyes back to the road. "I don't know for sure, and I shouldn't say things that are only rooted in my suspicions, not facts. Cahill's never given Olivia a reason to be dissatified with his work, and he helped her quite a bit after Joshua died. So, my daughter can vouch for the man better than I can. Cahill will find work somewhere — maybe he can be hired in that hotel you plan to build. Olivia said you want to raze her house and put one on that spot."

"That's something we discussed, if I don't resell that acreage. But she'd prefer I put a hotel somewhere else and remodel the house to make it into an inn."

Daniel smiled sadly, meeting Andrew's gaze. "I suppose she's still attached to the place — because of Joshua. But, it'll be your property. You can do whatever you want with it."

"I'd like to honor her wishes, so I told her I'd inspect it, and assess it's condition."

"That's kind of you." Daniel paused, then feeling awkward said, "Now — Andrew, there's something else — that we — need to talk about."

For a moment, Daniel looked forward feeling uncertain of how to proceed. Finally, he decided being direct was the best course of action, even though what he wanted to discuss involved a matter of the heart, not a business transaction. "I've seen the way you look at Olivia, and I've seen the way she looks at you. And I've heard the children...talking..."

Now Andrew's eyes moved from Daniel's to focus on the road.

"I'm concerned about my daughter," Daniel continued. "I don't want you sending any kind of messages that could be misconstrued by a female in a delicate emotional condition."

Meeting Daniel's gaze, Andrew said, "Daniel — I'd never do anything to hurt Olivia...as a matter of fact — I've fallen in love with her."

"Fallen in love with her — while you're still married to her sister?"

"Daniel — I know my current circumstances aren't ideal — but if she'll have me — after I'm divorced — I'd like to marry her."

Daniel remained silent for several moments, then blew out a deep breath. "I love Lavinia. I'm her father...but at the same time — I know that girl could drive a man insane. She caused her mother and me many a sleepless night, so I understand you wanting to end your marriage.

"Now, this situation of yours—it may not be right—but at this point—I just want to see Olivia happy again. She didn't deserve what happened to her...and if you can make her happy...you have my blessing. Maybe God will understand. But my wife might have a difference of opinion..."

Chapter 38

"He asked you what?!"

Olivia dreaded hearing what her mother would have to say. Trying not to roll her eyes, Olivia sat alone with her outside on the long front veranda. Her presence today seemed to make the salty smell in the air stronger than the fragrance of rose vines around them.

"Mother," Olivia said calmly, "you heard me the first time." She crossed her arms as they sat on a wooden porch swing. Olivia concentrated on the pleasant creak of the swing in an attempt to tune out the critical words.

Lori put her foot down to stop the swing from swaying. "Has the man lost his mind? He's still married! And what about you, Olivia? You haven't done anything foolish, have you?"

"No!" Olivia replied, insulted. She leaned back hard, to start the swing swaying and creaking once more.

"I trust you told him you couldn't possibly marry him. Besides, he isn't serious."

"Mother!"

"He just wants to charm your clothes off, then after he's damaged you, he'll say he's reconsidered things and come to his senses!"

Olivia clicked her tongue. "Andrew is an honorable man!"

"He's a man, Olivia—and worse yet, a white man!"

"Father's white!"

"That's different," Lori said primly. "Your father and I were practically raised together, and he grew up believing in abolitionist ideals."

"Well—Andrew's British by birth."

"They had slavery over there, too! British, skittish! That's how most white folks are about Negroes! The only white man I'd think suitable for you is Irving Pratt."

"The dentist?" To Olivia, he looked like a bean pole with spectacles.

Lori laughed. "Who else? Another man of medicine. Irving's from a fine abolitionist family. His people came out here from Kentucky after the war. All of them are well educated and I believe he'd make—"

"I'm taller than Irving Pratt."

"Not by much, and he's very handsome."

"He looks like he's fourteen!"

"He's thirty-three, close to your age, and the same age as Jesus was when he was crucified — and he's not old or widowed — *or divorced*," Lori added sharply. "Irving's a good man. At the last dance we attended in town, before the children came, he talked to your father about calling on you. But since Andrew's arrival, any party we go to, you're glued to that man's side. You waltzed and two-stepped with Andrew the whole time at the last dance."

"No one bothered to cut in."

"Why *would* anyone, when you look like you're in heaven while you're in Andrew's arms? Olivia, you need to stop thinking about Andrew and that foolish talk of his. Besides — provided he was serious — how could you hurt Lavinia like that?"

"Hurt Lavinia? She doesn't love him! He's divorcing her."

"Well, as of now, she's still married to him! And what about the children? If he says he wants to — *move here* and *marry you* — I assume he'd have the good sense to let Lavinia keep her children in the home where they were born with that nurse of theirs. But when would they see their father?"

"He plans on moving the children here too."

Lori looked at her daughter, appalled. "He'd tear Selina and Gabriel a million miles away from their mother?"

"Isn't that what you want—to have the children here, close by?"

"Of course I do—but not at Lavinia's expense!"

"They love California, Mother. They want to live here."

"They're four years old! They don't know what they want—but they'll want their mother!"

"Lavinia could care less about her children! *I* love them! Andrew says I've shown them more affection during this trip than Lavinia has during their entire lifetimes."

Lori pursed her lips. "You can't take her place, Olivia. She's their mother! I can't believe how selfish you're acting!"

Olivia tensed. "You probably wish I'd been the one to run off instead of Lavinia!"

"That's utter nonsense, Olivia, and you know it!"

"Then why are you always so concerned about her when she *despises* your very existence?"

Lori's eyes filled with tears. For several seconds she said nothing, but only gazed down at her hands. "I—I can't help but think—that Lavinia's the way she is—because of me."

"Mother, that's ridiculous."

"That's not what I think...I had the fever—and I could barely eat while I carried her.

Those things *must* have affected her somehow. But despite how she feels about me, she's still my child and I love her!" Lori wiped away her tears with a handkerchief. "You don't understand that because you don't have children."

Olivia looked away, feeling the hot sting of tears.

"Oh," Lori grasped Olivia's hand. "I'm sorry, dear. You don't have children *yet,* but you will one day, I know you will."

Silence hung between for a few moments, then Olivia looked at her mother. "Do you love me, too?"

Lori smiled sadly. "What kind of a question is that?"

"Does my happiness matter to you?"

Lori sighed. "Olivia, I want you to be happy. I want you to be married—I want you to have children—just not with Andrew."

Looking at the red and pink rose vines growing along the veranda railing, Olivia inhaled deeply. "I haven't made a decision yet."

"Decision? There is no decision! You tell that man you can't *possibly* marry him!"

Chapter 39

Olivia glanced at her wristwatch. It was just before seven in the morning. Lizbit, her chestnut mare, whinnied softly as Olivia climbed into the saddle on her back.

"Come on, girl." Olivia clicked her tongue, turning the reins in the direction of Charlton Place. Olivia rode Lizbit at a steady trot. Due to meet Johnny at eight for the cash flow meeting, she had more than enough time to get there.

A wide brimmed hat shielded her from the early morning sun, while brown leather gloves protected her hands from the roughness of the reins. Olivia hadn't bothered to dress stylishly for this early morning meeting. She'd freshen up when she returned to Rolando.

For comfort, Olivia wore blue jeans,

ordered from the Sear's and Roebuck Catalogue. Her mother thought them atrocious for a lady, and couldn't understand why Olivia refused to wear a full skirt over them. Olivia had also skipped the constraint of a corset. Under a loose fitting light blue shirt, she wore only a chemise, and savored the joy of breathing freely.

The last thing Olivia had strapped on was Joshua's gun belt, and she'd packed it with his Smith and Wesson .38. She always did that when riding alone.

Joshua had never used the weapon and hardly ever carried it. He claimed he'd be a hypocrite if he did. He wanted to save lives, not inflict harm or end them. But his relatives in Los Angeles had convinced him that he needed a pistol to protect himself from "crazy crackers."

Olivia's father had taught all three of his children how to handle firearms properly for their safety and protection. Although Joshua had never fired the S&W, Olivia, as a western woman, had. Yet she was thankful that killing rattlesnakes was the only thing she'd ever had to use it for.

Olivia rode enjoying the solitude and peaceful surroundings of the clear sky and mountains. She needed time away from Andrew, as well as her mother, so she could think. Andrew's visit would soon end. Olivia hated to see him go, yet felt relieved that she'd no longer be tempted by him. She hadn't given him an answer to his proposal, although Andrew had asked her to marry him several times over the the past week.

Father was understanding of what was happening between her and Andrew. Maybe that was because he resented Lavinia for hurting Mother all those years, Olivia thought. She suspected he liked seeing Lavinia get her comeuppance, although he'd never admit that.

Her mother's comments, however, were starting to annoy her, and worse yet, Olivia was beginning to believe them. "Only a woman with the morals of a heifer would steal her sister's husband," was the latest from Mother's repertoire. Perhaps it was foolish to think things could work between them, Olivia reflected, but whatever she'd decide, she couldn't leave Andrew hanging. And right now, she was leaning toward telling him no.

****

"Children," Andrew said, "you needn't complain, so. Aunt Olivia will be back soon enough. She said her meeting with Mr. Cahill wouldn't take that long." They sat in the dining room eating breakfast with Daniel and Lori.

"But when?" Selina whined.

"She said she'd take us to the beach again,"

Gabriel said.

"Aunt Olivia won't be gone any longer than necessary." Daniel smiled at the children. "She's eager to get back to her niece and nephew."

"*And* their father," Lori said with a disapproving look toward Andrew. She then glanced at the children's plates to see that they'd finished their tortillas filled with chorizo and scrambled eggs. "Maria," she called. When the girl appeared, Lori said, "Please take the children upstairs and get them dressed."

"Si, Meez Taylor." Maria smiled, as if knowing the children enjoyed hearing her speak Spanish, saying, "Vamos, ninos."

The children giggled, imitating her words as they quickly followed her from the dining room.

"I wanted to join Olivia for the meeting," Andrew said, "but she insisted I not go. Perhaps — she wouldn't mind if I rode over now. I could keep her company on the way back."

"Andrew," Lori said, addressing him sharply, "I don't approve of your intentions regarding Olivia, and since she's gone this morning, I'm going to voice my opinion."

"Lori," Andrew said, "I'm aware of your ill feelings, but I assure you, my intentions are honorable. I love Olivia very much. But it is unfortunate that I've met her at a rather — difficult and unaccommodating time in my life, and — "

"Difficult and unaccommodating indeed!" Lori raised her chin, a trait he'd seen in every Taylor woman, including Selina, to express dissatisfaction.

Though a genteel southern woman, Andrew thought, Lori seemed hard as granite beneath the surface.

"Lori," Daniel said slowly, "don't be so hasty to pass judgment."

"I'm not passing judgment, Daniel, but I thought you didn't approve either!"

"I never said that. I said it wasn't an easy situation, but I've talked to Andrew — and I know Lavinia." Daniel paused for several seconds. "As I see it, Olivia and Andrew are hurting right now...they need each other."

"But what about Lavinia?"

"Well," Daniel hesitated, "she doesn't feel hurt the way normal people do."

"Even though she is — different," Lori said, "Lavinia is our child! And despite what you think, this — this predicament is a disgrace! Andrew married one of our daughters, now he's divorcing her and wants to marry the other one! Can you imagine? What will people think?"

Daniel was silent for a few seconds, then took a deep breath. "A long time ago, a young white boy risked his life to save the slave girl he loved. They married, then ran off up North...I imagine...tongues wagged quite a while after that..."

Lori's mouth opened in protest for a brief moment, but then she pursed her lips, suppressing a smile.

"Andrew," Daniel said, "go on to Charlton Place. Olivia'd be pleased to have your company on the ride back, wouldn't she Lori?"

Andrew didn't wait for her to respond. "Then I'll be on my way. Excuse me." Relieved, he left the table.

****

Olivia sat in the dining room at Charlton Place, sipping coffee while perusing a list she'd just completed. She'd planned on discussing the cash flow statement with Johnny over the coffee and cinnamon bread her housekeeper had prepared for them, but he was late, by over forty-five minutes. As punctual as he was, that was out of character. Perhaps he'd forgotten about the rescheduled time, Olivia thought, but that too, wouldn't be like Johnny.

Since Cahill was delayed, Olivia had walked around the house, inside and out, trying to determine what could best convince Andrew not to raze it. She was sure it would make a charming inn, and had listed several reasons why.

Olivia sighed, pushing the list aside. Who was she fooling? Andrew was a businessman. If he agreed not to raze the place, he'd lose money. And if this land was on acreage he'd eventually resell, it would be razed anyway. The thought of the house being demolished devastated her, since memories of her marriage and life with Joshua were there.

Moving from the dining room to the foyer, she looked at the photo taken on her wedding day, as a bride on Joshua's arm. It sat on the credenza near the entrance foyer. Walking toward it, she realized with finality that her season of life with Joshua was over. Olivia hesitated, then decided to put the picture away.

She carried the wedding photo to a small office at the end of the hall. Olivia opened a closet, then pulled a box from the top shelf. Opening it, she gazed at the other mementos and pictures from her time with Joshua. Aside from his portrait in the parlor, this was the last keepsake she had to place there.

Tucking the box away, Olivia heard the front door open. She'd left it unlocked for Cahill. By now he was over an hour late.

"Johnny?" Olivia called, as she approached the entranceway. Seeing him, she said, "Why are you so late? Is something wrong?"

Johnny closed the door and locked it, then turned to face her. "There ain't nuthin' wrong,

Miz Cummins." He hung his cowboy hat by the door on a hat rack made from oak and deer antler. He shook blond locks from his eyes, then ran fingers through his hair to neaten it. "I need to talk to you 'bout somethin'."

"We were supposed to have talked an *hour* ago," Olivia said, "about the cash flow statement."

"There's somethin' else—more important—I wasn't sure quite how to begin...I needed a little somethin' to..." He began walking toward her, appearing slightly unsteady on his feet.

"Miz Cummins—" He stopped about a foot away from her. He wore his usual working attire of canvas trousers and a long sleeve cotton shirt, but he was unshaven—and Olivia could smell the alcohol on his breath.

"Johnny, you're drunk! You should be ashamed, drinking at this hour. I didn't know you drank."

"There's a lot you don't know about me, like how I feel about you."

"I assume you respect me as an employer and value my time."

"You're more than an employer to me, Miz Cummins. I see us as a team."

Olivia crossed her arms. "In a way we are a team, Johnny. But we won't be much longer if you continue to indulge in ignorant oil, begin running late and neglecting your responsibilities!"

"Look, me bein' late...it won't happen
again...and me drinkin'...I had to...this
mornin'...to help me tell you what I been
thinkin' about." He paused, staring at her, but
failed to go on.

Olivia exhaled. "Johnny, go home. Sleep
off your," she waved a hand, "condition.
We'll reschedule when you're sober."

"Miz Cummins, there's more I ain't tol'
you yet. You gotta listen. I can take care of
you — and your land...you've seen how I can.
I've proved myself to you, and —"

"Right now, you're rambling, only proving
that you're inebriated."

"I ain't so a — a — nibrated I don't know
what I'm sayin'!"

"You're wasting my time, Johnny. I have
guests to attend to."

A sneer curled Johnny's lips. His brown
eyes narrowed. "Your eastern dude?"

"If that's what you want to call Mr.
Standish."

"He ain't what you need," Cahill snarled.

"I beg your pardon?"

"Miz Cummins — Olivia — I deserve you —
and this ranch. I know you've always wanted
me —"

"I've always wanted you to be a top-notch
general manager, that's *all*, Johnny. Right now,
don't say another word. The alcohol is talking,

and I don't want you to embarrass yourself any further."

"Lemme finish!"

"You *are* finished! So stay quiet. You'll thank me later." Olivia began to laugh. "You don't actually believe — "

Cahill grabbed her shoulders. His fingers clutched her like claws. "What's so funny?" He scowled.

Surprised, Olivia pulled from his grasp. "Johnny!"

"I'm not good enough? Not refined and all like that Standish? He's just itchin' to get into your drawers."

"How dare you speak to me that way! As of now, you're dismissed! Get out! Have your bags packed and be off my property by sundown."

"I ain't goin' nowhere."

Olivia quickly pulled the S&W from her holster. "Out!" She aimed at him with both hands.

He stepped back a few paces, holding up his hands, smiling. "Go ahead, shoot. But I know you won't. You're too nice, and skittish, just like a jackrabbit. Didn't take much to scare you away from here."

Olivia cocked the pistol, but Cahill lunged forward, knocking her arms to the side. Olivia's ears rang as she fired off a loud blast. The smell of gunpowder stoked the air, but the bullet burrowed into the hardwood floor.

Cahill latched on to her wrists, laughing. "Sassy little spitfire." Wrestling the gun from her, he threw it across the room. As Cahill held fast to Olivia's wrists, his blood-shot eyes lasciviously appraised her body. "What're you gonna do now? I got you sweatin' like a whore in church, scarder than a sinner in a cyclone, and you ain't got your eastern dude here to protect you."

Olivia squirmed, trying to free herself, but Cahill's hands gripped her wrists even harder. "And you ain't got your big black nigger neither."

"Let me go!"

"I took care uh him reaaal goood..."

When Cahill loosened his grasp, Olivia yanked her wrists away. "What?" she cried.

He grabbed her tightly again, this time by the arms. "After he died, you was actin' sweet on me—'til that city slicker done come along."

Cahill's hands burned as he twisted them deeply into her flesh and the smell of his hot whiskey breath repulsed her. Olivia jerked free. "Sweet on you? You're insane!" She reached quickly with both hands to scratch his eyes, but he restrained her hands.

"Callin' me indispensable and all."

"I was only being nice!"

"Now you don't hardly give me the time a day! But you will."

Seizing her roughly by the shirt, he ripped it open, scattering buttons across the floor. Constraining Olivia's arms behind her, Cahill leered like a hungry animal. Ogling her breasts beneath the lace trimmed chemise, he smiled blackly. "They're even bigger than I thought."

He kissed her mouth ferociously, his unshaven face burning her skin. Olivia struggled to free her arms from his calloused hands and the shirt fabric twisted behind her back. With arms finally freed, she fought wildly, striking at Cahill, until he gripped her wrists again.

"Yeah, you go ahead and fight." Cahill tightly squeezed her wrists, hurting her, as she continued to struggle against him. "I could care for you, marry you — but now you don't think I'm nothin' but trash!" He kissed her again, but this time Olivia bit his lip, drawing blood.

"Oh, you're a feisty one, bitch." He slapped her backhanded with such force, she was thrown to the floor. Olivia landed face down, the wind knocked out of her. Cahill dug the heel of his boot into her spine. Olivia gasped breathlessly, then forced herself to scream.

"Go ahead," he said, "scream all you want, 'cause ain't nobody around to hear you. All the men are workin' and I seen that greaser housekeeper and her man ride off."

Cahill eased the pressure on Olivia'a back. She tried to rise, but once more, Cahill slammed her to the floor with his foot. I'm gonna kill you — just like I did Uncle Tommy and that black monkey of yours! And it'll look all accidental like. Highfalutin yalla wench. You think you're so much better than me. It'll make me feel good to see you dead! But first, I'm gonna do to you what I wanted to do since the first day I seen you, then had to swallow my pride to work for niggers."

Olivia, squirming under his foot, looked back to see Cahill unbuttoning his trousers. She managed to scoot forward a few inches, then flipped over on her back and kicked Cahill in the knee.

"Damn it!" he exclaimed.

Olivia scrambled to her feet running. Yet in seconds, Cahill corralled her around the waist and wrangled her to the floor again. Straddling her, he pulled at her jeans, trying to rip the buttons open, even as Olivia struck him furiously, scratching his face.

Restraining her hands, Cahill leaned close to her face. "You better stop fightin', or I'll knock every last tooth down your throat."

"No!" Olivia fought to free her arms. She tried to overturn his body, but he was too heavy, too solid. "God, help me!" The Almighty was her only hope.

Chapter 40

As Andrew approached the adobe, he heard screams and began running. Unable to open the locked door, he kicked it in. Seeing Cahill attacking Olivia on the floor, Andrew sprinted toward them. He pulled Cahill away, spun him around, then slammed him against the wall. Cahill tried to fight back, but in his drunkenness, only managed to grab Andrew around the waist in a bear hug.

Breaking from his hold, Andrew delivered a swift punch to Cahill's gut. The man grunted, slouching in pain. Then Andrew threw an uppercut to Cahill's face. Blood from the man's nose and mouth splattered through the air and on to Andrew's shirt. Cahill stumbled backward, crashed into the wall, then collapsed unconscious in a massive heap.

After witnessing Cahill's pummeling,

Olivia staggered to her feet. Turning away from Andrew, she leaned against the stair railing and began to sob, burying her face in her hands.

Cahill had torn away her shirt. Its abalone buttons glistened in tiny rainbows across the floor. Above the waist, Olivia was clad only in a chemise. As Andrew quickly approached her, he removed his shirt. But when he draped the garment over her heaving shoulders, she circled toward him, clutching him tightly around the neck, causing the shirt to fall to the floor.

Holding his hands out to embrace Olivia, Andrew hesitated to touch her. He wanted nothing more than to hold and console her. But he didn't want to be accused of being a cad while she was oblivious to her state of undress.

Clinging to him, Olivia pleaded, "Andrew, hold me!"

Gingerly, he enfolded her in his arms.

"Tighter," she cried. So he held her as snugly as possible. "Andrew, I was so frightened. I'll never be able to thank you enough. I don't know what I would have done if you hadn't come through that door. The only time I've ever been afraid like that—was the night Joshua was killed." Andrew glanced toward the credenza where her wedding picture had been, but noticed it gone.

Olivia pulled slightly from Andrew's

embrace, glancing beyond him in Cahill's direction. "Is he still out?" Her eyes met his, frantic.

Andrew turned briefly to gaze at the unconscious man. Blood streamed from Cahill's nose and the corner of his mouth. "Yes. But even if he were to stir, he wouldn't hurt you again. *I'm* here."

"But—"

"Olivia, you're safe. I'll protect you." Andrew said.

Olivia nodded, then angled away from him. The moment she did, Andrew quickly reached for his shirt, and once more placed it over her shoulders. She was still shaking and disoriented. The shirt hung loosely on her, but Olivia failed to notice that he'd placed it around her.

"Andrew, Johnny killed Joshua—and he wanted to kill me, too." She turned to face him, arms braced tightly across her chest "But first he wanted to..." The shirt was closed, but unbuttoned, and when she extended her arms to express herself, the garment opened completely, revealing her near naked breasts, of which she was still unaware.

Andrew immediately dropped his eyes to the floor. "You saw what he wanted to do to me! Andrew, why won't you look at me? Do you think *I* did something to provoke his attack?"

"Of course not," Andrew said, still gazing downward. "And there's nothing I'd rather do than look at you."

"Then why won't you?" She sniffed, still in tears. "And where's your shirt?" she asked, as though just realizing Andrew wore only an undershirt.

Still studying the floor, Andrew cleared his throat. "Trying to—keep you covered."

Olivia gasped. He imagined she'd looked down, appalled by the display of her bountiful bosom beneath the thin cotton fabric. When Andrew slowly raised his gaze, Olivia had turned her back to him. Clumsily poking her arms through his shirt sleeves, she muttered, "I've never been more embarrassed."

Feeling embarrassed for her, Andrew said nothing, though the heavenliness of her body had left an unforgettable impression in his mind. He walked to a closet near the front door. "Is there rope in here; perhaps a knife, too?" He opened the closet and glanced on the shelves.

"Look to the right, on the very top shelf," Olivia called over her shoulder, while fumbling to button the shirt.

Andrew grabbed the items needed and walked to Cahill, smelling the alcohol wafting from the unconscious man. His nose had swelled considerably. Andrew was sure he'd broken it. He used his booted foot to turn

Cahill on his stomach, then knelt down to tie the man's hands behind his back. Cahill's nails were embedded with a thin layer of grime. Afterwards, Andrew moved to Cahill's large feet. They were covered by a pair of almost new looking cowboy boots.

"Darling," Andrew said, unwinding some rope, "I'm not sure when he'll regain consciousness. But I'm staying here and keeping watch." After he'd securely restrained Cahill's feet, Andrew strode to Olivia. She was now decently attired in his blood splattered shirt, a collarless blue and white stripe. He gently placed his hands on her shoulders. "Are you all right now?"

She nodded silently, then took a deep breath. "I think so."

"Good. We need the authorities."

"That means going to Los Angeles."

"Then I'll need you to go back to Rolando and get your father. He and I — and Cahill — need to make a trip to the sheriff's office."

Olivia wiped her tears, then grabbed Joshua's gun from the floor. Shoving it into her holster, she said, "I'll ride as quickly as I can."

Chapter 41

Lori stood by the window in the parlor, wringing her hands, as she waited for Andrew and Daniel to return from Los Angeles. Though still sunny outside, it was past six in the evening.

Glancing toward her daughter and grandchildren on the sofa, Lori saw Olivia put an arm around Selina and Gabriel and then give them a gentle squeeze.

"Aunt Olivia," Selina softly touched her aunt's cheek, "I'm sorry you were hurt."

"Me, too." Gabriel snuggled closer to Olivia.

"Well...Mr. Cahill — didn't mean to hurt me," Olivia stammered. "He — he wasn't in his...right mind."

Lori sighed quietly. Olivia put on a brave face for the children, but she was still shaken from this morning's ordeal. Drained from it, she'd spent most of the day in bed.

"What does that mean?" Gabriel asked.

"His mind was sick," Lori said. "He was acting loony."

"Where is he now?" Selina said.

Both Lori and Olivia hesitated.

"Grandfather — and your father," Olivia forced a smile, "they took him to a special doctor."

"So he won't hurt anyone again?" Gabriel asked.

"That's right." Olivia stroked his hair.

"I wish he hadn't hurt you," Selina said.

"Thank you, sweetheart. But I don't want either of you to — to worry about me, okay? I'm fine now." Olivia nodded a little too vigorously, as though trying to convince herself.

"You don't look fine," Selina said. "Your lip's a little fat and there are scratches on your cheeks."

The wooden smile left Olivia's face. She pursed her lips for a moment. "I'll — I'll look more normal tomorrow."

Lori turned her gaze back to the window. "Finally!" She exclaimed, seeing Daniel and Andrew drive the buckboard into the courtyard. "The men are back." She rushed to the back door.

"Father's here!" The twins sprang from the

sofa and scampered after their grandmother.

"Maria!" Lori yelled. The girl appeared in seconds, her bright purple skirt swishing about her hips, as Lori neared the door. "Take the children outside to play."

Maria tried to corral the children, but giggling, they ran to the door, eluding her grasp. Pushing them aside, Lori opened the door. The men were just starting up the steps to the veranda. Daniel had driven the buckboard home from the train station. He and Andrew glistened with sweat and brushed dust from their clothes. They rolled up their shirt sleeves and stopped at the metal wash tub basin to cleanse their faces and hands.

"Children, settle down!" Lori admonished, as the twins ran out on to the veranda, screeching and squealing. Maria followed them, and finally managed to grab each child by the arm, but they pulled free of her. Selina and Gabe skittered past Lori in the doorway, then rushed by Daniel, with a quick hello. They stopped at Andrew, throwing their arms around his waist.

"Father, Father!" both children shouted.

"We missed you!" Gabriel said.

Andrew laughed as he washed his hands. "I missed you, too."

"Aunt Olivia's hurt," Selina added.

Looking grave, Andrew said, "I know."

"Children!" Lori clapped twice to get their

attention, "it's time for you to play outside with Maria."

"Vamos!" Maria's tone was sharp, but the children ignored her.

"We don't *want* to!" Selina objected.

"We want to know what happened to Mr. Cahill!" Gabriel said. "Aunt Olivia and Grandmother said he was acting loony and you had to take him to a special doctor."

****

Daniel's eyes met Lori's briefly, as he dried his hands with a cloth. "That's right, children," he said. "Now listen to your grandmother and run along."

Looking up to Andrew, who'd just finished wiping his face and hands, they pleaded together, "But Father, do we have to?"

"Yes," he said sternly. "Now, go play like your grandparents told you."

The children looked sad. "Alright, Father." Selina pouted, then reached to hold Gabe's hand.

They turned from Andrew and began to walk toward Maria, who said, "We play hide and go seek."

Instantly forgetting their troubles, the children squealed delightedly, bolting past her. "You're it!" Gabe yelled as he and Selina ran down the veranda steps and off into the yard to hide.

As Maria covered her eyes and began to count, Lori ushered the men into the house.

"Where's Olivia?" Daniel asked, as Lori closed the door.

"In the parlor," Lori said.

"How is she?" Andrew asked.

"Coping." Lori grasped his arm. "Andrew, I can't thank you enough for all you've done. And I realize now that—if I'd prevented you from going to her ranch this morning—we would've had to endure another tragedy."

"So," Daniel said, "now you're sorry for being difficult?"

"I am sorry, Andrew, and I hope you'll accept my apology."

"Apology accepted," Andrew said. "But I should've insisted I go with her to that meeting this morning, then she never would've been alone with Cahill."

Through clenched teeth, Daniel said, "And *I* should've insisted that she and Joshua never hire that character to begin with."

Lori took a deep breath as she led them to the parlor. "We can't change the past, but we *can* be thankful that we still have Olivia. She'll want to hear about what happened. Of course, she's—not quite herself. Oh—you all must be starving! It's been a long day." Lori called to Diego and instructed him to bring two plates of food.

Upon entering the parlor, Lori hurried to

Olivia's side. She sat next to her on the sofa, then gently placed an arm around her. Daniel kissed his daughter's forehead before taking a seat across from her in a wingback chair.

Andrew squeezed one of Olivia's hands in both of his, then kissed it, before sitting next to Daniel in the other wingback chair.

"Where is he?" Olivia asked.

"Behind bars," Daniel said.

"He confessed to everything," Andrew added. "The man's insane. He —"

"There's no need to go into all of it now," Daniel interrupted.

"I want to know everything," Olivia cried. "He said enough for me to figure out some of what he did!"

"Olivia," Daniel said, "the important thing is that he's locked away."

"He killed Joshua! He killed his uncle! He tried to rape me and wanted me dead!"

"Daniel," Andrew said calmly, "I believe for Olivia's peace of mind, she needs to know all the details."

A spicy aroma filled the room as Diego carried in huge plates on a tray and set them down on the coffee table in front of Daniel and Andrew. Although the plates were heaped high with baked chicken and black beans over a fragrant herbed rice, neither man touched them.

Daniel leaned forward and placed his

elbows on his knees. Folding his hands, he said, "I thank God Andrew was there. I would've killed Cahill! I never did like that fellow. Olivia," he sighed loudly, "you're too trusting—just like Joshua was."

"Joshua had integrity and a good heart!" Olivia's voice trembled and tears filled her eyes. "He's not here to defend himself! All he did was give Johnny a chance."

Leaning back in his chair, Daniel said, "Cahill made the noises that frightened you from the ranch—but that was the least of his offenses."

"Olivia," Andrew said, "it turns out he murdered Joshua in order to make you more dependent upon him."

"Tragic..." Lori squeezed her daughter's shoulder. "How could he do that to Joshua and Olivia after all they did for him?"

Tears rolled down Olivia's cheeks. "He rigged the explosion...to make it look like someone wanted to destroy the press? But all along...he wanted Joshua..."

Andrew nodded as Olivia stifled a sob.

"But before that," Andrew said, "he'd killed his uncle."

"His own uncle," Lori said, astonished. "Tommy was a decent man—a good friend to us—but he lost his life to his own kin? Why?"

Daniel hesitated. Andrew was about to speak, but Daniel stopped him, then began slowly, "Johnny and Tommy...were shot—and robbed, that day in LA...but Johnny wasn't hurt seriously. His uncle was alive but unconscious. Johnny played dead...then...when the coast was clear...he finished off Tommy...with rock a to the head."

Lori and Olivia gasped.

"He did that so he could steal his job," Daniel said.

Olivia hugged her mother and began to cry. "It's all my fault—everything!"

Lori rubbed her daughter's back. "It's not your fault, sweetheart. Johnny had us all fooled. Even your father was surprised by what a good manager he was."

"But I never should have ignored my intuition!" Daniel said angrily.

Olivia pulled from her mother's embrace. "Apparently, I have no intuition, not when it comes to business, which is why I make a better teacher! So the sooner I'm free of the ranch, the better. Andrew, best of luck to you in all your endeavors with it." She stood abruptly, then left the room in tears.

Chapter 42

In the darkness, restless and unable to sleep, Andrew stared at the ceiling of his bedroom. In just a few days, his visit would come to end. Then he and the children would return to New York. He'd need to tie up all loose ends with Julian, and start arranging his relocation to southern California, as well as his six month stay in Nevada to finalize the divorce.

However, what prevented him from sleeping was what Olivia had said earlier, "best of luck to you in all your endeavors..." Those words played again and again through his mind, as well as her hasty departure from the room.

Was she angry with him? Did she have no interest in a life with Andrew at all? If she chose not to be his wife, perhaps moving here would be a mistake. With Olivia, he and the children could live happily as one family. Yet, if she refused his proposal, Andrew knew he could never forget her.

Time was not on his side. He had to know if she'd marry him. The children loved the sunny state of California, as well as their new relatives. They were enthusiastic about living here, and Gabe enjoyed pointing out that he and Aunt Olivia were the same color. Olivia pampered and doted on the children, while their grandparents spoiled them senseless.

During this visit, he and the children had attended church every Sunday. Julian and Serene did the same with their children, but Lavinia had refused the idea of ever going to church, even on Christmas and Easter, the two times a year Andrew felt an obligation. "Are you supposed to go to church so much?" Gabe had once asked his grandmother, to Andrew's embarrassment.

Attending church on a regular basis and living among these God fearing relatives, Andrew believed, could only benefit Selina and Gabriel. He couldn't deny it being something good in his life as well. But what dangers would Selina and Gabe face here— aside from being labeled as Negroes, as Lavinia had so snidely pointed out one time. Would they be impervious to racism, and its dangers, because of his money?

This was the Wild West he'd read about, and it lived up to its reputation. In the brief time Andrew had been here, he'd faced an altercation with a wild cowboy — and triumphed. So he could manage. And since the closest lawman was in Los Angeles, he'd follow Daniel's advice and purchase a firearm after settling here. He *could* protect his children *and* Olivia.

Andrew felt invincible for a moment, but he needed rest so he could think clearly in the morning, approach Olivia, and somehow convince her to provide an answer for him.

His guestroom was down the hall from the parlor, where a large collection of books was shelved. He rose from bed, grabbed his bathrobe from behind the door, and quietly headed there. Perhaps he could find some non-stimulating literature that would lull him to sleep. As he walked softly into the room, a voice stopped him.

"Who's there?"

Surprised, Andrew fumbled for a moment in the dark to light a brass gas floor lamp by the doorway. "It's only me." Andrew smiled.

Olivia sat alone on the sofa. Her robe, a light pink silk, with a large ruffled collar of pale green, gracefully draped her body. She held a white handkerchief, wrinkled and splotched with the stain of tears. With red swollen eyes, she gazed at him, then smiled slightly. "Good morning." She sniffed, dabbing the hanky at her runny nose.

Andrew stood stiffly, wanting to comfort her somehow, but only replied, "Good morning." After a few moments of silence, he nodded toward the opposite end of the sofa. "Do you—uh—mind if I join you?"

"Not at all." Yet when Andrew sat down, Olivia stood up, stuffing the handkerchief into her pocket. Tightly crossing her arms, she turned her back to him. "I thought I'd be the only one who couldn't sleep tonight." The grandfather clock in the corner read one thirty-five. "Why are you up?"

"Olivia...let's not talk about me...How are you?"

She sighed, turning to face him. "As well as can be expected—I guess."

Even though her cheeks were scratched and bruised, and her lip slightly swollen, she was still beautiful. Her hair, usually pulled back, now fell freely, its curls framing her breath-taking face.

"What happened today—or yesterday, I mean—will only contribute more to my sleepless nights. I can't stop thinking about what—what Johnny tried to do to me—and all the things he *did* do." Her voice trembled.

Andrew attempted to think of something to say without sounding feeble, but could only manage, "You needn't ever worry about him again." He could kick himself for sounding so ineffectual.

Olivia nodded, then dropped her gaze to the floor. "Before, thoughts about Joshua — and the baby — kept me awake. But sometimes, the mornings are worse for me." She played with the ribbon at her neck tied in a bow.

"Why?" Andrew asked.

"The pain." She gazed at the silk in her fingertips, then untied the bow and retied it. "It can be so bad, I can barely manage to get out of bed. Yet, God gives me the strength to go on."

Olivia's eyes welled as she met his gaze. "My baby...he was so beautiful — and perfect. I held him...before they took him away." She wiped away tears with the back of her hand.

"Andrew, I was such a fool. Why didn't I see that Cahill was up to no good? Why didn't Joshua see it? I still can't believe he killed my husband, after all we did for him! We *paid* him well — trusted him — and gave him huge responsibilities!" She blew out a deep breath, raking hands through her hair. "Now that I know he murdered his uncle, it shouldn't surprise me that killing Joshua meant nothing to him.

"And what he said to me — his words — they were vicious. Andrew, you get used to hateful things being said when you're colored — you develop a thick skin. But to hear those words from someone you know — and trust — that's betrayal of the worst kind.

"Then what he wanted to do to me…" she trailed off. "He was a different person. I'd never seen him drunk, but it took the alcohol to unmask his true character." She paused briefly. "People aren't always what they seem — are they?"

"No." Andrew thought of Lavinia. "Your sister…seemed sweet and demure when I first met her. Yet not long into our marriage, she shed those layers — like a snake sheds its skin."

"Johnny was an actor just like she is!" Olivia said angrily. "If we hadn't hired him, I'd have my husband and my baby right now. But — I have to put this behind me — and move on…God will help me do that."

Still not understanding completely her faith in a circumstance like this, Andrew said, "Olivia — one time you told me you'd forgiven whoever killed Joshua. Now you know…so…do you forgive Johnny?"

"As hard as it is for me — I do. God wants us to forgive others as He forgives us. I'm still devastated — hurt — and angry. I can't help being human. But I know — in time — God will heal my wounds…"

Olivia sat back down on the sofa. "I have been struggling, though…The Bible says that God brings good things out of bad. But how can anything good come out of what's happened?"

Andrew could think of much, like the chance to marry her and raise his children with her, make love to her and have even more children...

"I have to force myself to remember," Olivia continued, "that God's purpose is greater than my pain. But that's so hard." Tears slid down her cheeks. "And envy has gotten the better of me..."

Hugging herself, she said, "I've been praying to overcome these feelings, but why did Lavinia have two children — when she didn't want any at all — and why was my one child taken away when I wanted him so badly? I keep thinking, why couldn't I have had those two living children and not her? I know that's terrible," Olivia looked down, embarrassed, "and I don't blame you for thinking less of me because of it."

"I don't think any less of you," Andrew smiled. "When my brother married his wife, I had similar feelings."

This brought a sad smile to Olivia's face. "Good. I've never told that to anyone." She sniffed. "I've been too ashamed to admit that I really feel that way."

While biting her lower lip, a look of distress crossed Olivia's face. "Andrew, there's more — that's been eating away at me —

I—I feel like such a failure."

Astonished, Andrew said, "Olivia, you're anything but a failure—"

"A failure," she interrupted him, "as a woman—I mean. Not being able to carry a child—" her voice broke as fresh tears flowed.

Andrew moved closer to her and held her hand. "Olivia, you shouldn't feel any less a woman. Joshua didn't feel that you were, did he?"

"No," she said through her tears. "He said he married me because he loved me, not to have children...He loved me," she said wistfully, "and I loved him—I don't understand why he had to die."

Pulling her hand from his, she stood up, again turning away. "If God didn't plan for me to have Joshua or children, he must have a better plan for me." Olivia wept softly at first, however, in moments she began sobbing uncontrollably. "That was my heart's desire." Andrew rose from the sofa and moved to embrace her. "This is the last thing I wanted to do—" she said between sobs, "cry in front of you like this."

"Shh..." he said. "Cry as long as you need to."

Olivia continued to weep, nestled snugly against his chest. After several moments, she pulled away slightly and looked up, into his eyes. "Andrew—I'm sorry—I've mussed your clothes. This is the second thing you've worn today that you've let me use."

He smiled. "My clothes are happy to be of service."

"Andrew," she continued to hold his gaze, "I'll — I'll miss you, when you leave. You'll have to hurry back."

"I'll miss you — more than words can say, Olivia. Today...I noticed your wedding picture — was gone. Did you put it away?" She nodded. "I'd like to think — that was for a reason..."

"You." She squeezed his arms. "You had something to do with that...and...it was time." After a long pause she said, "Thank you — for your comfort tonight."

"I'm glad I'm here to console you." Andrew lifted her chin, then kissed her tenderly on the lips. However, when she kissed him back, he pulled away. Kissing her at so vulnerable a moment wasn't wise. "Olivia, I shouldn't — "

"Andrew," Olivia said breathlessly, tugging him back, "don't stop." She pressed her body firmly against his, kissing him fervently, as if drinking life from his lips.

Andrew pulled his lips from hers. Vulnerable or not, he'd ask again. "Olivia, marry me. I love you. I have two children who love you, and I want nothing more than for us to have children together. But even if we can't, I'll still love you. I can't replace what you lost, but I can give you all of me — and everything I have. Marry me, Olivia, please."

She said nothing for several moments. Then, looked away. "I — I can't."

"What?" Andrew felt as if his heart had stopped beating. "What do you mean, you can't?"

"I — I'm no good to anyone — Joshua, Tommy, my baby — all dead because of me...Maybe I'm cursed — or something..."

"Olivia — you don't really believe that?"

She hesitated. "No — I don't — that was just an excuse — a bad one — but I *am* confused — things seem impossible — we can't — it wouldn't — "

Andrew grabbed her again, and kissed her long and hard.

When he released her, she felt limp. After slowly opening her eyes, Olivia said, "Why'd you stop?" She sounded almost drunk.

"Look at me, Olivia. Tell me again that you can't marry me."

With her gaze locked on his, Olivia remained silent. Tears welled in her eyes. After several seconds, she finally whispered, "Andrew, I — I can't — I can't tell you that — because — I *do* want to marry you."

His heart pumping rapidly, Andrew asked, "Are you — actually saying yes — to my proposal?"

Olivia nodded, then hugged him tightly. "Yes!"

A part of him feared her confusion was the main reason she'd said yes, but then, with the feel of her arms around him, he realized he didn't care.

"Andrew, I love you—I can't pretend I don't anymore! I want to spend the rest of my life with you! I don't care what Mother thinks—I don't care what anybody thinks—not even Lavinia!"

They kissed, passion bursting between them, while Andrew's hands glided ravenously over the silk that covered her body.

Relishing the warm softness of her curves, he said, "Olivia, you've made me so happy...you're everything I want—everything I've ever dreamed of."

"Andrew," she touched his face, his hair, "love me..."

"I do love you. More than—"

"I mean," Olivia kissed him with desperate need, "*love* me." She was breathless, filled with desire. "We can go to my ranch, then come back here before daybreak."

Andrew hesitated, looking at her with longing, ready and willing to leave with her, but said, "Olivia—as much as I want to—I can't do that." However, if he could, he'd rip every stitch of clothing from her, and ravage her right then and there on the floor. So was he really saying this? "You'd hate me afterwards for taking advantage of you in a time of distress. I couldn't hurt you like that—and I'd hate myself even more for it. Also—I'm not yet divorced. Right now—I have to think rationally—for both of us."

Olivia glanced down. "You're right." Her eyes met his, glistening with tears. "I can't believe what I asked of you." She stepped a few paces away. "I'm so sorry—and so ashamed I—"

Pulling her back, he said, "Don't be."

"But you must think—"

"That you're the woman I love. I've got to go back to New York and get my affairs in order. Unfortunately, before the divorce is finalized, I'll have to set up residency in Nevada for six months."

"That's an eternity," Olivia sighed.

"It seems so..." Andrew kissed her softly. "But at least I'll be close enough to visit you without it taking a train ride of several days to get here. And after it's all behind us, I'll marry you—then love you until *beyond* the end of time."

Chapter 43
New York City
Late Summer

With one hand placed over her heart, Lavinia rushed down the stairs. "Oh, my darlings!" she cried upon seeing her children for the first time in over two and a half months.

It was just past ten in the morning. Selina and Gabe stood with their father in the brownstone's foyer watching their mother's dramatic descent. Once next to them, she opened her arms wide. Leaning down, with breasts nearly spilling from her clothes, she scooped them close. Holding their heads to her bosom, while giving Andrew only a mere passing glance, she said, "How I've missed you — and how you've grown!"

To Andrew, Lavinia smelled wildly sweet,

her perfume scented by violet, lilac and
jasmine, and a bit stronger than anything
Olivia would wear. Lavinia's waist length hair
fell in smooth waves down her shoulders and
back. Although she'd barely acknowledged
Andrew, Lavinia had dressed for the occasion
in what appeared an attempt to rekindle his
desire. She wore a dark blue satin robe, and
beneath it, a low cut, lace trimmed negligee.
Catching himself, Andrew averted his eyes
from the lavender lace webbed alluringly over
her cleavage.

Despite her play at feminine wiles,
Andrew was astonished to see that Lavinia had
truly missed her children and was happy to see
them. Then again, he reflected, perhaps she
was acting. In the role of mother, she appeared
as sweetness and light, overcome with joy
upon seeing her long lost children.

"Darlings," Lavinia led the children into
the living room as Andrew followed, "I want
to hear all about your trip! And afterwards, I
have a special surprise for you!"

"What's the surprise?" Gabe asked.

"It won't *be* a surprise if I tell you," Lavinia
said.

"Please tell us, Mother," Selina begged.

"Oh...all right," Lavinia relented. "Your
bedroom, it's full of new toys. And one is a
beautiful porcelain doll for you!" Selina
gasped and clapped her hands. "And there's a

Lionel train set for Gabriel."

"Wow!" Gabe exclaimed. "Lina, let's go!"

When the twins started to run from the room, Lavinia stopped them. "No, children! Tell me about your trip first."

"We had fun with our grandparents," Selina said quickly, "even though they don't look alike."

"And we met a cowboy who wore a gun and had lots of bullets in his belt!" Gabe said, "but he got sick."

"We picked oranges right off the trees," Selina said, "and ate them! We went to a carnival—"

"We went to the beach—"

"And the sand was white!"

"We learned how to speak Mexican and we ate Mexican food!"

"We went to Aunt Olivia's ranch!

"We saw deer and lots of cows!"

After they'd prattled on a few moments longer, Lavinia said, "Are you really looking forward to moving there...that far away from me?"

"We'll miss you, Mother," Selina said, "but we'll have a *new* mother—"

"Selina!" Andrew said sharply. "You've said enough! This is your mother," he nodded toward Lavinia, "and she always will be."

Selina's lower lip trembled at her father's tone. He rarely raised his voice to her.

"Selina, darling," Lavinia bent down to her daughter's level, "just what were you going to tell *your mother* about a...*new mother*?"

"I think this would be a good time for the children to explore that room full of new toys," Andrew said.

"No. We'll make this a game," Lavinia said. "Selina *has* to tell me what she was going to say *before* she and Gabriel get to see all those new toys." Lavinia stroked her daughter's curls. "You wouldn't want to deprive your brother of all that fun, now, would you?"

When Gabe looked at his sister with wide-eyed anticipation, Selina shook her head. "No."

"Then I'll tell you what," Lavinia smiled slyly, "every time you tell me something about the new mother, I'll tell each of you about another new toy waiting upstairs. Doesn't that sound like fun?"

"She's very nice!" Selina said enthusiastically.

"I see." Lavinia raised a brow. "Well, there's a cobalt blue tea set for you, just like the one Mother has that you love so much."

"With the pretty gold flowers?" Selina smiled, excited.

Lavinia nodded. "And there's a Gilbert erector set for Gabriel."

"Yippee!" the boy shouted. "Can I play the new mother game, too?" he asked.

"The more the merrier," Lavinia said with artificial warmth.

"She looks like me!" Gabe shouted happily.

"Oh?" His mother's lips curled in a glowing smile, but her emerald eyes flashed tundra cold.

"Stop this game now, children!" Andrew said. Gabe and Selina looked at their father, startled by his anger. "This is a *bad* game and you mustn't play it any longer!"

Lavinia stood upright to face him. "Andrew, you're ruining our fun." Her tone was as frigid as her eyes, and a smile no longer graced her lips.

After taking a deep breath, he said, "Lavinia, I insist they go upstairs. We have an important matter to discuss."

The children stood quietly. Their wide eyes darted from Father to Mother.

"An important matter, indeed!" Lavinia swept her arms through the air dramatically. "*More* important, I take it, than you moving my children a *world* away from me!"

"It's somewhat related to that," Andrew said tightly.

Lavinia fumed for several moments, a look Andrew had seen many times. Her bosom heaved rapidly in a series of short fiery breaths while she tightly pursed her lips.

"Very well," she finally said, glancing

toward the twins. "Go upstairs while I talk to your father about his *important matter.*"

****

The children, however, didn't move.

"Father," Selina looked at Andrew, "I'm sorry—if I said something wrong."

"Upstairs, *now!*" was all he responded.

Gabe grasped his sister's hand and the children slowly left the room. Selina glimpsed over her shoulder as their mother closed the pocket doors behind them.

"Gabe," Selina said as they started up the stairwell, "I—I hope I didn't get us in trouble."

Half way up the staircase, Gabe sat on a step. Tugging his sister down next to him, he said, "Lina, let's listen. Maybe we can find out if we *are* in trouble."

For the first few moments, Selina could only hear muffled voices. But then her mother's voice grew louder and louder. Selina heard the words "married" and "Olivia", because Mother said them in a very loud and angry way.

Then, from behind the doors, came a loud noise—a bang—a crash! Alarmed, the twins looked at each other. Gabe's eyes widened. So did Selina's. Feeling frightened, she bit her lower lip. "Come on." Gabe whispered loudly. He took his sister's hand, then ran up the stairs, pulling her behind him.

Once safely in their bedroom, Gabe closed the door. "We'll play," he said, walking to Selina's bed. He reached for the new porcelain doll propped on pillows. "Here's your dolly." Gabe handed the toy to Selina.

She gazed at the blond doll in blue satin for only a moment before taking it from her brother. He didn't seem to be at all afraid, Selina, thought. But she was. "Gabe...what do you think happened in there?"

The boy shrugged his shoulders, then wandered to the new train set assembled in the middle of the floor. He plopped down and began to play, rolling the miniature engines and freight cars back and forth on a circular track. Not removing his eyes from the tiny locomotive, he said, "Everything will be fine."

For the first time in a very long time, Selina wanted to suck her thumb. She wondered if Gabe felt that way, too. She couldn't ask him, though, because if he didn't, he'd tease her for feeling like a baby. Besides, she wouldn't dare suck her thumb now, not with Mother around and the threat of quinine. But if only she could...it would feel so good...

She wished Brigid was here. Father had said she was traveling from Ireland. She'd been there visiting relatives and wouldn't be back in New York until tomorrow.

Selina sighed, then hugged the doll. She walked to Gabe and sat next to him. Rocking back and forth, she said softly, "Whatever happened, it's all my fault."

****

"Getting *married*?! To *Olivia*?!" Lavinia picked up a large Rookwood vase filled with roses. Andrew's jaw dropped as she took aim and threw it. He ducked, partially covering his face with his arm, then heard the pottery crash into the wall.

Water and roses lay scattered across the Oriental carpet, along with tiny shards of pink and green. Lavinia looked for something else to throw. But as she reached for a marble figurine of the goddess Athena, which surely would've rendered Andrew unconscious, he grabbed her firmly by the shoulders and forced her down into a gilded chair.

He'd expected a strong reaction, but he hadn't been prepared for war. The weapon of choice for a woman was her tongue, and Lavinia's was as sharp as any double-edged sword. To ward off a verbal assault, he'd armed himself with reason and rationale regarding his and Olivia's parenting capabilities.

Of course the rage that confronted Andrew wasn't as much about raising the children as it was about Lavinia losing him to Olivia. There really was no reason or rationale to that. No one can explain why two people fall in love.

He knew Lavinia would be angry, and he'd steeled himself for whatever words she'd fire at him regarding his pending marriage. Yet he'd never expected her to resort to physical violence.

"You fell in love with Olivia and plan to marry her?!" Lavinia squirmed against his grasp. "And you accuse me of 'alienation of affection'?"

"Nothing inappropriate transpired between us," Andrew said, then thought to himself, aside from a bit of passionate kissing that led to some rather titillating and extraordinary fantasies on his part. He released Lavinia's shoulders and stepped back a few paces.

"So you mean to tell me," she said, "that you fell in love from afar, with no physical contact whatsoever? Not a kiss or a touch of any kind?"

"We danced on occasion, but—"

"But nothing! I could destroy you, Andrew Standish! I could drag your name though the mud!"

"Then we could destroy each other," Andrew said, casually, "but what would that accomplish? You, a deceitful Negress, and me, a less than perfect man."

"A less than perfect man? You know there's more to it than that!"

"If you insist on dragging *both* of our

394

names through the mud, then I won't stop you, to be with Olivia."

"OOHH!" At this, Lavinia sprang from the chair, lunging for his eyes, her nails poised like claws.

Grabbing her wrists, Andrew said, "Lavinia, contain yourself. We mustn't upset the children."

He forced her down into the chair again. She struggled wildly against him as he restrained her. Lowering her voice for a moment she said, "So you cast me aside like garbage and then chase after someone else in the blink of an eye. Dark, homely *Olivia* at that! She's nothing but a silly, *stupid* girl—one who'd be smarter *without* a brain! *You*, Andrew Standish, are a fool!

"What's possessed you to want to do such a thing? You'll have to become a Negro if you marry her! You just wait and see! And the children—their lives will never be the same with you *choosing* to turn them into Negroes! And what about me? If word gets out that you've married my *black* sister, my life will unravel!

"If I could kill you, I would! First you stab me in the back, then Olivia, now a widow, you say, and childless, steals you away from me and takes *my* children because she can't have any of her own! She was always Father's favorite and now she's taken you! She's

395

nothing but a black hearted skink!"

Rather than slap her, as he wished to, Andrew shook her by the shoulders, violently, as though trying to shake reason into her. Aside from the time months ago, that he'd grabbed Lavinia brusquely from the vanity, he'd never laid a hand on her. Now, after a few seconds of throttling, she appeared surprised, gaping at him in saucer-eyed disbelief. Andrew ceased the shaking, but still held fast to her shoulders.

"Lavinia," he said firmly, "our marriage is over. Soon, I will no longer be your husband. We will be divorced. Rest assured, I will do everything in my power to keep word of my marriage to Olivia out of the papers. I will never associate your name with that of your family's. You have my word that I will do my best to protect your secret.

"Now," he removed his hands from her and stood upright, "there's nothing black about Olivia's heart. She hasn't taken your children. They'll visit you as often, and for as long as you like. But it's best for me to raise them, and Olivia couldn't love them more if they were her own."

Lavinia stood up quickly. "Well they're *not* her own! And it's not fair that she'll have them! No matter what, *Selina* should stay with *me*!"

Andrew was surprised by this. He

thought Lavinia would be happy to be free of children. "That's out of the question. Besides, they're too attached to each other. And just — why are you so eager to keep Selina?"

"Why? She's *my child*, of course!"

Andrew clenched his fists. He could feel his blood boiling, but tried to remain calm. "What about Gabe? He's *your child*, too."

Lavinia hesitated. "Yes — and I *do* love him — and *because* I love him — I think — I think that perhaps he *would* be happier living with his relatives — in California. He looks like them. And he'd be with you — his father. But Selina — she's mine — my little me. She looks white — like me — she shouldn't *have* to become a Negro. Why ruin her life?"

Andrew paused for a long moment, then inhaled deeply. "Listen to me — *woman*," he said sharply, "and remember that's *all* you are, even if you are as shrewd as any man and more treacherous than most. Legally, *everything* you have belongs to me — our children, your theater, the property you brought into our marriage, and every penny of income you've earned since. Stand in my way regarding *either* of my children — and I *will* take everything you have."

"Andrew," Lavinia's voice trembled, "you wouldn't! You're not one who'd do such a — "

"Don't challenge me. And remember, I'd expose you, as well."

Lavinia raised her chin. Her eyes watered but she held back the tears.

For several moments, Andrew said nothing, feeling somewhat amazed that Lavinia didn't respond. Her hands were tied. He'd won, although he despised himself for using such a deplorably underhanded tactic. Trying to soften the blow, he said, "Selina knows you're her mother, and she loves you...but she's very excited about living in California near her grandparents, whom she adores...as well as...Olivia."

"Her 'new mother'? Is that what they'll call her—Mother?"

As cold and unfeeling as Lavinia was, Andrew sensed a genuine hurt in her voice. "No," he said gently. "They'll call her Aunt Olivia."

"Good! As well they should!"

Exasperated, Andrew realized he'd been fooled again by Lavinia. Any hurt he'd heard earlier was replaced by spite.

"She's their aunt, not their mother. And it doesn't sound like she'll ever be *anybody's* mother!"

Chapter 44
Summer, 1906
Four Years Later

Andrew stroked eight-year-old Selina's long dark curls. She leaned against him on the sofa in his private rail car.

"Father, visiting New York isn't as much fun without Gabe," she said, "but it's still a grand adventure!"

Andrew smiled at her, then glanced up to see George, his Pullman Porter, about to leave the car. The Negro man was about twenty-five, and uniformed in a white coat, black pants and cap. He'd just turned down the beds in the sleeping quarters.

"Goodnight, George," Andrew said.

"Goodnight, Mr. Standish," he nodded, "and Miss Selina."

"Goodnight, George." Selina waved as he left the car.

The train trip from southern California to New York City would take about four days. They were on day two.

"Pardon me, Mr. Standish." Another servant appeared at the drawing room entrance. This was Millicent, the maid charged with Selina's care. Red-haired and freckle faced, the young woman wore in a simple black dress with a white apron and cap. "It's Miss Selina's bedtime."

"Father, can I stay up just a little longer?" Selina whined.

"Give us a few more minutes, Millicent," Andrew dismissed her, turning his attention back to Selina. "So, my princess, what do you enjoy most about our adventure?"

"For one thing," Selina smiled and hugged her father, "I get you all to myself! And our Pulley car—"

"Pullman car," Andrew corrected.

"Our Pullman car is just like a palace on wheels!" Selina giggled, fingering a gold tassel hanging from the arm of the sofa she shared with her father.

Selina enjoyed the spacious compartment of Andrew's private car. It had bedrooms and a large drawing room and bath. The furniture was covered in red velvet with gold braid, while the carpet was a thick forest green with an extravagant floral design stitched in a circular motif.

"Why can't we take the train to Paris when we visit Uncle David?"

Andrew laughed. "You know why, Selina. We have to cross the ocean."

"But can't you design a bridge so we can get there in a Pulley—I mean, Pullman Car?"

"I'm afraid I can't. We'll have to go by ship."

Coughing, she said, "Well, at least there won't be any dust! That's the only thing I don't like about our train ride."

"That can't be helped, darling. It gets sucked in from the cinder rail bed below."

"I don't care where it comes from, I hate it all the same! Gabe told me he hates the dust too, but he misses riding the train to New York. But Father, when I asked him if he missed visiting Mother—he said he didn't! Then he said the only thing he really misses about New York is Brigid."

Andrew shifted uncomfortably on the sofa. "Well—Gabe does love his mother."

"Does she love him?"

"Selina—of course she does."

"Do you know *why* Gabe doesn't want to visit Mother anymore?" Selina asked.

Andrew said nothing. Until the previous year, he'd taken both of the children to visit Lavinia, twice a year, for three weeks at a time.

Now only Selina traveled to New York.

When Andrew didn't reply, Selina said, "I do. Mother hurt his feelings the last time he was there. He said that she told him not to play out in the sun before he visits her again."

Gabe had become browner as he'd grown older, and the California sun had baked him even darker.

"Now Gabe thinks Mother doesn't like the way he looks," Selina pouted. "So he said he'd rather play out in the sun all he wants than be with her."

Unfortunately, Lavinia had said something to that effect, and now Andrew was unsure of how to respond to his daughter.

Andrew hadn't forced Gabe to go back to New York after that exchange with is mother, especially since Lavinia's only reaction to his decision never to visit again was a thoughtless, "Oh, well, perhaps he'll change his mind."

Thankfully, Andrew was spared having to continue this conversation because Selina changed the subject.

"Father — I don't want to stay all three weeks this time."

"Why not?"

"Aunt Olivia might need me."

"She will need you, darling, you're a big girl now and she's counting on your help. But she's only seven months along. The baby's not due for another two. And the doctor assured me that she and the baby are just fine, so it's safe for us to be away for a few weeks."

"I want to hurry home anyway! I can't wait to be a big sister! I need to finish organizing all the games and toys I want to give the baby!"

"Selina, the baby won't be ready for those things for a very long time."

"I know, but I'm so excited—and I love feeling the baby move!" She laughed. "I'm sure Mother won't mind if I'm not here for as long this time. Does she know Aunt Olivia's going to have a baby?"

Andrew drew in a deep breath. "She knows—I wrote her all about it."

Selina smiled contentedly, then snuggled against her father. "Then she should completely understand."

Chapter 45
New York City
Two Weeks Later

When the carousel music began, Lavinia said, "Hold tight."

"Giddy up!" Selina giggled, holding on to the metal bar attached to her life-sized mechanical horse. The white animal, ornately carved with a tail and mane of gold, its neck and torso decorated by brightly colored flowers, undulated to the festive rhythm of calliope whistles. "Mother, this is so much fun!" Selina shouted over the excited screams and squeals of the other children in Central Park.

"Of course it is, Selina, darling." Lavinia smiled at her daughter, then looked past her toward a group of fans gathered at the merry-go-round. She revolved past them as they stood in awe, waiting to catch a glimpse of the one and only Lavinia Standish. Sitting side saddle on the back of a majestic purple horse, embellished with roses, cupids and jewels, she waved every few moments to appease them.

After three minutes of turning round and round, the carousel gradually slowed.

"Mother, one more time, please!" Selina said. Her horse slowly sank as Lavinia's rose high and stilled when the machine came to a full stop.

"No, Selina, we've ridden five times."

At eight years old, Selina was the perfect child, but Lavinia couldn't endure yet another go round on the carousel surrounded by other little brats joyfully expressing themselves by way of shrills and screeches.

"Pretty please!" Selina begged.

"I said no. Now mind your mother. Let's speak to these nice people." Lavinia looked toward her admirers. "They've been waiting to see me. Then we'll have ice cream before the concert starts."

Selina sighed her consent as Lavinia gracefully alit from her horse, then helped Selina down from hers.

A young couple approached Lavinia first, as she stepped from the merry-go-round holding Selina's hand. The man wore a dark blue suit, while his white gloved companion was dressed in lavender.

"Lavinia Standish!" the young man said, removing his boater. Other adults who'd ridden the carousel with their children and hadn't initially recognized her, as well as several park goers now passing by, turned to stare. "My wife didn't believe it was you, but I knew it was!"

"And you were right," Lavinia said, shaking hands with the young man and the woman.

"There's no one else as stunning as you in New York!" He gushed. His spouse, however, dipped her head, allowing her wide brimmed hat to hide her face. Noticing this, he hastily added, "with the exception of my wife, of course."

"It's a pleasure to meet you, Mrs. Standish." The wife's smile was stiff, yet she tried to sound gracious. "And your daughter is as pretty as a picture—just as beautiful as you are."

"Why, *thank* you," Lavinia smiled broadly, admiring her "little me."

Selina wore a large straw hat decorated by an enormous multi-layered bow of pink satin. Her knee-length pleated dress was also pink, and the same color as her mother's, though not nearly as flamboyant.

Lavinia's gown was long, adorned with two tiers of lace edged ruffles and slightly puffed sleeves. Its low neckline was also trimmed in lace with a bow at the center. Lavinia's colossal hat was embellished with an abundance of pink silk roses and greenery.

"Selina *is* a beautiful young lady," Lavinia stroked the little girl's curls that spiraled down her back, "and I'm quite proud of her." About three dozen fans and onlookers had gathered around now. "I have my acting," she projected as though performing, "but motherhood is my greatest achievement!" A pleasant summer breeze swept over them, carrying the fragrance of lilies and a generous whiff of dung.

A mocking bird trilled loudly, but Lavinia's audience laughed and smiled. A bearded older gentleman, suited in black tipped his top hat. "You were absolutely splendid as Imogen in last season's *Cymbeline!*"

"Oh, thank you," Lavinia replied. "In my opinion, that's one of Shakespeare's works that isn't performed enough."

The people praised her acting, doted on Selina, complimented Lavinia on raising such a fine young lady, asked Lavinia about her upcoming fall performances, and expressed their best wishes. Lavinia shook hands, threw kisses and wished them well.

"Mother, can we have ice cream now?"

Lavinia laughed at Selina's remark, as did her admiring public. "Duty calls," Lavinia waved to her fans. "A mother's work is never done."

"Mrs. Standish," a large matronly woman
called, "where's your son?"

Lavinia froze. Smiling through clinched
teeth, she pushed aside a very faint pang of
guilt. "Out of town—with his father," she
replied. "Now, I must say goodbye." Lavinia
slowly strolled away from the crowd, leading
Selina by the hand toward their waiting
carriage.

Gazing up at Lavinia, Selina said, "Mother,
people sure do love you."

"Yes, darling," Lavinia smiled, "they do."

****

"Selina, are you enjoying your visit with
me?" Lavinia asked, shielding them from the
sun with her parasol. Pigeons waddled by
cooing, as she and Selina sat on the rim
surrounding Bethesda Fountain. Towering
high, it gurgled loudly in a steady flow behind
them.

A bronze angel stood at the very top of the
structure. With wings spread gracefully, she
held a lily in one hand, while the other was
outstretched, blessing the water below. On a
lower tier beneath her were four cherubs
symbolizing temperance, purity, health and
peace.

One of the largest fountains in New York,
and unquestionably the crown jewel of Central

Park, Bethesda Fountain provided a dramatic backdrop for Lavinia, who waved every now and then as passers-by slowed in recognition.

Selina nibbled on the last of her second chocolate ice cream cone. She'd been so good during the concert they'd attended at the bandstand pavilion on the Mall, that afterwards, Lavinia had rewarded her with another ice cream.

"Yes, Mother, I'm enjoying my visit very much."

"Are you happy?" Lavinia asked. Her daughter had grown into a civilized well-behaved young lady and Lavinia rather enjoyed her company. Like a nymph, Selina was wispy thin. Thick dark hair spilled down her back and shoulders. With the exception of her eyes, which were wide and brown, rather than green and slanted, Selina's resemblance to her mother grew stronger each year. And Lavinia couldn't overlook the added attention her daughter attracted. As for publicity, this was an extra bonus.

Selina was quiet for a short while before answering Lavinia's question. "Yes, Mother. I'm happy."

To Lavinia, Selina sounded unsure. She probably didn't want to upset Lavinia again, like last time, when she'd suggested not staying in New York for all three weeks. Lavinia hadn't liked that idea at all. "What a dreadful notion!" Lavinia had balked. "Do you want to deprive your *real* mother of your company?" That had put an end to that discussion.

"More ice cream?" Lavinia asked sweetly.

Placing a hand on her stomach, Selina declined, shaking her head.

"You know, my darling," Lavinia said, "I miss you very much when you're not here. Would you ever consider — coming back to New York — to live with me?"

Looking down, Selina wiped away cone crumbs from the stiff pleats of her dress. She remained silent for several seconds, then finally said, "I don't know."

Selina had mentioned more than once, her mother reflected, that she loved living in California and that she looked forward to becoming a big sister in a couple of months.

Lavinia had never been fond of children, yet she did love her own. She hadn't wanted to be around either Selina or Gabriel while they were little and did nothing but squeal, shriek and cause mischief, but now her daughter was akin to a little adult. And although her son was better off in California, Lavinia harbored resentment about her situation, and seethed thinking about it.

Olivia had stolen her husband and taken her children. Now Olivia was expecting a baby and she and Andrew and Selina and

Gabriel, were living as one happy family — at
Lavinia's expense! Olivia had no right to such
happiness — it wasn't fair! Besides, Selina
didn't need to be turned into a Negro when
she didn't have to be.

"Darling," Lavinia held one of Selina's
hands. "I'm so happy while you visit me.
When you leave, I can't *begin* to describe the
pain — I miss you so much. Please stay with
me, Selina, for good. Don't go back to
California with your father."

Selina's eyes widened. "But Mother, I
can't stay here! Aunt Olivia's depending on
me. After the baby's born, she'll need my help.
And remember what I told you we'd be doing
after it comes?"

Lavinia released her daughter's hand.
"*After* the baby comes?"

"Yes. After the baby's born, we'll be going
to Paris to visit Uncle David."

Lavinia raised a brow. "Oh, yes...now I
remember..."

"I can't wait to meet Uncle David — and
Aunt Janine, and our cousins!   And we'll get
to see all the sights — the Eiffel Tower, the
Louvre, the palace at Versailles — Aunt Olivia
and Gabe and I have been reading lots of books
about Paris and what we'll get to see.

"Is that so?" Lavinia asked, unsmiling.
"Your father has talked to me about that.
Sounds like an exciting time for you. Along

with *Auntie* finally being pregnant," she added in an ugly tone.

"Why do you always call Aunt Olivia, 'Auntie'? That makes her sound so old."

Lavinia ignored this. "It's about time for Auntie to be with child! She's been married to your father for four years now. It doesn't take brains to get pregnant, but she could barely manage that." Then she muttered, "They were made for each other — Andrew a fool, and Olivia an imbecile."

"What did you say?"

"Nothing," Lavinia snapped.

Selina bit her lower lip, then asked innocently, "Did — did Aunt Olivia — really not know *how* to have a baby? Is it — really hard or something?"

Lavinia smiled, then laughed in spite of herself. "No, sweetheart, I was only teasing. It's been very difficult for Auntie to become pregnant; something wasn't right in her body for making babies...but...now she seems fine..."

Selina nodded, then gazed toward the fountain.

A few moments later, Lavinia said, "Here, darling." With pink gloved fingers, she placed five coins in Selina's hand. "Make some wishes."

Selina stood on the rim of the fountain and smiled. She closed her eyes, then tossed a coin into the water, watching it splash by the lily pads scattered along the surface. Then she closed her eyes again and repeated the ritual four more times.

While Lavinia watched her daughter, she said nothing. After several seconds, she'd quickly constructed a script. Selina, now out of coins, stood mesmerized, gazing toward the angel.

When she looked down at Lavinia, Selina giggled. "My last wish was that all my other wishes would come true!" Gasping, she covered her mouth with both hands. "I wasn't supposed to tell!"

"Your secret is safe with me." Lavinia smiled, then grasped her daughter's hand. "Now sit down, sweetheart, there's something very important we need to talk about." With Selina seated next to her, Lavinia began to perform the cunning production she'd created moments earlier—just for Selina's sake.

"Darling—since it—has been so difficult for Auntie to have a child, this baby will mean the world to her—*and* your father. That's why I'm hoping you'll stay with me. You see, Selina, when the baby comes, there'll be no room for you."

Startled, Selina's mouth opened, but for several seconds, she said nothing. "What— what do you mean?"

"Well—let's start with the *real* reason you're going to Paris."

Selina fidgeted uncomfortably on the fountain's rim. "The real reason is to visit Uncle David."

Lavinia looked down and sighed. "Selina, dear, they haven't told you. You see—you're father doesn't want you to know."

"Know what?"

"Well, going to see Uncle David is just an excuse to make you *want* to go to Paris." Squeezing Selina's hand, she said, "Darling, they're going to leave you there—in a boarding school."

"A—a boarding school—like in *A Little Princess*?"

"Yes. They're putting you in a school far, far away from home, where you'll stay for several years, just like little Sara Crewe in that story."

Frightened, Selina's eyes grew wide. "But Sara had to live in the attic—and work as a servant!"

"Well...sometimes...bad things do happen at boarding schools. And since you'll be in France, you'll have to learn how to speak French. Not a soul will know how to speak English. And what's worse—you'll have to eat things that French people eat," Lavinia crinkled her nose, "like frogs and snails."

Selina's eyes sheened with tears. "Father and Aunt Olivia wouldn't send me away—not to a place like that!"

"Oh, but darling, they will! And it's
important that you know why." Lavinia
paused for effect as her daughter's pleading
eyes begged her to go on. "Auntie Olivia —
doesn't — *want* you anymore."

Selina's lower lip trembled. "That's not
true! She loves me... and she's told me how
much I can help with the baby."

"The baby is *why* you'll be going off to the
boarding school in the first place."

"What are you talking about?"

"Auntie has tolerated you long enough.
And now that — now that she and your father
are having their own child, and perhaps more
in the future — you'll be in the way."

"I'll be in the way? Aunt Olivia's never
said anything like that...what about Gabe — will
he be in the way, too?"

"Darling, your brother looks like Aunt
Olivia." After peering around to make sure no
one could overhear them, Lavinia dropped her
voice to a whisper for a moment. "He's brown,
like she is. It's only natural that she'd want to
keep him, and not you. Perhaps — she loves
him more than she loves you. And, I
suppose — she's willing to raise one of my
children — but not both."

"But what about Father?" Selina's voice
broke as she choked back sobs. "He wants
me...doesn't he?"

Lavinia paused for a slim moment. "I

don't really know about that. He's married to Auntie now. He'll do whatever it takes to make her happy. And if that means Auntie only raising one of his children from his marriage to me, then that's how things are going to be. Do you understand?"

"No!" Selina pouted, stomping a dainty, pink-slippered foot.

"Then let me explain," Lavinia said sharply. "Auntie Olivia is his new wife, *not* your new mother. Now your father only cares about her happiness, not yours. It's a good thing she does want Gabriel, though, because a father always has a special bond with his son. And besides, Gabriel is much more — intelligent than you are, Selina — at least in things that interest your father. So — I believe — your father — has always enjoyed him more."

Large pools welled in Selina's eyes, and in seconds, fat tears like glycerin drops, rolled down her cheeks.

"And besides, darling," Lavinia said, "Father doesn't love me anymore. So the more you look like me, the less he'll like you over time, because you'll remind him of me."

Selina sniffed while her face creased in despair as more tears flowed.

"I know hearing this is unpleasant, but you're just leftovers from your father's first marriage — leftovers that he doesn't want —

because of his new wife. And if Auntie has a girl, your father won't even give you a second thought. He'll forget *all* about you in that big, old drafty boarding school. And most likely," Lavinia lowered her voice to a whisper again, "when they *do* have more children, they'll be brown, like Gabriel and Aunt Olivia. *You* won't fit in."

When Selina began to sob, Lavinia embraced her.

"I want to go home," her daughter cried.

Lavinia gave Selina a handkerchief, then stood with her. They walked across the red brick paving on the lower level of Bethesda Terrace. Selina's tears evoked sympathetic stares from onlookers as she and her mother ascended an elaborate granite staircase to the upper terrace where their carriage awaited on the Mall.

Ronan Moran, Lavinia's carriage driver, opened the coach door for them. Ronan was a stout man with ruddy cheeks. He wore a dark suit and bowler hat. "I'm sorry to see Miss Selina look so sad," he said with the touch of an Irish brogue.

"Take us home, Ronan," Lavinia instructed. "I'm sure Miss Selina will be fine after a bit of rest."

"A good laugh and a long sleep are the two best cures." Ronan winked.

Once Lavinia was seated comfortably with

Selina inside the enclosed coach, Ronan drove the carriage from the park down a wide avenue lined with towering elms.

Lavinia soothed Selina, holding her in her arms. "There, there, darling. You'll always fit here with me—we look just alike. Selina, you're a beautiful girl, and smart enough for me. We can go to Paris any time, and I'd never run off and leave you there. Remember, I'm your *real* mother, not Auntie, and no one could ever love you as much as I do."

"But—but Aunt Olivia said she loved me," Selina cried, "and that I'd grown in her heart like a real daughter. Why would she say that if she didn't mean it?"

Lavinia released Selina from her embrace. "Those were only empty words. But, darling, what's true is that you grew inside me." Lavinia placed Selina's hand below her heart. "Right here, under my heart, and my love for you will always be true."

****

With tear stained cheeks, Selina glanced from the carriage's open side window. Leaving the park, the horse clip-clopped loudly onto 79th Street. Paved with macadam, the busy city street was noisy, crowded by horse drawn vehicles, automobiles, trolley cars, pedestrians and a few men on bicycles. The heavy air was thick with the smell of petroleum and manure.

Feeling bereft, and unsure of what to think, Selina held the handkerchief to her eyes, then buried her face in her hands and continued to cry. Lavinia lovingly rubbed her back. Her mother acted as though she loved her now, Selina reflected, but in the past, Selina hadn't believed so. Why else had she run off to the theater so much?

And what about Father? Selina thought she was his princess. That's what he'd said. Were his words empty, too? She couldn't believe he didn't want her anymore. But is that what happened when people divorced? Do some children, like her, from a father's first wife, become unwanted leftovers when a new wife has babies?

Lavinia stroked Selina's hair. "Darling, you will stay with me, won't you?" Selina raised her head from her hands, but didn't answer. Instead, the girl's eyes wandered to the window again. Their coach rolled over uneven ground just as a large delivery carriage pulled by two horses rumbled by.

"You'll be with me, in New York," Lavinia said, "the most wonderful and exciting place on earth. Or do you want them to leave you in Paris at that horrible boarding school?

"You're eight years old now. You need your mother—your *real* mother. Someone you can love and trust. Someone who'll never desert you. Your father promised to stay with me in sickness and in health. That's what a wedding vow says. But he left me—just like he'll leave you."

Selina met her mother's gaze. "But if I *do* stay in New York, will I ever see Father and Gabe again?"

"Your father will come and visit you."

"Gabe, too?"

"We'll...talk about that."

Selina was silent for several moments. "What about you, Mother? Will you be at the theater all the time and touring in your shows?"

"Darling, I promise—I won't be working as much so I can be with you. And do you know what? I'll talk to Brigid. I know how much you and Gabriel love her. When she came to visit you last week, she told me she wasn't working for anyone. Later today, she'll be back to see you again. I'll talk to her then and see if she can come back and help me care for you. How does that sound? She enjoys visiting you when you're here, and she'd be tinkled pink if you chose to stay. I'm sure she'd love to work for me again just to be with you."

Still finding it difficult to believe any of what her mother had said, Selina didn't respond. But what if everything *was* true? In the end—she'd at least have Brigid. When

Selina and Gabe had first moved to California, they'd actually missed Brigid more than Mother.

As Selina weighed her choices, an automobile flew by at blinding speed, honking its blaring horn. Did Mother really love her? Selina asked herself. She said she did, and Selina wanted to believe that. But if Mother got tired of her, she'd probably run off to the theater again. And what about Father and Aunt Olivia? If they didn't want her, because she'd be in the way, Selina would rather live in New York—not a French boarding school. Brigid would be in New York. And the one thing Selina was sure of, was that Brigid loved her.

"All right, Mother," Selina said softly, "I'll stay."

Chapter 46

"Oh, my precious!" Lavinia squealed, embracing Selina tightly. "How happy you've made your mother!"

When the metal carriage wheels trounced over a large bump, Selina wriggled from her mother's arms, then looked her firmly in the eye. "But I'm going to ask Father if any of what you've said is true!"

Lavinia gasped. "No, darling! You mustn't! *Please* don't tell your father any of what we've discussed. He'll send you away to Paris immediately if you do. And he'll..." Lavinia paused for a moment, then glanced down. "He'll hurt me," she said quietly.

When Selina looked at her mother with unbelieving eyes, Lavinia extended her leg, then inched her dress and petticoats high above her white silk stocking. Beyond her lace garter, Lavinia revealed a large purplish bruise on her thigh.

"You *see* what he did to me yesterday!" Lavinia said. "He'd brought you back from Uncle Julian's and you'd run upstairs to play. While you were out of sight, I asked him to let me keep you here in New York, instead of dumping you in that boarding school and he — he exploded!" Lowering her dress, she sighed sadly. "Your father claims that *he* knows what's best for you — not me. And when he's angry with me, he hits me — in places where the bruises won't show."

Selina crossed her arms tightly. "I know my father! He wouldn't do that!"

"But, darling," Lavinia implored, "you've never seen him when he's angry. He's on his very best behavior when he's around you — at least now, anyway. I hope he never hurts my sister, especially now in her condition."

Selina shook her head rapidly. "He'd *never* hit Aunt Olivia! All he ever does is look at her or kiss her."

"Well — since he doesn't love me anymore — and since I'm just leftovers, I suppose he thinks it's alright to strike me. *Both* of us, Selina, *leftovers*! I hope he never beats *you* one day." Appearing terrified, Selina's brows rose and she gulped, visibly. "When we were married," Lavinia went on, "your father never laid a hand on me, but now — I — I suppose things are different.

"Darling, all you have to do is tell your father that you want to stay with me, then you needn't worry about being sent away. Tell him it's your choice. If he suspects I had a hand in your decision," she placed a hand over her heart, "I'm afraid of what he might do to me. One day, you might fear him as much as I do! People love me, Selina! You said so yourself. Do you see crowds surrounding your father like they surround me?"

As a trolley roared by their carriage loudly ringing its bell, Selina slumped, hanging her head. For a moment, Lavinia turned away to gaze from the window. She smiled, feeling victorious. During the night, she'd bumped into a table on her way to the bathroom. That bruise, the unexpected prop for her scenario, had helped her win.

"Now, darling," Lavinia angled back to Selina, "there is something else we need to discuss...You being here — living in New York with me — that's the best possible thing for you right now. You may not completely understand why, but you will one day. I promise you, Selina — your life here is better than it ever could be in California."

"Why is living in New York better?" Selina asked.

"Well, it's not so much New York — as it

is — being with me." Lavinia paused. "Being
white. Now, darling, don't mention any of
what I'm about to say to your father. But
you'll have more advantages in life living with
me as a white person. You already understand
that being white is far better than being Negro,
don't you?"

****

Selina thought about this. She'd overheard
Aunt Olivia and her grandmother talking
about what Mr. Cahill had done when his
mind was sick. He'd called Aunt Olivia a
nigger. When Selina later asked what that
meant, she was told the meaning, and that it
was a bad word. Mr. Cahill was white, but
even though he'd worked for Aunt Olivia, he'd
called her "nigger", and that showed he looked
down on her and hated Negroes. He hated
them so much he'd attacked Aunt Olivia.

Then Grandmother said that even if Mr.
Cahill's mind hadn't gotten sick, he 'd
probably always felt that way inside, he just
never would've said what he did say out loud
and he wouldn't have hurt Aunt Olivia. Selina
wondered how many other white people felt
like that inside. Did Uncle Julian and Aunt
Serene? Did Ronan and all their other
servants?

Thinking further, Selina concluded that
white people were treated better than black

and brown people, and that lots of poor people were black and brown. Rich people were white, and most people were white, so white must be better. Selina looked white, but even though Gabe was her brother, he was dark like a Negro. Was he a Negro since their grandmother was a very dark Negro? Was Mother a Negro, too? Was Selina, herself, a Negro? She hoped she wasn't. Selina liked being white—white *was* better. But she really wasn't sure what she was supposed to be.

Selina slowly nodded her head to answer her mother's question. Yes, she agreed silently, white was better. But she felt befuddled as she asked, "Am I a Negro?"

"Darling, you may not look it, but since your grandmother is, you are, too. Unfortunately, just one drop of Negro blood makes you a Negro. However, the way I see it, I *look* white so I *am* white. But if people knew about my Negro blood, they wouldn't speak to me—they wouldn't *love* me! And I'd never be allowed onto the stages I play except to scrub them.

"So you must always keep that part of your background a secret. Never tell a soul. If you lived out West with those colored relatives of yours, you couldn't very well hide the fact that you're colored, too.   It's best to forget about them. Don't visit them, and pretend they don't exist."

"But I can't forget about them!" Selina cried. "And what about my brother?"

"You *can* forget them and it's best that you do! Don't worry about Gabriel! He'll be fine. Now that he's older, he's darker — and he looks like a Negro. He'll fit right in with his grandmother and Auntie and all their Negro friends in California. He'll have a good life. *And* — he has his father — your father would *never* send his son off to a boarding school."

Selina was silent for a moment, staring sadly at her mother. "Are you going to forget about Gabe?"

Lavinia took a deep breath. "No, darling, he's my son. I know he'll be well taken care of, but he can never have the advantages of being white looking the way he does. He's better off where he is. He'd just ruin our — *your* life, being around you, living here."

"Why isn't Father concerned about his own life being ruined?"

"Your father's made a choice, a foolish choice. And when people make foolish choices, that proves they don't know what's best. He's chosen to marry my sister. She's dark and appears as Negro, and being Negro puts you in a lesser place. Your father has chosen that place with Auntie and the future children they'll have that will look like her. There's no reason for you to go to that place and live a lesser life — in addition to being

subjected to boarding school and possible
beatings by your father."

Selina sat quietly for several moments
absorbing this, while their horse, as well as
several others pulling carriages and wagons,
clip clopped in a steady powerful rhythm
along with the blustering roar of trolleys and
automobiles whizzing by them. Then a
memory from years earlier resurfaced.

When they'd come back from California
the very first time, something bad had
happened in the living room behind closed
doors. That loud crash. Could her father have
hurt her mother even then? Was it just a
matter of time, Selina worried, before he'd hurt
her, too?

"You deserve better than what you could
ever have in California," Lavinia said, " and
you'll have it here with me. Do you
understand, Selina?

The girl hesitated. "So I deserve
better...because I *am* better...and here...I'm
safe..."

"Yes," Lavinia said in triumph, "you do
understand! Safe from your father and safe
from any ill feelings towards Negroes! You'll
never have to claim that part of yourself—it
can disappear!

"Now, your father's coming by tomorrow
to take you to church at St. Patrick's with Uncle
Julian's family. We'll tell him then that you

plan to stay here with me—for good. I'll talk to him first—alone—in the living room. But, Selina, dear, after I've shut the pocket doors, you come downstairs and make sure to listen in."

Chapter 47

Lavinia escorted Andrew to the living room the next morning when he'd arrived to take Selina to church. After locking the pocket doors, Lavinia gingerly explained that Selina wanted to stay in New York.

"What do you mean, she wants to stay with you?!" Andrew asked incredulously. "That's preposterous. If she did say anything remotely close to that, it was only to make you happy. I can assure you, she didn't mean whatever it was she said."

"Andrew," Lavinia fluttered her lashes in a look of ingénue-like innocence, "you can scoff all you like — yet — when Selina first told me I — I was just as surprised as you are. She practically *begged* me to let her stay — but nevertheless, I'm thrilled — because that's what

I want, too."

Andrew squinted his eyes at her with intense skepticism. "When were you ever a mother to her? When were you even ever *here* for her?"

"Well — for the past four years — when she's visited — Selina and I have spent lots of time together. Now that she's older — she's realized that she needs her *real* mother — and I need her, as well..." Andrew crossed his arms as Lavinia prattled on. He didn't appear convinced by his ex-wife's staged sincerity. "...So I've promised her that I won't be working as much so I can be with her. Besides — I've conquered every role I want to play, and I've made lots of money in the process. But even lots of money gets rather monotonous."

Andrew said nothing for several moments as he studied Lavinia. "You're giving up the theater, so you can conquer the role of Mother?" He laughed. "I don't believe it! And since when has money *not* been important to you?"

"I didn't say it's not important, and I won't give up acting entirely. I just won't do it as much."

"Being a real mother is entirely different to playing one on stage."

"I'll have Brigid to help me," Lavinia said.

"I thought you didn't like Brigid."

"Selina does. And I rather admire her myself."

Andrew breathed in deeply. "Let's end this discussion now. *I* know what's best for Selina."

Lavinia paused, then raised her voice, knowing her daughter was listening outside the door as she'd been instructed. "Are you referring to—*Paris*."

"Not only Paris, however, that trip—that experience—will benefit her greatly. She needs everything that's been planned for her and—"

"She needs her *real* mother!" Lavinia interrupted. "So, despite what you have waiting for her in Paris, that's what she wants—and *I* want my child. Would you deprive a mother of her own flesh and blood?"

Exasperated, Andrew rolled his eyes. "I would never deprive a real mother of her child, but you've never seemed like one."

"How can you say something so hateful?" Lavinia sounded on the verge of tears. "And you're being extraordinarily unfair to me in all of this! You don't think that after being deprived of my children for the past four years that I haven't grown a real mother's heart?"

"Lavinia, I won't fall prey to your dramatics. I won't let Selina stay here."

"But that's her heart's desire."

"Since when?"

"It doesn't matter! What matters is that

she doesn't want to leave with you!"

Andrew hesitated. "It makes no sense for her to change her mind so suddenly. She was looking forward to the baby....and Olivia would be heartbroken if she didn't return with me. Has Selina thought about that?"

Lavinia's chest rose and fell rapidly. Forcing herself to whisper, she said, "Who cares about Olivia? Selina is *my* child."

Andrew's eyes narrowed in suspicion. "Is that what this is all about? Are you using our daughter like a possession, or a pawn in some sick game of yours?"

"No, no—of course not," Lavinia said calmly, trying to cover the vitriol that had spilled from her lips seconds earlier. "But if it's Selina's wish to stay with her real mother, you shouldn't stand in her way."

"Lavinia—the thought of my daughter living here disturbs me—tremendously! Without my constant presence, she'd be exposed to a lifestyle I consider inappropriate."

Lavinia splayed a hand over her heart. "How dare you! I'd make sure Selina continues to go to church every Sunday with Julian's family, and I'd never expose her to anything vile!"

"I was referring to your theater people!"

Lavinia stood next to a white marble top table. A large Cloisonné urn sat on top. "*My* theater people?" She made a sweeping gesture with her hands. One hit the urn and it crashed loudly to the floor. "Oh!" Lavinia screamed. "Not my —"

"What the devil is wrong with you?" Andrew said.

"You don't have to yell at me, too!"

Andrew looked at her strangely. "I wasn't yelling."

"Stop it!"

"Stop what?!" Andrew's voice rose in frustration.

"*Torturing* me!" She shouted, then dropped her voice, "by not allowing me to keep my daughter."

The pocket doors began to rattle. "Mother, Mother!" Selina cried frantically from outside the room as she tried to open them.

"You've upset her!" Lavinia huffed.

"Nonsense," Andrew said angrily, "*you're* the one who's been raving like a banshee."

Insulted, Lavinia said, "Stop it!"

He looked toward the broken urn. "And a clumsy one at that."

"Stop it!"

"Mother!" Selina's rattling of the doors grew louder.

As Andrew started for pocket doors, Lavinia yelled again, "Stop!" Then lowering her voice, she said, "*I'll* let her in."

As Lavinia slid the doors open a few feet, Selina burst through them, grabbing her mother tightly around the waist. "Mother!" She looked up to her with eyes wide and frightened. "Is—is everything all right?"

"Yes, darling, everything's fine. You're father and I were just having," she paused to rub her upper arm as if it were sore, "a discussion."

Selina peeked at Andrew from behind her mother.

A few yards away, Andrew knelt down on one knee. "Where's my hug?" He smiled, opening his arms.

Selina stiffened, but Lavinia said coolly, "Go on."

The girl walked toward her father warily. He gave her a kiss on the cheek and a snug squeeze. She only returned a weak embrace.

He stood to his full height and looked down at her. "How's my princess today?"

"Fine," she said quietly.

"Selina, your mother," he nodded toward Lavinia, who stood near the pocket doors, "tells me you wish to stay with her in New York, and not return to California."

"That's right."

"Why?"

"It's just that I miss her—and—I need her."

Andrew turned toward Lavinia angrily. "Just what have you said to her?!"

"Why—why—I haven't said anything to her. Be—besides that fact that I love her dearly and miss her very much." Her voice trembled.

"You must have said something else!" Andrew walked toward Lavinia as his voice grew louder. "She's never wanted—"

Before he could continue, Selina ran to her mother and stepped protectively in front of her. "It was my choice. I want to stay," Selina said. Lavinia pulled her daughter close, hugging her tightly from behind.

Andrew quieted his voice. "Lavinia, would you please—leave us alone?"

Selina swallowed hard as she looked back at her mother.

"Of course." Lavinia slowly took her arms from around Selina. She stepped from the living room, then began sliding the pocket doors together. With just a sliver of her face visible from the door panels, she assured her daughter, "I'll be right outside this room." Then she closed the doors completely.

****

Selina looked fearfully at her father after Lavinia left them alone. "You're not cross with me, are you?"

He stooped down next to her. "Darling, no."

"You won't—hit me, will you?"

"Have I ever hit you?"

"No."

"Did your mother say I would?"

"*No*," she said emphatically. "But you just seemed — so angry a moment ago."

"I was, but I wasn't angry at you, and I'd never hurt you." Andrew was quiet for a moment as he searched his daughter's face. "Selina, do you really want to stay here?" She nodded silently. "Darling, your mother's not here. Tell me why."

"I already did. I miss her, and she misses me."

"Selina, are you sure this is what you really want?" He looked deeply into her eyes. "You don't have to stay if you don't truly want to. And you'll miss out on Paris."

Selina's eyes widened. "Do you really want me to go there that badly?"

"Of course. In addition to meeting your uncle, I have all kinds of exciting things planned for you. You'll love it so much, you won't want to come home."

Feeling her heart beat quicken, Selina blurted, "I'd rather stay with Mother. She said she'd take me to Paris."

Andrew lowered his gaze for a moment. "Selina, I never knew you missed your mother so much."

"I do, Father, so please don't make me go back with you."

"Selina, I'd never force you to do anything you don't want to do."

"Then let me stay in New York!"

"Darling, what is it that you're not telling me?"

"Nothing! I've told you everything!" She started to cry. Andrew hugged her, but Selina pushed him away. "Let me stay with Mother!"

Andrew looked at her with hurt in his eyes. For a long moment, he said nothing, then took her gently by the hand and led her to the gilded sofa. When they sat down, she pulled her hand from his and wiped her tears away with the tips of her fingers.

"Selina," Andrew said slowly, "I didn't mean to upset you. I didn't realize staying with your mother—had become so important to you, nor that it meant so much. But if you do stay here—I'll miss my beautiful princess. And all of your relatives in California will miss you. Have you—thought about them? Gabe, Aunt Olivia, your grandparents..."

Selina dropped her eyes to the floor. "Yes," she mumbled. "I'll miss them, too...but I need to be with Mother now."

Silence hung between them for several moments until Andrew said, "Aunt Olivia will be very upset when she learns you're not coming back."

Selina played with her fingers. "She'll be so busy with the baby, she won't realize I'm not around. Besides, I'd just be in the way."

"That's not true. She was counting on your help."

Selina's eyes quickly shot to Andrew's. "Father, will you and Aunt Olivia have more babies?"

"I hope so."

"Oh." Her gaze dropped again.

"I'd like for you and Gabe to have lots of brothers and sisters." Selina remained silent. "Darling—I will let you stay here—but know you can come back to California at any time. Write me, or tell Uncle Julian, and I'll be on the next train out to get you. Understand?" Selina bit her lower lip, nodding.

Andrew began to put his arm around her, but when Selina tensed, he stopped.

"Darling, I love you. And always know that I want you with me, and so does Aunt Olivia, but if it's your wish—your true heart's desire to live here—then I'll allow you to stay."

Selina raised her chin. For a moment she looked deeply into her father's eyes. Moving her gaze to the window behind them, she said, "I want to stay."

****

Andrew clasped his hands, looking down defeated. Selina would change her mind, he thought. A year with Lavinia would be long enough, then she'd be more than ready to come back to California...he hoped...

Keep Watch for
Revelation
Book III of the Unchained Trilogy

Will Selina remain with her mother permanently? How will her decision transform her life? Will she acquiesce to Lavinia's demand that she disassociate herself completely from her black relatives?

When Selina meets a southerner, the man of her dreams, will she ever reveal the truth, or, afraid of his reaction, follow in her mother's footsteps and live a lie?

Find out in *Revelation: Book Three of the Unchained Trilogy,* due out in late 2014!

ABOUT THE AUTHOR

Maria McKenzie is the author of the Amazon bestseller *The Governor's Sons:*

> "...tender and touching, and also quite terribly and frighteningly true. Maria McKenzie is definitely a young novelist to watch." - Stephen Birmingham, *New York Times* bestselling novelist and social historian

and *Escape: Book One of the Unchained Trilogy:*

> "...I do see definite potential for [McKenzie] to be one of the brilliant authors of our time..." - Desere Steenberg, *Historical Romance Reviews*

Maria is currently at work on *Revelation: Book III of The Unchained Trilogy.* Look for it in late 2014! Maria lives in Cincinnati with her husband and two boys. Before becoming a stay-at home mom, small business owner and author, she worked in Georgia and North Carolina as a librarian for several years.

To visit or contact Maria, go to www.mariamckenziewrites.com. Find her blog, interviews, reviews, novel excerpts, help for writers, published articles and more!

39118220R00251

Made in the USA
Middletown, DE
05 January 2017